George J. Galloway

The Code of Aquinas

Published by REGINA Press

A Division of Regina Foundation of Oregon

REGINA Foundation of Oregon

12042 SE Sunnyside Road

Suite 486

Clackamas, Oregon 97015

ISBN 978-0-9966479-5-3

Dedication

To my mom, who taught me love of language.

To my nanny who predicted it.

Acknowledgments

Sometimes, I think, editors and publishers rank
right there down the ladder with the major media and
members of congress. Editors and publishers are
a bane on anyone who has the audacity to call themselves a
writer. I have been blessed to say the editorial team at
Regina in the publishing of this novel has been
stellar. From now on I will have to look up the ladder.

Thanks to Harry and Beverly Stevens for sailing this ship
into a safe harbor. Thanks also to Kelsey Hintzman for a
yeoman's job editing. Without them there wouldn't be a
Gilly Morrison. And that would be a real shame.

"The war of revolution is won,

but the war of independence is yet to be fought."

- *Benjamin Franklin*

"There are three things necessary for the salvation of man: to know what he ought to believe; to know what he ought to desire; to know what he ought to do."

- *St. Thomas Aquinas*

Part I

"To know what you ought to believe…"

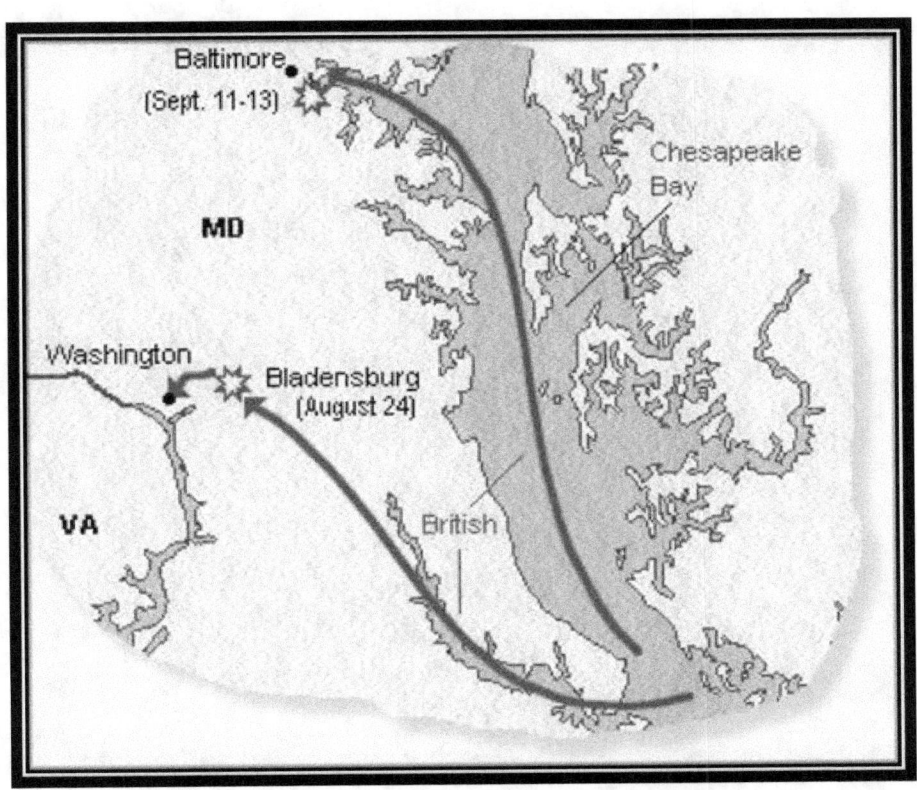

(Image Source: *Wikimedia Commons*--public domain)

Chapter 1: Blood Brothers

Fells Point, Baltimore, Maryland

Christmas Eve, 1813

"Tough" Gilly Morrison shed a tear. From a distance he watched his best friend Michael Dooley, Jr. ship out on the proudest privateer ever to leave Baltimore. Gilly wanted to be on that ship more than anything in the world. She was the Baltimore clipper *The Chasseur*, captained by the luckiest and most audacious seaman in the War of 1812 – Tom Boyle. Dooley was fortunate to get a berth assigned as a powder monkey, running gunpowder from the magazine below and amidships to the cannon on deck.

On any ship, gunpowder was treated with extreme caution. The safest place on board for gunpowder was below decks towards the center, away from any incendiary objects and enemy fire. It took agile young boys to quickly replenish the cartridges of the gun crews by running down the ladders

1

to the magazine and back up again. In battle, this was a highly dangerous job because the powder monkeys were expected to deliver their precious packages without incident while being exposed to enemy sharpshooters firing from their masts.

If the privateer's cruise was successful, young Dooley would earn a small fortune. Every sailor on board was entitled to a share of the prize money in capturing British merchant ships and the cargo they carried in their holds.

But Gilly knew his friend didn't sail on *The Chasseur* in search of prize money. Dooley's father was impressed by the British months earlier and forced to enter into their navy. Impressment was a scourge to every seafaring American town. Because of their continuing war with France, England relied on their naval superiority for its very survival. The availability of men to work these ships was becoming scarce. American seamen were increasingly compelled to serve in the British navy to fill the gap. Impressing a sailor was like pronouncing a prison sentence. This meant Mike Dooley, Sr., might never again see his son or the beautiful Baltimore harbor he had come to love since leaving his home in Ireland many years before.

Michael wanted to make the English pay for his father's impressment and, in an innocent, adolescent way, help to end the war sooner so his father could come home to him. Gilly understood this more than anyone. Still, it left a hole in Gilly's gut just the same.

Gilly was supposed to be "tough" or resilient enough to withstand

2

just about anything. He was an orphan abandoned shortly after birth and left in a basket on the steps of St. Patrick's Church on Market Street, in Fells Point, swaddled in a blanket. A note was attached that read: "Please baptize and raise my baby because I cannot. God forgive me. His name is Gilly Morrison. His father was lost at sea and I have no means to provide for him. He will always be in my prayers." The note was signed "Mother."

What made Gilly so "tough," however, was more than the fact that he was an orphan. He was crippled since infancy. When he was old enough, Doctor Williams explained to him that he had suffered a broken femur in his left leg before he was abandoned on the steps of the church. The leg had never healed and this left him growing up with a severe limp and considerable pain. Gilly bore this handicap with a smile, hence his nickname. This was also why he couldn't join Michael on the privateer. Walking on land was difficult enough; trying to traverse a ship's deck, even in calm water, would be altogether too painful, and possibly a liability for other members of the crew. Gilly never used a crutch or cane; he simply accepted the pain as a fact of life. Watching Michael Dooley about to sail away was a different kind of pain entirely.

At five-foot-eleven Gilly was tall for his thirteenth year. He had a lithe body, weighing no more than one hundred and twenty pounds. His soft, blue eyes — the color of a cloudless sea-sky — offset perfectly his curly, rust-colored hair, and his pearly-white teeth which burst out when he smiled, as he often did.

He was raised by Father John Francis Moranvillè, the French Sulpician cleric, who was the pastor of St. Patrick's Church and the director of St. Patrick's Free School and Orphanage. Father John was assisted by the St. Patrick's Benevolent Society, a group of compassionate women who raised funds to support the church, school and orphanage. Despite his left leg, Gilly grew into a fine, strong young boy thanks to loving, instructive care.

The Chasseur was about to weigh anchor. Wives, children, parents, sweethearts, and friends of the ship's seamen waved and wept goodbye. Unexpectedly, an elegantly covered chaise, pulled by a white pony, clip-clopped onto the quay. Gilly groaned in disbelief. It was Desiree, the daughter of William Pechin, the aristocratic editor and owner of the *Baltimore American and Daily Advertiser*. Known to readers on the Point as *The American*, it was the most influential newspaper in all of Baltimore and a consummate supporter of the republican administration of President James Madison.

Leaning on the door outside the Dooley family cooperage, Gilly heaved a long sigh of dismay. "Leave him alone you rich brat ... Michael, why did you have to fall for this pampered princess?"

Desiree descended her carriage and waved at Michael Dooley. Michael quickly looked at Captain Boyle anticipating his approval to leave the ship. Boyle nodded, reluctantly. Every other member of his crew had already

4

said their goodbyes. Michael scampered over the side to Desiree's carriage. She presented him with a perfumed, silk hankie, and curtsied. Michael removed the blue bandana he had tied around his neck, gave it to Desiree and bowed. This nauseated Gilly because he knew the rich young beauty was using Michael for her own amusement and he couldn't stand it anymore.

"Thank God you're shipping out, Michael," Gilly whispered to himself. "Thank God."

Michael had met Desiree working as a newspaper boy for *The American*, selling papers for the past year. Desiree possessed all the attributes of Venus. Her deep, chestnut-colored eyes were complimented by her light, auburn hair, which she wore loosely, in ringlets around her shoulders. She was blessed with rosy cheeks and permanent dimples that became even more evident when she smiled. She always wore dresses that were cut low displaying a swan-like neck, and pert breasts. Her waist was so small she didn't require a girdle. Standing erect she was a statuesque five-foot-seven, taller than most of the boys she knew.

Of course, Michael Dooley fell in love with Desiree. Boys his age have a tendency to be entrapped in the web of manipulative young girls, especially when the boys believe the attraction to be mutual. A smile from a pretty girl, a pat on the hand, perhaps a well-timed sigh and a flutter of eyelashes may just be routine social skills for a blossoming debutant; to boys like Michael, however, it was concrete evidence of undying affection. Hence, he was at her beck and call and almost begged to be toyed with.

But, when war was declared and after Michael's father was impressed into the British Navy, his priorities changed. Michael's mother had died of "The Fever" that had swept Fells Point the summer before. After his father's impressment he was all alone in the Dooley's fine red brick house on Thames Street. His feelings for Desiree had not changed drastically; they were just knocked down a peg or two.

Michael felt the need to contribute, in some way to the war effort. His chance came with the opportunity to serve aboard Boyle's privateer. Desiree didn't like that. She was used to having her way when it came to suitors, not that she needed more of them. Yet, she acted like the brave girl on the docks bidding adieu to her hero as he sailed away risking life and limb for the cause he ardently believed in. This was the reason for Gilly's nausea. Desiree had duped his best friend with guile intentions and now had him in the palm of her hand.

"Go away, Michael, and Godspeed to you. Go away and forget the likes of Desiree Pechin forever."

*****

As *The Chasseur* got underway, Gilly remembered how Michael became his best friend. It was the year before war was declared, right after Michael's mother died. They knew each other since they both attended St.

Patrick's Free School. But there was an invisible wall between them. Gilly was an orphan. Michael was the only son of the most successful tradesman in Fells Point and the owner of the Dooley Family Cooperage. Gilly knew he was nearing the age where he would be contracted out as an indentured servant for a period of years to one of the trades in the city.

This was the lot of both boys and girls at the orphanage, who had no money or family to support them. Father Moranvillè instructed the St. Patrick's Benevolent Society to arrange for civil and compassionate indenture. He would have the final say before any contract was signed. The contract would always insist on apprenticeship, so that the child would learn a trade and be able to make a living after the contract had expired. For a boy, this would include a roadmap into becoming a journeyman and later, a master of his craft. For a girl, servitude could never extend beyond the age of eighteen, when the servant, the family she served, and the Benevolent Society would discuss options such as marriage, religious vocation, and business opportunities.

Religious freedom was a must, and so was time for continued schooling. In many instances Moranvillè refused placing his orphans in servitude at all, instead negotiating a daily wage until the orphan was capable of making their own decision as to what they wanted to do for the rest of their life. If circumstances permitted, there were other possibilities besides indenture: moving out West, where land was plentiful and where skills in the arts of agriculture, horticulture, and husbandry were desperately needed; service in the American Army or Navy; or the vast opportunities to make one's living from, or on the sea. There was one, big difference between orphans at St. Patrick's and elsewhere: education. Students at the school—both boys and girls—were instructed in English, penmanship, mathematics, Latin, poetry and prose, navigation, and religion.

If not under contract, the orphans were sent out to families and businesses throughout the city in the afternoon before they were required back for dinner and independent study. In short, their minds were expanded, their skills developed, and their prospects greatly enhanced; all within the context of a religious discipline that would guide their lives.

Yet, there was always the wall between servant and master. So the children at the Free School, innately, avoided close association with "their betters." Gilly could easily become an apprentice at the Dooley Cooperage. That would mean he would be working for Michael. Nobody talked openly about it – it was just there – like a line that shouldn't be crossed.

That line was inadvertently crossed one day at St. Patrick's Church. Both Gilly and Michael were serving as altar boys at Father John's Sunday Mass. Gilly noticed Michael was having a problem with the mechanics of the Mass and stumbled in his Latin responses. Gilly also saw that there were tears in Michael's eyes. One of the orphans who worked as a servant girl at the Dooley's home on a per diem, Jessica Farmer, a favorite of Gilly's, had let everyone know that Mrs. Dooley had died of "The Fever" the day before. Why Michael was serving the Mass today, Gilly couldn't fathom. He should be with his family in mourning.

The funeral Mass was well attended. Artisans, craftsman, seamen, ship owners and captains crowded St. Patrick's to pay their respects. Teresa Dooley was well liked on the Point and would be deeply missed, especially by Jessica Farmer who saw Teresa as a role model.

During the funeral Mass, Gilly glanced at the front pew and found Michael's forlorn face. How must it feel to lose your mother? Gilly, of course, had no memories of his own mother. He wished he had and he often wondered about her: about what she looked like, what she did, whether he had a brother or sister or a father, any kinfolk at all. It seemed strange coming from nowhere.

He had always planned on having a big family with lots of kids he could take fishing or on a family picnic. Growing up at the orphanage wasn't bad; he knew that, especially at St. Patrick's where there was indeed love and protection. Yet he couldn't help but picture a stable home with parents and siblings; what they would do together and what they would share. In his daydreams, his imagination would soar and he would think about holidays, especially Christmas, with everyone gathered around the table - a hot turkey basting on a spit, pastries cooling in the pie safe, maybe even a decorated tree with presents underneath. But then he would wake and shake off these desires.

Orphans shouldn't feel sorry for themselves. They were surrounded by other orphans who had the same dreams, the same desires, and the same experiences. Yet they didn't talk about them. Their lives were a patched quilt of quiet disappointments. To survive, one had to rise above self-pity.

Gilly rang the bell at the consecration of the Mass. All eyes contemplated Jesus in the host that Father Moranvillè raised over his head. Jesus had a mother, Gilly thought. In the Good Book, it's said He gave her to everyone as their mother, too. This gave him immense comfort, and brought a smile to Gilly's lips.

A few days later, Gilly penned a poem for the school newspaper. Mr. Pechin gave his permission for the school paper to be printed at the offices of *The American*. Gilly, the best writer at the Free School, was also the school paper's editor and wrote:

Love is a gift.

Freely given, joyfully accepted,

freely given, oft spurned;

freely given just the same.

It is an anchor, a tether, deeply rooted.

Oblivious to tide, distance, tempest.

Freely given, it simply is and always is.

Death?

What death?

At St. Patrick's, Michael approached Gilly. Michael was holding the school newspaper; his hands were shaking and his eyes moist. "Gilly, this is wonderful. It reminds me so much of my mother. Thank you for writing it."

"Thanks Mike. I wrote it after your ma's funeral."

"Michael, if you don't mind, Gilly. That's how they can tell us apart - me and my pa I mean. Everyone calls me Michael and everyone calls my pa, Mike."

Gilly smiled, stretching his tanned cheeks, and revealing a dazzling set of white teeth. A line was being crossed but neither Gilly nor Michael was conscious of it.

"All right then, Michael it is, if that's what you want. Listen, I was just about to make my way to the wharf to see the regatta. It should be a fine competition. Would you like to join me?"

Michael hesitated, remembering he had to check on the family business about incoming orders. "Sure Gilly, I'd love to. Do you mind if we stop at the cooperage first? I've got some work to do with my pa."

Gilly and Michael walked down Market Street to the wharf on Fells Point. Michael took note of Gilly's limp and shortened his stride a bit. At the family business, Michael introduced Gilly to his father, Mike Dooley, Sr.

"Ah, so it's yourself is it," Mike bellowed in a soft, Irish brogue.

"My son tells me you're a story teller and a fine poet, the best on the Point."

"Thank you, Mr. Dooley. I do like to write now and again."

"Keep it up then, boyo. This country needs more voices who can truly speak to a man's heart and give comfort to his soul as God is my witness."

Michael and his father reviewed the books of the cooperage as Gilly looked around at what might someday be his fate. There was nothing there to be afraid of. The business was alive with work and honest industry. He could, if need be, choose this living after all. He could sign a contract that would make him indentured for five or seven years or so. Suddenly, the fear of servitude left him. Only, there was something that troubled him - what about his writing? That, after all, was his love, his reason for being.

"Are you ready, Gilly? My pa and I are finished here. The race on the river is about to begin isn't it?"

"In about fifteen minutes. I've got a penny on the red sail. She's faster than anything on the water," Gilly said, confidently.

"No bets for me, Gilly. I know near nothing when it comes to competitive sailing. But, I'll cheer for your red sail anyway."

Before leaving the cooperage, Gilly looked back on Mike Dooley working up a good sweat creating barrels and casks for the sea captains and their ships. He immediately developed a sense of kinship with him. Working with a teacher like him, Gilly thought, wouldn't be bad after all.

The red sail won the regatta and Gilly was jubilant. Michael invited Gilly back to the Dooley's red brick house on Thames Street for dinner. Jessica Farmer was there preparing the meal.

As Michael and Gilly entered the front door, Jessica, who had been reading from the Dooley family Bible, quickly put it back into the large cedar chest in the living room.

"Well hello, Michael. Do we have a guest for dinner tonight?"

"Yes, Jess, we do. You know Gilly Morrison, don't you?"

Gilly smiled, sheepishly. Somehow, he knew, he had crossed over a line. "Good evening, Jessica. Can I help you with something in the kitchen?"

"No, everything is already done. I've made chicken and dumplings. Michael, will your father be joining us for dinner?"

"He was finishing up some work on the barrels when I left him a couple of hours ago. He should be here shortly, I think."

At that moment Mike Dooley entered the door. He had a somber look on his otherwise cheery face. He took a seat in front of the fire in the small living room and lit his pipe, which wasn't his custom. He would usually do this only after dinner. "Well, lad, let's get to the point. I'm not one to be beatin' around the bush. I've got sad news for you, Michael."

Jessica listened from the kitchen door. Michael and Gilly took the two remaining seats in front of the fire. "What you saw at the cooperage today was the last of the orders for casks and barrels." Michael had seen earlier this afternoon that no more orders were listed in the books, but he hoped it was a temporary lull in business.

"The war between the Brits and the French has ruined our sea trade. If we can't ship our products to foreign ports then there is no need for barrels and no need for a cooper."

Michael gazed, trustingly, at his father's face, wondering what that would mean. "The British have us stopped up like a cork in a bottle," Mr. Dooley continued. "If we can't send our merchant ships abroad with the God-given resources of this country to freely trade with other nations then we, as an international seafaring community, are done for. Why, even when we do try, the British Navy stops our ships and impresses our sailors with impunity. I fear there is no other course for this country than war. Until then, to save our business and the home we live in, I must go to sea as a ship's carpenter."

Now, Michael knew why his father lit his pipe before dinner. Life would be different from here on in.

"The *Mary Lynn* ships out in two days. She's a fine brig with a worthy captain and crew. She'll sail close enough within our own borders to

14

avoid bumpin' into the English and French. Then, if all looks safe enough, we'll sail down to the Caribbean and fetch some molasses. With the profit from this ship's voyage we can keep the cooperage and our home. Michael, I know you're busy with selling your papers and with school, but I have to ask you to do double duty. Check on the cooperage every day. Make sure we fill the few orders we are given. Our reputation depends on it. You know I can't trust your Uncle Bob to do this."

Michael's Uncle Bob was a great salesman and fighter. He had sailed with the legendary Joshua Barney in the Revolutionary War. But he was also a drunk and certainly no businessman.

"Jessica, darlin'," Mr. Dooley called into the kitchen.

"Yes, Mr. Dooley?"

"Are you willing to stay on here at the house while I'm gone? It'll be a month or so."

"Yes, sir, I'll be here for as long as you need me. I owe your wife that much, anyway."

"Good lass, you're a good girl and will be sorely needed. Michael, my son, while I'm gone I may miss the opportunity to give you the code of our family, the treasured Code of Aquinas. I know you're looking forward to it being revealed to you on your thirteenth birthday."

Mr. Dooley rubbed his nose and eyes in extreme disappointment. After all, he was looking forward to it, too. "I know, my son, these are hard words for you to hear. You know I wouldn't put this burden on your back if I could help it. I'll ask Father Moranvillè to give you the words for me if I haven't yet returned."

The father saw the sadness flash upon his son's face.

"When I come home we'll talk about it, I promise you. As God is my judge, I make this vow."

Mr. Dooley clapped his hands together to dismiss the melancholy that had filled the space between father and son. "Well, now, enough business and bad news. If my nose is any good at all, I'd say it was time for chicken and dumplings. Let's eat."

From that day forward, Gilly and Michael became fast friends. There were few secrets between them. When they had leisure time, which didn't occur often, they spent it together fishing on the Patapsco, always talking about whatever was on their minds: girls, school, girls, fishing, girls, the upcoming school athletic competition, and girls.

After stopping in to see the pastor of St. Patrick's Church and visiting Teresa's grave, Mr. Dooley sailed on the *Mary Lynn* with the outgoing tide and little fanfare. There were only a few souls on the docks to say goodbye including Michael. With his mother dead and his father headed down the Patapsco towards the great Chesapeake, Michael felt completely alone. Is this how an orphan feels all the time, Michael wondered, thinking about Gilly?

A few days later, Gilly stopped by the cooperage to see how Michael was coming along. What he saw surprised him. Michael and his uncle Bob were busy filling new orders that came pouring in after rumors out of Washington reached Baltimore that war might soon be declared against Great Britain. War meant businessmen, ship owners, and investors in the shipping industry might soon see opportunities they've never dreamed of before. A war would necessitate the building of ships for immediate coastal trading, for privateers to capture and confiscate enemy merchant vessels, and for American naval defenses. All of these ships would need barrels for water, food, and a hundred other things stowed upon ships that needed to be kept for long periods of time.

Michael wiped the sweat from his brow and spied Gilly standing in the doorway. "Gilly I'm glad you're here. I need to talk to you about something."

"Sure Michael, whenever you've got time. Looks like you don't have much now."

"No, I don't. I sure wish Pa hadn't shipped out on the *Mary Lynn*. If he could only have known about the war talk out of Congress last week I'm sure he would never have gone. Even I didn't realize how serious it all was

17

and I read my newspaper every day!" They both laughed at this.

"Listen, Michael, you go back to work and help your uncle. We can talk any time after things quiet down." Walking back to the orphanage, Gilly was convinced Michael was going to ask him to apprentice at the cooperage. Gilly recognized this would be an ideal opportunity for him – for any penniless orphan. He could learn a steady trade that would always be in demand along the wharves of Fells Point or any coastal community in America or even around the world. He should jump at the chance to join the Dooley family cooperage.

The increase in business at the Dooley cooperage was overwhelming Michael and Uncle Bob. Gilly wondered why Michael didn't send for him. Surely, the cooperage needed help. But, Uncle Bob hired a clerk by the name of Samuel Snipes and two brothers by the name of Smith who were farmers in search of fortune in the big city and who would work in the back room fashioning barrels out of shaped staves and iron hoops: Dooley barrels, guaranteed to be, as was the mainstay of the Dooley reputation, completely air tight and waterproof.

And then the lights went out in Michael's young life. The *Mary Lynn* returned to Fells Point, but without Mr. Dooley. He had been impressed into the British Navy. Even though he had fought with Washington and Lafayette at the siege of Yorktown; even though he had established a popular business in Baltimore and ran it successfully for over a decade, he was impressed because he had a slight Irish brogue and for no other reason.

News of the impressment swept the Point. Michael was devastated and sunk into a deep depression. No one could talk to him. He did his work, faithfully, for it was in his blood. But he avoided all human contact if possible, not Gilly, not Jessica, not even Desiree. He worked at the newspaper, went to school, and labored at the cooperage as he always had. His spirits were cheered a bit when he was named as a member of the Deptford Hundred, the volunteer fire brigade that was the pride of Fells Point. Uncle Bob, who was the foreman of the brigade, made this happen. After a fire on the docks destroyed a local tavern, Michael, sooty and sweaty from fighting the blaze into the morning hours, dragged himself home and washed his slight body in the back of the house. An unexpected knock on the door startled him. It was Father John.

"Good morning, Michael, and a blessed birthday." Michael had forgotten all about his birthday. Father Moranvillè then proceeded to relate to him the Code of Aquinas that has guided the Dooley family for over five hundred years. The code his father should have given him. The words of which his father had sworn they would talk about. "As God is my judge, I make this vow," his father had said.

*****

Michael was swamped with hawking *The American*, his schoolwork, and keeping up with the avalanche of orders at the cooperage, even with the

19

addition of Samuel Snipes and the Smith brothers. But there was one thing he desperately needed to tend to. One autumn morning Jessica Farmer arrived early at the Dooly home to make breakfast before Michael reported to the offices of *The American.*

"Hey, Jess would you do me a favor?"

"Of course, Michael, do you want something special for dinner tonight?"

Michael shrugged his slight shoulders. "Sort of, Jess. When you get back to the orphanage would you ask Gilly Morrison if he would like to go fishing after school today? We could meet at the pier and maybe bag some rock fish and bring them home for supper. Would that be okay with you, Jess?"

Jessica turned from the fire and wiped her hands in her blue apron. "But why don't you just ask Gilly yourself at school today?"

"I'm not going to school today," Michael stated flatly. "There's too much to be done at the newspaper and a lot more at the cooperage."

Jessica served him his breakfast. There was too much of Teresa in her not to hold her tongue. "You never miss school, Michael. Not before or after the war was declared. Not before your mother passed away or after your father was impressed. I know you're extremely busy. You know your mother, the Lord rest her soul, and your father, God help him, would not approve of this. You also know Father John will not stand for it. Talk to him this morning or he'll come looking for you. Oh, and you two had better catch something for me to prepare for supper or you'll be dining on strawberry jam on stale bread tonight."

Despite the backload of orders at the cooperage, Michael took the afternoon off to go fishing. He did take Jessica's advice, however, and stopped by the rectory to explain to Father John before going to the wharf. It was early November, and the wind off the waters of the Patapsco spoke of a cold and damp winter season in the offing. Gilly arrived silently behind him.

"Fishing at this time of year, Michael?" Gilly whistled between his teeth. "Do you suppose there are any fish left for dinner?" He sat down on the pier and prepared his tackle and bait.

"Jessica says they'll be no dinner tonight unless we bring it home ourselves."

They both laughed. As they cast their hooks into the water, watching the corks on their lines bob gently in the ebbing tide an odd silence overtook them. But Michael knew that for him time was precious and he needed to speak out.

"Gilly, I want to talk to you about something very important to me."

"The fish aren't saying a word, Michael. So go ahead."

"I've just received the code of the Dooley's thanks to Father John."

Gilly nodded. "I heard your father mention something about it before he shipped out on the *Mary Lynn*. He said if he wouldn't be back in time, Father John would give you the words." Just then, Gilly whistled and started giggling.

Michael was annoyed. "This is nothing to laugh about. This is serious."

Gilly put his arm around Michael's shoulder. "I know it is. I'm sorry but I thought you wanted to talk to me to sign on as an apprentice at the cooperage. Jaysus, Michael, I was that certain of it. I also tried to reach out to you after your father was impressed, but you were despondent and needed time alone. I respect that. Sometimes an orphan needs that, too."

Michael was astonished. "You, Gilly Morrison, signing a contract to be indentured for, what, the next five to seven years with all of your God-given talent? Why you're the best writer and poet at the school, maybe even the whole of Baltimore."

"Michael, I've turned thirteen, too, and It's time for me to start to consider what's to become of the rest of my life. I have no money and no family, and I cannot continue to be a burden to the good people at the orphanage."

The fish weren't biting at all. But their thoughts were far away from fishing. Gilly still had his arm over Michael's shoulders. He was older only by

two weeks, but had all the attributes of a big brother.

"Hey, Michael, wouldn't you want me to apprentice at the

cooperage?"

"Of course, Gilly, who wouldn't want to have you working in their

shop? But, I was thinking about something else besides apprenticeship.

Something I really can't explain right now. But certainly something I want to

talk to you about later.

Gilly was confused. "Then why did you want me to go fishing at this

time of year? I haven't had a nibble by the way and I'm getting mighty cold."

Michael reached into his basket and pulled out a sharp fishing knife.

He placed the knife over his index finger and sliced his skin. He winced from

the sharp pain. Then he handed the knife to Gilly.

"I need you to be my brother, Gilly. I can't explain it all now, but if

you agree to do as I have just done I will be eternally grateful."

Gilly had heard of the ritual but had never performed it. It was as if

Michael was reading his mind. He needed a brother, no – he longed for one.

With tears in his eyes he took the knife, extended his finger and sliced it just

as Michael had done. Michael firmly shook Gilly's hand. They both smiled as

the blood oozing from their fingers intermingled and became one.

"Gilly Morrison, you are now my brother. In all the trials and triumphs that come into our lives, you will always be my kin and I yours. And because of this I can now freely share with you the code of the Dooley clan."

"Tough" Gilly Morrison remembered all of what his "blood brother" had told and entrusted to him as he watched *The Chasseur* slip out of the harbor and gently make her way down the frigid Patapsco River and onward to adventures unknown.

Chapter 2: The Code of Aquinas

There were five things Michael Dooley asked Gilly to do for him before the departure of *The Chasseur*: take Michael's position as paperboy selling *The American* at the busy corner of Market and Bank Streets every morning before school (any boy would die for this because sales here were brisk); move into the Dooley house on Thames Street and keep it in good order until Michael returned; manage the cooperage and review the books with Samuel; watch over and help Desiree Pechin in whatever she needed; and, most importantly, ponder on the Code of Aquinas so that upon Michael's return they could compare experiences and discuss if it really did change a person's life.

But difficulties, some anticipated and some not foreseen, popped up. First, Gilly had to figure a way to pull his wagon full of newspapers down

Market Street, especially where the street turned from smooth, hardened dirt into bumpy cobblestones. A horse or an ass would be the ideal solution, but neither Michael nor Gilly possessed these work animals. Gilly could ask for assistance, of course, but that would injure his acute sense of pride, so that was out. He resolved the issue by using a shoulder harness. It would be painful, especially trying to pull his wagon over the cobblestones. Yet pain was something Gilly saw as more of a challenge than an obstacle.

Before shipping out, Michael had talked to Father John. The good Moranvillè had to give his blessing for Gilly to leave the orphanage and live off premises. What Michael and Gilly did not know, and Father John did not tell them, was that Jessica Farmer would no longer be working as a servant girl at the Dooley home. This meant Gilly would have to learn how to cook and clean for himself.

The third request wasn't all that bad. Gilly, who was the best student at St. Patrick's Free School, excelled in every subject including mathematics. He had spent time with Michael and Samuel, the clerk, going over the books at the cooperage, so Gilly was somewhat familiar with the accounting. For his efforts at this, Gilly was to receive a per diem, at the insistence of Father John, who would not condone an apprenticeship at this time.

The fourth request was almost impossible. Gilly detested Desiree Pechin. He thought she was an obnoxious, spoiled brat who flaunted her natural beauty and her father's wealth without regard to other human beings.

Gilly never told Michael about his opinion of Desiree because he didn't want to hurt his friend's feelings. Gilly knew Michael was enamored with her and he couldn't find it in his heart to dissuade him.

As for the Code of Aquinas, Gilly found equally as difficult as dealing with Desiree Pechin because both were hard to comprehend. The code read: "There are three things necessary for the salvation of man: to know what you ought to believe; to know what you ought to desire; to know what you ought to do."

Gilly thought that the very simplicity of these words was what made it so hard to understand. He also wondered how these words could possibly change anyone's life. Michael had recommended his friend consult Father John to help him understand the code's meaning, but first warned him that, apparently, the code was something one digested slowly over time. Michael Dooley, himself, hadn't yet understood its meaning.

As Gilly struggled to live up to all of these newfound responsibilities, America faced her own difficulties. The war was not going well, and the attempt upon Canada had failed miserably. Forts in the northwest had surrendered needlessly; Congress began to rethink their passage of the declaration for war; and factions in New England began considering even more radical actions such as a separate peace with Britain and a possible secession from the union.

It was supposed to be a cakewalk. Prominent men Like Henry Clay

27

of Kentucky viewed the war as a natural expansion opportunity for a young America. After all, the British and all of Europe had Emperor Napoleon to contend with. Considering everything else that was going on in the world, America was just a flea bite in the schemes of the great British Empire. Yet, the United States failed to take advantage of its own obscurity and no significant progress was made against the enemy.

To Gilly, the war against Britain was as far away as the Canadian frontier. He didn't know it now, but the distant guns of battle would soon creep ever closer upon his world and change him forever.

*****

One day after school, Gilly made a point to see Father John to discuss the Aquinas code. "I am surprised, *mon ami*," the old priest declared. "The Dooleys never discuss the code of their family except with family members."

"Michael and I became blood brothers before he shipped out, Father. He did this so that he and I could talk about the code. You see, with his father impressed and his mother dead, there was no one he could turn to - except you, of course. You know yourself that Michael's uncle Bob, who turned away from the code years ago, would be of no help in this matter."

"*Oui*, Gilly. Bob Dooley is an unrepentant sinner who is as much a danger to himself as he is to anyone else. So, do you know the words of the ancient code?"

"Yes, Father. Michael and I briefly discussed this. He warned me that the meaning of the code might take some time to sink in – that one could not immediately understand just what it means right away."

Father John paced the floor of the rectory in deep study. "Michael is correct for the most part. The code is a gift. In fact it is many gifts. Gifts are given, they cannot be demanded. The code of the Dooley's is taken from the writings of the great and gifted St. Thomas Aquinas. It is from his *Two Precepts of Charity*, written in the year of Our Lord 1273."

Gilly nodded. "Yes, Father, Michael told me."

"*Oui, mon ami*, but Michael has told you mere words. These words are important. Yet words mean nothing if they don't produce fruit. And good fruit takes some time to develop and mature. This is as it should be from the beginning, unless providence decides otherwise. Tell me this, Gilly, does an apple or a peach taste good when it is just a seed or a bud on a tree?"

Gilly shrugged, "Why no, Father. It takes a whole season to grow from a blossom and years from seed."

Father John stopped his pacing and grinned at his best student. "Then why do we need to taste the seed before it has become what it was meant to become? Can we not, instead, enjoy its maturation? Savor and revel in what it will be?"

"That's the best part, Father," Gilly admitted. "It's the anticipation every farmer dreams of, and every eater, like me, looks forward to."

Father John stood in front of an ice-glazed window at the rectory and gazed out at the snow flurries gently wafting down upon the Point. He decided he was not yet finished with his Socratic lesson. Moranvillè firmly believed that education and self-enlightenment were impossible without utilizing the methodology of the ancient Greeks philosophers, especially Socrates, and the moral dictates of Augustine and Aquinas. Even in the case of young artisans where hands-on-experience was crucial, there was still a critical need for the Socratic Method.

"Gilly, what will help in the growth of the apple or the peach?"

"Ample sunlight, water, and good soil, I suppose."

"And tell me from your religious studies, what are the seven gifts of the Holy Spirit. This is not an examination, *mon ami*. Take your time. Can you remember them?"

"Yes, I think so: wisdom, understanding, counsel, fortitude, knowledge, piety, and fear of the Lord."

"*Tres bièn*! Gilly. Then please consider how the code of the Dooley clan can enter into your life and your heart."

Gilly had to think about this. "Well, slowly, I guess. But surely, if I concentrate upon it and pray that I be given this gift, if I let it take its time and not try to rush it then, perhaps, it can happen. Father, is it the same thing as the seven gifts of the Holy Spirit?"

"In the manner of a gift it is. But take it as three different gifts. First, as Aquinas said, 'know what you ought to believe.' Digest this inspiring quote in little bites. The Holy Spirit is the Paraclete: the advocate and defender of mankind. He is the Helper Jesus promised us before his ascension into heaven. He will never abandon us if only we rely upon His help and always call out to Him in sincerity and faith. This is certain. Think of a sailor who relies upon the stars and the sun to fix his position in a sea of confusion and to guide him in his journey, slowly, confidently, one nautical mile at a time. The code is meant to help you reach a heavenly destination. It is a map used in the journey of a day or one of a lifetime."

"So, I should continue to ponder over the words in my mind one phrase at a time," Gilly concluded.

Father John beamed brightly, "until the day comes when you marvel over the changes in your heart."

*****

For Desiree Pechin, life could not have been better. After Michael Dooley took his position as the powder monkey aboard *The Chasseur*, Desiree decided to pursue Gilly and make him one of her many romantic conquests.

31

Desiree usually got bored over the winter months. Most of her beaus were away fighting the war; this could prove to be a pleasant diversion. Gilly may be lame, but he was handsome. Furthermore, each day when Gilly was gathering up his papers at the *American*, he would always ask Desiree if she needed anything.

"Mistress Pechin, is there some service I may do for you today?"

But, there never was. Desiree had her servants and her father's money. Still, she wondered why this boy was so attentive. Being selfish, spoiled, and pampered she expected this from her servants, but not from a boy she hardly knew. Somewhere, deep inside, this annoyed her.

Desiree was used to getting what she wanted. Ever since her mother's death in childbirth – Desiree's birth – Mr. Pechin had lavished his daughter with the finest material things life could offer. Mr. Pechin was a wealthy aristocrat as well as the owner and editor of *The American*. His passion was, unquestionably, republican politics, but his downfall was his daughter.

Desiree took Gilly's attention the wrong way. He only meant to be civil and fulfill one of the promises he had made to Michael Dooley. But, Desiree saw an opening for flirtatious fun. She quickly plotted a subtle campaign to capture his heart.

One frosty morning in February, Gilly arrived at *The American* with his wagon and shoulder harness ready for a brisk business selling newspapers. The snow had increased in the early hours before dawn. Now it poured down in soft buckets, blanketing Baltimore in a white quilt. Desiree was seated outside her father's office sporting a pouting look on her face.

"Good morning, Mistress Pechin," Gilly said as he always did with a bright smile on his face. "Is there any service I can render you today?"

"Yes Master Morrison, you may wipe that silly smile off of your face. It's too damned cold for anyone to be grinning this morning."

Desiree was dressed in a lacey lavender dress covered by an ermine coat and matching hat.

"You're right of course," Gilly responded, innocently. "It is downright cold this morning. But it gets my blood up. I like to keep active in frigid temperatures. It makes me want to do things and get them done. That way, at night by the fire, I can appreciate what it really feels like to be warm. Don't you feel the same way?"

"I certainly do not," Desiree protested. "I ought to be kept warm and comfortable at all times. A girl of my station should expect no less."

Not understanding Desiree's remarks, Gilly peered out the window. The snow continued to fall and covered the streets up to the shin bones. Gilly was worried about his trek with his shoulder harness and wagon all the way down to Market and Bank Streets. It would be an arduous and slippery job.

33

Desiree softened her harsh tone. "What I like on a day like today is a nice cup of tea. Why don't you come over to my house, let's say at three o'clock. I'll have my servants fix us some scones and biscuits."

"I'm sorry Mistress … "

"You may call me Desiree, Gilly."

"Yes, thank you Desiree. And I appreciate the informality. But I have to work at the Dooley Cooperage after school. I really don't have time for tea."

Being raised in an orphanage had at least one advantage in life. It engendered in the orphan an instinct for possible danger. Not just in life's events and circumstances, but specifically with the people an orphan interacts with. A sort of rearguard action that helps defend the heart against emotional trauma. In Desiree, Gilly sensed a threat. Although he had promised Michael Dooley to watch over her, he wisely did this from a wide berth both physically and emotionally.

Desiree felt a peculiar sensation up her spine. She sensed an honesty in Gilly. Something different from her other suitors and conquests. She was used to winning a heart without even trying. But, this boy was different. Why, she had no idea. Internally, she detected a raw, untamed independence that both irked her and fascinated her at the same time. He, of course, was nothing. He had no social standing in the world. Yet, he was also quite intriguing. He was a young man who had an undeniable mystery of purpose and mission. Desiree, instinctively, wanted to be a part of it, whatever it was.

Gilly loaded his newspapers into his wagon and pulled them with his powerful shoulders like oxen in a yoke plowing a new field. Desiree, watching him from the window, felt, at first, confused, and then slighted. Why would a boy diligently ask after her welfare on a daily basis and not pay her the adulation and attention, if not the affection she deserved?

After school, Gilly stopped in at the cooperage as the snow continued to fall. Samuel and the Smith brothers were huddled around the Franklin stove seeking comfort and warmth against the nor'easter pummeling the city. Having fulfilled the orders for the next day, the Smith brothers went back to their lodgings on Shakespeare Ally. Gilly and Samuel turned their attention to the accounts.

"Master Morrison, may I ask you something?" Samuel inquired after their business was concluded.

"Sure, Samuel, I'm all ears."

Gilly sat back in his chair and made a mental assessment of the Dooley clerk. He was a giant of a man in his late twenties, maybe six-seven and a good eighteen stone, if not more. His brown hair was accented with premature gray around his temples. As he removed his spectacles, Gilly could see the gentleness of his green eyes. He would be tough in a fight, because of

35

his physical stature, only Samuel was a Quaker and didn't believe in fighting.

"I could not help but hear you and Michael discussing the Dooley family code before the young master shipped out on *The Chasseur*. You both seemed decided that the influence of the code upon one's life must take time."

"Yes, Samuel. Father John and I were talking about that very same thing the other day."

"But has there ever been an occasion where the code has been immediately received into the heart?"

Gilly thought about this, but didn't know the answer. After all, he only received the code from Michael not that long ago. Both Michael and Father John, however, talked about the need for time before the code could begin its work. It seemed unnatural for it to take effect upon the first hearing.

"I'm not sure, Samuel. It doesn't seem likely, though. I mean, I suppose, if God willed it, it could. Why do you ask?"

"I'm not sure either, Master Morrison. But ever since I heard you talking about it my mind and my heart have been bursting with an ardent desire to fulfill its dictates. I don't have to think about it because it thinks for me. Everything I do is balanced by its precepts."

Gilly whistled. "Whoa there, Samuel, don't you think you should back off a bit? I'm much younger than you and don't have your wisdom and

36

experience, but I think you're rushing into things a might fast. Why would the code come into you so quickly? Did you want it to? Perhaps you convinced yourself into believing it to be so."

Samuel shrugged, "I did not convince myself of anything. It simply happened that way."

"How did it happen that way, Samuel?"

"I opened my heart to God. This St. Thomas Aquinas of yours cannot be dismissed. His logic is undeniable. To not see it is pure folly."

Gilly sent Samuel home and locked the doors of the cooperage. He trudged through the snow wondering how Samuel could have gotten the meaning of the code so quickly. He decided not to go back to the Dooley home just yet and slogged his way up to the rectory of St. Patrick's Church. Maybe, if there was a light on, he could ask Father John to explain it all.

It was not quite eight o'clock. There was a dim light burning from the window of Father John's study. Gilly rapped on the door and knocked the snow off his well-traveled boots. Father John invited him in.

"In this terrible weather, Gilly, why do you come to me?"

"It's because Samuel had heard Michael and I talking about the Code of Aquinas, Father, and he is certain in his heart that it has made an immediate change in him."

"Ah, so the Code again is it? Come, Gilly, warm your body by the fire."

Gilly removed his hat and coat and knelt before the fire place, wincing at the pain in his left leg and stretching out his hands to warm them. He turned his head back to Father John with an inquisitive look.

"Why is it Samuel gets the meaning of the code right away and Michael and I have to struggle with it? Why, as we talked about before, do we have to digest it in little bites? Is it because he is a Quaker or a better person? I don't understand, Father. I mean have we done anything wrong in our assessment of the words of the code? They seem so simple to me. I can't fathom why they don't just reach out and grab our attention; why they don't have an immediate impact upon our lives as it did to Samuel."

Father John moved his chair closer to the fire and sat next to Gilly. "Are you a little jealous, *mon ami?*"

This question disturbed Gilly. "In a way, I guess I am. Maybe it's like the first time I met Mr. Dooley. Having a father is something I've always wanted. Ever since I met Michael's father I immediately admired him. He seemed to me so self-aware and assured of his standing in life, but never boastful or proud. Like he knew, instinctively, what he … Oh, I get it. 'What he ought to believe.'" Gilly laughed at himself.

"And I've strived to be like him. You know, responsible and reliable,

38

someone you could count on in any situation. I pictured myself being married someday and having children. Then I could tell them about the code and pass it on to them when they came of age. Mike Dooley was … " at this tears welled into Gilly's eyes and he briefly sobbed, " … was everything I dreamed my father would be."

"*Oui*, Gilly. Monsieur Dooley was like that when I first met him after the Battle of Yorktown. He came to this city in search of a better life. He had, through self-discipline and hard work, internalized the gift of the code. It became a part of him you see. He no longer dwells on its words or what they mean. He doesn't have to. The code is inside him, as real as his heart and mind and soul."

Gilly was perplexed. "By your own admission, Mike Dooley had to work at it. It didn't just immediately change his life."

"For certain, it did not."

"Then how do you explain Samuel?"

Father John smiled. "You mean how is that Samuel, as you have described, is struck with a bolt of wisdom beyond our comprehension like Saul on the road to Damascus?"

"Why, yes, Father that's exactly how it seemed to happen. He was given an immediate insight."

Father John shrugged his shoulders. "I have no idea. Perhaps Samuel was in dire need of spontaneous understanding. Perhaps he must have it now because there is no time to acquire it. I do not know, nor do I care to know what is not in my purview to know. That's the Lord's work. Thankfully not mine, else I should be up all night debating the question."

Father John yawned. "I tire easily in old age, Gilly. This is the prerogative of ancient souls such as me." The good priest cradled his chin upon his slight chest and began to breathe deeply in sleep. Gilley kissed his forehead and crept out into the night.

On his way out of the rectory of St. Patrick's, Gilly noticed the storm had hurried off to sea after depositing another cold blanket for the residents of Fells Point to wake up to. He sat in front of the hearth at the Dooley home and lit a fire. He opened the cedar chest and removed the family Bible, searching for the passage about St. Paul's encounter with the divine. Father John was right about one thing. Gilly was jealous of Samuel's immediate understanding of the Dooley code. Unlike Father John, he would be up all night debating the question.

Chapter 3: The Test

The British Navy had succeeded, not just in blockading the entire

Chesapeake Bay, but under Admiral Cockburn had terrorized villages and

towns, burning homes, ships and port facilities, and seizing crops. Cockburn

sought the names of all the men on the rolls of local militia companies. For

these men justice was swift and horrible. Their homes and barns were torched

and everything they possessed was confiscated. This was "total warfare" on

an unprecedented scale. American citizens were not in rebellion against the

British crown, they were a free people defending a free nation. Cockburn

didn't care. He was sent to the Chesapeake to punish and punish he would.

Gilly was hawking more newspapers than ever before. Every

Baltimorean wanted to know the latest dispatches from Washington and news

of the American military efforts on land and sea. The people of the city needed information to plan, possibly even evacuate. If Cockburn burned and pillaged other towns, they thought, he most certainly would torch Baltimore. The city's privateers, like *The Chasseur*, under the command of "Mighty" Tom Boyle, were the bane of British commerce. In London, insurance rates for merchant shipping soared to an all-time high. It wasn't a question of if Baltimore should be attacked, only when? Gilly stood on his wagon and shouted the headline from this morning's paper. Referring to Admiral George Cockburn it read: "THE GREAT BANDIT LOOMS."

As the days passed into the spring of 1814, the city was alive with defensive preparations of an alarmed and alerted citizenry. But all this was beyond the ken of Desiree. Her focus was on Gilly Morrison. Pride, or even more than that, a smug and supreme sense of vanity continued to lead her on a quest to capture Gilly's heart. Despite constant invitations to tea at the Pechin home, Gilly refused every offer. For Desiree, infatuation now turned into an obsessive desire. If her astounding beauty and her best flirtations could not entice Gilly, maybe some espionage would help.

A few days later, a letter arrived at the cooperage addressed to Master Morrison. Gilly fumbled with the seal in anticipation. It was from Michael Dooley.

Hudson Hotel, New York City

Dear Gilly,

I hope this post finds you well. Jessica and I have had bizarre and extreme adventures on board *The Chasseur*. We sailed across the Atlantic after picking up several prize ships and sent them into New England before making the crossing. It was incredibly cold and incredibly beautiful. I received a slight knock on the head as we attempted to escape a British frigate off Cape Henry after she gave us a broadside. Don't worry, everything is fine now.

We arrived in Ireland and quickly went to work securing a coastal town in the County of Donegal. There we stayed for three days and shared our prize money with the residents who were so pleased to see us. After that we were almost caught by the British Navy sailing in the Irish Sea. But, Captain Boyle delivered us to safer waters in the south, off the coast of France. Then we made the crossing back, towards the southern coast of the United States. Before we could reach our destination, a hurricane blew in on us. It was touch and go, Gilly. The crew had found out that Jessica Farmer was a girl acting as a Master's Mate. She had pulled off the ruse for almost the entire voyage before she was ratted out.

I don't want to go into all the particulars, but we

almost bought it when a mutiny erupted aboard ship because the crew thought Jessica was a "Jonah" who brought them the bad luck of the hurricane that threatened our lives. We braved both the storm and the mutiny but there were many lives lost.

Captain Ken sends his regards. You remember him, don't you? He's the friend of my father who used to scare us with stories of a giant squid that would swallow whole ships.

Jessica has done a fine job as Master's Mate. She really is quite something and all the crew has now taken to her and trusts in her ability to con the ship. She sends her love and wishes you all the best.

Uncle Bob and I took up daily conversations on the Code of Aquinas while the ship was crawling in the doldrums sailing across the mid-Atlantic. He hopes to make it part of him as my father has these many years. I don't know if that will ever materialize, but I'm praying for it. He seems something of a changed man.

How are the Smith brothers and Samuel? Is the cooperage holding up? We heard about the blockade and I suspect we're not filling too many orders. And that's okay.

With the money I've made on this cruise I'll be in good shape for a long time. But, there's something way more important than money.

Gilly, you know I didn't ship out and leave you and the cooperage for mere money. Captain Ken says there's a slight chance that my pa might be with the British invasion force that is sailing down the St. Lawrence River to invade New York. He says this because my pa is both a cooper and a carpenter and that these skills would be needed by the British who are building a fleet there. Captain Ken figured my pa was sent to Halifax after impressment. So, broadly speaking, he's in the neighborhood. However remote the possibility is, I can't pass up the chance to be in proximity to my father.

And, here it is Gilly: Jessica and I, Uncle Bob and Captain Ken, have all volunteered to join Commodore Macdonough in the defense of Lake Champlain. It's a long stretch of water situated between New York and Vermont. The thinking is that now the war is over in Europe and Napoleon defeated, the British will send an army of crack soldiers through Canada into our country. Lake Champlain is vital in any effort to invade New York. Without this waterway, Captain Ken tells me, it's impossible. You can't invade New York without controlling the lake, he says.

Captain Ken served with General Benedict Arnold in the Revolution before Arnold turned traitor. Still, Captain Ken loved Arnold, who he swears saved the colonies in our fight for independence on Champlain and at Saratoga. But, that's a story for another day. Anyway the British tried this way back when, and Captain Ken says they're going to try it again.

So we're traveling up the Hudson River to Lake Champlain and a town in Vermont to help build and then sail Macdonough's fleet. Many of the hands from *The Chasseur* are going to join us. I know it sounds crazy but it's as if we all suddenly recognized that this is what we 'ought to believe.'

It's very strange. Either we will be laughing about this whole thing or crying about it in our grog years from now. It's ironic when I realize that as we go north to confront and repel the enemy, you face possibly a worse threat on the shores of our home city.

Stay strong, Gilly, because with God's help we can overcome the invasion of the enemy and save this country from the arrogant bastards who still think we're one of their colonies.

Oh, and by the way, if you're wondering why I haven't inquired about Desiree Pechin it's because of Jessica.

Gilly, apparently this comes as no surprise to anyone but me. I was so enamored with Desiree that I could not see the affection Jessica had for me. We fell in love with each other on the crossing to Ireland. It happened when I looked into her eyes on a cold, starlit night and knew that she is what I 'ought" to believe in. It is my firmest hope that, one day when this is all over, she will become my wife, and, if we get through the coming battle, to return to Baltimore and raise a family. This, then, releases you from my request to watch over Desiree.

Jessica is my love and my life from here on in. Desiree, I now know, is someone who uses people for her own purposes. Take care, Gilly, you don't fall into her trap as I did. She can be highly controlling and persuasive.

And how are you getting along with the code, Gilly, my blood brother? Have you consulted Father John? I can tell you it has already had an immense impact upon my life. Perhaps it's because I've experienced the heat of battle, not knowing whether I would live or die. Thus the code becomes more intense and relevant. I told you before I shipped out that the code works slowly and quietly below the surface of your conscious mind. I'm told it takes years to acquire a mastery of it, or, rather, allowing it to master you. I hope we can compare notes on the code when I finally return home. Maybe then we can try our luck baiting for rock fish and talk of the code and everything that's happened to each of us over the course of this war.

Pray for us Gilly, as I assure you I will keep you in my prayers. You and I are about to enter into the teeth of the gale as the British juggernaut descends upon us. This cannot be a coincidence. It is meant to divide American forces between New York and Maryland. It's like we're fighting two wars at once. If our nation can pull this off, it will be remembered as akin to the victory at Yorktown.

Please let us hear from you. The mails are slowed by the war I know. Any correspondence from you will be directed from the hotel we're staying at in New York City to Commodore Macdonough's shipyard in Vergennes, Vermont.

Your brother by blood,

Michael

Gilly shared the contents of Michael's letter with Samuel. The clerk proudly read it to the Smith brothers, who, thanks to Samuel, were just beginning to learn how to read.

*****

Desiree had her servants follow Gilly everywhere. He was so busy he didn't even notice. The servants reported back to their mistress the truth of what Gilly said: he lived in the red, brick house of the Dooleys on Thames Street; he was kept occupied selling papers until school started; he attended St. Patrick's Free School and was a star pupil, excelling in poetry and prose, and mathematics; after school, he checked on the cooperage, examining the books and arranging orders for the coming day; he returned to Thames Street to cook a simple meal and clean the Dooley home, then retired early. There were no girls in his life and few friends. Gilly led a solitary life.

And then it dawned on Desiree how to manipulate the situation. One morning, after Gilly had left *The American* to sell his papers on Market Street, Desiree paid a visit to her father. She knocked gently on the editor's door. Her plans were laid out perfectly in her mind and her countenance was set in confident determination.

A raspy bark replied from behind the door. "Alright, damn you, alright, come in if you must." With her chin up and a rosy smile on her dimpled face, Desiree swooshed herself and her dress into the office.

"Why, child, you're up and about early this morning."

"I needed to speak to you father."

"Is it your tutor, again?"

"No, the tutor's failings are a discussion best left for another day." At this, Mr. Pechin sighed in relief. Keeping a tutor for his daughter was a constant struggle. Either the tutors quit in frustration or Desiree had them fired.

"Father, I just noticed Gilly Morrison leaving the newspaper strapped to a harness of some sort." Desiree rolled her eyes and feigned a look of compassion.

"Yes, it's his shoulder harness. He's lame, you know, and the harness helps him in his work."

"But he looks as if he was a beast of burden."

"We're all beasts of burden, Desiree, whether we want to admit it or not. There's nothing wrong with devising a mechanism to help you in your work. Why it's downright American ingenuity."

"Ingenious or not, it pains me to see him under such circumstances.

50

Father, I've read Gilly's poems. They are brilliant. Father Moranvillè says his prose is even better."

"The good priest knows more about French poetry than he does about running a newspaper. Now, what is this really all about? There's a war on, child. I've not time to discuss poetry and prose."

Desiree clasped her hands together and raised them in urgent supplication to her father. "Couldn't you hire him as a writer for *The American*?"

"News reporting is totally different than poetry," Pechin asserted. "I need factual information for my readership – not schoolboy notions of what the world should be or some sort of romantic gibberish like that."

"Talk to Father John, he would tell you of Gilly's talents. All of Fells Point knows of Gilly's character and he knows everyone in Fells Point. They trust him implicitly, father. You could use a writer like that. Your readership will increase and your republican agenda will triumph."

"Desiree, a reporter's job is to get around and cover a story without delay. Gilly, well, Gilly is a cripple. No harness in the world could help him with that."

"Yes there is father. You could give him one of your horses from the stable. The horse would be his legs."

"I can't set a precedent like that. The other reporters, my staff, they will all want a damned horse."

Desiree used her last strategy, but a well-timed and a proven one: she stomped her foot and raised her voice. "The Pechins should be above all that. We should set an example in helping the impoverished, especially those as talented as Gilly Morrison."

William Pechin relented. He always did because he could never refuse his daughter when she wanted something so badly; although, her sudden compassion for the needy of Baltimore was somewhat surprising and quite puzzling.

Desiree left *The American* and took a seat in her elaborate carriage. As it made its way into Old City she sported a mischievous grin. With Gilly hired as a writer for the newspaper he could only be grateful to her for her benevolent largess. Besides, her father was the editor and Gilly would never want to compromise his new found position by denying her overtures.

To Gilly's surprise, Mr. Pechin asked to see him the very next morning. Gilly sat nervously in the editor's office clueless as to the purpose of the meeting. Pechin came right to the point.

"Gilly, you've done a fine job selling our newspaper on the Point. It has not escaped my attention. I always like to reward hard work. It was recommended to me yesterday – an odd but rather interesting proposition

52

which I wish to pursue as long as you and Father John agree."

"Certainly, sir, may I inquire as to who made the recommendation?"

"Yes, my daughter, Desiree." Gilly sunk a little lower in his seat. "But, be that as it may the offer is this: would you be interested in working as a reporter for *The American*?"

Gilly's eyes popped out of his head. Never had he dreamed of such an opportunity. He tried to answer without stammering. He desperately tried not to whistle. "Yes, sir, I would. I appreciate your consideration of my humble talents and promise to work very hard."

"I have no doubt you will. But, tell me Gilly, and I know this is sudden and you haven't had time to formulate yours ideas properly. Have you any notions on how the newspaper can increase circulation?"

This question, however, was something he had given a lot of thought to, only because as he was selling his papers in the morning, the average reader had already expressed them. Gilly decided to be honest about this.

"I do, Mr. Pechin, but these are not entirely my ideas. They're the readers' ideas. Every day they ask me questions. Not about the dispatches, everybody knows all of the newspapers in Baltimore carry the latest dispatches. But what they want even more are the stories behind the dispatches." Gilly had gotten Pechin's attention.

"And what do you mean by the stories?"

"Every reader knows the names of the soldiers and sailors behind the defenses of the city. What they want to know is who they really are. Should they trust them? Will they stand and fight or will they run?"

Mr. Pechin waved his hand in front of his face. "Good heavens, that's sounds like a lot of claptrap to me. Gilly you know, don't you, the difference between objective reporting and subjective narration? How can one know if a man is going to run or not at the sight of a British bayonet? How can a reporter, or anyone for that matter, prejudge a man's fortitude before the action takes place. Unless there's a documented history of disservice and cowardice, this could be grounds for a libel suit. Worse still, *The American* would be accused, and rightfully so, of causing an unfounded panic in the populace."

Gilly nodded, enthusiastically. "I've no intention upon making those judgments, sir. The readers will come to their own conclusions if given the right information. And information to make critical decisions now, before the coming battle, is important to them. They ask each other the same question: 'should I take my family and evacuate or stay and support the war effort?' This is what the readers want to know. What they *need* to know."

The editor sat back in his leather chair and mulled this over. "And how are we going to make all this happen, Gilly?"

"If I may, Mr. Pechin, I'd like to make *you* a proposition."

"Highly unusual from someone so young and inexperienced, however proceed."

"Grant me the authority to go beyond the dispatches. To tell the stories of the men and women, yes, women, who will figure in the equation of the expected hostile actions by the British upon Baltimore City. By using my pen as a sword, because the battle we all expect is coming is being fought *here and now*, not just when the first shot is fired. There's a story behind each and every one of the defenders of Baltimore and I firmly believe it is this newspaper's responsibility to tell the whole story. And, most importantly, to make *The American* the storyteller to the city before rumor and innuendo captures the minds of weak-minded people who will run before we can put up our best defense."

Pechin knew, when war was first declared, that if the republican press did not control the dissemination of information to the public, the war could be lost. Pechin was now convinced to have *The American* tell the story of the war through the eyes, ears, and pen of young Gilly Morrison.

"Go and sell your papers, Gilly, for perhaps the last time. You'll be busy with a different kind of selling from now on. Sharpen your pen and let it become a sword. I will find a replacement for you. In the meantime I must procure Father John's permission. In any event, report back to me at this time tomorrow."

As Gilly sold the last of his papers at Market and Banks streets, his mind began to swirl in a dozen different directions. Could this really be happening to me, he asked himself? Am I dreaming?

Gilly had always imagined using his talents as a writer and poet to advance himself in life. He had always admired the biographer whose job it was to tell his audience, in a compelling way, the story of someone in history who made an impact on the world. Or the poet, who could capture the essence of an idea or an ideal in a few well-chosen words and thus command immediate understanding. But he was an orphan. Orphans had no right to dream such things.

At school, Father John asked Gilly to step outside so that they could talk privately. "This morning, I received a note from your esteemed editor asking for a meeting this afternoon. It concerns you, *mon ami*. Can you enlighten me as to its purpose?"

"He's asked me to be a writer for the newspaper. It's an excellent opportunity, Father. Something I feel, perhaps, I don't deserve. But one I would very much like to try."

"And, how did this all come about, Gilly. You are a student capable of scholarly achievement no doubt, yet this is not generally known outside the confines of this school."

Gilly frowned and bowed his head. "Desiree Pechin recommended me," he said, dejectedly.

Father John clasped his hands behind his back in a most clerical fashion. "You are aware, my son, of the capabilities and intentions of Mistress Pechin? You know, I'm sure, of the machinations she applied to Michael Dooley."

"Yes, Father John, she used him like a puppet for her entertainment. She collects lovers like I used to collect butterflies when I was a kid."

The priest compressed his lips and put his arm around Gilly's shoulders. They walked for a short spell before Father John stopped and faced Gilly once more. Moranvillè sensed Gilly was on fire for this opportunity and wanted him to digest the full implications of his decision before the priest gave his approval.

"All of our actions have consequences, *mon ami*, some apparent, others hidden and unseen to our conscious minds and innocent hearts. When our decisions are truly our own, after careful reflection and prayerfully pleading for the guidance and inspiration of the Holy Spirit, then we can act without self-incrimination. But if our decisions are tainted by our own sense of self-satisfaction, or avarice, or envy, then they become corrupted. And, worse still, if our decisions are manipulated to satisfy the evil objectives of others, we surrender our free will and become pawns to be toyed with on the chessboard of life."

Gilly's head was still bowed down to the ground. Tears streamed from his eyes and down his cheeks. He felt every one of Moranvillès words in his heart, to the very depths of his soul. He knew the priest was right. His desire to have this position was influenced by both his own ambition and the wiles of the editor's daughter. Still, if he could only get the chance …

Suddenly, something occurred to him in his heart and mind. It was subtle but ran deep into his very veins. He knew what he "ought to believe." God had given him the gift of communicating to others truth. And, now, he knew it to be true.

Father John pulled a handkerchief from his cassock and put it into Gilly's hands. "I'll speak to Mr. Pechin this afternoon and tell him that I give my approval for you to be employed as a writer on a *per diem* basis. But the final decision is in your hands. You and I both know a ransom must be paid. Go and check on the cooperage and then go to the Dooley house. Make yourself a fine meal. Then reflect on what I have just told you and pray. With a good night's sleep and proper consideration of the Code of Aquinas, which I can already see working in your mind and heart, you will come to the right decision in the morning. You are a good boy, Gilly, and will become a fine man. No harm will come to you as long as I live. And even after I'm gone, if you internalize the code, which I'm certain you will, there will be no danger."

Gilly was comforted by Father John's words of encouragement. The priest believed in him. The code was working in him. Yet the danger posed by

Desiree was all too real.

Chapter 4: Consequences and

Compromise

Gilly checked on the cooperage and found Samuel behind the counter going over the accounting in his systematic manner.

"Hello, Master Morrison, it's good to see you." Samuel noticed Gilly's somber mood and the puffiness of his eyes. Something wasn't quite right. Gilly was always bright eyed and smiling.

"Samuel, where are the Smith brothers?"

"They're off drilling with the City Brigade. There's no work to be done. Should I dock their wages?"

Gilly shook his head. "As long as the business can afford it, everybody remains on payroll. That goes for you, too. Whenever you volunteer at Fort McHenry to help construct the new fortifications Major Armistead has ordered, you'll still be on the books of the cooperage, understand?"

Samuel nodded. "Yes, sir, that is most generous. Before the British blockade we had done quite well. We filled more orders than I've ever seen before. There is still, as you know, a solid, positive balance on our books."

"Good. The work you and the Smith brothers are doing in the defense of the city is more important than you realize. If the enemy takes Fort McHenry and overruns Hampstead Hill, one of the first buildings to be put to the torch will be this establishment. We've outfitted more privateers with barrels than anyone else in Baltimore and there's a price on our heads.

"And yet, Samuel, be aware that our business might not remain as dire as it appears right now. If the British threaten Baltimore we'll see more militia pour into town, more militia means more barrels. Then our orders will skyrocket like the munitions on one of those damned British Bomb ships the dispatches hinted were coming into the Chesapeake."

"What on earth are bomb ships?"

Gilly knew Samuel was a pacifist and unaware of military matters and jargon. "An evil invention if there ever was one, Samuel. You saw the fireworks over the Patapsco at last year's Fourth-of-July celebration didn't you?"

"Oh, yes. It was magnificent, and according to the dictates of my Quaker faith, a peaceful and proper use of gunpowder, I dare say."

"Well keep that memory in your head and picture those shells directed into Fells Point. What do you think would be the likely result?"

Samuel didn't enjoy making the picture. "It's a horrible thing, Master Morrison. The result would be pandemonium - utter terror. Do you think such a thing could happen? Would the orphanage be threatened?"

"I don't think the British have turned into madmen, not yet anyway, except maybe for Admiral Cockburn. They know all about our city because they have spies everywhere. They wouldn't fire upon the orphanage because they don't make war against children. Besides, it has no strategic importance. I make this analogy only to stress the point that their objective is terror. Now picture those same rockets firing over and into Fort McHenry, and the defensive line – our last defensive position that is Hampstead Hill. What would the militiamen do?"

Even Samuel knew what they would do. "I'm afraid they would run away, sir. The militiamen are there to protect the city, but they have homes, farms and families. I've talked to a great many of them since this whole nasty business began. They consider themselves patriots and brave men – and they certainly are. But unlike the regulars, they aren't paid to die."

"That's what I think, too. I asked you this Samuel because it's going to be my job to change that scenario you just portrayed."

"How is that possible?"

Gilly paused to catch his breath. So much had happened to him today. He tried to keep things in proper perspective. "Well, let's go back to the increase in business I expect to happen soon. We won't be filling orders for the shipping trade of course, there is little of that. But as a battle for the city seems imminent we can expect an increase in orders, especially dry barrels for gunpowder. We've got to keep the reputation of this cooperage as high as it has ever been. Those barrels must be able to withstand the worst kinds of weather so those risking their lives will find comfort in a Dooley-made barrel.

"Remember also, Samuel, the Smith brothers are going to be called to muster at all hours of the day or night. They may not be available for work. So, keep an eye out for additional help. If anyone comes in here looking for a job, take their name and address so that we can get ahold of them when we need to. I can get a discount rate at *The American* for any advertisement we want to run. I'll have Bartlett, Pechin's assistant and copy editor, put it on the front page. That will certainly bring prospects to our door."

Samuel, diligent as ever, began to take notes.

"Now, I'll be checking in on the business from time to time, but not every day."

"Are you leaving, Master Morrison?"

"In a sense, yes I am. I've taken a position with *The American* as a writer."

Samuel beamed. "Congratulations, sir. This is, indeed, a momentous occasion! I know of your great interest in writing. I have read your poetry and it inspires me. Is this what you meant when you said it will be your job to instill confidence in the militia, enough, possibly so that they will not run away from rockets?"

"Sort of, Samuel. My thinking is that if I can inspire self-confidence in the militia, I might finally be able to do something to contribute to the war effort. I can't drill like the Smith brothers and I can't help build ramparts as you are doing. My contributions will have to be made from the sidelines of battle and well before the battle begins, you see?"

"Yes, indeed I see. What I don't see, and forgive me for this, is why your nose and eyes are red when you have always had a cheery disposition. Do you believe in your own self-confidence?"

Gilly lowered his head. "I thought I did. But now I'm not quite sure. Father John and I had a long talk this afternoon. He warned me of the consequences should I take this position."

They were both silent for a time. Then, Samuel put two and two together. "Sir, does this compromise you in some way? Think on the Code of Aquinas and what it means to you."

"I've done nothing else these past few hours."

"Master Morrison, does this compromise I suggested - this consequence Father John spoke of - is it driven in a collapsible chaise, have dimples and long, auburn hair, and hides its perfect face under a pink parasol?"

Gilly could only grunt. "She was here already? And, I thought I finally started to really think I've gotten the code."

"She's been here twice, Master Morrison."

"I must have been with Father John at the time. Boy, she works fast. What am I to do Samuel? You've understood the words of the code since it first reached your ears and I have just grappled with fragments of it."

"Trust in yourself, Master Gilly, if I may be so informal. Trust in who you are because there are many of us who admire you *because* of who you are. The code is just coming into you like a spark to dry kindling. You will not be compromised. This, in my humble opinion is what 'you ought to believe.'"

Gilly nodded his head and smiled at the clerk. "Thanks, Samuel, you've read my thoughts, realized my doubts, and yet, like Father John, you still trust in my judgment."

"I will always do that, Master Gilly."

As Gilly opened the door to the cooperage he turned once again to the Dooley's loyal clerk. "Lock up and go home my friend."

*****

Finally, after perhaps the longest day of his young life, Gilly limped his way to the red, brick house on Thames Street. He clasped the bright brass handle and opened the heavy oak door. Gilly suddenly felt a deep pang in the pit of his stomach and heard it give a long-drawn out growl. He descended into the cool root cellar with a candle and found the crude ice box covered with straw and containing perishable food items like the fresh milk he had bought just yesterday. Coming back into the kitchen, he sat at the table and fixed a butter and jam sandwich, with extra butter and strawberry jam. He devoured the sandwich in just four bites, and then washed it down with the still cold milk. This brought some sense back into him. It was the "fine meal" Father John had foreseen. He rushed upstairs, undressed, and put on a warm pair of wool socks, a flannel nightgown, and a nightcap. Then, he sat at the desk and began to write a letter:

Dear Michael,

Thank you for writing to me. I received your much

anticipated correspondence just the other day. I marveled at the adventures you and Jessica endured across the Atlantic in cold weather. I wish I could have been there with you.

I was surprised at your decision to travel up the Hudson River to Lake Champlain after the long and dangerous voyage you've just come through. But, I understand your reasoning. I agree with old Captain Ken that the British invasion of New York can only be successful if they build a strong fleet of ships and control the lake. Not being familiar with the geography or topography of the area, I stopped by the library and looked at all the maps.

Whether your father is among the company of carpenters and coopers the British have on the Lake is a mystery to me. I certainly hope, for your sake, Captain Ken's assessment of this situation is true. My Lord, Michael, can this possibly be happening? Are you really within proximity to the father you love and lost so unfortunately to the evils of impressment, and at this critical juncture?

As you wisely pointed out in your letter, Michael, you are poised to face the British assault by land and lake in

New York; we are facing the same challenge in Maryland, but by land and sea. Don't you see the irony? Or should I say the chilling destiny?

In Baltimore, the city is planning for a strong defense. The Smith brothers have joined the City Brigade and frequently leave the cooperage to drill with the town's finest militia. Samuel, our gentle Quaker, spends as much time as he can in helping out with the construction of fortifications at McHenry.

Oh, before I forget, Michael, I gave my permission to keep them on the payroll while they volunteer their efforts. I didn't think you'd mind. You, more than anyone, know their personal quality and untiring work ethic. If orders pick up, and I suspect they will as battle approaches us, I trust they will do double duty. In the event they cannot, I told Samuel to find additional help to get us through the much expected British onslaught.

Also, apparently, Samuel had heard us discussing the code before you shipped out on the *Chasseur* with Captain Boyle. He heard the words and they immediately made a deep and lasting impression upon his heart. It's true, Michael, I wouldn't lie to you. Samuel, although always a kind and simple man, has exhibited some amazing capabilities. He has developed an inner sense of awareness to the things around him. It's as if he is reading your thoughts. I confess I was jealous of this, because I've struggled to understand the code as you have. Father John says it might be that Samuel needs to interiorize the code quickly because this is something he 'ought to believe' and there may not be much time to accomplish it.

Anyway, I'm so glad you and Jessica have found romance. You will be the perfect couple, I have no doubt. Please give my love to her, and my respects to your uncle Bob and Captain Ken.

There is only one more thing. I have left this for last on purpose. Desiree Pechin has been after me since your departure, as you suspected when you wrote to me. She pulled an unbelievable ruse on me and I fell for it. She suggested to her father I be hired as a writer for *The American*. Although I knew she proposed (probably demanded) it of her father, I quickly accepted without thinking of the consequences or the fact that my integrity would be compromised. I'm convinced both consequences and compromise threaten me and I am distraught. Still, the code has worked in me and I've decided to accept the position as scared as I am of the consequences. Michael, you know more than anyone on earth what this means to me. Please, pray God will give me the strength to withstand her wiles. In the meantime I will pray for you and Jessica. Keep safe, Michael, and please write while there is still time.

Your blood brother,

Gilly

*****

The sun was just up and gleamed off the blue wavelets of the Patapsco when Gilly arrived at *The American*. Gilly smiled at the boy who had taken his place hawking papers in Fells Point. The boy's name was Gabriel Johnson. Michael knew him as Gabe, a fellow orphan from St. Patrick's. Father John must have arranged his appointment, Gilly thought.

Gabe was about to make his exit and start his first day at Market and Bank Streets, but hesitated and walked over to his older, fellow orphan. There's a strong sense of camaraderie and often affection among orphans, especially between younger children and the older ones. After all, they considered themselves almost like siblings. Gilly saw himself in this very position not long ago.

Gabe was the epitome of an orphaned waif. He was small, skinny, and somewhat unkempt. He sported a jaunty cap with the brim listing over his right eyebrow. HI was evident he had been crying because there were black streaks trailing down his gaunt cheeks. As he wiped away his tears with his hands stained with fresh newsprint, the impression of the pitiful ragamuffin was even more exaggerated. Gilly wasn't going to mention anything. Sometimes a forlorn countenance was good for sales.

As Gabe neared, he broke into a run and wrapped his slight arms around Gilly's waist. "Gilly, I'm so terribly happy. I finally have a position and can make some money on my own. Thank you, Gilly."

Gilly whistled. "Don't you be thanking me, Gabe Johnson. I'd wager it was Father John who recommended you to Mr. Pechin."

"Yes, but if you weren't promoted - and everyone at the orphanage cheered by the way - I would never have had the chance."

Gilly chuckled, "You'll do fine lad. But let me give you some advice.

"Oh please, Gilly, do so."

"Never, ever, be late for work. In fact be early." Gabe nodded, absorbing every word from the celebrated senior orphan. "Watch your accounting. Know and have documented every paper you leave here with and then make sure that squares with the amount of money you bring back. Save your money, especially the tips you get around the holidays. Put it away

71

without thinking. Give it to Father John and he will have an account opened for you at the bank. After a couple of years you will be amazed at how much money you have put away."

"Oh, Gilly, will it really be that much?"

"It will, indeed, if you don't spend it." Gilly grinned and showed his gleaming white teeth. He was almost as excited as Gabe was. "Except for maybe a new cap, lad; this one's a little frayed. Now go and do your job and do it well wee one."

Gabe needed no further encouragement. He dashed outside to his wagon. While he strained to pull his load his heart pounded, his brow broke out in a fine sweat, and his imagination reveled in new possibilities beneath a frayed, listing cap.

Mr. Pechin ordered Gilly to proceed to the Pechin Stables and select a horse so that Gilly could cover the city and beyond in his duties as a writer. Gilly was about to object, taking this, at least initially, as something of a slight due to the impediment he endured in his leg. Pechin noticed his young reporter's downturned expression and immediately understood.

"So far in life, Son, you have not only coped with your disability, but have endured the pain in silence and with great dignity. This is why I have chosen you." Gilly couldn't help but think Desiree was somehow behind the idea of a horse.

"Sir, I have always been able to perform my duties despite my leg."

Pechin's compassion was beginning to wan. "You've never worked for me as a reporter!"

"Writer, sir," Gilly said, timidly.

"Yes, all right, damn you - writer. But I will require you to cover a vast territory, sometimes on short notice. Good God, man, you can't limp your way through this war. I require immediate information – err – stories, when and if I need them for publication. The presses won't wait for anyone, sir."

Gilly capitulated. "I will obey your orders to procure a horse from your stables. I can ride, although I haven't had extensive experience."

"Have no fear, Son, the master of my stables is more than qualified to see to your needs. Just follow his instructions and report back to me as fast as you are able. Things are moving rapidly now. This will be the battle summer the British have been anticipating. They will not fail to let it slip out of their hands."

*****

Maryland had always been "horse country." Some of the finest horses were bred and raised on the farms of the state's affluent families. The Pechin Stables were located south of the city and was home to some of the most prized horse flesh in America.

Gilly took the ferry from Fells Point across the Patapsco and ascended Federal Hill overlooking the entire city and its extensive harbor. He paused to rub his aching leg. "Mr. Pechin was right," Gilly thought, "I need a horse."

Atop Federal Hill, Gilly could see all of Baltimore and admired its beauty. He immediately saw its strategic importance in the war. "Of course the British would come to capture and subdue our city," Gilly talked aloud to himself. "Nowhere in America, not New York City, not Philadelphia, nor Boston, has the war been waged more successfully by our private navy." Gilly was suddenly beset with a sense of pride in his hometown.

He cupped his hands over his blue eyes and stared east. Major Armistead had his command up early. They were busy in the fort, on the walls, in the ramparts. The new writer for *The American* felt a story being born in his mind. I'm definitely going to do an article on Armistead, he thought.

Gilly slowly walked down Federal Hill and finally arrived at the Pechin Stables. He presented the editor's letter of introduction to the Master of the Stables, Istvan. Gilly didn't know it yet, but the Hungarian horse trainer was about to make a unique difference in his life.

Chapter 5: Princess

Istvan was as protective of Pechin's horses as if they were his own. He looked at Pechin's letter of introduction with an air of skepticism. This was primarily because he couldn't read English. Still, he paused here and there as he pretended to read just to make it look like he could. He did, however, recognize Mr. Pechin's signature.

He walked around Gilly and inspected him as if he was sizing up a new horse for purchase. Gilly assessed him, too. The Hungarian master was short in stature with a long, aquiline nose and bushy, gray eyebrows, matching the gray around the temples of his head. He sported a long, black handlebar mustache, which was well groomed and greased. His spine was so erect one would think him two inches taller. His clothes were crumpled yet very clean. Even his leather riding boots were well polished. His steps were taken deliberately, in a military fashion. In the nook of his right armpit he carried a mahogany riding crop with a leather strap.

"What is name?"

"My name is Gilly, sir. Gilly Morrison."

"Why you here," the master demanded more than asked.

Gilly pointed to the letter. "I haven't read Mr. Pechin's words, sir. I just assumed this was all explained in the correspondence from my editor."

Istvan shook his head in the negative and grunted. "Why you here," he repeated.

Gilly shrugged his shoulders. "I'm here to procure a horse."

"Why?"

Gilly became agitated. "Because I'm lame in my left leg and I can't walk without pain. As a new writer for *The American*, I need to be able to get around the city and beyond. I also need to write my stories and have them published in the newspaper on a timely basis. I can't cover the war on foot. I need a good horse to help me. The British are everywhere up and down the Chesapeake Bay and I have to keep up with their movements."

Istvan understood this as the pillaging and burning of towns and villages had become common knowledge and the local populace scrambled to

76

take every measure to avoid a similar fate. Indeed, Istvan was just about to move Mr. Pechin's horses to a safe haven, west of the city, when Gilly arrived. Rumors were whispered about that the British did not have the one thing necessary to achieve total victory: cavalry. Istvan knew, from his service in the Hungarian army a decade ago, that horses were essential in battle. He would do anything to prevent the British from capturing the Pechin Stables.

"This is jó, Gilly Morrison. But how much time is it before lobster crawls into Baltimore and squeezes us with big claw and stabs us with black bayonet? Istvan not got time to train. Must move horses to safety."

Gilly had to make a few assumptions. What he heard as "yo" meant good, or fine, or something like that. The lobster would be British infantry.

"Soon, Master Istvan, but we aren't sure. The enemy may decide to go against Washington or Annapolis before they set their sights on us. Yet there is no doubt in my mind they will attack Baltimore this summer. They want to destroy us. My guess is late summer, maybe early fall."

Istvan pressed his lips together. Perhaps, he thought, there will be time to train a crippled boy on an important mission before he evacuated the stables and headed for higher and safer ground to the west.

The stable master took Gilly by the hand and walked back and forth among the stalls of the stables. Istvan suddenly stopped at the stall of a spirited palomino. Gilly was apprehensive about the choice. He had ridden a

77

few horses in his life, but always ones that were docile. This mare seemed a little feisty – almost like she had never been broken. The horse, Gilly thought, had something of a surly attitude and bearing. It was almost as if she was looking down on him. Given the fact Gilly could not walk without pain, let alone saddle a horse and use his left leg to direct a horse's gait and direction, he shook his head in disapproval.

Istvan, however, was not deterred. He had made a preliminary decision.

"It is jó."

He led Gilly to a small cottage. There was a fire in the kitchen where a pot was boiling containing veal, potatoes, carrots, and onions, flavored with basil and paprika. "Gulyas," Istvan exclaimed. "Jó, igen? Is important to eat before making decision on horse, or on anything else in life, igen?"

Gilly was exhausted after his trek to the stables and desperately wanted to lay down some ground rules. "Istvan, when you say 'yo' you mean 'good,' is that correct?"

"Igen, that is correct. My English is not what you call fluent. I sometimes love the words of my native tongue to your English, but I try to speak American."

Gilly nodded and sat down at the table. He took a spoon and scooped up a bite of the aromatic Goulash from a bowl Istvan placed on the table. It watered his mouth with its succulent combination of herbs and seasonings. He was famished after his long trip from Fells Point. Sopping up the gravy with a slice of fresh bread smothered with sweet butter, he uttered a long, satisfied sigh.

"Istvan, that was absolutely delicious."

"It is jó?"

"Oh, yes, it is very yo."

After their meal, Istvan lit his pipe and took a turn around the stables. Gilly followed him. The stable hands had all retired for the night. The horses were fed, washed and groomed. Istvan stood before the palomino and smiled.

"Let us stroll outside Gilly Morrison. I need talk to you in private." This confused Gilly. There wasn't anybody else in the stables. The sun was just setting in a cloudless sky and Gilly felt a sudden sense of peace within him. To the north rose Federal Hill, and just beyond that the busy Baltimore streets and its forty thousand residents. Here, however, all was quiet and lush. He sniffed the air. Even though it was late spring there was still a touch of lilac lingering on a slight breeze.

"Istvan, why did we leave the stables? Everyone else has gone."

"They have big ears."

"Who has big ears?"

"Horses, Gilly Morrison. They can sometimes read thoughts."

"Horses can read thoughts? You mean they know what I'm thinking in English?"

"I think in Hungarian, you think in English. It doesn't matter what language we think in, the horses know all."

"What do they know, Istvan?"

"The palomino knows you don't like her. You must change this."

Gilly tried to make some sense out of what Istvan was telling him. "Can she read my mind from here? Because, if she can, she must know I don't really dislike her. I guess I'm just a little intimidated."

"Ah," Istvan balked, "this is worse than not like. She must see you as leader. You have to be strong, Gilly Morrison. Not to dominate her, you see. This one cannot not be dominated or ruled over in any way. She is too proud to be told what to do."

"Then, how do I make her go and stop and turn?"

Now it was time for Istvan to pause and collect his thoughts. "You are young, Gilly Morrison. You have not – what do they call it – experience with women or girls yet."

"Talk about intimidation! I can hardly speak around them.

Sometimes I can't even think, Istvan."

"It is natural, Gilly Morrison. It is very natural for boy of medium age to get a twist in the tongue around girls, igen? I was same when medium age so many years ago." Istvan smiled as he remembered his boyhood. "But, this could mean problem."

"Why's that?"

"With this female you have to bring her flowers and candy. Well, maybe apples and carrots. But don't spoil her, not at first. This will come later, after she has made her decision."

"What decision?

Istvan faced Gilly and looked into his eyes. "The choice is not for Gilly Morrison to make. The choice is for palomino. If she accepts you, all is fine. If not, then it is impossible."

"Then why did you … ?"

"I didn't choose anything. I felt something. She knows you don't like her or you have an inner fear. But, she likes *you*, this of utmost importance."

Gilly put his hands on his hips in frustration. "And why does she get to make all the decisions?"

"Ask God, not me. Things not change since beginning. Eve takes bite

81

of apple. Adam takes bite of apple, with no questions. Things not change. We are men and we are stupid when we meet women, igen?"

"I guess that's the way it is. I know I'm that way, although I'm trying to be better at that."

"Good luck. Maybe you find a better apple. But, there is one thing palomino has that you do not."

"What's that?"

"Horse sense."

*****

Gilly bunked with Istvan in the small cottage behind the stables. Altogether, it was a long and warm day. The goulash Gilly delved into was now digested and putting him to sleep. Gilly yawned deeply yet he could not find it within himself to nod off. Istvan was already buried in his blankets.

"Okay, so I don't have good horse sense." Gilly said, staring at Istvan's body somewhere underneath the covers. "Although I think I do. And the horse has all the sense in the world, fine! - yo! Then why would I put my life in the hands of a horse who could throw me off her back whenever she wanted to?" The stable master poked his hand out from under the blankets and waved it in the air dismissing the question. "Okay Istvan, you go to sleep. But, before you do, can you at least tell me her name?"

Istvan whispered "Sarika," and promptly fell asleep.

*****

At sunrise, Gilly was awakened to the enticing aroma of frying bacon, fresh coffee, and potatoes. It was a cold spring morning. He stretched his body atop the comfortable feathered mattress and thought about rolling over and shutting his eyes once more. But the allure of the kitchen was too strong. After dressing in a new flaxen shirt and white duck trousers, he reached underneath the bed and pulled out his sack. Gilly couldn't help but admire the shiny riding boots he purchased from a second-hand shop in the city just before he left Fells Point. The stable master will be impressed with these, he thought.

Istvan set the table with wooden plates and spoons. Then he lifted his cast-iron skillet from the fire and laid it on the table. Fresh bread and butter, and hot coffee and cream completed the morning repast. Gilly said not a word but dove into his breakfast with gusto.

Istvan enjoyed his meal, too, but couldn't help occasionally glancing at his new student. The boy reminded him of someone long ago; someone who for years he had tried to put out of his memory. Their breakfast finished, Gilly helped with cleaning the dishes at the washstand in back of the cottage.

"You are ready then, Gilly Morrison?"

"Yes, see my new boots?"

Istvan grunted. "They are not new and not needed."

"But I thought we were going riding?"

"Today we train. I train you - you train horse – horse train you. This day not for saddling and riding. Horse not ready for this. Today is for talking to horse. She needs, how do I say, get acquainted with you. Just you and her. Would you let stranger get on Gilly Morrison's back first time you meet?"

"Then you aren't going to talk to me and coach me?"

"Me not talk to you. You not talk to me. You did enough talking last night. Today you talk to horse."

As Gilly walked to the track, Istvan had one of the stable boys fetch Sarika. The track was impressive. It was a quarter-mile in circumference and shaped like a rather large egg. A seasoned fence surrounded the whole of it. There were no other animals exercising on the track right now. The master wanted Gilly and Sarika to be alone.

Istvan led Gilly through a gate onto the track. The stable boy guided Sarika on a solitary rope strung about her long neck. Sarika was used to exercising on the track and was let in easily. Istvan put the tail end of the rope in Gilly's hands and proceeded to his other duties.

At first, Gilly just stared at her. She was beautiful in the morning light. Her coat was pure gold with a snow-white mane and tail. Her large, chestnut-colored eyes stared back at him beneath long lashes with a curious intensity.

Gilly shrugged his shoulders and raised his eyebrows. "Okay, girl, let's take a walk." He led her around the track by the rope and then stopped for a moment. "Don't let me do all the talking, Sarika. You're the female here and I bet you can talk it up with those stable mares of yours as well as the best of them."

Sarika stood about fifteen-hands tall. She was not a great steed in the Arabian line but she thought she was. She walked proudly with her head held high, prancing occasionally like a champion with high steps, each leg acting independently of and yet in sync with each other. She seemed to instinctively know she was special.

In their walk Gilly reached up and grabbed the rope from directly beneath her chin. "You know you're a pretty girl, Sarika. What does your name mean anyway? I know a pretty girl in Baltimore. Her name is Desiree. She has the same color eyes as you do. But, she's not my girl and I don't think you would like her. She's rich and pampered and privileged. She doesn't see anything around her but her own selfish wants and desires." Gilly laughed at himself while showing his dazzling white teeth in a broad grin. Sarika decided she liked his teeth.

"But what am I doing talking to you about another girl?" Gilly didn't know it yet, but his sense of intimidation was now completely gone. Sarika sensed it immediately. After an hour, Gilly started to limp badly. Sarika stopped and scratched the ground with her left hoof. Holding her head up in supposed indignation, she snorted heartily. It was as if Sarika knew Gilly was in pain and wanted to halt the easy exercise for his sake.

Gilly was more than happy to comply. While rubbing his sore leg he opened his mind to the mare. He told her things he had never told any living creature, not even his blood brother, Michael. Everything Gilly had bottled up in his heart was now uncorked and spilled out onto a dirt track before a horse with knowing and compassionate chestnut eyes.

Sarika listened attentively. She nodded her head and snorted whenever Gilly paused in his heartfelt discourse. Gilly reached as far back into the depths of his soul as he was capable. Tears welled into his eyes as he told Sarika his life story: of his abandonment as a baby; his life at the orphanage; and his longing for love and family. Gilly lowered his head and quietly sobbed. Sarika nuzzled her nose atop his head, played with his curly, red hair, and licked the tears from his face. Gilly swore she was crying, too.

Suddenly, Istvan appeared behind them. "Jó!" he exclaimed. "You have nice talk. This is jó. The first step always hardest step. Like baby who must crawl before walk."

"What does Sarika mean in English?"

Istvan smiled broadly. "In my country she is 'Noble Lady' – she is

'Princess'."

Gilly nestled his head into the mare's mane and shrugged his shoulders. "I didn't need to ask you, Istvan. I already knew. I love you noble lady. I love you my Princess."

While Gilly rested his leg upon a cushioned chair, Istvan prepared a simple lunch of root vegetables, fresh berries, bread, and strong tea. "How long do we continue with the walking and talking, Istvan?"

"Not long now. You will do this for rest of day. You make much progress, Gilly Morrison. I never see such progress in short time. Sarika has come to love you. I not know what you talk about, but I know she has made decision. She has chosen you. Not as master but as child. She wants to take care of you. She knows you love her just as much. This is jó. There is not time to train as Istvan would like. I must move horses to safety. We try saddle tomorrow. See how it go."

During the afternoon session, Gilly talked to Sarika about different things. He constantly called her his Princess. He told her of his plans on writing for *The American*. And then something dawned on him.

"Wait just a minute, Princess. If I can do half of what I just told you; if I can put together a string of stories and have them published, I could *prove* my worth. I could convince Mr. Pechin of my ability to tell the story of the battle that is to come and possibly increase sales. If I could do that before

87

Desiree tries to compromise me then I could be my own man. Free from her wiles. Don't you see it Princess?"

Sarika did see it, but not in the way Gilly intended. What she saw, or rather sensed, was an abiding confidence - an uncompromising assurance in the heart of her rider. She needed this from him. This was the leadership she desired. She was, after all, of noble breed and birth and required at least this much in her prince.

*****

The British army and navy were poised to attack at all points along the Chesapeake after establishing a base and building Fort Albion on Tangier Island in the center of the Bay. The question was where would they strike next?

For Southern plantation owners came disturbing news that the British were training black slaves, who had been freed by British forces or who had run away, as army infantrymen. The former slaves responded well to army discipline and training. Some British officers even thought they would be a match for seasoned redcoats.

William Pechin was anxious for his star writer to return to his duties at the newspaper and write the stories they had talked about. He sent a message by courier to Gilly urging him to return to Baltimore. At dinner, Istvan and Gilly discussed the pressing dispatch. Istvan insisted that Gilly remain long enough to be able to ride Sarika properly.

"You love horse. She love you. This all plain to see. But you need instruction. She wants to please you. She know you have bad leg. She will do, because she love you, what you want her do. But you must be taught how to ride a horse like in Hungary. What you call your Princess must be ridden with all respect and dignity. She is noble lady and deserves this.

"As for training, you must first learn proper deportment. Attitude is everything. Sit with firm back. When you ride Sarika, you must ride like prince. Like all world is looking at two of you. This is how Sarika sees things. Work on posture, igen? Never show fear. Sarika will know all this in heart. We start at dawn."

They ate in silence. Istvan had fixed sausages fried in olive oil with onions, peppers, garlic and paprika. He stuffed these in fresh bread and served it with cold milk. Knowing time was of the essence, they retired early and fell fast asleep.

It was sometime in the middle of the night when Gilly heard Istvan shouting in Hungarian. His screams were eerie and chilling. Gilly lit the lantern and awakened the stable master. Istvan was sweating profusely. It was apparent to Gilly that he had experienced a terrible nightmare.

"What is it Istvan? What made you into a raving maniac at this ungodly hour?"

"I go to kitchen, Gilly Morrison, and make tea."

The dry kindling was already in the hearth waiting for the breakfast meal. Istvan lit the twigs and put a kettle over the fire swinging gently from a crane. In the soft glow of the lantern, Gilly noticed that Istvan was ashen colored and deeply distraught. They remained silent as the tea came to a boil. Gilly fetched the cups from the cupboard and sat down at the table waiting for Istvan to speak first.

"I need explain, Gilly Morrison. I knew this would happen first time I saw you. When you present me with letter of introduction from Mr. Pechin, I pretend I read. This was foolish pride on me. I cannot read English. That is why I ask you many questions." Gilly sipped his tea and remained attentive despite the early morning hour.

"I watch you eat. I watch you sleep, though you not know this. And, I watch you with Sarika. How you talk and walk with her. This all brings memory back to me, a memory of my own son. His name was Andras. In my language means 'warrior.' And so he was. My father and his father before him were Master Horsemen. Andras would follow in our footsteps. He was just about same age as you. He struggled at first, only because he knew more about horses than his officers did. He was expert rider. Andras quickly rose through ranks, achieving victory and promotion in Hungarian forces. There was nothing on earth to stop him.

"It was cold winter. Napoleon was defeating kingdom after kingdom,

90

like dominoes on game board. Hungary and Russia joined each other in last try to stop French and their terrible thirst for conquest at Austerlitz.

"Andras, now captain, led his men on frontal assault against Napoleon's cannon in center of enemy lines. He fell, Gilly Morrison … Andras was killed. Whole command wiped out. It was brave they said. It was glorious I was told. But it was also foolish. This is why I cry out in night when all is quiet except screams of my soul."

"Come on, Istvan," Gilly cajoled, "let me take you back to bed. You might sleep better after getting all this off your chest." They headed back to the bedroom, but Istvan stopped and searched in his locker for something.

"I want you to have this, Gilly Morrison." Istvan produced a locket and chain. "You are of Irish descent, igen?"

"I don't know. I'm an orphan and never knew my family or where we came from."

"You got red, curly hair and fair complexion. Last name of Morrison suggest such Irish lineage." He held up the locket between them. "This was given to me by my mother many years ago. It was her dearest possession. Sit, Gilly Morrison, and Istvan tell you little story.

"When devil, English General Oliver Cromwell, invaded Ireland and crucified Christ all over again, Roman Catholic Church - priests, nuns, bishops, all were martyred and died for faith. Hungary, too, has had such persecution.

"During this time, a certain Irish bishop managed escape and made way to Hungary. This bishop was holy man. He was welcomed and dearly loved by all people of Hungary. He brought with him portrait of Virgin Mary – Madonna and Jezuska. Madonna wept tears of oil and blood. For hundreds of miles, all went and pray before Irish Madonna. This continue even today. My mother touch face of Our Lady with little part of dress. She put in locket for me. I should have given for Andras so he wear into battle, but my faith was weak after my mother and wife died.

"Now, Gilly Morrison, I give for you. Wear about your neck. You are like Andras, strong and determined to have own way. Like Andras, you charge into battle with sabre held high. This is what you ought to do. You not fear death. You fear dishonor. I know you only little time, but I see your truth. This locket will protect you against British monsters who mean destroy you." Istvan slipped the chain over Gilly's neck. "May Irish Madonna protect you against all evil and harm."

Chapter 6: The Race Begins

For the first time, Gilly mounted his Princess upon a leather saddle. "Remember, Gilly Morrison, talk to horse. Keep back straight so horse will be proud of you. From now on you and horse are two of kind. She knows this and expects you act like royalty on throne. Then she not be ashamed. She is proud lady and she needs be proud of you, too. Remember, posture always most important. Do not slack shoulders. Remember proper deportment is expected."

As Istvan had suggested earlier, Gilly rode Sarika close to the fence and used it as a guide for both him and the horse. "You are doing so well, Princess!" Gilly reassured her, stroking her mane. "I bet you are the best horse in the stables. You are certainly the prettiest. Everyone in Baltimore will be jealous of me, sitting a horse with such beauty and charm. And wait until

Desiree sees you. She will turn green with envy. She thinks she is my princess. But I only have one and that is you my noble lady."

Istvan stood outside the railing with a few of the more curious stable hands. They knew Sarika better than anyone and were astonished that the palomino was responding so obediently. Istvan signaled Gilly to step up the pace, "Give her kick, little kick."

With both heels Gilly applied some pressure, almost like a slight nudge, to the horse's midsection. Sarika answered his command and cantered regally around the track. Sarika was now showing off. She kept her head up with little or no movement. She pranced as if she was on parade.

"Little more kick, Gilly Morrison!" Again, the horse replied to the command and increased her gait into a steady trot. Gilly had Sarika holding close to the rail by the simple use of his rein. He was using very little pressure with his thighs and knees. His left leg was simply too weak. Istvan turned to the stable hands in absolute amazement. "Boys, have you ever seen miracle before?" They shook their heads in wonder.

"One more kick!" A trot turned into a gallop. Sarika sprinted with a free rein, Gilly was just trying to keep on his saddle. "Pull back rein!" Istvan shouted. "Talk to horse and pull back rein!"

Sarika slowed her gait to a proud saunter, her head still held aloft, her breathing quick but not labored. She had just put on a show and she knew it.

She glanced back at her prince who was sweating much more than she was.

Istvan was more than pleased. He had indeed sensed something intangible between the boy and the horse. Yet he had no idea such acute solidarity was possible between man and animal in so short a time. Istvan, who did not believe in chance, knew this was providence.

A stable boy took Sarika for her bath, grooming, and a well-deserved meal. Istvan and Gilly walked back to the cottage, proud of the morning's accomplishments. The boys and stable hands talked about nothing else. Prince and Princess were now one. But Istvan was right, it was always her choice: the choice of a princess to give herself to her prince.

The next day there was a celebratory feast for everyone at the stable. Istvan prepared a large kettle of 'gulyas' and purchased a keg of refreshment. Meanwhile, Sarika enjoyed a generous helping of early spring carrots. Before Gilly left, he and Istvan shared a tankard of pale ale and talked about everything that had happened since Gilly's arrival at the stables. As Gilly mounted Sarika and gently stroked her snowy mane, he was choked with emotion.

"How can I express my gratitude, Master Istvan? You have made my dreams come true."

"And you have made mine more than come true. You have brought my son back to me. This is great gift. Thank you, Gilly Morrison. Remember my mother's locket. Keep it with you always."

Gilly turned Sarika towards Federal Hill. Istvan called after his prized student. "Remember stay rigid in saddle, remember deportment, posture!"

*****

Gilly arrived back at Fells Point with Princess in agreeable tow. He fixed a stall in the lean-to in the back of the house on Thames Street. Sarika seemed comfortable and content. Gilly walked up to the docks to check on the cooperage. He noticed his leg felt better but his bottom was very sore.

It being late afternoon, Samuel and the Smith brothers had already left. All the citizens of Baltimore felt required to assist in the defense of the city. The whole town was alive with activity to repel a British assault. Gilly saw these things both on his journey to the Pechin Stables and upon his return. Although militia from as far away as Philadelphia and federal forces, both army and navy, did respond, Baltimore was determined to defend itself with or without assistance. Still, there was much work yet to be done both at Fort McHenry and at the fortifications on Hampstead Hill.

When Gilly entered the front door of the cooperage he saw Father Moranvillè pouring over the accounts of the business. "*Très bien, mon ami,* you are home once more to assist me in this work of debits and credits which I have no head for."

Gilly looked over the books and was satisfied with the accounting. He was amazed, however, at the amount of business the cooperage had acquired since his departure just a few days ago.

"How on earth are we going to fill these orders?"

"Do not upset yourself. Samuel and the Smith brothers are returning after their military duties are finished for the day. They will work all night if they have to."

Gilly looked at the clock behind the counter. "Good, then what I will do is ride out to Hampstead Hill and check on the Smith brothers then double back and see what Samuel is up to at McHenry. When they return to the cooperage I'll go to the Dooley house and make some sandwiches for their dinner. Then, I've got some writing to do before my meeting with Mr. Pechin tomorrow morning. I will also work all night if I have to."

"You have been given a good horse to accomplish all this?"

"Oh, yes, Father. You should see her. She is magnificent and noble. I call her Princess." Moranvillè clasped his hands behind his cassock.

"Gilly, there was another princess here to see you today. She arrived only an hour before your return."

"Oh, no, Father, not again. Why, I was only gone a couple of days."

"The consequences I mentioned to you before are about to begin.

Mistress Pechin is a wily girl. She seems determined to conquer you by all means necessary. So far you have done an admirable job in deflecting her most obvious endowments, vis-à-vis, monsieur, her physical attributes. This has only enraged her. You have gazed upon the goddess and found her wanting. A woman with her vanity cannot accept this. Not from any man or boy, but especially not from one who is so far down, *pardonne-moi*, the social ladder."

"Careful, Father. I may be a penniless orphan but I know that beauty is only skin deep. *Oui?*"

"*Oui*, Gilly. Michael Dooley knew this, too. Yet he succumbed nevertheless."

"Michael did, yes. It was because he did that I learned not to make that mistake. I saw what she did to him - using him like he was a toy made for her amusement. That won't happen to me, Father."

"I know it will not. You are still known as 'tough' and so you are in more ways than one, *mon ami*. Mistress Pechin is also tough. She will not give up easily. Her pride is at stake."

"Mine, too, I think."

"Then this may require some interference to allow you to breathe. She will use your new position at *The American* against you."

"I'm aware of that, Father."

"Perhaps I may take it upon myself to enlist her support for some project which will keep her busy. Maybe I could ask her to help with raising money for some well-needed supplies at the orphanage?"

"Thanks, but no, Father. This is between Desiree and me. I've been talking this over with my Princess … "

"With your horse?"

"Yes, well, it's a long story. Anyway, I've come up with a strategy."

"You have a plan then, *mon ami*?"

"Yes, Father. I'm going to write my first story tonight and place it on the editor's desk before Desiree even gets up tomorrow. Then I will lay out my plans to Mr. Pechin about stories I will write in the coming weeks. If I can engender in him a belief in me before the inevitable collision I will have with his daughter, perhaps I can beat her at her own game."

The good priest smiled. "And I will be praying for you to accomplish just that. Now go on your mission to feed Samuel and the Smith brothers. And then do exactly what you just told me."

Sarika had seen Gilly safely home from his early evening mission. Her reward was a sponge bath, a good grooming and a feed bag. Gilly had managed to pick up a bale of Timothy hay for her dinner. This was the finest hay in the city, but nothing was too good for his Princess.

"Now you eat, noble lady. Then get some rest. We will be very busy tomorrow and you will soon know the streets and dirt roads of Baltimore as well as I do." Gilly gently caressed her mane and kissed her wet nose. "Everything depends on tomorrow for you and me, Princess. So, let's do our best, igen?"

Sarika pawed her hoof and rubbed her nose in her prince's red, curly hair. She savored the sweet Timothy hay while Gilly entered the back door of the house to prepare a simple supper. Gilly wondered if Mr. Pechin would send someone over to the Dooley home to construct a better abode for his Princess than a simple lean-to.

In his bedroom, with quill pen in hand and a full bottle of black ink sitting securely in the well of the desk, Gilly began to write his story:

It is my intention to bring to the readership of *The Baltimore and American Daily Advertiser* the stories of the people who will guide this city over the coming weeks and months in the common defense of our great city. Some of these people will be well known to you, although I hope to discover things about them that perhaps you didn't know before. Others will be complete strangers. Yet people who are at this very moment critical to our very survival.

Three times weekly you can count on me to deliver to you a story of integrity, compassion, duty, sacrifice, and patriotism. No matter who the story is about, a great name or a hidden jewel that cares not to shine in public adulation, you will come to understand their value and importance to you and to our fair city.

Let me begin today with a story of three people who wish to remain in anonymity, yet their story is as compelling as any of our great leaders. They could be your friends or neighbors. Perhaps you have seen them in church or in the marketplace. Maybe they are members of your own family, or by chance, one of them is you....

Gilly then wrote about Samuel and the Smith brothers. He wrote about their work ethic and the fact that they were sacrificing all of their free time for the cause of the common defense. His story focused on the importance of sacrifice. How there was a cost to freedom and how each generation must pay that price. How some paid for it with the ultimate sacrifice.

It was near two-o'clock-in the-morning before he finished his piece. As he nestled into his feathered mattress and covered himself with his quilt to ward off the damp early morning air, he patted the locket of Istvan's mother hanging from his chest and immediately fell into a deep sleep.

His dream was very colorful and most life-like. He was at the Pechin Stables. It was early morning sometime in September for the leaves and just begun to turn. Heavy dew soaked the ground and a deep fog enveloped the stables so it was difficult to see very far.

Istvan was pleading with Gilly, imploring him to do something important. Gilly had no idea what was expected of him. Finally, Gilly took Istvan by the shoulders and began to shake him. "What is it Istvan? What do you want me to do?"

"I want you to win!"

Istvan pointed to the track. Sarika was there saddled and waiting for him, snorting and anxiously pawing her hoof. Gilly could see there was to be some kind of contest. He entered the gate and mounted his Princess. The fog was so thick he could barely make out the railing. A British officer appeared next to Gilly. He was dressed in full military regalia. He sat upon an enormous black stallion.

"Are you ready?" the officer asked with pleasant smile.

"Ready for what, sir?"

"Are you ready to lose, my boy? Everything is at stake, you know."

"What's at stake?"

The officer pointed his riding crop around the Pechin Stables. "Every horse here will be mine when I win; including the palomino you sit upon. Then, I will give it to the army and they will, at last, have a cavalry. After that we will sweep all of Baltimore into the sea where my ships will be waiting. I never lose, you know. And when I win, I punish the loser severely. What is the fun of winning if you can't subject the loser to abject humiliation?"

Suddenly, Gilly was aware of the costs if he lost. For a moment he panicked - something Istvan instructed him never to do while riding a horse. He reached down and patted Sarika's white mane. "It's okay, Princess. I will never leave you. You know I love you. Do your best to win this race. No one will ever ask more of you than that. It'll all be my fault if we lose. Everyone will blame me because of writing my stupid stories."

Gilly turned to the officer who was still smiling at him. "To whom have I the pleasure of racing against, sir?"

The officer bowed his head and replied "George Cockburn, Rear Admiral of His Royal Majesty's Navy."

Gilly stared in horror at *him*: the monster that had pillaged and plundered the Chesapeake's villages and towns with impunity. "You're the Great Bandit!"

The report of a handgun signaled the race had begun. Cockburn pulled ahead. In the fog, Gilly could barely make out the shape of the admiral's stallion. Within a second, he could see absolutely nothing.

How long was this contest? Was it a half-mile? Sarika knew what she must do for her prince and galloped with abandon. Gilly caught a glimpse of the stallion's tail. "We are close, my Princess!" Gilly shouted.

But then the wind started to blow in from the southeast in gale force. Gilly could hardly sit his palomino. The wind lifted him from the saddle and raised Sarika's body off the ground, although she still kept her legs moving in a fierce gallop. The horizon in front of him turned black, then deep blue, then yellow, red, pink and green, almost at the same time. The entire sky was ferociously spinning like a living pinwheel. Men were screaming – horrifying, terrible screams. Bullets from musketry and black balls from booming cannon were whizzing all around. Rockets were exploding in the sky.

Suddenly, without reason, the storm disappeared without a trace and all was clearly visible. Gilly could see the finish line. He also spied Desiree under a pink parasol. She had taken the arm of a British army officer. She pointed at Gilly and both she and the handsome redcoat began to laugh hysterically.

This made Gilly angry. Sarika sensed his fury and raced to the outside of the admiral's stallion that had possession of the inner lane. They were now dead even. Both horses were not a nose apart. As they crossed the finish line there was a tremendous roar from a crowd of people Gilly could not see, only hear. Somehow, he knew the race was over but he had no idea who had won.

"Who won?" Gilly screamed. "Who won?" He struck out with his fists into the darkness demanding to know the answer. He pummeled his knuckles into something soft. It was his pillow. Just then the distinctive sound of a rooster filled his bedroom. Gilly woke from his dream soaked in sweat and still very angry.

Chapter 7: The Purser

Gilly arrived at the newspaper office and waved hello to Gabriel. He noticed Gabe had a clean shirt on, a new cap, and was as happy as any orphan could be who had been given the freedom to make some money and plan for the future without having to totally rely upon someone else.

Gilly firmly rapped on Pechin's door. "Come in, damn you, but it better be good."

Gilly smiled at the sound of the gruff voice and opened the door. He walked to the editor's desk and plopped down his story.

"Well, it's about time, young man, I was beginning to worry. Now, what's this?"

Pechin scanned Gilly's piece. "I like the introduction. It speaks of the people. And your description of the three volunteers reads well and invokes a perfectly idealistic notion of patriotism."

Gilly frowned. He thought he was just being honest, not pandering to overly sentimental nationalism. Samuel and the Smith brothers truly felt a clear sense of duty and were proud of their efforts.

Pechin finished reading and slammed his fist on the table. "This will appear on the front page of tomorrow's paper! Well done, Gilly, I dare say. But what comes next? You promised a story three days a week and a promise printed in my newspaper must be kept, unless it is from a politician of course."

"I have planned a campaign to write a series of stories about the flag that will fly over Fort McHenry."

"What do our readers care about a damned flag? Where is the human interest in this story, boy?

"Have you ever heard of Mary Pickersgill?"

"I have not, nor has anyone else. What on earth has Mary Pickles have to do with the war?"

"Mary Pickersgill, sir. She is sewing both the battle flag that will be used when the British attack us, and another flag that will be hoisted after our victory. Major Armistead, the commander of the fort, has taken the foresight to order a victory flag so huge in its dimensions that the British will see it from the Chesapeake itself after their withdrawal from our waters."

"Pure arrogance, I dare say, Gilly. How can the major spend extravagant taxpayer funds on a foregone conclusion that is neither prudent nor yet to be proven? On what basis has he to act with such extravagance?"

Gilly lifted himself out of his seat and placed his palms on the editor's desk. "That's it exactly, sir! But is it just mere arrogance to profess to his men and this city, volunteers who perhaps have misgivings and are, as I am, somewhat daunted by the approach of a professional fighting force that has bested Napoleon, that we can win? Don't you see the perfectly simple ruse of a leader who dares to tweak the whiskers of the British lion before a terrible confrontation? Very few people know of Armistead's victory flag. I plan to tell the story from the beginning. To interview Armistead himself and all the other ordinary people engaged in this arrogant and necessary project.

"I told you before, Mr. Pechin, my intention is tell stories that will resonate with readers' hearts. Not just dispatches full of facts and figures, but stories that evoke both an emotional and intellectual response. Stories such as these will challenge the reader's mind and may engender a heartfelt investment in the defense of this city."

Pechin remained skeptical. "And then what do you plan to write about?"

"Stories that would help raise confidence and hope in our people. I want to interview the legendary Joshua Barney, who now commands the flotilla of gun boats built right here in Baltimore and has been sent to defend Washington. His story will be crucial to our readership since he was a hero in the last war. But, the possibilities are endless. There are the three commodores who grace us with their presence in our city: John Rodgers, David Porter, and 'The hero of Lake Erie,' Oliver Hazzard Perry. The question begs how is it that these three competent naval officers are here with us now in the very hour of our desperate need?"

"Go on, Gilly, I like this."

"The only other commodore I am aware of is Thomas Macdonough who commands the fleet on Lake Champlain and who is now facing what we in Baltimore are anticipating: a British juggernaut which will stop at nothing to destroy us. You know Michael Dooley, sir?"

"Why, yes, a fine boy who confided in me after his father's impressment. He sailed out with Captain Boyle on the *Chasseur* months ago."

"Yes, sir, I heard you had something to do about that?"

"At the insistence, young man, of the esteemed pastor of St. Patrick's Church, School, and Orphanage, Father Moranvillè. It seemed the right thing to do at the time as Michael was determined to sail anyway."

"Michael is now in Vermont helping Commodore Macdonough build

109

his fleet. We are in correspondence since he is my best friend."

"You're confusing me, Gilly. Why would the defense of Lake Champlain, of New York and Vermont, have anything to do with us in Maryland?"

"Because it is all connected, sir; it was a plan devised in London months ago after the defeat of Napoleon on the European Continent to coordinate an attack on America. They mean to stretch out our defenses, especially American federal forces, so that we are vulnerable."

"How can a boy possibly know this? Neither you or Michael Dooley have any military experience."

"Michael Dooley has relied on the expert advice of Captain Ken Russell. You remember him, sir. The ancient one who could still best any young man at arm-wrestling? It is his opinions Michael and I rely on, not those of our own."

Pechin recalled Captain Ken and the service he had seen in the revolution. Yet it was still not clear to the editor what all this had to do with Gilly's writing here and now in Baltimore.

Gilly suspected Pechin's doubts. "Sir, writing occasionally about the war on other fronts will take the peoples' minds off their own difficulties here at home. This is a war bigger than our own problems. We, as a nation, are all in this thing together. It would soften the blow to know that our fellow

110

citizens suffer a similar plight and mean to stand and fight against it."

William Pechin was more than convinced. "Go, Gilly, and tell your stories. I will send a courier to the Dooley home at sunset every other night to collect your latest story. Remember, you must produce quality material for the Monday, Wednesday, and Friday editions. Oh, by the by, how is the horse, satisfactory I presume?"

"No sir, not at all. She is perfect. Thank your daughter for her kind suggestion. The horse will be my legs from now on. But, sir, may I beg a personal favor?"

"You can if it's not expensive."

"The beautiful palomino your servant, the Stable Master Istvan, has chosen for me is tied up in a lean-to in the back of the Dooley home on Thames Street. Would it possible for some of your workmen to construct something more comfortable for the horse? Then she can eat and sleep without discomfort from inclement weather and be of more value to me and this newspaper."

Pechin scribbled a note and gave a grunt in the affirmative that Gilly did not hear. He had hurriedly scampered out the door knowing he had already used up any additional benevolence the editor was capable of for one day. As he mounted Sarika, he looked around the street for any signs of the dangerous Desiree, but she was still nestled in her bed scheming and planning her next move.

*****

Gilly stopped at the cooperage to see how things were going before his work at the newspaper completely overwhelmed him. Samuel was behind the counter as usual sipping some tea. Gilly heard the pounding of mallets in the work room. Samuel eyes were somewhat blood-shot. He could not cease from yawning.

"You were at in all night, then?"

"Yes, Master Morrison, the job is finished. These are new orders that must be filled."

"Who ordered them?"

"The Committee of Vigilance and Public Safety headed by his Excellency the Mayor, General Smith, and Commodore Rodgers." Samuel paused to make sure the noise in the workroom continued. "They have plans on building a flotilla of gun boats and barges to be fitted with cannon." Samuel motioned Gilly to come to the counter and took out a paper and charcoal pencil from the top drawer. "They will stretch a line across the Northwest Branch of the Patapsco from Fells Point to Whetstone Point." Samuel drew a line and then penciled in HH at the north point of the line and WH at the south. "It will lie nearly on the same line of longitude with the defenses on Hampstead Hill. In this way the gun boats and barges can support

112

both Fort McHenry and our fortifications on Hampstead Hill."

"Samuel, how do you know all this and why, for God's sake, are we whispering?"

"Commodore Rodgers, himself, was here early this morning with these orders. He knew who I was because my services were suggested to him by Major Armistead. He also knew who you were. He seemed very informed about everything."

"Samuel, why would they need more laborers on Hampstead Hill?"

Samuel removed his glasses. "Not as a laborer, Master Gilly, but as the commodore's secretary with the rank of purser." Samuel waved his hand in front of his face and smiled. "It is only a formality. He knows I am a pacifist and cannot fight. The commodore assured me I would never have to pick up a rifle. After the battle I will be furloughed and will officially leave the service." Samuel frowned and set his jaw firm with a look of determination. "As to why we're whispering, the information I just gave you is confidential. I don't know the new hires in the back room and must take every precaution."

Gilly's head swirled, he whistled between his teeth and took a seat on a stool at the counter. He pointed his thumb in the direction of the work room. "That's not the Smith brothers in there?"

"No, Master Morrison, it is not them. I told them to go home and get some sleep."

"Hold it, let's get this straight … err … no, let's start at the beginning."

"But don't you have other duties for *The American* today?"

Gilly shook his head in the negative. "This is Thursday, my story is already filed for the Friday edition and I have all weekend to write another story, at least until Sunday evening when my story will be filed for Monday's edition. Besides I have to understand this whole thing. I owe this much to Michael Dooley and his family.

"Now, and slowly this time, how is it that Commodore Rodgers asked you to become his secretary?"

"I have had many discussions with Major Armistead while I was working the entrenchments at McHenry. He knows I was a schoolmaster for a few years before I made my way to Baltimore. He knows my work ethic. Last night, Commodore Rodgers, while dining with Major Armistead in the city, enquired if the Major knew of anyone who could possibly help him keep up with the enormous correspondence, both official and unofficial, the commodore has to deal with on a daily basis. Armistead immediately suggested your humble servant."

Gilly whistled. "This isn't looking good for me. Okay, now what about the new hires?"

114

"They came in yesterday morning after seeing the advertisement on the front page of *The American*. I took their names and addresses and made enquiries as to their experience. They are immigrants from Ireland, a city by the name of Cork. They had worked as coopers for many years along the docks of that city. They are both older men and remember, as young lads, a Dooley cooperage in that city. They asked if it was the same family. I didn't know any of this. But I took their information and had them report for duty today as the Smith brothers were tuckered out from working all night. Their names are Sean O'Casey and Liam Dailey. I checked their papers and contacted the bank where they have an account and also at the boarding house. So far as I can see, Master Gilly, they are what they claim to be."

"When are the Smith brothers to return to work?"

"This afternoon, then they will complete the work the new hires have started. There is to be no drilling today, I understand."

"Keep the new hires on, Samuel; we could use some good help. But never, I repeat never, show them the orders from our clients. They need only follow instructions. And do not let them deliver our products to their intended destination. The Smith brothers can see to that. There are spies everywhere, Samuel, and we must take every precaution. We supply our army, navy, and militia with barrels, casks, kegs, hogsheads and other items necessary for the defense of the city. If a spy could figure out who ordered these things and where they are to be delivered, it could provide the enemy with important intelligence as to where our strengths and weakness are, do you understand?"

"I do indeed, Master Morrison."

Gilly pondered for a moment as a memory struck him. "I remember Michael Dooley telling me his grandfather was from Cork and had run a successful cooperage there for many years. This was before Michael's father and his Uncle Bob came to America and joined Washington's Army at the siege of Yorktown. Strange, how these new hires knew about the Dooley cooperage in Cork. The world is becoming smaller all the time, isn't it?"

Samuel cleared his throat. "Now about the commodore's offer that I be commissioned in the American Navy and serve him as his private secretary?"

Gilly could not help but express disappointment on his face. He also knew Samuel would not propose this if he had not already set his heart on it. It reminded him of his own decision to leave the bulk of the work at the cooperage to Samuel and take his new position as a writer for *The American*. Besides, Gilly thought, Samuel would have used the code. He would have already discerned this in his heart and within his soul. Like St. Paul, Samuel knew what he "ought to believe."

"Samuel, how can I ever replace you at this late date with a battle for the very survival of our city looming over our heads?"

The clerk clasped his hands before his chest in a pleading gesture. "I would never leave my post at this critical juncture unless a very plausible solution is more than attainable."

"Samuel, you were just offered the post this morning. How can anything plausible be possible?"

"Providence, Master Morrison. My cousin, Richard, has come to town looking for a position. He is staying with me at my lodgings. Like me, he was a schoolmaster at a Quaker Meeting House before the opportunity war sometimes brings drew him into the city. Also, like me he is a pacifist. The work ethic passed down to us in our family is as important to him as it is to me. Richard is an erudite and scholarly man and was always quicker at his slate in arithmetic than I was. He can communicate in a variety of different languages. I sent for him this morning after the commodore left. Richard is more than eager to take my place at the cooperage, at your discretion of course. I can show him the books and leave him in charge with only a few hours of instruction, he is that quick a learner."

"Can we wait until tomorrow morning, Samuel? I'd like to meet Richard in person before I make my decision. But, I will miss you my friend."

"I will never be but a step away."

"Make that a short step, Samuel. With my position at the newspaper keeping me on my toes all day, I won't have the time to check on things here as much as I would like to. I sure hope your cousin works out. He has very big shoes to fill."

"You are most kind, sir."

"And as for the new hires, I'll just have to trust your judgment. See to it that Richard keeps a close eye on them."

Chapter 8: Beyond Reason

When Gilly reached the Dooley home he led Sarika out back to the lean-to. It was no longer there. In its place stood a small barn with double doors and roofed with cedar shake shingles. It was more than big enough for Sarika and would keep her dry and comfortable all year long.

Gilly opened the doors. On the left hand side bags of oats, bales of Timothy hay and barley lined the wall. A stall was constructed and lined with fresh straw and was situated on the right. Gilly smiled, Pechin works fast, he thought. Either the editor was just protecting his investment in the palomino or he was demonstrating to his new writer the importance of quick, decisive action; perhaps it was a combination of both. In order to win the editor's favor and keep one step ahead of Desiree's traps, Gilly intended to be both quick and decisive as well.

119

On the way home, Gilly had picked up a cut of choice veal, carrots, onions, garlic, mushrooms, potatoes, and paprika. He started a fire in the kitchen and selected a large cast iron pot from an array of cookware neatly stored on a cart near the hearth. He poured some olive oil into the pot and liberally greased the sides. As the fire got hot, he sliced the veal in small chunks and coated them with flour. Then he attached the pot to a crane and swung it over the fire. He added the meat and while it browned, he cut the vegetables and added them to the pot and covered the contents with water. After that, he raised the crane so that the pot was far enough away from the fire that it only simmered. It was Gilly's version of "gulyas". He had saved some of the carrots and brought them out to the new barn for Sarika. Returning to the kitchen, he lifted the lid and added some cream before covering again.

As the "gulyas" simmered to perfection, Gilly sat at the kitchen table with paper, ink, and quill. First he laid out his plans for his next story: where he must go, who he needed to interview, and all the questions he had to ask to get the story he wanted to write. With this accomplished, he took some more writing paper and started a letter.

Dear Michael,

So much has happened since last I wrote you. Mr. Pechin sent me to his stables on the south side of Federal Hill to obtain a horse that would help me get around town in

120

the performance of my duties as a writer for the paper. There was an old Master Horseman in charge by the name of Istvan who, underneath his icy military guise, was as warm a soul as any I have ever met.

He selected a horse for me. A spirited palomino by the name of Sarika, who I never thought I could ride due to my sore leg. Somehow– and I don't for the life of me know how– my leg feels fine when I am riding her.

Sarika and I bonded so quickly, Istvan and the stable hands were amazed. I call her "Princess" because she comes from royal stock and because that's how much she means to me. I asked Mr. Pechin to send over some of his workmen to fix up the lean-to in the back of the house. Tonight, to my surprise, a small barn appeared before my eyes. My Princess resides there now, dry, warm, and quite comfortable. Pechin never mentioned anything about cost, and if he ever does the barn will be my gift to you for your generosity in allowing me to stay here.

And now, Michael, here's the rub: Samuel has been asked to become Commodore Rodgers' private secretary. He will enter the navy with the rank of purser. I know what you're thinking. Samuel is a pacifist. But

Rodgers has promised him his duties will be relegated to using pen and paper. Samuel's cousin, Richard Snipes, is in town and I will interview him tomorrow morning to be the new clerk. Samuel swears by him, so I am at ease tonight knowing the cooperage will be in competent hands; although no one, in my opinion, can ever replace Samuel.

There have been two new hires, and this you might find interesting. They are Irish coopers from Cork and remember your grandfather's business along the wharves of that city. Their names are Sean O'Casey and Liam Dailey. They are older gentlemen and quite skilled. Perhaps Uncle Bob will remember them.

The Smith brothers are burning the candle at both ends and can use the help. Business, as I suspected, is picking up as hundreds of soldiers and sailors pour into the city and are in dire need of supplies and provisions, most of which have to be barreled.

I've told Mr. Pechin that I would correspond with you to keep the citizens of Baltimore informed as to the preparations Commodore Macdonough is making on Lake Champlain. Have you seen any action?

If you write to me about the preparations on the

Northern Front, I can keep my readership engaged in reading something other than their own very considerable fears. This might help to unify us, knowing there are Americans determined to fight our enemy all across the country. As we already know, The United States has had unprecedented victories at sea, both with our small federal navy and, as you and Captain Boyle well know, the crippling of British mercantile trade. Michael, you are facing the same lion we are. This beast is hungry and means to devour us. Please keep me abreast of your activities. After all, you are a son of this city and people will be interested in your exploits.

By the way, how are you making out discerning the code? Father John says he can see it working in me, but I have my doubts. Samuel, I know, used it in making his decision to serve under Rodgers. It all seems so simple to him. Perhaps I should stop trying to analyze it so much and let it work its grace silently and in its own good time.

Please give my love to Jessica, Uncle Bob, and Captain Ken. Please also keep me in your prayers; the inevitable confrontation with the editor's daughter has not happened yet, but will any day - any hour now. Stay safe.

Your blood brother,

Gilly

The delicious aroma of "gulyas" filled the room and Gilly could stand it no longer. It wasn't as good as the Hungarian stable master's, but it was good enough.

As he prepared for bed, the laced curtain in his bedroom blew out and flapped noisily from a strong breeze. Gilly doused his oil lamp and began to close the window when a streak of lightning lit up the room. After that a crackling thunder burst rolled, piecemeal, over Fells Point alerting its residents that it was now summer, possibly their battle summer. As sheets of torrential rain poured down upon the city, Gilly felt serene. Sarika would be dry and comfortable tonight. He yawned once more and said a quick prayer not to have another dream like he did the night before. "No more races, Master Istvan, igen?" Then he caressed the precious locket and fell fast asleep because he finally knew what he "ought to believe."

*****

Gilly awoke refreshed from a dream-free slumber. He saddled Sarika and headed for the cooperage, stopping on the way to buy a newspaper from Gabe.

"Congratulations, Gilly! Everyone is talking about your story. I'm almost sold out." Gilly smiled back at Gabe and tipped him well, but did not

124

look at the paper. That would be just for him in the privacy of the Dooley home. Moreover, Gilly sensed something more than just accomplishment. He suddenly remembered what he had internalized in his heart and soul the previous evening, just before he surrendered to sleep: the meaning of the first part of the code: "to know what you ought to believe." Maybe it was Gabe. Maybe it was something else. But, for the first time in his life he recognized that self-sacrifice, hard work, and self-denial could accomplish marvelous things. That the first part of the code had to do with giving up one's selfishness for a greater good.

As he rode on he noticed that his leg did, indeed, feel better and stronger. He was now able to use his left thigh and knee to help direct Sarika over and along the wooden wharf leading to the docks of Fells Point. It was a gorgeous morning. The Baltimore heat had abated after the storm and both prince and Princess enjoyed their ride in the fresh breeze.

When he opened the door to the cooperage, Gilly saw Samuel going over the books with someone who looked like his twin. "Good morning, Samuel. Is this your cousin?"

"Yes, Master Morrison, Richard is already absorbing the details of the business. We had a long talk last night and I filled Richard in on all the current orders. Oh, and thank you for the most excellent story I saw in *The American* this morning. You did as I requested and kept me anonymous."

"This is yo, Samuel."

This is what?"

"Sorry, I've picked up a liking for Hungarian expressions and cuisine. But, it's of no importance. Are you ready Richard, to take over your cousin's duties?"

Richard smiled agreeably. "I am, sir. But I will have inquires to make from time to time. My abilities are limited to languages and the study of mathematics. Not the practical applications of the artisan such as the cooper and carpenter."

Gilly was curious. "What languages, Richard?"

"The romance languages, sir - French, Italian, Spanish, and the classical languages of Latin and Greek, although my studies have expanded recently to both Eastern and Western Slavic languages, including Finno-Ugric language studies."

"Would that, perhaps, include Hungarian?"

"Certain dialects, yes sir."

"When we have time on our hands, I have to introduce you to someone. But, for now the only time we have is for filling our orders."

The creaking door of the cooperage swung open as the Smith brothers and the new hires, Sean O'Casey and Liam Dailey, entered. They stopped talking after spotting Gilly and the new clerk .

Elijah Smith, the older of the twins by at least five minutes, approached Gilly with hat in hand. "Sir, we read today's newspaper and was honored you saw fit to write about us, me and Ethan. We're just small change to the war effort, we know that. But it was mighty kind of you to mention us in your story - even if you didn't use our real names or anything. Why it's as if we was like regular heroes. But we're not Master Gilly. Every man in our brigade knows that. Thanks for not mentionin' our names. It'd be a tall order to live down in the brigade.

"Anyway, Master Gilly, we was talkin' last night, I mean my brother and Sean and Liam." Elijah paused, working his hands back and forth along the brim of his hat. He wasn't used to talking to people in authority. "Well, sir, Sean here said he would like to join up in the City Brigade. Liam, who never shouldered a weapon before, would like to volunteer at McHenry, maybe takin' Samuel's place."

Gilly frowned and took a step toward them. "Sean and Liam, you were hired so that the Smith brothers could fulfill their military obligations. If Sean and Liam join up who is going to fill these orders?" Gilly held a stack of new requests in his hands and banged them on the counter.

Sean, Liam, and Ethan Smith all lowered their heads and said not a word. Elijah, however, put up a large, callused, right hand. "Master Gilly, we were thinkin' on takin' turns. When they drill, we work. When we drill, they work. When orders are backed up we work together and do double duty."

127

Gilly glanced at Samuel, who sat silently behind the counter. Samuel knew Gilly was looking for advice, although he would never voice it in front of the men. Samuel nodded in assent. Gilly breathed out a loud sigh.

Just then a courier arrived from *The American*. It was a note from William Pechin. "Good job, Gilly, my edition has sold out for today. In Fells Point people are still clamoring to get a copy of today's paper. You have done it! The mayor, the Committee of Vigilance and Public Safety, even the military have all offered me congratulations and are anxiously awaiting more of your stories in the days and weeks to come. Are you satisfied with the new housing for your precious palomino? It only shows you what speedy and determined action can accomplish."

Gilly was pleased, but didn't let it go to his head. This, after all, was only the first of many writing assignments. What would come next may not be received as well. He turned his attention to the business at hand.

"Richard, see to it that the schedules of these men are in complete agreement with each other and their duties here at the cooperage. If there is ever a slip up, for any reason, then all bets are off. Keep me informed of any infractions. Okay boys, you can have a go at it. But your primary duty is here in the production of our wares and nowhere else unless and until this city is under actual invasion. Does everybody understand this?"

The coopers shuffled back to the work room to begin their day. Gilly cocked his head at Samuel as if questioning his judgment.

At that moment, Desiree's carriage bumped across the wooden pier in front of the cooperage. Gilly lifted his head and pleaded with the Almighty to help him endure the inevitable encounter he had dreaded so much. Samuel, who could guess, by Gilly's expression, what this was likely to be, and Richard, who had no clue, both stared in frozen angst.

Desiree descended from the perch of her carriage as if all of Fells Point was watching her. With two fingers she delicately touched the gloved hand of her driver and proceeded to the door of the cooperage with her head held high and her lavender dress swishing with every practiced step of her most feminine gait.

As she entered, she immediately saw Gilly, yet pretended to ignore him. Instead, she curtseyed to Samuel and Richard. The room was suddenly overwhelmed by the sweet scent of jasmine. Finally, Desiree raised her laced-gloved hand to Gilly. He patently disregarded it.

"You should be ashamed, Gilly Morrison. Any gentlemen in this city would be pleased to pass his lips upon my hand, especially one who is indebted to me for his current position."

Gilly was amazed at himself. The moment he had feared for the past week-and-a-half produced no anxiety, no palpitations of his heart, no confusion. He stood in front of the counter with almost a sympathetic expression upon his face.

This look took Desiree by surprise. She thought she would have every moral advantage over him. She quickly recovered knowing she was in the right and proceeded to take the high ground.

"If it wasn't for me, Master Morrison, you would still be a peddler hawking newspapers on the street every morning with a harness strapped around your shoulders like any pack animal on the streets of Baltimore. It was I, and I alone, who convinced my father of your supposed worthiness in, not just reporting for *The American*, but becoming a first-class writer. It was because I believed in you. And now you have the audacity to stand there and not take the hand of your benefactor? How dare you, sir?" Desiree expected not just gratitude, but undivided attention and devotion.

"Are you some kind of princess, then?"

Desiree stomped her foot in protest. "I should be your princess for everything I've given to you."

"No thank you, Desiree, I already have one."

"What! You have no one! No girl, no mother, no father, family, nor home – you have nothing! You're just an orphan who is indebted to me for all I have done for you."

Gilly handed the new orders to Richard. "Do not show these to the new hires. Just tell them what they and the Smith brothers have to accomplish today. Never let anyone know of the destination of our wares. If delivery is expected, have the Smith brothers do the job."

Gilly had his back to Desiree. He wasn't pretending to ignore her - he was actually doing it. "Samuel, what can I say to you that you cannot already read in my heart? I wrote Michael Dooley last night and told him of your decision. I'm sure he will be as proud of you as I am right now. Thank you, my friend, for everything."

"It has been my greatest pleasure to clerk for the Dooley's, for you, and even the holy and oft times amusing Moranvillè. Thank you, Gilly, for taking on Richard. He shall not disappoint you."

Gilly walked quickly to the door and opened it. Then he pivoted, without a trace of pain in his left leg and took two steps in Desiree's direction, his piercing blue eyes riveted upon her. His face was not more than six inches from hers.

"I have earned everything in my life by myself, except what the good Lord has given me in the love of caring people who never knew me when I was first laid upon the doorsteps of a church many years ago. They, and only they, are my benefactors. I am deeply grateful to you for suggesting to your father that I be engaged as a writer for *The American*. If it was your idea for me to ride a horse in my duties, I am even more appreciative. I have no time for tea. Please don't invite me again. As Samuel will tell you, I know what I ought to believe, although I don't yet know what I ought to desire, nor what I ought to do."

Gilly closed the creaking door behind him and mounted his Princess. Desiree stomped her foot in total frustration. "Samuel! What does he mean? Who is this princess? What in God's name was that last thing he said to me? What did he mean by knowing what he ought to believe and other such nonsense?"

Samuel and Richard and been pretending to be occupied working on the books of the cooperage during the confrontation. The Clerk, soon purser, removed his glasses and gave Desiree an inquisitive look. "Why, Mistress Pechin, don't you know? In all matters of the soul one should seek the advice of the Pastor of St. Patrick's. It is in him that both Michael Dooley and Gilly Morrison have complete reliance."

Desiree left the cooperage in quite a huff. She considered having a long talk with her father. But thought that would be premature. After all, it was upon her recommendation that Gilly obtained his promotion. She would look silly seeking his firing after her convincing performance to have him hired as a writer. She had already heard the accolades about Gilly's first story. No, to undermine this now would be counterproductive. Desiree, stripped of her schemes, was close to bursting into tears. In the blink of an eye, however, she rallied. After all, she was Desiree Pechin.

*****

Gilly and Sarika boarded the ferry that would take them to Fort McHenry. The waters of the Patapsco were calm under a searing summer sun

132

which was tempered by a delicious breath of clean wind. Gilly could imagine where the line of gun boats and barges were to be placed in the river between Fells Point and Whetstone Point. It would be a good strategic maneuver, and yet, Gilly felt something else must be done to protect the city should the fort fall to the British. He sighed realizing the complexity of the defense of the city given its vulnerabilities by both land and water. Yet, he knew, it also possessed natural protections. The Committee of Vigilance and Public Safety and the military were taking every precaution against anything the British could possibly plan. In the end, Gilly thought, everything would ultimately depend on proper preparation and the integrity of the men and women who would, or would not, hold to the last.

*****

Desiree left the docks at Fells Point and ordered her driver to go the offices of *The American*. There was simply nowhere else for her to go. She had no friends to pour her heart out to. She had burned too many bridges in her short life to sustain a friendship. She would not, she decided, directly confront her father about Gilly. She needed to assess the situation slowly and then make a determination on how to proceed. She also needed money to go shopping in the afternoon.

"Good morning, father, how is your war going today?"

"Badly, daughter, very badly, and on all fronts, including the Chesapeake I fear. Do you need money again?"

"Yes, father, a little. I fell in love with that blue bonnet I saw yesterday and I positively must have it." Mr. Pechin opened his purse and put some gold coins on the edge of his desk. "Oh, how did Master Morrison's story go over this morning?"

"Capital! Everyone in Baltimore is talking about it. I must congratulate you, my dear, on your wisdom in seeing Gilly's promise as a young writer."

"Thank you. I do take an interest in developing talent, especially in the arts. But this was only one story. His true worth will be judged over the course of time as you well know. By the way, I stopped at the Dooley Cooperage this morning and saw our protégé. It struck me as strange, but he was entirely full of himself. He didn't give me the time of day. Do you think this is all going to his head?"

William Pechin leaned back in his leather chair and carefully observed his daughter. "Desiree, it was *you* who recommended *him* to me. Are you now in doubt about an outcome you were so adamant about just a few days ago?"

Desiree shifted in her seat. A crease appeared on her forehead. "No, father, I am not. But his whole damned attitude incensed me this morning to no end." Desiree had wanted to keep this conversation close ended. She came here looking for information, not to reveal it. Her supreme weakness, however, had always been her superior sense of self-pride, and that was checked severely at the cooperage.

"Tell me, daughter, exactly what you were doing on the docks of Fells Point this morning and do not proffer an evasive answer."

"Father, how could you ask such a question? I was simply there to see how Gilly was getting along, especially after he acquired his horse, which, you doubtless remember, was also my idea."

Pechin was not satisfied. He was an editor of a major newspaper and could smell diversion, although not oft times in his daughter. "And you were not received well from what you tell me."

"No I was not. Gilly treated me cruelly and with contempt. He asked me if I was some kind of princess. Can you imagine such impudence from a homeless orphan who would not have anything if I didn't intercede on his behalf?"

William Pechin was a man of action and preferred direct confrontation to the arts of diplomacy. This had been the reason he had acquired so many enemies in his life. It was also the reason for his success.

"So, *you* - have fallen in love - with *him*."

"Father, how dare you say such a thing?!"

"I don't blame you, my dear. He is most handsome. He can express

135

himself– a quality most men do not possess. This makes him even more attractive to the feminine sex, since there are no secrets hidden in the dark recesses of his heart. With Gilly Morrison you get what you see: an honest, intelligent, and compassionate young man with a bright future in front of him, despite all the obstacles he has suffered. Obstacles he has overcome and defeated while building a bridge across the void to the possible.

"No, dear, I don't blame you at all. It somehow reminds me of myself when I was a youth and your mother chose *me* instead of I *her*. She saw things that I could not see. I was so full of doubts about myself and my abilities. We didn't always come from money, you see. That was earned over many years of trial and error. But there was never a doubt in my mind that she loved me with all her heart. With her help and her constant fidelity and belief in me, we prospered. Not only financially, which is only a byproduct of hard work and a little good fortune, but, most importantly, in our love for each other."

For just a brief moment, Desiree became misty-eyed. "Father, you never told me about you and mother. Thank you for that, I will never forget it."

Then, Desiree awoke from the trance her father's memories had put her under. "I can't be in love with Gilly Morrison! I can't! He's an upstart nobody. I just expected him to pay me more attention, that's all. After today, I know he has only one love – his writing. And I am never, ever, going to replace that in his life. Unlike mother, I did not and do not choose Master Gilly Morrison."

"Sometimes, my dear, one chooses without being fully conscious of the choice. What you need to do is to explore the possibilities within yourself. I can see the truth in you quite clearly. Gilly Morrison has done something to you that I should have done years ago, but could not."

"And what is that, father?"

"To stop spoiling you, which I have been doing since you were born because I felt guilty that your mother died giving birth to you. Now, however, you are an adult woman. A woman who cannot obtain the one thing in life needed for happiness."

Desiree was not pretending anymore. She earnestly desired to know how her father expected her to achieve happiness. "Pray, father, do go on. I so desperately want to know."

Mr. Pechin sat back in his chair and gazed at his daughter's eyes that were, for the moment, as sincere as his own. He had spent so many years placating her every wish that he had denied her a father's duty to provide loving guidance touched with simple truth. The thought occurred to him that perhaps it was too late. And yet he could plainly see that his daughter needed that kind of guidance now more than ever.

"Go and talk to Father Moranvillè at St. Patrick's. He may shed some light on our frank discussion that I cannot. He is, I believe, in this world and yet not of this world. Some call him senile, some a dreamer. I think he is a portal between this world and the next. I am not a religious man, Desiree. I deal in facts, logic, and reason which has led us to an era of freedom man has never known before. This is the glory of our revolution, and why we fight the war we fight today to keep our independence from European monarchs and emperors. Moranvillè possesses something that goes beyond facts and reason. He bridges gaps between the here and now – and, eternity. Go and see him my dear. Listen to his words and see if he can bridge the gaps in your life."

Part II

"To know what you ought to desire…"

Chapter 9: Roses

Desiree left the offices of *The American* depressed and disoriented. Her father's words were like darts thrown directly at her heart. She was so disheartened she didn't stop to buy the blue bonnet her father had given her the money to purchase.

She had manipulated people, especially boys and men who sought her company, even her own father, for so long now she simply wasn't capable of acting any other way. She told her driver to take her home. She would have a cup of tea and, somehow, this would make everything right again.

At home, she ordered her servant to prepare tea and scones. She took these on the veranda in the back of the huge house. The veranda overlooked a fragrant garden filled with gardenias, imported from China, and a well-manicured lawn, perhaps the best in the city. Desiree composed herself and shrugged off her father's comments as if they were never mentioned. She dismissed the emotions that welled within her heart when her father confided to her about the love he shared with her mother.

No one could tell her, she convinced herself, who she was in love with. The truth was that she had never been in love before. Infatuated at times perhaps, with young men in uniform since the outbreak of the war, but only in a schoolgirl fashion, nothing serious – nothing approaching what people called *love*.

What is love anyway? Is it as they say a burning desire for another? Is it just physical attraction? Or does it involve something deeper? Something beyond what one could see or hear or touch?

How could she possibly be in love with an orphan? Marriages should be arranged according to the financial assets each party could contribute to the other. This obscure idea of love had little or nothing to do with that.

The question, still gnawing in her belly, however, was what did Gilly mean when he said he already had a princess? This was a downright lie! He had no girlfriends. He was a loner who read and wrote when he wasn't working his fool head off. How dare he say he had a princess! The very thought of it was ludicrous. Desiree had him spied upon. There was no one in his life. How could anyone dare to be called his princess?

Despite the tea and scones, Desiree was simply not herself. She yearned for more than the beauty of the veranda and the comfort of her pampered life. She ached for intimacy. For sharing her dreams with another. For a future – no – maybe just a few hours of joy and happiness and closeness with the one she loved. At the present time this was impossible. Unconsciously, however, deep within Desiree's heart, Gilly Morrison was no longer an absurd obsession, he was part of her.

*****

Gilly reached Fort McHenry and entered the gate without any obstruction from the sentry. Everyone knew who he was. McHenry was a large citadel commanding the confluence of the North West and Ferry Branches of the Patapsco River. Any enemy ship must pass its guns before approaching Baltimore's harbors. It was unusual in design because it was star-shaped, and nicknamed "The Star Fort." It looked just like the shape of a starfish. It was heavily armed and carried a garrison of over a thousand men.

The officer of the guard approached him after he entered the gates. "Can I help you, Gilly? You look a little lost."

"I'm here on an assignment for *The American*. I would like to interview Major Armistead if he isn't too busy."

"He's always busy, Gilly, but he might make time for you. Oh, now that you're here, I wanted to say that was a great story you wrote in the newspaper today. Was that Samuel you were talking about?"

Gilly grinned, "I can't say it was lieutenant, and I won't say it wasn't."

"Have it your way, then. But we're sure going to miss Samuel around here. I never saw such a workhorse. Word is he joined the navy, for God's sake, and is working for Commodore Rodgers. Our mistake, the army should have pegged him a long time ago." The lieutenant pointed to the northeast star of the fort. "You'll find the major sighting cannon below the ramparts. It's not hard to find, but … " the lieutenant waved to one of the men, "McGuiness, come here would you?" McGuiness sauntered over like he meant to take his time doing it. "Take Gilly to see Major Armistead. I'm sure the major won't mind if his dinner is a bit late. Good luck to you, Gilly, and keep writing those stories. The men really enjoyed your piece today."

Gilly dismounted his Princess and climbed down the steps to the northeast star fortifications along the water with McGuiness leading the way. Gilly noticed the man wore and apron, not a uniform. "What's this about dinner for the major, are you a cook?"

"I'm the major's chief cook and bottle washer all right. If there's anything the officers can't do without getting their precious fingers dirty they calls on me. I was the cook for the county sheriff before he kicks me out for sleepin' on the job, between meals mind ya. Since then I comes here and looks after the major. He lets me sleep in the guard house, the jail I calls it. I've got some chicken soup on top of the stove right now. The major doesn't

144

much care for it, but it's the best I can do with what they give me isn't it? Hell, let it simmer until it boils down to nothin'. I could care less. Chicken soup is just chicken soup."

Above the high tide line Gilly saw Major Armistead peering into a telescope towards the likely approaches the enemy might take in trying to overtake the fort. "I'll be okay from here, McGuiness. Thanks for showing me the way." The cook saw a flat stone warmed by the sun at the water's edge. He didn't want to go back into the fort only to be given another assignment by one of the officers. He climbed down onto the stone and stretched out his body. To make things more comfortable he removed his apron and used it as a pillow.

Armistead was a veteran soldier who had served with distinction at the capture of Fort George, near the mouth of the Niagara River in Canada, in May of last year. He proudly presented the Fort's flags to President Madison and was immediately given command of Fort McHenry. He was a quintessential military man, with short, brown, curly hair, a broad forehead, long sideburns, and a ruddy complexion. His uniform was immaculate and featured a dark blue jacket, shiny brass buttons, gold epaulettes, a wide red sash adorning his midsection, white pants and shirt, and dark stockings.

"Well, well, if it isn't Gilly Morrison," Armistead said as he shook Gilly's hand. "Am I your next victim then, for the curiosity of your readership?"

"Something like that I suppose, Major."

Armistead resumed his reconnaissance, diligently studying his defensive positions. "Do you have any idea how complex our defenses must be to deter an all-out British assault on this fort and upon this city?"

"No sir, I really don't. I tried to imagine it in my mind, but I can't quite get a clear view of it. We are so vulnerable on both land and sea. How can we possibly plan for every contingency?"

"Gilly, is this for the newspaper or your own edification?"

"Everything we say to each other as far as strategic defenses of this city and this fort will be between us only, sir. My story will be about you, as an individual, as well as a military leader, about the men who serve under you, and the citizens you rely upon, nothing else I promise you. The enemy will gain nothing from reading my stories except, perhaps, what they might not bargain for: a clear understanding of the resolute determination of Baltimoreans to fight for the city that they love."

"Well said, young man. I know now why Samuel loves and appreciates you so much. You are aware, of course that I recommended your Quaker clerk to serve as personal secretary to Commodore Rodgers?"

"I am, major, and I will miss him a great deal. Thank goodness his cousin, Richard, will take his place at the cooperage. Capable and quality help is so difficult to find. But tell me major, your command, does it extend

146

beyond the fort and its entrenchments?"

"A bit, yes, although very important nonetheless. Here, Gilly, take my glass. Due east now, just across the channel, do you see it?" Gilly focused the glass but couldn't quite pick out the fortification the major was referring to. "Two points southeast, son," Armistead said.

"Yes, I see it. It's very small, though."

"Large enough to deter the enemy from landing troops under the very belly of our defenses on Hampstead Hill."

"Okay, major, I'm beginning to recognize the strategy. Now if you complete preparations for a line of gun boats and barges from Fells Point to the northern portion of Whetstone Point ... "

"Whoa, there Gilly, how on earth did you know about that? It's supposed to be confidential information."

"Commodore Rodgers paid a visit to the cooperage and ordered barrels for the boats. He told Samuel what they would be used for."

"Dear Lord, we can't keep a secret for more than a few hours in this damned city."

"I will keep it secret, I promise. Now, how about the back door, wouldn't the British try to sneak south of our defenses into the Ferry Branch and take us by surprise?"

"You mean a flanking maneuver, don't you? While we're facing the monster directly in front of us, they send a landing party and take us from the rear."

"Yes sir, isn't that a possibility? "

"Gilly, I'm glad you're on our side. Don't bother turning the glass, you can't see from here. We're planning on building two forts that will be called 'Babcock' and 'Covington.' They will be situated to the west and southwest of this fort."

"Good, I'll sleep better tonight knowing that, major. Still, there's something else I thought might be of some benefit, if I may dare be so bold?"

"Go ahead, Gilly, I'm getting used to it. No wonder you are where you are today at such a young age. Did you ever think about petitioning the War Department for a commission in the army? Maybe even for a berth as a midshipman?"

Gilly laughed, but not without a pang of regret. "With this lame leg of mine, major, that was never a possibility. Thanks for asking anyway. Seriously, though, did you ever consider another line of naval defense?"

"Such as a fleet of newly built frigates, perhaps, with captains and crews equal to face His Majesty's finest?"

Gilly recognized the sarcasm, but dismissed it with one of his winning grins. "I was thinking about the channel, major. Did you think about blocking the channel with scuttled ships? In this way the line of gun boats and barges wouldn't have to bear the total burden of the last naval line of defense. Ship owners of Baltimore are sure to agree since if we lose this contest there will be no ships or docks or anything else that won't be put to the torch or captured. Even if the British succeed in silencing your guns at McHenry, they wouldn't be able to sail into the northwest branch and storm our harbors and homes. It wouldn't stop them entirely, but it may save Hampstead Hill from a flanking and devastating fire. It could buy us time."

Armistead thought about this without comment. After a moment, he took back the glass and turned his attention again to possible avenues of British encroachment upon his fort. "Gilly, my friend, mention what you just told me to no one else. I will bring this up with Commodore Rodgers, and Generals Smith and Stricker." He collapsed his spyglass and sat down on a barrel of gunpowder, a Dooley barrel. "Now, Gilly, proceed with your interview. I will answer your questions with candor and humility, both of which are not my strong suits."

Just below the rampart, McGuiness, the cook, finally dozed off. The Major's dinner would wait.

*****

Desiree's carriage pulled up in front of the rectory of St. Patrick's Church on Market Street. This time she descended without fanfare. She was in too much of a hurry. The French cleric was busy tending his roses in his garden in the back of the rectory, which was his simple joy in life. He cared for his roses as meticulously and lovingly as the greedy care for their wealth. Moranvillè saw in his roses all the possibilities life could offer: germination, sprouting, growth, budding, and, if nature was kind, a beautifully scented blossom.

He cupped his hand over his eyes and took in the deep blue, windswept sky. He was at one with creation and could not help but to break out into song. It was his favorite hymn, based on Psalm 148:

> "Praise the Lord! Ye heavens adore Him;
> Praise Him angels in the height;
> sun and moon, rejoice before Him;
> Praise Him, all ye stars of light.
> Praise the Lord! For he has spoken;
> worlds His mighty voice obeyed;
> laws which never shall be broken for their guidance he has made."

Nestled among the pastor's rose bushes stood a small, marble statue of St. Francis of Assisi with the saint's arm extended and a sparrow perched on his hand. Moranvillè had fostered, since early childhood, a great devotion to St. Francis. Crouching in his garden he folded his hands in front of his slight chest and prayed.

Desiree had heard singing and followed the sweet, monastic tenor voice to the rear of the rectory. She saw the cleric in deep prayer and paused, not willing to disturb his meditation. As she waited, she noticed the gaunt features of his face. His neck was stretched to the breaking point upwards towards the sky. His skin was ivory colored and taut revealing bony cheeks and a firm chin. There was an aura about him that emanated total serenity. Then he blessed himself and breathed an audible sigh from the depths of his soul.

He turned to greet his visitor. "An angel tapped me on my shoulder a moment too late, Mistress Pechin. Please forgive me for not giving you a proper welcome."

He could see in her face that she was distraught. After nearly fifty years in the priesthood, reading expressions was second nature to him. Yet, he made no comment. It was Moranvillè's practice to let the sinner or seeker of help open them self to him without unnecessary prodding or awkward questioning. After all, the seeker sought him, he did not, necessarily, seek them, and this was the first step towards personal redemption.

Desiree, who was not religious, began the conversation with a typical and annoying tone of arrogance. "Father Moranvillè, I have come to see you about a most serious matter which must be dealt with immediately."

Father John nodded solemnly, acknowledging what Desiree considered serious, but then turned back to his roses and began pruning again.

151

"*Oui*, mademoiselle," he said, innocently. "What then is troubling you?"

"It concerns Gilly Morrison and Michael Dooley and this stupid code they care so much about. How could Gilly possibly pay more attention to that than to me? I am the most desired and eligible girl in all of Baltimore. Any man would be lucky to have me on his arm." Desiree's answer to her own question wasn't meant to sound so obviously conceited. In her mind it was the plain truth.

Moranvillè listened until she was finished. He then started humming to himself Psalm 148. Desiree lost her temper. She stomped her foot demanding Father John's attention. But the priest patiently continued his pruning. Desiree's eyes filled up with tears; she sobbed silently into her silk handkerchief. The old man leaned back on his haunches away from his flowers and sighed contentedly.

"*Mademoiselle*, have you noticed the roses this year?" Desiree was taken aback by this comment. She wanted to talk about almost anything but roses. "They have not yet come into full bloom and it is so late in the season. A fact I pointed out to Jessica Farmer at this very time one year ago."

"Oh, that orphaned waif again," Desiree scoffed. "I heard she sailed off with Michael Dooley on *The Chasseur* disguised as a boy. Can you imagine the impertinence?"

Moranvillè ignored her comment. "Like you, she, too, was impatient,

152

as is natural for the young at heart. But the good Lord works in divine ways that we cannot and should not judge. I carry a letter in my pocket from Jessica Farmer, the orphaned waif, praise be. She and Michael have fallen in love on the long passage across the sea. She had always been in love with Michael. But the young cooper's son was infatuated with the editor's daughter – you *mademoiselle*.

"Michael's mother, Teresa, on her death bed, made me promise to see to it that Jessica and Michael would be together always. It was her last prayer and dying wish, which makes it God's work.

It was this humble priest, who crouches upon the earth before you, who convinced Jessica to dress like a boy and sail with Captain Boyle as a master's mate on the privateer *Chasseur*."

Desiree had totally forgotten why she was even standing there. This story sounded incredulous, yet she believed every word of it.

"It had it all been arranged, you see. I called a meeting of everyone concerned, except for Jessica and Michael. Along with the esteemed Captain Boyle, Captain Ken, the Dooley long-time friend, Bob Dooley, members of the crew of the privateer, and, this may surprise you, William Pechin, we finalized our plans before *The Chasseur* left Fells Point."

Desiree took a step back in astonishment. "My goodness, I had no idea. You mean my father knew of everything?"

153

"Not only knew, my dear, but heartily approved of it. Michael Dooley, you see, had a great respect for your father. He turned to your father after finding out about his own father's impressment. Knowing this, we sought your father's opinions on behalf of Michael. All went smoothly and according to plan. Jessica played her role remarkably well. She is a brilliant, young mathematician, excellent in navigation and seamanship. She berthed with Captain Ken and was kept apart from the crew. Being an officer, she was insulated from just about everyone on deck and below. She kept her watch on the quarterdeck, where only officers were allowed.

"On their return across the Atlantic Ocean, Jessica was finally found out. As a hurricane threatened the ship, the crew was inspired by a few evil men to blame Jessica for their run of bad luck - you know how seamen are prone to superstition. They accused Jessica of unspeakable crimes and labeled her a 'Jonah,' the worst possible accusation one sailor can lay upon another. But, the leaders of this witch hunt had ulterior motives. The ship was carrying an enormous amount of specie and treasure. Each hand was deserving of a share in the profits of the privateer's cruise. Yet, greed is, as Aquinas said, one of the deadliest of the seven sins. Greed is a cancer that cannot be cut out or cured. Left unchecked by men it eats into their souls and destroys them.

"Their plan was a simple one - mutiny. To kill Jessica, Michael, Captain Boyle, Bob Dooley, Captain Ken, and any other loyal crew members, including Boyle's young steward, David.

From the outset of the voyage, Captain Boyle had told David of Jessica's true identity, even before the ship slipped out of its berth here at the Point. David, who had never known love in his tragic life, soon fell in love with Jessica. But the boy mastered his emotions and with a pained heart accepted the fact that Jessica belonged to Michael and no one else. Strange, irony is perhaps the best teacher. David was lame in his left leg, a result of countless beatings he received from his father before Captain Boyle rescued him and gave him a purpose for being. David was the only victim of the insane mutiny. He was slain standing guard outside of Jessica's cabin protecting her life and virtue. A candle, Jessica has requested, burns in the church this day for David's soul and all children who are subject to the evil desires of men.

"The mutiny failed. The storm passed, and Michael and Jessica are alive and well preparing for a battle against the British on a skinny stretch of Lake called Champlain between New York and Vermont. They will have their test as we will, *mademoiselle*. All of us, no matter what our station or circumstance in life must face a test, at least one test."

Desiree's tears of vanity were all gone now. She stumbled to the garden bed and collapsed next to Moranvillè. She had forgotten everything that had brought her here. She cared nothing about the manure she now knelt upon.

The priest turned back to his roses and finished his pruning. "A rose

155

bud flowers according to the dictates of its own nature, outside the time frames of foolish men like me. We can, and we do, plan and dream as we work for the fruition of our goals. There is nothing wrong with this. It is in the nature of man since the beginning to be stewards of the earth and everything within it. But, it is also true, I cannot be the rose and the rose cannot be me, *oui?*"

"I think I'm beginning to finally understand, Father John." She looked at the roses and breathed in their sweet smell. "Roses never impart such a delicious aroma until they are in full bloom. Why then, do these roses emanate such a perfect fragrance while they are still budding?"

Father John shrugged, "I can ask you a better question, *mon amie.*"

"Yes, Father?"

"Do you love Gilly Morrison, my daughter?"

"Yes – yes – oh yes, I love him!"

Moranvillè took his soil stained hand and patted her auburn head. "Then let this bud bloom in its own time. Its scent may be deceptively alluring today, but imagine the bounty of its fragrance when it finally blossoms."

"But, Father, what must I do now, while I wait for the bloom of this rose?"

"Look up to the sky tonight. It will be clear, moonless, and star-

156

filled. Think on what or who makes this all possible. Is it the machinations of men? The planets and stars move with a purpose because they are under authority. Are you under authority? Do you move with a purpose or are you independent of such designs?"

He then took his hands and placed them on Desiree's cheeks. "Both Gilly and Michael are men of the Code of Aquinas. They are determined to know what they ought to believe; know what they ought to desire; know what they ought to do. Nothing in this world will deter Gilly in this quest, because it is now a part of him.

"You are not a creature of greed, like the evil ones on board *The Chasseur*. But you are, *mademoiselle*, a foolish and pampered girl with little or no regard for human frailty. This is because of your father's guilt after your mother died in your childbirth. Now, you are of an age to recognize these things and make amends. You must first look to yourself and your own soul before expecting to pursue another soul such as Gilly Morrison or any other man. This is the one great thing you must accomplish to achieve true joy in your life."

Moranvillè then laid his hands upon her head, quietly prayed, and blessed her.

Chapter 10: Epiphany

Desiree's carriage and driver were waiting on Market Street outside the church. She told the driver she was going to walk down to the docks. The driver raised his eyebrows in surprise. It was almost a quarter-mile. The driver was careful to follow her footsteps at a safe distance so that she did not hear the horse's shoes slap the cobblestones and possibly disrupt her thoughts – or, God forbid, because the cobblestones were uneven, break a heel on her shoe.

When she reached the waterfront she gazed upon the gentle chop of the Patapsco and winced slightly as the noon sun shimmered across the expanse of river from Fells Point all the way to Whetstone Point. Desiree closed her mouth and breathed in a lung-full of clean, salty air through her nose. Slowly exhaling, she felt a sense of peace.

Walking back along the wharf, she decided to stop into the

cooperage. Richard was behind the counter studying the orders. "Good day, Mistress Pechin, what may I do for you today?"

"Is Master Morrison here?"

"No, mistress, he is working on a story for the newspaper."

"How about Samuel, is he here at all?"

"He has joined the navy and is now the personal secretary of Commodore Rodgers. I am his replacement, Samuel's cousin. My name is Richard Snipes. We saw each other earlier, mistress, but you were … " here Richard paused to find the appropriate words, " … engaged in a conversation with Master Gilly."

Desiree smiled brightly. "That was no conversation, Richard. That was a horse whipping if ever I saw one. And it was one that I so justly deserved!" They both laughed. And then Desiree adopted a more serious attitude. Her dark brown brows were raised in a questioning manner. "I know Samuel has worked so hard as a volunteer at Fort McHenry. I was hoping he might be able to help me find something to do as I desperately need to pitch in and do my part for the war effort. I know I have little to offer. Nothing in the way of skilled labor, but I can sew! I used to design and sew clothes for my dolls when I was a child."

Richard was completely dumbfounded. No genteel young woman from the upper class had ever put such a question before him. Then he remembered something Samuel had told him about a flag being constructed for Fort McHenry that was so large in its dimensions it could be seen by the naked eye for miles.

"Mistress, have you heard of the flag being sewn to fly over the fort, the really big one?"

"Why, no Richard, I have not."

"It is supposed to be as large as a sloop and will be flown by Major Armistead after the British are defeated and scurry back down the Patapsco towards the bay, pray God. Samuel mentioned that it was so big the seamstress in charge, a Mrs. Pickersgill, I believe, had set up shop in the basement of a brewery here on Fells Point because it was the only place large enough to accommodate the work. I think that if you made proper inquiries, you would find the place and Mrs. Pickersgill in the bargain."

"Oh, thank you, Richard. You are a dear. This is of great help to me. I will go at once, locate Mrs. Pickersgill, and offer my services, if she will have me." Desiree quickly exited the cooperage. Richard, behind the counter, rubbed his hands into his face and breathed out a long sigh.

Desiree informed her driver she was looking for a place where they made malt beverages along the wharf and where a gigantic flag was being made. As her carriage clip-clopped along the wharf she was amazed at the amount of activity to be seen everywhere. The dock boats were plying their oars back and forth across the river delivering provisions and armaments for the thousands of militia, and the regular army and navy. Funny, she hadn't noticed that before.

Desiree ordered her driver to stop at the first brewery they came upon. It was only a few hundred yards away. Before entering, she glanced back at the men, women, and children who scurried about with purpose, each one determined to defend their city. Desiree wanted to join them. She, too, wanted to act with a purpose for the common good. She didn't know if it was Father John's blessing or hearing the words of the Code of Aquinas, but she was suddenly awakened to something greater than herself.

Father John had finished his chores in the garden. He wiped his hands on a towel while walking toward the front of the rectory. He could see Desiree heading to the riverfront on foot, her delicate chaise and coachman trailing behind. There was no doubt in Father John's mind as to the sincerity of Desiree's contrition. She was immensely sorry for acting selfishly. Yet, she was still Desiree: innately strong and stubbornly defiant. Now even more so because she recognized that there was a job to be done and no time to waste.

"She will be in a hurry to make up for lost time, Lord," the priest said aloud. "You know the quality of this one. She won't be long in - how do the English put it? Crying over spilt milk? Yes, that's it exactly. Oh, she will lament from time to time. She wouldn't be human if she did not rue the days. But, Moranvillè is warning you, Lord. This one you just touched with your

161

mercy is going to lay siege to the very gates of heaven. And don't blame the child, Lord. Remember Luke, Chapter Nine? You, Yourself, said don't look back after putting your hand to the plough!"

*****

After his interview with Major Armistead and his men, Gilly checked on Richard at the cooperage. The information he received from the major was going to make a good story in and of itself. Still, he had to track down Mrs. Pickersgill to make his story complete.

"Good evening to you, Master Morrison. How did everything go at the fort? Satisfactory, I hope?"

"Yes, Richard, and then some, now let's take a good look at these books. The boys are working in shifts, I see."

"They are, the Smith brothers are in the back cleaning up. We've completed all the work for the past week and now are looking to fill the orders for next week." Richard removed his apron and unbuttoned his shirt. He removed a key and chain from around his neck and unlocked the top drawer of the counter. "These are the requisitions for the coming week."

"Oh my, Richard, things are really picking up around here. Do you think we can keep up with demand?"

"It won't be easy, I admit, sir. If we have to work all hours into the night we will." Richard was about to mention Desiree's visit this afternoon, then thought it best to keep it quiet for now. He could see the strain on Gilly's face and did not want to add to his burdens. He also didn't want Gilly to be overly concerned with filling the new orders. He needed Gilly to be confident in his new clerk.

Suddenly, Gilly remembered something that had unconsciously bothered him last week, when Desiree made her unannounced visit. "Richard, pass me the orders from the week before." There, Gilly thought, that was it. Every page of last week's orders was smudged with a thumbprint. Samuel would never have been this careless.

"Richard, is there anything else in the drawer?

"No more orders, sir. Samuel tells me you take old orders back to the Dooley home to be put into the yearly business ledger. There's just this simple sketch. Looks like Samuel's doodling."

Richard handed Gilly the charcoal drawing Samuel had made showing the plan to construct a line of barges and gun boats across the Patapsco from Fells Point to Whetstone Point. There was the same thumbprint at the top of the page. It wasn't there when Samuel drew the sketch.

"Is this drawer always locked?'

"Yes, sir, my cousin gave me explicit instructions to keep it locked under all circumstances. Is there anything wrong, Master Morrison?"

"No, it's nothing, Richard. Just keep that drawer locked. You and I are the only ones with a key. I'll take these papers with me back home. Let me know if there's anything amiss, however small or seemingly inconsequential, understand?"

"Yes, sir, and by the way should I have the men come to work on Sunday to start our preparations for the week?"

Gilly giggled and pointed his finger at his clerk. "And do you, Richard, want to explain that to Father John when he bangs on this door after Mass on Sunday? I know he is a good and peaceful man, but I've also seen him in rare fits of holy righteousness where he would take a club over a man's back to put the fear of God back into him. Remember he is the pastor of a tough harbor town, and sometimes that means being tougher than the sinners who inhabit it."

Richard's face reddened in obvious embarrassment. "Master Morrison, consider my suggestion withdrawn, never to be spoken of again in this or any other lifetime."

*****

Father John's real name was Jean Francois Moranvillè. He was the Abbè of a large monastery on the southeast coast of France. He escaped to Spain after religious liberty and the Catholic Church were threatened by the French Revolutionary government. Many Catholic clergy and religious, especially those who held title, such as bishops and abbots, were condemned to death by the guillotine in the brutal and bloody attempt to rid France of the faith that had sustained them for centuries. Tens of thousands of priests were exiled, many were slaughtered. Father John managed to escape and made his way across the Atlantic to a settlement in French Guiana, off the coast of Brazil. Here, the ugly arms of the revolution threatened him once more and he fled again, this time to Baltimore.

Archbishop John Carroll, the head of the Roman Catholic Church in the United States, appointed Father John as pastor of St. Patrick's Church, in Fells Point.

Father John was only four-foot-eleven and weighed less than ten stone. Despite his lack in physical stature he commanded reverence and respect. This was because of his saintly acts of compassion, and his tireless efforts for the poor and the orphans on the Point.

At times, he was also feared by the sailors and innkeepers along the wharves. If a wife and mother cried to him in his confessional about her husband, who had just returned from a long voyage at sea, yet refused to give his spouse money for food, medicine, and rent, Father John would go searching for the sailor among the inebriated in the saloons and bordellos. Upon finding the man, Father John would threaten him both with damnation and with a strong whack of his "war club" across the back unless he did his duty to his family first. His club was a crozier, really, make of mahogany and topped with a silver cross; a designation of his former office as Abbè, years before.

Thus, after ten years of such active and pious service, Father John had succeeded in gaining the love of his parishioners and the cautious deference of fence sitters everywhere. He had aged a great deal during that decade, but only in body. His spirit still soared to lofty heights and his intellect was as acute as ever.

On that Saturday night, Father John took stock of the situation of his parish and his parishioners. He often did this when he sensed trouble brewing among his flock. Michael Dooley and Jessica were safe for the time being, yet facing unforeseen dangers as a massive invasion from Canada threatened New York.

Gilly Morrison had shown tremendous fortitude in directly confronting Desiree Pechin even though all his hopes and dreams lay in the balance. Desiree showed true remorse for her past. He couldn't read her heart, of course, but he saw her kneeling in manure and that was as fine a start on the path to humility as any.

The good priest walked out the front door of the rectory. It was getting late. There was little illumination emanating from the city of forty thousand souls. He looked to the heavens and saw a panorama of celestial delights: planets fixed in an ancient march from horizon to horizon; stars clustered together in constellations appearing to the imagination as clearly as pictures on a canvass; falling stars and streaming lights with blue and white tails. Moranvillè yawned and shifted his shawl over his slight shoulders and closer to his neck. There was a damp chill in the air. He reentered the rectory ready for sleep. As he nodded off he hummed his favorite psalm: " … laws which never shall be broken for their guidance He has made."

*****

While Gilly and Richard were discussing Father John that afternoon, Desiree Pechin walked into the brewery and inquired after Mrs. Pickersgill. She was led down a flight of steps into the basement. It was here that she saw the flag for the first time and it took her breath away. It covered the entire breadth of the basement floor. The fifteen stars in the dark-blue field were already in place with pins and measured two feet in diameter. Most of the fifteen stripes were sewn and attached with heavy thread densely stitched at seventeen threads per inch. This was needed to endure the gale-like winds over Fort McHenry that would punish a flag weighing over fifty pounds and rising to the top of a ninety-foot pole.

Mrs. Mary Pickersgill was taking a breather and talking to her mother, Rebecca, who sat watching and observing the work from her rocking chair. Mary massaged her hand and forearm muscles and continually stretched her fingers.

"I don't know ma," Mary said with some doubt in her voice. "The British might be here to burn this flag before we ever get it done and hand it over to the major."

Rebecca rocked silently, smoking a pipe and taking everything in. "You're doin' fine daughter. Don't be frettin' about every final stitch. Wasn't it me who taught you how to ply a needle?"

"I know ma, but my back's just about to give out on me. If we only had a few more girls to help get the job done I'd feel better. Have you ever sewn anything as big as this before?"

Rebecca drew on her corn cob pipe, stuffed with good Carolina tobacco and let the smoke exit her mouth and nose. "No, daughter, I ain't. But when I was in Philadelphia during the revolution, George Washington wanted me to sew a flag for him to fly over his first command, in Cambridge, Massachusetts, after congress appointed him Commander of the American Army. He was in a hot bother to skedaddle with his troops to the relief of Boston. He said iffin' I couldn't do the job in twenty-four hours, he'd get Betsy Ross to do it."

Mary Pickersgill rolled her eyes toward the ceiling. She was too busy to endure another story about how her mother and Betsy Ross were competitors in Philadelphia. "Let me guess, ma. You did it on time."

"Damn right I did. Showed that hussy Ross up and got well paid for it."

Just then Mary noticed a vision walking towards her. She took off her glasses and huffed upon the lenses and wiped with her apron before putting them back on. "Can I help you with something?"

Desiree flashed a stunning smile showing a perfect set of white teeth and exquisite dimples. "Why, yes, I'm looking for Mrs. Pickersgill."

"That's me, missy, has been for going on forty years now."

"Mrs. Pickersgill, I came here to ask if you needed any help sewing the flag."

"Well, I wouldn't deny it, missy. My fingers are so sore it's hard to open them at all in the morning. I have to warm a blanket by the fire and wrap them up and then sit on them till they get normal again. I could sure use a good hand or two around here. You got a good seamstress in mind? Or would it be one of your slaves or servants that has hands of iron and is handy with a needle?"

Desiree blushed, something she rarely did. "Why, no, Mrs. Pickersgill, I was thinking of myself. I would very much like to volunteer and help in any way I can. I've sewed an entire wardrobe for my collection of dolls when I was a girl."

Mary turned to her mother to see if she had heard the same thing from the pretty mouth of the socialite. Rebecca was inhaling at the time and began to choke on the smoke from her pipe. Mary whacked her mother on the back a few times until Rebecca's wind pipes were cleared.

"Are you okay, ma?"

"No. You, daughter?"

"No, ma, I don't reckon I am." Mary turned to Desiree and managed something like a smile, but not really. "Missy, did I hear you say something about a doll collection?"

"Yes," Desiree beamed. "I even fashioned my own designs and patterns ... " While Desiree explained her experience, Mary and Rebecca exchanged confusing glances with knitted brows and open mouths. " ... and then I cut the patterns and matched them to the silk cloth and snipped and sewed.

"I do appreciate the opportunity to assist you in your work, Mrs. Pickersgill. I've been absolutely dying for a chance to contribute to the war effort. But, I can't very well shoulder a shovel or a rifle and go off digging and drilling with the boys, can I? When I heard you were making a flag the size of life itself, I knew in my heart that this was the place for me. Believe me, Mrs. Pickersgill, when I really put my mind to some endeavor I am as ferocious as a lion and no one can stop me." Mary and Rebecca's mouths were still agape.

Desiree looked over the flag and thought there were too many stars pinned to the blue field. Her jaw dropped and she pressed her hand to her ample bosom. "Oh my, Mrs. Pickersgill, I'm afraid there's something terribly wrong!"

Mary leapt to Desiree's side and felt her forehead. "What is it missy? Do you feel faint?"

Desiree pointed a well-manicured index finger at the flag. "Oh, my dear Mrs. Pickersgill, I'm so sorry to tell you … "

"Tell me what, child?"

Desiree was almost weeping, she was that distraught. "You have two too many stars on that flag!"

"Oh my good Lord, this is horrible! Think of the time it will take to make the corrections! Ma, how could I have done something so stupid? The major was adamant – he said make sure there are fifteen stars and fifteen stripes. Oh my God, ma, what can we do now?"

Rebecca relit her pipe and rocked slowly in her chair. "Daughter," she said coolly, "count the damn stars."

Mary did so. Then she faced Desiree with an angry glare. "Missy, you've got some explaining to do. You nearly gave me the apoplexy. This here flag is exactly according to order: forty-two feet in length, thirty by width, with fifteen stars and fifteen stripes."

Desiree was confused. "But I was taught a flag had only thirteen stars and thirteen stripes. You know, after the number of the founding colonies."

171

"Missy, I have no idea what castle you just walked out of, but did you ever hear of the two new states that have joined the union?"

"No, I never did, Mrs. Pickersgill."

"The folk in the states of Vermont and Kentucky will be very glad to hear that. Ever since they joined these United States, the Congress said our flag should expand as new states come in to the union." Mary Pickersgill put on her no nonsense face and used a sterner tone in her voice. "Now, let's not beat about the bush. You say you want to help?"

"Yes, please, madam."

"Let see those hands of yours." Desiree obediently lifted her palms for inspection.

"These hands haven't seen a day's work since the day you were laid in a cradle. Now, missy, take a gander at mine."

"My goodness, Mrs. Pickersgill, they're terribly calloused and bruised."

"Are you willing, then, for your delicate hands to look like these? Make no mistake, missy, you'll do more than break a nail or two. This here's rough, back-breaking work. You'll be crawling on your knees most of the time. Girl, are you sure this is what you desire to do?"

This couldn't be happenstance. Not here and not now, and, certainly, not under these circumstances. Mary Pickersgill used the exact words of the Code of Aquinas. There was no doubt in Desiree's mind that this is what she "ought to desire." Wait until Father John hears about this, she thought. Why, it was as if St. Thomas Aquinas was speaking directly to her. This was not just the code that had changed the lives of Michael Dooley and Gilly Morrison anymore. It was Desiree Pechin's code, too.

"Yes, it is exactly what I ought to desire, Mrs. Pickersgill."

"Then lose the fancy dress. You can't work in a rig like that. Tie some lose rags around your knees and elbows. Put a bandana around your curly locks to keep your hair out of your eyes. Get ready to suck the blood from your fingers when you accidentally stick your fingers with the needle you'll be sewing with, which will be at least a dozen times a day. Missy, do you understand everything I just told you?"

Desiree grinned in anticipation. "When do you want me here, tomorrow?"

"When the sun rises and the rooster should be shot for all the noise he makes."

Desiree bowed her head, trying to hold back grateful tears.

Mary Pickersgill stretched out her hardened hand and lifted Desiree's chin. "Don't cry now, darling. Where you come from and why you're doing this I swear I haven't a clue. I have a daughter of my own and three young nieces. I'm no stranger to the longings and dreams of young girls. Somehow, and don't answer me now, there's a handsome young man involved with this business. Or a change of heart because of some past wrongs your young mind is wrestling with. I'm thinking a combination of the two." Mary turned to her mother, still smoking her pipe and rocking contentedly in her chair. "Ma, you got anything to say?"

Rebecca removed the stem of her pipe from her mouth. "Tell me, girl, what is your name?"

"My name is Desiree, madam. Desiree Pechin, I live with my father in Old Baltimore Town."

Rebecca nodded and took another puff on her pipe. "Desiree, I'm real fond of tea and scones in the morning. Maybe your servants can rustle up some of that for me tomorrow. And maybe some jams and jelly."

Before Desiree went to bed that night, she walked outside the front door of the Pechin house. It was as Father John had predicted. There was no moon and the stars in the heavens glimmered brightly. Knowing nothing of astronomy, she could only gaze at the wonderful sights that befell her tired eyes. She thought to herself, is it really the way Father John said it was?

As she gazed at the heavens and saw the miracles in the night sky, tears welled in her eyes. Desiree saw something she had never seen before - she saw the magnificence of the universe under authority. She suddenly realized something quite astounding. That she was under authority, too.

Chapter 11: The Road to Damascus

Gilly couldn't sleep. It was now August and the heat and humidity building up in the horseshoe harbor of Baltimore was unbearable. He lit a candle and worked his way down the steps toward the kitchen. He sat at the oaken table and cradled his head in his hands. A flash of white lightening that lit up the kitchen was quickly followed by a clap of thunder that shook the little red brick house on Thames Street to its foundation.

Gilly grabbed a towel from the closet and opened the Dutch door leading to the back of the house. He stripped off his clothes and walked outside. The lightning and thunder had abated but torrents of rain still pelted Fells Point with a vengeance.

He heard Sarika whinny in her stall and opened the doors to the new stable. "Hello, Princess, you're all nice and dry I see. Good for you, but I needed to get naked and wet, it was so damned hot in the house and I just couldn't sleep a wink."

Sarika seemed to understand and used her nose to push some hay in Gilly's direction. He rubbed himself dry with his towel and gathered some more hay around him.

"This is a good idea, Princess. I think I'll sleep here tonight with you." Sarika nodded her head in approval. Gilly made himself a nice dry bed of straw and hay and laid his head up against Sarika's stall. The palomino jutted her magnificent mane between the rails. As she played with his curly, red hair, Gilly fell asleep.

His dream was as colorful as it was before when he raced against the British admiral. This time, however, there were no horses. Gilly was in the crow's nest of a ship, high atop all the other masts with a clear view of everything in front of him. He reached down to pick up a glass and peered ahead at a fleet of ships off the starboard bow. The ships he saw were all flying the Union Jack.

Gilly yelled down to the deck trying to warn the captain of the oncoming threat. He shouted at the top of his lungs "sail ho!" But none of the seamen or officers on deck seemed to take any notice. Desperate, Gilly started to descend the main mast but lost his footing because his left leg lacked the strength to take his full body weight. He clung for dear life to the mast fearing another step might be his last. Still, the crew must be warned about the British fleet.

Gilly attempted to just use just his right leg in his climb down, but this, too, failed. No one will warn the Americans of the threat coming towards them. They will be surprised, routed, and beaten. He hugged the mast and started to sob. The wind picked up and dislodged a block and tackle from the standing rigging. It dangled just over his head, swaying to and fro like a pendulum. Every time it passed over his head it grazed his hair. He wished it would stop. Then it laid itself upon his head and snorted. Gilly opened his eyes. He put his hand to the top of his head and felt Sarika's nostrils.

The storm had blown over by dawn and sunlight filtered through the cracks in the door of the stable. Gilly yawned and stretched his arms and legs. He roused himself from the warm straw, and then wrapped the towel he had used last night around his waist.

"My breakfast first, Princess, then I'll be back and give you yours. Thank you for waking me. We have a full day today."

After saddling Sarika, Gilly rode to the wharf on Fells Point and tied Princess to a post outside the brewery. He was informed that Mrs. Pickersgill and family were in the basement. Before Gilly even saw the flag, he smelled the delicious aroma of tea biscuits and scones. Maneuvering his way down the steps, the sight of the huge flag astonished him. Mrs. Pickersgill welcomed him and introduced her family: her mother, Rebecca, smoking her pipe and enjoying a cup of tea while sitting on her cushioned rocking chair; her daughter of thirteen years, Caroline; nieces Eliza and Margaret Young, both in their early teens; and a black, indentured servant, Grace Sher, who was learning to be a seamstress.

"And who is that girl?" Gilly asked, pointing to a young woman with her back to them, feverishly stitching the two foot stars into place. She had rags wrapped around her elbows and knees. Her hair was hidden by a bright, blue bandana. She wore a simple tunic and white-duck trousers. Upon her feet were Indian moccasins.

"She's new to our little group. Not much of a hand with a needle, but what she lacks in experience she makes up for in stubbornness. Says her name is Desiree and her father is a big wig in town that runs a newspaper." Mrs. Pickersgill whacked Gilly on the back. "Say, you must know her; you said you're writing a story for *The American* or some such paper."

Gilly could only mumble "Yes, Mrs. Pickersgill." He walked towards the stars and stooped over the hard working figure.

"Hello, Desiree."

Desiree picked up her head from her work and sat back on her haunches. Gilly noticed that a few locks of her auburn hair had fallen down into her eyes. She blew them aside with the corner of her mouth. He also noticed that her nails were badly chipped, her hands were red and sore

179

looking, and she had developed calluses on her fingers and palms.

"Gilly, what on earth are you doing here?"

"I'm working on a story for the paper about the flag. But what, in God's name, are you doing here?"

"I'm working, too, as you can plainly see. We need only attach these stars and add two more layers of bunting for the states of Vermont and Kentucky and then all will be accomplished. The flag is desperately needed at the fort as soon as possible. The British could attack at any time now."

Gilly was tongue tied and stammered incoherently. He could not fathom how Desiree was actually in front of him on her hands and knees in workman's clothes doing manual labor.

"Are you all right, Desiree? Should I contact your father? I cannot, in all honesty, understand what you're up to."

"I'm contributing to the war effort, Master Morrison. In my own way I'm doing whatever I can to be of some simple service. Is this so hard for you to understand? Now, if you'll be so kind, please leave me as I'm behind in my work as it is and have no time for idle conversation. Oh, and mister, do not, under any circumstances, mention my name in your story! My father knows nothing about this. I'll tell him about it later. And after you've stopped gawking at me and wonder why I've come to the realization that I've been a spoiled rotten brat for more years than I can count, just go and ask Father

180

John. You're not the only one who has been in search of spiritual guidance."

Gilly got his story and then some. He didn't mention Desiree. He did, however, tell the story of a seamstress who was the daughter of a competitor of Betsy Ross when Rebecca resided in Philadelphia during the revolution before moving to Baltimore. Rebecca made sure Gilly was informed about this over a cup of tea and scones before his departure. Gilly told his readership about the brutal work on hands and knees the women had accomplished in the final completion of the flag that required over 350,000 stitches to do the job. A flag designed to ensure in the soldiers, seamen, militia, and populace of the city that victory was within their grasp if only they believed in it.

*****

Late that night, Desiree was taken home by a very bored driver who had been waiting for her since sunup. She twisted the brass handle of her front door. She was hungry and exhausted beyond belief.

William Pechin was seated at the dining table finishing a late night meal. He had been in his offices going over the latest dispatches from Washington and reports of newspaper headlines along the eastern seaboard from Maine to New Jersey. None of it looked good for the republican cause.

He was aghast at his daughter's appearance. Never in his life had he seen her like this. She smiled at him and took a chair at the table. A servant placed a plate of chicken and rice in front of her and decanted a glass of sherry, fearing Desiree might faint from exhaustion. Desiree grabbed the crystal glass and drained it with a satisfied sigh. Then she tore into her dinner until nothing was left but the bones of the chicken.

"I owe you an explanation, father. Please be patient with me as I try to explain."

"You owe me nothing, my dear, and you need not explain."

Desiree fought the desire to close her eyes from fatigue. "I saw Father John. He opened up in my mind something I've never dreamed of before."

"And what is that my daughter?"

Desiree tried to think, but thinking is difficult when one is overwhelmed with the need to sleep. "To the possibility that even I can now make a difference, though the time is late and my opportunity is quickly slipping away."

"Desiree, what were you up to today?"

"Helping Mrs. Pickersgill and her family sew the flag Major Armistead ordered for Fort McHenry. It's beautiful, you should see it. Gilly was there researching his next story. I asked him not to mention anything about me. I needed to talk to you first."

"From the looks of your hands, I'd say you put in a long hard day."

182

"We were at it since sunup. It's almost done. Maybe another few days and then I can worry about my hands." Desiree wished to draw attention away from herself and changed the subject. "Father, you were working all day, too. Is the war progressing well? Do we have a chance in the fight that's coming?"

This time it was Mr. Pechin who reached for the sherry. He poured himself a generous glass. "No, dear, I'm afraid things are looking pretty badly. New Jersey has just passed a resolution condemning the war. The governors of Connecticut, Rhode Island, and Massachusetts have refused to comply with President Madison's request for militia troops. There is even talk of a convention to assemble in New England to sue for a separate peace with the British. If this happens, our country and everything it stands for will face complete destruction. It might even cause a civil war." Pechin poured another glass and stared blankly at the palms of his hands. "And everything your father has worked for these many years will be brought to naught."

Desiree hadn't heard a word of her father's discourse. Her head was lying on the dining room table. Mr. Pechin gathered his daughter in his arms and carried her to her bedroom where her chamber maid was patiently waiting. He hadn't done this since his daughter was two-years-old.

*****

After interviewing Mrs. Pickersgill and family, Gilly mounted Sarika and rode in the direction of the cooperage. He couldn't get the picture of

Desiree, working like a sweaty stevedore unloading a ship's hold, out of his mind. Sarika noticed a change in Gilly's attitude and whinnied, bobbing her head up and down as she did so.

Gilly opened up his mind to his Princess. "There is something not quite right about all of this, my noble lady. People don't change in a blink of any eye, horses either for that matter.

"Yet, I've never seen Desiree like this before. It's as if she were a completely different person. She was ... she was sublime." He pulled on the reins and Sarika came to an abrupt stop. "I have a change of plans, Princess. Let's go and see if Father John is at the rectory. I need to seek the advice of a higher authority."

Moranvillè was in the church relighting Jessica's candle for David, Captain Boyle's steward who was murdered on *The Chasseur*. Gilly genuflected before the altar and asked the priest for a moment of his time.

"No doubt, *mon ami*, you are here to question me about Desiree Pechin."

"Yes, Father, I'm at a loss to understand what has happened to her. It can't be an act. I saw her on her hands and knees stitching stars on a flag. She was dressed like a dock hand. Her fingers were bleeding from sticking herself with a needle."

Father John took a seat in a side pew and motioned for Gilly to sit

184

next to him. "Sometimes, what you see you cannot understand. Since you are a devotee of Aquinas, I will put it in his words: 'We are more certain, therefore, in believing the things of faith than those things which can be seen, because God's knowledge never deceives us, but the visible sense of man is often in error.' What you see is a prissy, self-centered, rich young woman who has no regard for her fellow man, *oui*?"

Gilly nodded in agreement. "Yes, Father, that's it exactly. How could she change so much? It's not within her to reform so quickly and suddenly dedicate herself to the war effort. She didn't give a ... "

Moranvillè wiggled his finger in front of Gilly's face to silence the oath about to be spoken.

"Okay, I'm sorry Father. But Desiree is an arrogant, manipulative creature who plays upon innocent hearts and uses them to accomplish her own selfish designs."

"This is certain, she was everything you say."

"What do you mean she *was*? Surely she couldn't have had a monumental change of heart in a matter of days, let alone hours." Gilly put his hands to his face and rocked his body in the pew. "Oh, Father, are we talking about St. Paul again? Are you saying she had a moment of the soul like Samuel did and all of a sudden realized the meaning of the Code of Aquinas and internalized it in her heart in a matter of seconds? I can't believe this.

How on earth did she find out about the code anyway?"

Moranvillè shook his head and laughed. "Don't trouble yourself, Gilly. Desiree's transformation is completely unlike your former clerk's. Samuel had a lifetime of reflection and soul searching before the veil was lifted from his eyes.

"Desiree had no such advantage. On the contrary, she has lived, as you aptly describe, a life full of venal pursuits. Her 'Road to Damascus' has been so subtle that she had not one conscious thought as to where it would lead her. Are you following this, *mon ami*?"

Gilly shook his head in the negative. He understood, vaguely, Samuel's instantaneous conversion. But, Desiree's was totally beyond his ken.

"Mistress Pechin told me she had a long talk with her father; a discussion which disturbed her to the very core of her being and lit a fuse within her soul. Believe it or not, Desiree loves her father very much. The capacity to love was always in her. It was given to her by the mother who gave her life, who willingly sacrificed a mother's life for her daughter. This is a special level of love that cannot be kept hidden forever. The Creator of love would never permit such a thing to happen."

Gilly put up his hand to stop Father John until he had time to digest everything he had just been told. "So, it was Mr. Pechin, my editor, who lit this fuse in Desiree's heart?"

186

"Yes, it was certainly her father. She seeks to please him to prove her love, you see?"

"I'm trying to. I really am. But what does all of this have to do with the Code of Aquinas? How could Desiree, of all people, allow this to change her hardened heart?"

Moranvillè sighed, not out of frustration, but because he must reveal to Gilly a truth that would be very difficult for him to accept. "We talked about the Dooley code at her insistence. She could not understand why you and Michael Dooley cared so much for the words of Aquinas. I explained this to her.

"*Mon ami*, her father lit the fuse because he confessed to his daughter the love he had for his wife. Now, however, a fire burns brightly within Desiree's heart and will not and cannot be extinguished."

Gilly nodded in understanding. "So, she now burns with a desire to help her country in its hour of need. Praise be, Father. Desiree now has a clear vision of the world around her. Something, I think, until this moment has never dawned on her before."

"*Oui*, so it appears. Yet there remains a certain question as to why her heart burns so. Gilly, Desiree now sees things through the lens of another. She sees them through the eyes of the one she loves. And because she has this deep and abiding love, she will never see things any other way. The reason

187

she has accepted into her heart the Code of Aquinas is because her lover has, too. How can she possibly satisfy her lover if she has not accepted into her heart the one thing that means the most - to him? This was her 'Road to Damascus,' and this is truly the wisdom of Aquinas."

"What are you trying to tell me, father?"

"That *she* is in love with *you*, my boy!"

Chapter 12: Rumors and Conspiracy

Gilly's story appearing in Monday's paper was a huge success. Mary Pickersgill and her mother could not have been more pleased. Again, *The American* was sold out, this time, in less than an hour after kids like Gabe hit the streets. Mr. Pechin sent a courier to the Dooley house with a note of congratulations.

What Gilly had wanted to accomplish with his story on the making of Armistead's flag was to engender a sense of stubborn determination in the minds of Baltimoreans to withstand the British invasion no matter how ugly things became after the attack began. "The flag of victory," Gilly wrote, "would fly over Fort McHenry if for no other reason than the sweat and tears of a few women and girls who painfully sewed so many closely knit stitches." Now, all of Baltimore knew it.

189

Gilly didn't take satisfaction from the accolades that came his way. He was already gathering information for his next story in the Wednesday edition. He wanted all of his stories to coalesce and build upon one another; each story reinforcing a frontiersman-like resolve to endure and survive despite the odds.

Gilly rode Sarika past St. Patrick's Church towards the tip of the American lines on Hampstead Hill. It was a long ride because he had to take a detour through Old Town before turning east. He was half tempted to stop at the Pechin house and see how Desiree was getting along but remembered she was probably at the brewery finishing her work on the flag. Besides, he had best give Desiree a wide berth after what Father John had told him.

The sun was almost at its zenith when Gilly rode down the lines to his destination at Rodgers Bastion, which was situated at the very center of the American defenses. The sun bore down with relentless heat upon Gilly's hatless head. Sarika felt it as well. Her prince was determined to make sure she had her fill of water once they found Commodore Rodger's headquarters.

The City Brigade had just finished morning drill and took cover from the sun underneath makeshift lean-tos covered with straw. They stoked their fires and were preparing a well-earned meal when Gilly spied the Smith brothers among their company.

Gilly waved and rode up to their lean-to. Ethan and Elijah were both happy to see him. But that changed quickly.

190

"Master Morrison," Elijah said with great concern in his voice, "why have you mistreated this palomino so cruelly?"

Gilly dismounted his Princess and shrugged his shoulders. "I just rode up from Fells Point, boys. I knew she needed some water but I didn't mean to harm her in any way."

The Smith brothers were raised on a farm and knew about the proper care of animals. Ethan Smith checked Sarika's hooves. "Sir, when is the last time you picked these shoes?"

"I didn't know anything about picking shoes; I thought the farrier would take care of that in about a month or so."

Elijah took Sarika's reins and led her underneath the lean-to. "Ethan, get me a bucket of water, a sponge, and some dry straw." He turned toward Gilly, a look of consternation in his knowing eyes. "Sir, this is an excellent horse, you should take better care of her."

Suddenly, Gilly felt extremely guilty. "Elijah, I swear I would have taken better care of Sarika if I had only known. Would you teach me?"

Elijah smiled at his employer. "Sir, if you're not raised up livin' with horses and cows and sheep your never gonna know what they need and how to take care of them. It's not your fault."

Ethan came back from the lean-to and added his farm-grown

191

wisdom. "Master Morrison, this here horse is not an ox or a bull or a quarter horse fit for nothin' but pullin' a plow. She's somethin' special and needs treated that way. When you sponge her down at night make sure you give her fresh, dry straw to stand on after her bath. And, always, I say always, check her hooves to pick out stones or anything else which might cause discomfort at first and lameness later iffin' you don't do this."

Gilly was truly relieved to hear this advice. "Thank you, boys, I won't forget what you taught me. Now, if that beef stew is ready in the pot over that fire and is half as good as I smell it is, can I join you and share your meal?"

As Sarika cooled down from her sponge bath standing upon fresh, dry straw and lapped up plenty of cold water from a bucket, the Smith brothers shared their stew and their thoughts with Gilly.

"It was a great story you wrote in *The American* today, sir," Ethan said. "I wish the other militia drilling with us in the City Brigade could read and write like Samuel taught us."

"What do you mean, Ethan? Don't others read the newspaper for them like Samuel did for you at the cooperage, before you learned how?"

"No, they don't. All they do is talk and talk and talk some more about the officers. Seems like they got nothin' else to do but complain about the officers."

"I thought it was commonplace for soldiers to gripe about things, especially their officers. But, I'm curious. What about the officers?" Gilly asked.

Ethan was hesitant to say anything and looked to his brother for help. "They say the officers are all thieves," Elijah responded. "There's talk of the officers runnin' off with all the money the federal government has given to the city to fend off the British. We don't believe a word of it, Master Morrison. But the rumors the men are talkin' about, and not just the militia mind, but the regular army and navy is outta control that's all."

Gilly whistled. The very thing he was trying to do with his stories in *The American* was being sabotaged among the fighting men and he didn't know why.

"Elijah, when did you first hear these rumors?"

Elijah scratched his unshaven chin trying to remember. "Just a few days ago, I think. Before that everythin' was just fine. The boys had every trust in the officers and then all of a sudden like, things changed."

Gilly wasn't going to let this go without finding out more. "Were there any specific officers mentioned in the talk among the men?"

Ethan, who was as distressed as his brother to relate this news, chimed in with his opinions. "Yes, sir, Master Morrison, they said Commodore Rodgers stole a pack of money outfittin' a bunch of gun boats and barges that they say were to be strung across the harbor from Fells Point to Whetstone Point. But the boats were gonna be made outta green wood so they would take on water. And that Major Armistead concocted the whole idea, so that when the British did attack he'd surrender the fort and be promoted to general in the Brit's army."

Elijah found his tongue. "That's not the half of it. They say General Stricker turned tail at Brandywine in the revolution."

Gilly was astonished. "What! Washington nearly lost the whole of his army at Brandywine Creek. The Americans had an orderly withdraw after the British flanked them left and right. It was a miracle they even survived. If Stricker turned yellow at Brandywine, then how did he continue fighting in Washington's army?"

Elijah wasn't finished. "They say General Smith turned tail at Brandywine, too. He was a money-grubbin' Mick merchant who sold American supplies to the British at Valley Forge. After the revolution he bought his way into politics."

"General Smith comes from an illustrious family who were crucial to the American cause in the revolution," Gilly insisted. "Smith was a 25-year-old lieutenant colonel who was ordered to command Fort Mifflin by Washington himself. With two other forts on the Delaware River, Smith was literally blockading Philadelphia after the British took the city! Fort Mifflin endured the heaviest enemy bombardment in the history of the war!"

194

Gilly was incensed, now. "For nearly sixty days, Smith and his men held the fort against a tremendous siege! Time and again they repelled the British Navy which gave Washington time to carry his ragged army to Valley Forge for the winter. At last, Smith was struck by a spent cannon ball and was wounded. He was carried from the fort and transported to Valley Forge to heal and recover. Days later the fort fell. And all of this happened after the Battle of Brandywine! For God's sake, boys, he's a United States Senator from Maryland. What kind of politician puts his life on the line in two wars!

"As for Commodore Rodgers, there isn't a schoolboy in this whole city who doesn't know of his heroism and bravery in *this* war. His family's from Havre de Grace, just up the bay. Last year Admiral Cockburn had his house burnt to the ground and everything the family owned was plundered or destroyed.

"And as for Major Armistead, you've read my story on him didn't you? Last year he took Fort George from the British and presented the Union Jack to President Madison and that's why he was given command at Fort McHenry. Boys, can what you tell me possibly be true? Who would tell such lies? And, worse, who in their right mind would believe them?"

The Smith boys had their heads bent down looking at their boots. Ethan tried to answer and apologize at the same time. "That's what everybody is sayin' anyways. Look Master Gilly, we didn't mean to make you so gosh darn mad or nothin'. Elijah, what did you have to bring all this up for?"

Elijah stammered, "M – me, you was the one who went on and on about this whole darned thing!"

Gilly was still steamed, but tried to keep his composure. "Is there anything else, boys? Did these rumors mention Joshua Barney or President Madison?"

Ethan shrugged his shoulders. "Only that Madison was too short to command anything and that Barney was an old man way past his prime and was foolish to think he could battle British frigates with a flotilla of no good gun boats."

"Ethan, Elijah, pay attention to what I'm about to tell you. You know, of course, that these are all lies." The Smith brothers shook their heads in agreement. "Then, what I want you to do is to keep your mouths shut for the present. When you hear these rumors make a mental note of the person or persons telling you these things. Ask without appearing to ask, if you know what I mean, who they heard it from. We have to determine who is spinning these lies among the men and there's precious little time to do that. Do you understand these orders?"

Elijah answered first, "Master Gilly, do you mean for us to act as spies on our own brigade?"

Gilly shook his head in the negative. "No, absolutely not, Elijah, nor you Ethan; I would never ask you to betray your brothers in arms. I only plead with you to keep your eyes open. Please keep everything I just told you in strict confidence. Go about your business as if nothing has ever happened. I will instruct Richard to give you as much time in the field and away from the cooperage as you need. Don't worry, both you boys will be paid as if you worked full time. Sean O'Casey and Liam Dailey will fill the orders or I'll find other coopers to do the job. That's how important this is to me and to this country."

"We will do whatever you want us to do, Master Gilly," Elijah said. "Ethan and I owe you much, but we owe our loyalty to our brigade even more. If you need us at the cooperage let us know. For now, we'll stay here and find out as much as we can."

"Thank you, boys, for your trust in me and in your brigade. I'm going on to Rodgers Bastion and see if I can get to the bottom of all this. Oh, and thank you for your advice on caring for my Princess. Without Sarika, I wouldn't have the legs to do any of this."

Gilly saddled Sarika and bounded up to the center of the American lines in hopes of finding Commodore Rodgers.

*****

The British squadron was stationed off of the Potomac River awaiting orders from Vice Admiral Sir Alexander Cochrane who was expected to be sailing up the Chesapeake Bay with the rest of the fleet and army reinforcements. Soon, the decision would be made on when and where to hit the Americans first. As Captain Ken had suspected, the mission of the British was to stretch out paltry American defenses and relieve Canada of any undue pressure so that an assault could be made on New York and Lake Champlain.

The British in the Chesapeake could attack any number of targets in order to accomplish this, including Washington and/or Baltimore. Or they could forego these and sail south out of the Chesapeake and threaten Richmond, Virginia. They could even go north and attack Philadelphia or New York City.

But one man, Rear Admiral George Cockburn, "The Great Bandit," was determined to keep British forces in the Chesapeake. He had spent the past year probing, examining, and mapping every river, stream, creek, and brook. Anything he thought might be of use when the fleet arrived and a decision was finally made by the Vice Admiral. By the time the Commander of the North American Station arrived, Cockburn was ready with thoroughly laid out schemes.

He was also ready with a web of spies stretching from Havre de Grace all the way down to Virginia. They were imbedded securely with unbreakable ciphers, credible employment, discreet go-betweens, secret drop off points, reliable messengers, and all coordinated by Cockburn's chief of intelligence who was as anonymous to the rest of the fleet as all of his agents in the field.

Rear Admiral Cockburn was particularly proud of his network of spies in Baltimore. They had already paid off dividends. In addition to obtaining military information this nest of operatives was charged with destroying the moral of the formidable American fighting force. The best way to do this was to question the authority and capability of their officers: to circulate rumors and spread innuendo among the fighting men so that orders would be at least questioned and, in the heat of battle, possibly ignored, maybe even blatantly disobeyed.

Cockburn dressed in his finest to meet with his superior aboard the flagship. Before he did so, he directed his steward to send for his chief of intelligence.

"Ah, there you are, Henrik. I need an update from you before my meeting with Cochrane. He is as uncommitted as he always is on any assault whatsoever because he lacks clarity of mind and remains terribly indecisive. But, you and I, Henrik, know our plans for the destruction of Washington and Baltimore are fool proof." He turned from the mirror and winked. "Especially, if your network of spies is as effective and reliable in the next few weeks as it has been."

Henrik grinned. "Our intelligence is excellent, Admiral. We have people – men, women, and children, embedded in key posts all over the Chesapeake. They have infiltrated Washington and Baltimore, and are even

199

within earshot of Commodore Barney's flotilla that pretends to protect their capital. Our agents are already achieving success, as you know, in smearing the integrity of the most important American commanders. But there is one obscure item that must be dealt with in order for us to expand our success."

Cockburn glanced in his dressing mirror at the reflection of his secret intelligence chief and waved away his valet who was putting on the admiral's cummerbund. "Henrik, what is this obscure item? Deal with it, use all expedience and let's hear nothing more about it."

Henrik shuffled his feet before answering. "I'm not quite certain how one can expedite this particular situation. But, let me explain, my lord. All of our efforts in Baltimore and beyond may yet be undone because of the writing of one individual."

Admiral Cockburn took a crystal glass filled with fine Madeira wine his steward offered to him on a silver tray and waved it in the air, dismissing the difficulty. "So, Henrik, burn the presses, what? Accidents happen, fires and the like, as you are well acquainted from your years of experience."

Henrik sighed. "He's just a boy, my lord. His name is Gilly Morrison. He writes for *The American*. Every time he has a story published in the most popular newspaper in Baltimore, he's stymied our efforts in undermining the confidence of their leadership."

The valet carefully placed a powdered wig upon the admiral's head and stepped aside so that his lordship could appreciate its effect upon his appearance. "Bury him, Henrik, like you've done to so many others. Compromise him, if you must, and make him into what he is not. Threaten him then, if nothing else works, or make him disappear. But, stop him, Henrik."

Cockburn's assault on Baltimore had already begun, well before anyone could spot a Union Jack.

*****

Sarika was well rested and proudly pranced Gilly up to Rodgers Bastion. Headquarters was in a bunker behind the main fortifications. Gilly walked past the sentry and banged on the door. Samuel opened it and smiled in delight. "Master Gilly, this is a real pleasure!"

Gilly was ushered in and took a seat in front of the secretary's desk. "Samuel, I need your help."

"I hope nothing's wrong at the cooperage, sir?"

"No. Richard is doing a fine job."

"You wish to interview the commodore, then, for your next story?"

"Yes, Samuel, I do, but that's not all." Gilly fished into his pocket and pulled out the set of orders he had taken from Richard and the map with the thumbprints. "Is the commodore available," Gilly asked, pointedly.

"No, Master Gilly, he is occupied with his aide. I was told not to disturb him."

"Break your promise, Samuel. This is urgent."

Samuel knitted his brows and frowned. Gilly stared at him with unblinking, hard blue eyes. Samuel knew he didn't have a choice. He walked to Rodgers' office and rapped on the door, opening it before he heard an objection. There were a few indelicate words said inside before Rodgers appeared at the doorway.

The commodore looked over the shoulder of his secretary. "This better be good, Gilly. What do you want, and don't tell me you want an interview. Although, your piece on Armistead and the flag was well done; all of the officers have read it."

"I need to see you alone, sir, on a most important matter. The interview can come later."

Rodgers dismissed his aide. He was about to do the same to his private secretary when Gilly waved him off. "This concerns Samuel as well, sir."

Samuel walked outside and motioned to the marine sentry to stand guard at the door and told him to let no one enter, then bolted the door. "All clear, gentlemen, we won't be disturbed."

Gilly produced the papers in his hand to Samuel. "Do you remember these orders and the map you drew for me after the commodore arrived at the cooperage the morning of your departure?"

Samuel looked them over and nodded his head. "I do, Master Gilly, but there's something wrong with them."

"Tell the commodore what's wrong with them."

"There are thumbprints on the top of each page, including the map I drew. These were not there when I left your service at the cooperage, Master Gilly."

Gilly thought for a moment, and then something dawned on him. "Samuel, do you remember what the weather was like the night before your departure?"

Samuel bowed his head and then spoke as if that night was as vivid in his mind as yesterday. "It was bad. The storm poured buckets of rain and the wind was wicked."

"So if someone had broken into the cooperage that night, he would have touched the counter or the walls or the door which are always caked with sawdust and soot with wet or damp hands, is that right?"

"Yes, sir, this is the natural state of the cooperage. It also explains the thumbprints on both the map and the orders."

203

During this exchange, Commodore Rodgers waited impatiently. He did not have any idea what they were referring to. "What, on God's earth are you rambling on about? What's this about thumbprints?"

Gilly could see the frustration on the commodore's face. He asked Rodgers to take his seat and then he proceeded to explain everything that had happened since Rodgers' visit to the cooperage ordering the barrels for the gun boats and barges and what the Smith brothers told him about the rumors circulating among the men.

Rodgers put it all together and saw the danger to his command should this intrigue be left unattended. He told Gilly and Samuel to immediately see Generals Smith and Stricker. The Americans had their own network of spies. Perhaps the army could make some sense out of it. Rodgers would warn Armistead of the possible threat to McHenry himself.

Chapter 13: Mr. Peabody

Samuel and Gilly were greeted at Command Headquarters with skepticism. They carried a letter from Commodore Rodgers allowing them to enter army headquarters and see General Stricker. The General's aide stared at them with derision. Still, he couldn't deny the commodore's request and ushered the pair into the anteroom to the General's office.

The General's secretary doubted they could be seen at this time. But, when Stricker found out that Gilly Morrison was here to see him, he came to the door personally.

"Ah, Gilly, it's good to see you again. I can't tell you how much your stories have buoyed the morale of my command. I suppose you're here to include me among your illustrious conquests? I have no doubt you will do me justice."

Gilly flashed his winning smile. "I certainly do want to interview you, General. And General Smith as well, but there is something I need to speak with you and General Smith in private about first, if you don't mind, sir. It's important."

"This office is always open to a friend, Gilly. Please come in and ask your questions." Stricker waved to his aide. "Tell General Smith I would like to see him on a most urgent matter." Stricker looked at Gilly. "I trust, Gilly that this is as important as you just said it was. General Smith is not a patient man and, in spite of his long governmental service, he detests the press."

General Smith entered the office in a huff. He paused when he saw Gilly and frowned. "Upon my word, Stricker, I hope this has nothing to do with *The American* and has something to do with military matters?"

The last thing Generals Stricker and Smith expected to hear was what Gilly told them about the rumors circulating around the American camp. Gilly told the generals everything he had explained to Commodore Rodgers.

"The commodore said I should see you about this matter, sirs. He said you had people in charge of intelligence who might help me."

Stricker was peeved and it showed on his face. "Sam," he said to General Smith, "we've seen this before, in the Revolution. It happened to the best officers. It drove General Schuyler out of the army. It destroyed General Arnold and, I'm convinced, played a part in his decision to turn traitor. And now it's happening to us."

Smith sighed and nodded his head. "I know John. I saw it happen, too. But, thank God, things are different now. Malicious rumor mongering cannot affect us on a personal and professional level as it did Schuyler and Arnold. It can, however, undermine the confidence of our command."

He faced Gilly and pointed a bony finger at him. "Young man, I'll submit myself to your questions for your newspaper. General Stricker will do the same. You are doing more than you can possibly imagine counteracting the intrigues of British agents in our midst. But, I warn you, Gilly. Every time another of your stories appears in *The American* and thwarts British plans to undermine our soldiers and sailors confidence in their officers, you place yourself and Mr. Pechin at risk."

Gilly turned to Samuel, a look of pure astonishment on his face.

"Oh, don't be surprised at what they can accomplish, or try to. We've learned a thing or two since the last time we tangled with His Majesty's forces. 'Divide and conquer' has always been their way; here, on this continent, in Ireland, everywhere the English have touched dry land. Just look at what they're doing in New England throughout this war: secret negotiations with New England governors attempting to break the union of the states; special shipping privileges allowing northern ports unprecedented access to the high seas while our maritime trade is under strict blockade; there is even talk of a convention that will meet this autumn and openly discuss secession."

Smith grimaced and banged on the desk with a clenched fist. He regained his composure with difficulty. "But, gentlemen, let's not lose heart. The war isn't over yet. The entire country is watching and waiting for the British to mount an assault here, in the Chesapeake, and to the north, on Lake Champlain. If we can only hold, the New England states will blink. Because if we hold, the nation will rally behind the president; New Englanders will, too. Then there'll be no more talk of secession because that would mean civil war. In the meantime, gentlemen, let's take some initiative of our own, eh?"

General Smith's confidence soothed Gilly's mind, yet he was somewhat alarmed. "General Smith, are you saying that the British find my writing so much of a threat that they would take some violent action against me and my editor?"

Stricker raised both his palms. "Whoa there Gilly, the general is only using appropriate caution in telling you to watch your step. Talk this over with Mr. Pechin. He will advise you as to what precautions to take. Remember, in a war anything can happen."

"General Smith, you mentioned some initiative we could take?"

"Yes, son, my aide will direct you to Mr. Peabody. He is an expert in military intelligence and the wiles of those who practice that trade. He will advise you from here. For the time being, however, please keep writing your stories for *The American*. They may actually be the best counter-intelligence measure at our disposal. After you report to Mr. Peabody, General Stricker and I will clear our schedules for your interviews. Okay, by you John?"

"Yes, General Smith. But let's give Gilly's readership something worthwhile to talk about. Do you remember all the stupid mistakes the British made during the last war? They were so cock sure of success against us they blundered into thinking we were just going to roll over and surrender. But their officers forgot one thing: this continent cannot be conquered without the cooperation of the citizens who reside here. They may find some sympathy now in New England, as opposed to the last war, but not here in Maryland, or anywhere south of Pennsylvania. Let's put that doubt to rest in the minds of our soldiers, sailors, marines, and militia." Stricker winked at Gilly and Samuel. "Gilly, would you by any chance be thinking along the same lines I am?"

Gilly's raised his auburn brows revealing and innocent set of sky-blue eyes. "Why, General Stricker, are you honestly suggesting I report to my readership that, perhaps, the British military leadership has actually made some mistakes on this continent?"

*****

Mr. Peabody lived an obscure life in a small, brownstone house in Old Town as a collector and trader in antique manuscripts and books. Years of examining old parchments and maps had weakened his eyesight to the point where any direct sunlight pained him greatly. He answered his bell and led

Gilly and Samuel into his study.

Peabody took his seat behind his oak desk and motioned for his guests to sit opposite to him in a pair of well-worn leather chairs. The room was steamy, smelled of mildew and pipe tobacco, and was dimly lit save for an open window with its shutters drawn back that allowed a rectangular shaft of light to access the middle of the room which separated Peabody from his guests. Gilly showed him a note from General Smith. Peabody peered at the note with his thick glasses poised on the tip of his long nose.

"Where are the cooper's orders and the map with the thumbprints?"

Gilly produced them from his top pocket and handed them over the desk. Peabody opened a drawer and took out a curious device that looked like a tiny telescope. Using the shaft of light from the window to see better, he put the papers at the bottom of the device one at a time and examined them closely. He then reached behind him and took a small vial full of black powder. This he liberally spread over the papers and then gingerly worked an artist's brush back and forth across the surface of the pages. Finally, he gently blew on the powder.

For the longest time, Gilly and Samuel could only see the bald spot on the crown of Peabody's head as he proceeded with his examination. They noticed he wasn't using his glasses, for they were perched atop of his head. Gilly and Samuel exchanged perplexing glances.

"You are, I presume, the same Gilly Morrison who writes for *The American*?"

"Yes, Mr. Peabody, I am."

"Then, I trust you have the brains not to mention this meeting with anyone except the officers who sent you here?"

"Yes, sir … I mean, no sir. Mr. Pechin will have to be included. We will, of course, be very discreet."

"And your friend, here, he is a warrant officer with the American Navy, perhaps of Quaker sensibilities?"

"Yes, sir, his name is Samuel Snipes. He was my bookkeeper at the cooperage before Commodore Rodgers asked him to become his personal secretary. Before that he taught in Quaker schools in Elizabethtown."

"The thumbprints are not his."

"Why, of course they're not. Samuel would never be so untidy. He always took great care to be orderly and organized in his work."

"The thumbprints are not yours either."

Gilly became a little impatient. "Of course they're not mine! Why would I have brought them here if they were?"

Mr. Peabody looked up from his device and leveled a firm stare at

Gilly. "You would be the perfect candidate, my lad. The perfect suspect for a spy, I mean."

"A spy! Why everyone in Fells Point knows exactly who I am. I lived there all my life. I grew up in the orphanage at St. Patrick's. Why would anyone think I was a spy?"

Peabody smiled and cocked his head. "No one would, except for me. It's my business to know these things. It's always the most trusted, the most unsuspecting individual who is the best spy, my lad. It's my job to probe into things no other man would dare to investigate. I know all about you. You came from nowhere and became important in the eyes of many in a very short period of time. You are an orphan with no family and no family resources. You have unprecedented access to important personages who crave your attention. In short, Gilly Morrison, you would be my perfect spy; because you are so totally vulnerable to the voices of dark angels who would promise you wealth and the greatest of all enticements: vengeance."

"I can understand money as a motivation for someone in my circumstances, but not revenge."

"Ah, that's where you're wrong. You could easily have grown up feeling bitter and resentful of the events that led to your abandonment. By the way, I've also noticed you have a gimp left leg. It is not unusual for young people to harbor anger no matter what their situation in life. You have been dealt a raw hand from the beginning. This could have fostered a cynical attitude; as though you had been cheated from life's pleasures and pursuits. Your vengeance would be the worst and most dangerous kind: against the very God who made you."

Gilly thought for a moment, seeing the wisdom of Mr. Peabody's words. "So, why am I *not* the perfect spy?"

"Alas, my lad, it is a shame that you're not. It would have been so much fun catching you. But, since you were raised under the care of the pious Moranvillè you were given, excuse the pun, a leg up in life."

The writer in Gilly made him want to pursue the matter. Curiosity was his major character flaw. "Samuel is the personal secretary of Commodore Rodgers. Couldn't he be the perfect spy?"

"He could, yes. But I dismissed it entirely because of association."

"What association? Samuel, do you belong to any associations?" Samuel vehemently shook his head as if her were being accused of something.

"From the moment you entered my door, I noticed a certain sense of rapport between you and your friend. You share something, I think. Perhaps it is a bond of immense value; but only important to the both of you, and, possibly, a few others within your acquaintance. I suspected this because of the way you look at each other. There is complete and utter trust in your glances toward each other. It probably has nothing to do with the matter at hand. May I ask you, however, what this invisible bond might be?"

"You may, Mr. Peabody. It is a code we live by taken from the writings of St. Thomas Aquinas."

"Oh, do tell me," Mr. Peabody pleaded. "Codes are in my line of work, you know."

Gilly turned his head to Samuel as if asking him for advice. Samuel shrugged, innocently. "It isn't the kind of code used in your profession, sir. It is a treasured family relic passed on from one generation to the next. It is taken from Aquinas' *Two Precepts of Charity*, written in the year 1273: 'There are three things necessary for the salvation of mankind: to know what you ought to believe; to know what you ought to desire; to know what you ought to do.'"

Peabody considered this in silence for a moment. "Most profound, gentlemen, truly, this is most profound. I should very much like to delve into the meaning of this quote after the current crises dissipates. But, there is one curiosity that I'm sure I shouldn't go into. How is it that you live by a family code when you have no family? Next, how is it that a Quaker school teacher, usually a pacifist, turned naval warrant officer in war time, practices a code written by a Roman Catholic theologian?"

Gilly beamed his winning smile. "That's easy, Mr. Peabody. The code is a cherished and guarded Dooley family tradition dating back hundreds of years. I am Michael Dooley's blood brother, so he told me all about it. Samuel heard Michael and me talking about the code at the cooperage by

214

accident. He immediately saw its application to his own life. Father John describes this as a Pauline moment. He meant it was sort of like St. Paul in his journey to Damascus. So, you see it's all quite simple."

Mr. Peabody was not accustomed to being confused. "I knew I should not have asked. Now, however, I would like to know what you told our commanders in full. Please leave nothing out no matter how inconsequential in may appear."

Gilly communicated everything he had told Rodgers, Smith, and Stricker.

"This is an ancient story you tell me Gilly. The spy or spies took the information so carelessly left in the drawer at the cooperage and used it to good advantage. In order to spread a successful rumor there must be a thread of truth to it. The American plan to build gun boats and barges and string them across the mouth of the Northwest Branch of the Patapsco was not vital information and so could be used to divulge rumors to the men and make them seem credible. Do you both follow me?"

Samuel, who was silent until now, and who felt guilty for leaving the sketch in the drawer, spoke up at last. "Mr. Peabody, why was this information not vital to the enemy?"

"Because, Mr. Snipes, it was an expected and necessary defensive maneuver by the Americans. Any British naval strategist would have seen it coming. Why not, then, use it to create a falsity that would pay dividends at a later point?

"In the same way, the rumors spread against Smith, Stricker, Rodgers, and Armistead all have a touch of truth to them. This is what makes them valid upon the ear of the ignorant listener. These tactics are as old as Methuselah. They can be quite successful if these libels are planted in fertile soil."

"Fertile soil?" Gilly asked.

"Fear, gentlemen, fear of the unknown; fear of a superior enemy force; fear of one's own capabilities when they have not been tested. Fear is the most fertile soil in which any spy could possibly sow a rumor and watch it grow."

"But the accusations are so obviously absurd," Gilly protested. "Why would anybody in their right mind believe in such outlandish lies?"

"They may not believe in them at first. They may laugh them off as sheer nonsense. But, the human mind can play nasty tricks on us. The rumor is spread among the troops when they are at their leisure, eating and talking around the campfire, let's suppose. Suddenly, the enemy is sighted and the fighting begins. Combat is a horrendous human experience for almost everyone. Blood begins to flow. Comrades fall all around you. The noise is deafening: cannon fire, rockets, musketry, painful and ugly human cries.

216

Naturally, you are frightened beyond all belief. You question yourself. You question your leadership, not because you remember every detail of the rumors that had a ring of truth to them, but because of the insanity of the situation your leaders have placed you in. What do you do? Let me ask you, gentlemen. What would you do?"

Samuel spoke first. "I do not know, as God is my witness, what I would do."

"I don't either," Gilly said. I hope I would stand my ground and fight. Yet, I might also run like I was running from an angry bear, especially if I saw other men running. Would it be like playing with dominoes, Mr. Peabody?"

Peabody nodded his head. "It would be exactly the same; because somewhere in the back of your mind a doubt had been planted in the fertile soil of fear. It only takes one domino to fall. The rest follow in sequence because of proximity."

They were all silent for a moment. The threat of the rumors they had heard now becoming real.

"And what about the thumbprints, Mr. Peabody, can they shed any light on who the spy is?"

"For the moment they can't. They can only shed light on *who* the spy is not. Science has not progressed very far on this front. There are reputable

217

men who maintain that each individual has a unique fingerprint. I happen to agree with this theory. The use of fingerprints for identification purposes has been in use throughout antiquity: in Babylonia, China, Greece, even Rome.

"If I had a copy of the spy's thumbprint and I filed it my drawer, I could make a comparison with the print on the papers you brought me. But, I don't have a copy. Therefore, no comparison can be made. Perhaps, in this technologically advanced world we live in, someone somewhere will begin to start a collection of prints that can be used for individual identification and then the world will change. Until then, I will use this uncertain science as best I can."

Samuel was confused. "Mr. Peabody, how did you know our prints were on the papers and neither of us was the spy?"

"I saw both of your fingerprints on the papers you gave me by using common soot from the chimney mixed with starch. Using the microscope on my desk, I examined the prints. Yours, Samuel, were very faint. I take it you are a meticulous person as far as personal cleanliness is concerned?"

"Yes, I am. I like to keep things neat and orderly, including myself."

"And you, Gilly, have been riding all day in the hot sun. You'd have worked up a good sweat. Therefore your prints on these papers are quite distinguishable. As far as how I made a comparison with the large thumbprint, there are definite differences between the prints that an experienced eye can detect. When we have leisure time, I'll be glad to go into the science of it all."

Gilly was fascinated. "One of these days I'm going to write a story about your theories on fingerprints, Mr. Peabody. In the meantime, is there anything else we should do?"

"Let me know of any developments at the cooperage and within your scope of work for *The American*. Did the officers warn you about possible consequences that might occur from the publication of your stories?"

"Yes, I was warned that if I continued to have my stories published there may or may not be some sort of retaliation."

"Take their advice to heart, Gilly. You are a one-man threat to an army of well-hidden agents whose mission you threaten with every word you write. Let me know of any information the Smith boys convey to you. I have already heard the rumors from my contacts within the city and the militia.

"Mr. Snipes, if you can keep me informed of anything that crosses your desk I would be deeply appreciative; especially as it relates to this situation and the overall morale of the men under Rodgers command. Finally, Gilly, I would like to visit the Dooley Cooperage and conduct my own investigation. I gather you are closed on Sundays?"

"Yes, sir, Father John would have it no other way."

"Good. Then why don't you and I meet this Sunday and find out what we can before the barrel of a British musket is shoved down our throats."

Gilly nodded. "How about noon, if that is convenient?"

"Noon it is. Now before you go, I'm going to snip a sample of that thumbprint from one of these papers. I should have started doing this years ago." Mr. Peabody took his sample and placed it in an envelope. "There, I've begun my collection. The intelligence community may never be the same."

*****

On his way back to Fells Point, Gilly stopped at the Pechin house in Old Town. He had finished his interviews with Generals Smith and Stricker and Commodore Rodgers that afternoon after seeing Mr. Peabody. He would put pen to paper tonight. First, though, he needed to speak to his editor about everything that had happened today.

A servant opened the door and led Gilly to the dining room where Mr. Pechin was enjoying his dinner. "Good to see you, Gilly. Please come in and take a seat. Our cook has prepared some excellent lamb. Please join me for I have had my fill. Desiree has not come down to dinner and claims a lack of appetite. This, I'm told, happens to the young who have fallen in love."

Mr. Pechin said this without looking at Gilly, pretending to busy himself with his favorite dish. "I also have some delicious Portuguese wine here. It's a wonderful Madeira that will calm you nerves and then we can have a chat."

"Thank you, sir. I ate with the troops on Hampstead Hill earlier today and right now I really don't have much of an appetite myself. But, if you don't mind, I think I might taste some of that Portuguese wine, especially after what has happened today."

William Pechin was an extremely observant man. He saw the anxiety on Gilly's face but declined comment until his young writer composed himself.

"I interviewed Generals Smith and Stricken today," Gilly began, after sipping on his wine, "also Commodore Rodgers. But, the turning point of the day was when I talked to a few men in the City Brigade who work for me at the cooperage. I am concerned about the rumors I'm hearing."

Pechin put down his fork and reached for his glass of wine. "What rumors, Gilly?"

Gilly told him about the slanders in circulation against the American commanding officers, the subsequent meeting with Mr. Peabody, and his assessment of the situation.

"Can you believe it, Mr. Pechin? The Smith brothers, Ethan and Elijah, who work for me say the troops are eating this stuff up. They say many of the troops can't read and have never seen any of my stories printed in *The American*. All of the officers, even Mr. Peabody, warned me of some possible retaliation if I continued to submit my stories; not just to me, sir, but you as

221

well."

"And are you afraid, Gilly? Do you think that either you or I are in danger?"

"I don't know, sir. But even if we are, I wouldn't stop writing for you and *The American*. I always thought my stories would build a second front for Baltimore before any bullets were ever fired. Everything I've heard today only confirms that in my mind."

"Mr. Peabody was correct in his evaluation," Pechin stated plainly. "An attack is probable as you well know. Anything the British can do to undermine our people's confidence in their officers is to be expected. And, yes, Mr. Peabody is also right about how these rumors can affect the men. Not the regulars as much as the militia. As far as you and I are concerned, our profession has its risks as well as its rewards. Your stories are good, Gilly. You have, indeed, created a second front and boosted enthusiasm throughout the city. I'm glad to hear you're not intimidated. We need your stories now more than ever.

"As for the men not being able to read your stories, I am going to offer free copies of *The American* to every officer who wants one, as long as they read it to their men." Mr. Pechin smiled and raised his glass. "Gilly, I want to propose a toast: To the power of the press and seamen's rights!"

As Gilly raised his glass to return the toast, Desiree entered the room.

She was wearing drab clothing. Her hair was in disarray. Her hands were callused and dirty. And Gilly Morrison had never seen anyone more beautiful in his life.

Chapter 14: A Warning

Gilly rose from the table and immediately noticed the effects of the Spanish wine on his senses. He was simply not used to strong drink of any kind. He was also drained both physically and mentally and the wine enhanced his exhaustion.

Mr. Pechin saw his daughter standing in the dining room staring down at her callused hands. He felt his presence might be an imposition and made to exit the room. He turned back to Gilly.

"Next week, I want you to go down and interview Joshua Barney on the Patuxent River. After you submit your stories on the commanding officers we can forego another story until you get the lay of the land, so to speak, down there with the Commodore's flotilla. Send a courier back to me with anything you've got. Charge all of your expenses to *The* American. I'll send you an authorization before you go. Time's running short, Gilly. Oh – and watch yourself my boy."

"I'll be careful, sir. You do the same."

With Mr. Pechin gone, Gilly and Desiree stood awkwardly alone in the dining room. Gilly felt numb and tense at the same time. He couldn't say anything because no words formulated in his mind. Yet he was on edge, afraid she would walk away.

It wasn't long ago that he would have felt threatened in Desiree's presence. He was always wary of some sort of trap; of being caught in the web of one her plots. Those fears were all gone. Now, he feared only that he would not be able to tell her what was in his heart.

How did this happen? How could he fall in love with someone he had despised only yesterday? She was not scheming. He was not afraid. She had changed. He had, too. Yesterday was forever ago. Today was here – now – wonderful.

Desiree escorted Gilly out the front door. "What did my father mean just now?"

"That the British are poised for action?"

"No, I mean when he said to watch yourself. You're not in any trouble are you?"

Gilly smiled and shook his head. "He's just being cautious. Traveling anywhere right now is precarious. No one knows where the enemy might hit us."

Desiree eyed him suspiciously. Somehow she knew there was more to it. That's all right, she thought, I'll pry it out of father tomorrow.

Sarika, who was tethered to a hitching post in front of the house, snorted loudly. Gilly laughed. "It's time for her dinner. She's had a long day; I'm afraid I haven't been treating her as well as I should."

"She's your Princess. You should treat her like one," Desiree said. They slowly walked toward Sarika.

"Who told you I call her Princess?"

"Father John did. We had a long discussion about things."

"What else did Father John tell you?"

"That you're a man of the code. That it is working inside of you although it might not appear so just now."

For a moment, their eyes met. To Gilly, Desiree's eyes were now like a magnet; a delicious, chestnut magnet full of sweet fruit forbidden to him only yesterday. It was difficult not to look into them. Gilly thought he should break the attraction but it was almost impossible. "You've had a long day, too. Let me see those hands."

226

Desiree raised her palms. "The flag's finished. Now I need to find something else to do. I'll talk to Father John. I heard the orphans were being moved to a temporary shelter outside the city in case the worst happens. I think I can be of some assistance there. My father has connections. We can see to it the children are moved safely."

Gilly took her bruised hands and tenderly kissed them. "I can see the code has been working on you, too. And I'm not just talking about your hands. Goodnight, Desiree. Tell Father John I'll be by to see him soon."

Gilly mounted Sarika and relented one more time to look into Desiree's magnetic, chestnut eyes glistening in the moonlight. As Gilly cantered off on Princess, Desiree took a deep breath. For the past few minutes she had not been conscious of breathing at all.

"I think he loves me," she said aloud. She looked up at the stars and smiled. She wondered if Father John's roses were blooming.

Sarika rode Gilly home at a quick trot. Sometimes she meandered off to the side of the roadbed deliberately disobeying Gilly's commands. Sarika smelled competition. She didn't care for this new filly at all.

In addition to giving Sarika a meal, Gilly made sure to pick her shoes and provide dry straw after her bath. He thought about fixing something for dinner but found he was not at all hungry. He got dressed into his night gown and sat at his desk to write but nothing came to him. Besides, he had left his notebook in his saddle bag.

Gilly remembered Sarika's attitude in his ride back to Fells Point. She had been surly and somewhat defiant. This had never happened before. Gilly smiled as he recalled Desiree calling Sarika his Princess. It occurred to him now that his Princess might just be a little jealous. He decided he would write his story tomorrow. Tonight, he would sleep next to Sarika in the small stable under cool straw and start everything anew at dawn. Tonight, whether Sarika liked it or not, he would dream of Desiree.

He awoke with the sun, hungry and revitalized. Lighting a fire in the kitchen hearth, he swung a crane over the crackling kindling and attached both an iron skillet and a coffee pot to the crane. While he waited for the skillet to warm, he dashed out the Dutch door and gave Sarika her breakfast of Timothy hay and barley. Then he went to the chicken coop and snatched two fresh eggs from underneath a hen's bottom.

Balancing the large eggs in one hand, he grabbed his saddle with the other and brought them inside the house. The skillet was now hot enough so he poured a little olive oil over the surface and cracked in the eggs. The bread was stale but Gilly stomach didn't care and he buttered it anyway. The eggs didn't take long to fry. He removed the skillet from the crane and served the eggs onto a simple wooden plate. He removed his notebook from his saddle bag and sat down to eat and write his story while the aroma of delicious coffee wafted across the room.

As Gilly helped himself to a second cup of coffee, his story poured out of his mind and heart onto the pieces of paper in front of him. He told the story of two courageous officers, Smith and Stricker, who had served with honor and distinction during the revolution.

Gilly related how General Smith had served with George Washington at the battle of Long Island in New York and how it was Smith who had waited for the last boat before taking Washington across the East River from Brooklyn to Manhattan. All told, 9,000 American soldiers and sailors evacuated Brooklyn Heights without one single loss of life. It was a great British victory, and yet Washington and the Continental Army lived to fight another day thanks to men like Samuel Smith who did not run in the face of overwhelming odds, but bravely stood their ground.

Gilly wrote about how Brigadier General John Stricker, as a young cadet, had served under his father, a lieutenant colonel. The Strickers were part of the German Battalion, composed of Americans of German descent from Maryland and Pennsylvania. General Washington used this battalion effectively at the Battle of Trenton where soldiers from this unit yelled across the lines in German and persuaded the Hessians to lay down their arms. Cadet Stricker fought honorably at the battles of Princeton and Brandywine. At the battle of Monmouth, in New Jersey, the battalion held the line against an aggressive British counterattack. Monmouth may have been a draw, but the fact that American regulars, like John Stricker, stood toe-to-toe in hand-to-hand combat against redcoat bayonets proved to the world that Washington and his army were not the ragged rabble the British claimed they were.

Gilly pointed out the disastrous failures of the British army and navy in the War for Independence starting from the beginning on the bloody march from Lexington and Concord and the assaults on Breeds and Bunker Hills; at the evacuation of Boston, the Battle of Valcour Island, where General Benedict Arnold delayed the British invasion of Lake Champlain and the Hudson Valley, and at the surrender of General Burgoyne at Saratoga; all culminating in the British defeat at Cowpens and General Cornwallis' embarrassing surrender at Yorktown.

Gilly stopped writing and looked at what he had accomplished. Everyone old enough would remember, he thought. And those too young would learn a lesson in what true stubbornness and sacrifice on behalf of a just cause could accomplish.

Satisfied with what he had written, Gilly got up from the table while savoring the last of his coffee. He opened the kitchen door into the small living room. What he saw shocked him. Instinctively, he reached underneath his night shirt and clutched Istvan's locket.

*****

Desiree had a long day planned, starting with a stop at the rectory. She could hear the now familiar monastic tenor coming from the garden out

230

back. Father John was busy snipping his rose blooms.

"Bonjour, *mademoiselle*. I am collecting my treasure to place in a vase before our Blessed Mother. Have you heard anything from Gilly? I have not seen him for some time and I have been remiss in not checking at the cooperage."

"Why yes, Father. I saw him last night. He came to talk over some business with my father. He's to be sent south next week to interview Commodore Barney."

Father John pretended to examine his roses but there was a twinkle in his eye. "And is there anything else to report, *mademoiselle*?"

Desiree giggled. Her dimples spread across her cheeks in enchanting amusement. "Tell me Father John, deep inside, are you a hopeless romantic?"

"*Oui*, child, I am at times both hopeless and romantic. Now let us go into the rectory where we may take solace from prying ears and enjoy a civilized cup of tea."

Desiree told the good Moranvillè what had transpired the night before. To Father John's delight she even described Gilly's kisses on her callused hands. "So you see Father, the roses have bloomed as you said they would."

Father John shook his head. "No, daughter, I said my roses would bloom. I would never be so foolish to predict if and when Gilly's love would come to fruition. I have no gift of prophecy. Yet, I am grateful and I will give thanks and praise to the creator for hearing both of our prayers."

"As will I, Father. You have been as kind, understanding, gentle, and, may I say, pointedly direct with me as my mother would have been had she lived."

"*Merci beaucoup, ma chère amie.* That was most kind of you. Your mother has been in my prayers since our first intimate discussion." Father John approached the altar in his study and smelled the rose blooms in front of the statue of the Virgin. He clasped his hands in front of him and rubbed them vigorously.

"Now, let us pursue other business, *mon ami.* I have heard the work on the flag is accomplished."

Desiree breathed out a sigh of relief. "Thank goodness, Father. I thought my hands were going to fall off. They're so stiff I still have to sit on them to straighten them out just like Mrs. Pickersgill. But it was worth every stitch."

"Hard work in pursuit of a noble end is always satisfactory. It fulfills a basic human need to be productive. Ask any farmer. But, before I let you slip into idleness let me propose to you another worthwhile endeavor."

"Does it concern the orphanage, Father?"

232

"Indeed it does. We must find suitable and safe refuge for the children. Would you care to assist us?"

"Oh, yes! I would be more than happy to."

"Then, let's take a walk, *mademoiselle*."

The St. Patrick's Free School and Orphanage was only a few blocks away on Apple Alley. They arrived to see members of the St. Patrick's Benevolent Society busy packing bundles filled with books, clothing, and personal items for each of the orphans in burlap bags.

"Each of these children has their own material things," Father John said. "Because these are their only possessions, they covet them with all their heart. It is important that we treat these bundles carefully. We need to show the children that we will not abandon them or the things which have become part of them. After all," Father John shrugged his slight shoulders, "they have been abandoned once before and once is enough."

Desiree compressed her lips which she always did when her mind was actively trying to solve a problem. "Father, do you know where the children are going to be kept? Outside the city, I suppose?"

"As far outside the city as possible, *mon amie*. It is important to keep their innocent eyes away from the inevitable casualties of war. My order has a monastery … "

"A monastery!" Desiree cried out. "Father John, you're shipping these children off to a monastery!"

"*Oui*, is this problematic in your eyes?"

"It most certainly is a problem. These children need fresh air and sunshine, Father."

Moranvillè knitted his brows. "There are ample amounts of both at the monastery, mademoiselle."

"Yes, but where are they going to play? Where are they going to sleep? Not in some dank and dreary cell cornered in on all sides like a prison. Not if I can help it. The children are used to a wide open dormitory where they can laugh and sing and whisper secrets to each other. You can't imprison them, Father."

Moranvillè's forehead turned red and a sour look came to his otherwise cheerful complexion. "But, our time is short. We have no money for more spacious accommodations. And even if we could board the children at various inns and homes north of the city it would prove impossible, as half of the city's gentry has already vacated and now occupy all of these places. One cannot find an honest innkeeper who is not full up from here to Pennsylvania."

Desiree noticed the change in Father John's demeanor. His body had become ridged and his hands were clasped tightly behind his back. Her own father sometimes adopted this straight laced deportment, especially when she was insisting on having her way. She quickly made a tactical retreat and put on her best smile, her dimples dancing in the hot August sun.

"You are quite right, Father. It's a shame really. I can certainly see that you and the Benevolent Society have done everything in your power to watch out for the welfare of the little ones in your charge."

Father John's muscles relaxed a bit. He unclasped his hands. "*Merci, mademoiselle.* We have attempted all avenues available to us."

"Say, wait just one minute, Father," Desiree exclaimed, as if an idea was just coming into her head.

"What is it, my daughter? Tell me what has popped into your mind."

"Why I didn't think of this before, I'll never know. I must admit to you, Father, I really have no talent for planning at all. It is far beyond my poor feminine capabilities."

Father John started to laugh. He laughed so hard he doubled over. It was contagious and Desiree began to chuckle, too.

"What is it? Tell me, Father. I have no idea what I'm laughing at, but it's good to see you do it."

"It's you," Father John gasped, trying to catch his breath and wiping the tears from his eyes. "What – what do mean you have no head for planning? Next to Jessica Farmer, you are the smartest young woman I have ever met! I saw the intrigues you used on Michael Dooley, and on Gilly Morrison! If they would allow it, you could lay out a strategy that would send the British running back down the Chesapeake with their tails between their legs." Desiree stopped laughing and gave the cleric a stern glance. Moranvillè noticed and held up his hands as in self-defense.

"Don't be perturbed, *mon amie*, as I was a moment ago. Forgive this old man, please. I can see now you had an honorable motive for your objection to the monastery. Do tell me what you have in mind and I promise no more laughter with tears."

Desiree smiled. "So, I take it, you're not going to underestimate me anymore?"

"Not in this world, Ms. Pechin. It would be a serious miscalculation on my part."

"Good, then let me tell you my plan. My father has a summer estate, just north of the city at the mouth of Jones Falls where the hills slope down. It's nice up there. If it wasn't for the war, we would be there now. It's called *Tranquility*."

"Such a beautiful name, *mon amie*, for a country retreat. Tell me more."

Desiree sighed, remembering with fondness the joy of her childhood.

"It is very large with plenty of trees and green meadows. There's a small lake there for swimming, fishing and boating. The altitude is higher, so the nights are cooler except maybe this time of year. But that's okay because facing the lake is an extensive campground. The children could sleep under the stars if there's no rain or under tents and lean-tos if there is. There is a spacious ballroom for music and dancing. This would make an ideal dormitory, so we have to make sure we take all the cots and bedding we can. The children would love it, Father, as they would the monastery, I'm sure."

"I will stop underestimating the power of your intellect, *mademoiselle*, if you will stop pulling the leg of an ancient priest."

*****

What Gilly saw horrified him. The small living room was destroyed. The Irish lace curtain which was accented with a white scarf trimmed in gingham was ripped from the window and lay in tatters on the floor. Mrs. Dooley's spinning wheel was broken into splinters. Chaos was everywhere and it filled Gilly with distress and loathing.

The pride of the Dooley family was their Pillar and Scroll shelf clock from Plymouth, Connecticut. Its face was smashed in and its springs were scattered all over the room. Cushions and pillows were ripped open, their eider down feathers strewn in every direction; even the pewter plates etched with the faces of Jesus and Mary were bent and mangled and tossed haphazardly into the fireplace. He looked up above the mantel. Printed in

237

large letters was a message scrawled on the wall with red paint: "BEWARE MORRISON BEWARE"

Gilly stumbled across the room and shut the front door which was left open. Turning back to the inglorious mess before him he saw the wedding chest, where Mrs. Dooley kept her fine linen and family Bible. Kneeling in front of it he smelled urine. The Bible had been desecrated. Suddenly, his stomach started to churn. He ran out through the kitchen to the back of the house and retched.

*****

Desiree was having a fine time. She was a born planner and organizer. A fact Father John would not soon forget. She had so many ideas about how to accomplish the evacuation of the orphans she was hard pressed not to express them all. Father John stopped her outside the orphanage and gave her a stern warning.

"Be careful not to be so much in charge of things, *mon amie*. The women here are dedicated to this orphanage and its children. They have been with me for nearly ten years and I have no idea what I would have done without their support. Everyone here is committed. Your presence here, although a gift from God, could be taken the wrong way if you are in any way disagreeable.

"These women come from all over the Point. Most of them are wives

238

and mothers, but we also have some who operate their own businesses. They are all worthy of respect, and, since you are new to most of them, they deserve deference on your part. Take it slowly, mademoiselle. Suggest only, do not take command of the operation and you will be readily accepted, *oui*?"

"I promise, Father." Just then a loud, hoarse voice yelled from the second floor window of the orphanage.

"Well I'll be damned! Oh, sorry padre, didn't know you was here. Hey good lookin', how's my favorite debutante?" It was Mary Pickersgill.

Desiree waved back at the window. "Your debutante is none the worse for wear since she learned how to use a needle. How are you Mary?"

"I'm doing better, sweetheart, now that the flag is finally done and delivered thanks to pretty fillies like you. Now why don't you swish that skirt up here and give me a hand."

"Be right up, Mary! See Father," Desiree exclaimed, "I've already been accepted!" Desiree scooted in the door and ran up the steps.

Father John clasped his hands behind his back and whispered something beneath his breath, in French of course.

There were about thirty women working in the second floor dormitory. They all stopped what they were doing as Desiree bounded into the room and embraced Mary Pickersgill. Desiree was wearing a yellow silk dress

239

with elegant, black leather shoes sporting a two-inch heel. On her head was a blue bonnet tied with a bright yellow bow.

"How's that boy you were dreaming of darling. Have there been any juicy developments?"

Desiree's face broke into a dazzling smile. Her dimples could not have stretched her cheeks any harder. Mary took her hands. They both giggled like schoolgirls.

"He kissed my hands, Mary! He asked to see my palms because they were all calloused and bruised like you told me they would be and he kissed them!"

"What on earth did you do, dear?"

"I just stood there completely at a loss for words. Then he jumped on his horse and galloped into the night."

Mary turned to the other women who had not missed a word of the conversation. "Did you hear that, ladies? He kissed her hands and galloped into the night. Isn't it romantic?"

The ladies were all aflutter, laughing and yacking with each other and exchanging stories about their first love. Father John walked into the dormitory with raised eyebrows. Mary Pickersgill clapped her hands.

"Okay, girls, let's get back to work. Father, how are we gonna transport all of this stuff?"

"Wagons!" Desiree exclaimed. "I'm ordering six Conestoga wagons with teamsters to help us load them. They should be here in an hour." A hush fell over the dormitory. Desiree remembered what Father John had told her. She took off her bonnet and tossed in on the floor. Then she kicked off her shoes and started to fold a blanket. Mary quickly took the opposite end and helped Desiree fold it neatly before putting it into a burlap sack.

"Well," Mary stated flatly, her hands and arms upon her hips. "Those wagons aren't going to wait and the British won't neither. Let's get crackin'." In a second the dormitory was alive with women bent on finishing their work before the wagons arrived. Many of them kicked off their shoes.

Chapter 15: The Last Rose of Summer

Gilly lit a candle at the side altar in front of the statue of St. Patrick and knelt down in prayer. "There have been some snakes let loose on the Dooley home, dear Patron of Ireland. Please cast them out of our homes, our city, and this country."

Moranvillè, who was busy in the sacristy, came out when he heard the familiar voice. "Gilly, what brings you to the feet of our Patrick at this time of day?"

"Because I need him right now, Father. The Dooley home was ransacked last night. Everything is in pieces; even Mrs. Dooley's shelf clock. I brought this," Gilly held up the Dooley family Bible. "It's been desecrated. I wiped the cover with vinegar and let it dry in the sun. Would you bless it for me? The people who did this must be full of hate. It can't be just my stories that made them do this."

"When something holy is defiled, prayer and reparation are the sure remedy." Father John blessed the bible and then bowed his head in prayer. When he had finished, he put his hand on Gilly's shoulder and led him to a pew. "Now, *mon ami*, tell Moranvillè everything."

*****

Desiree visited her father at *The* American and began explaining to him how *Tranquility* would be perfect to act as a temporary refuge for the orphans from St. Patrick's. She ended up stomping her foot to ensure she would get her way. Some things never change, her father thought.

"Very well, Desiree. I agree it would be ideal but who's going to take care of the children up there?"

"Many of the women from the benevolent society have volunteered already. They are bringing their babies with them while their husbands fight for the militia. The Conestoga wagons have already departed for the estate. I sent a messenger ahead of them to let the staff know that the children's baggage was on the way and to set up a makeshift dormitory in the ballroom."

"Apparently, you've thought of everything. And before you even asked for my permission you sent the wagons with all of the baggage. Sometimes, my dear, you stretch the limits of my patience. But, since this is a project already launched and well underway my immediate question is, when

243

are the children going to be evacuated?"

"Tonight the teamsters will unload everything at *Tranquility* and make their way back starting tomorrow morning. Some of the women are working today packing sandwiches for the long trip tomorrow." Desiree breathed out a long sigh and sat in a chair. "At long last the orphans will be safe. Thank you, father, for your understanding and assisting."

"As if I had a choice," Mr. Pechin said, chuckling.

There was a loud knock at the office door. "Enter," Pechin rasped.

Gilly opened the door. Upon seeing Desiree he took a step backward. "I'm sorry sir. I can come back later."

"Come in, my boy. Come right on in."

Gilly put his story on his editor's desk. "I wrote it this morning, sir." He turned to the chair across from the desk desperately trying to avoid Desiree's eyes. "Good morning, Mistress Pechin."

"Good morning, Master Morrison." Desiree noticed Gilly's eyes were focused on the floorboards. She also noted the ashen color of his face.

Pechin perused Gilly's story, giving a judicial nod of the head as he read each paragraph. When he was finished he placed the papers on his desk. Without glancing up he folded his hands together and whispered. "This is the best work you've ever done, son. It is truly remarkable. You should be as

244

proud of your writing as I will be when this is published on the front page of *The American*." He looked up at his star writer and saw that Gilly's hands were shaking.

"What is it, son? What has happened to you?"

Desiree leapt from her chair and took Gilly's arm. She knew something was wrong.

"I had a visitor or two yesterday evening or early this morning before I got up." He explained to them what had occurred at the Dooley house. Everything except for the desecration of the Dooley family Bible; for now, he kept that between himself and Father John.

"My Lord, darling, you've had a terrible shock. Please sit down on the chair."

Pechin wisely ignored the endearing term his daughter had just used. He picked up Gilly's story again and flipped through the pages. "In light of this development, do you still wish me to publish this?"

Gilly gritted his teeth in anger and determination. "I want this story printed and distributed all over the city more than I want to take my next breath."

Pechin nodded his head. "Then, it will be done."

Desiree was beside herself. "Father, what does it mean - 'beware

245

Morrison beware.'"

Pechin inhaled deeply. "We were warned, my dear. Both Gilly and I were advised to tread carefully in our business."

"So, that was what you meant last night when you told each other to be careful."

Gilly rolled his blue eyes towards the ceiling. "If Princess had not had a fit of jealousy I would have been in my bed last night and not the stable."

The editor paused to digest everything Gilly had told him. Suddenly a wry grin appeared upon his otherwise dignified countenance. "Hah! Well, my boy, we've ruffled their feathers this time didn't we? There's no mistake now, is there, that the enemy sees us as a real danger. You've done it Gilly! You've stirred up a nest of hornets and made them sting you. We should not be surprised at whatever comes next. The threat, I believe, is real. Do you have a firearm at your disposal?"

Gilly had to think for a minute. "Mr. Dooley has a pistol in a case underneath his bed."

"Good, oil it and have it loaded. Keep it underneath *your* bed where you can get at it if you need it. Lock both front and back doors as soon as you go home, and no more sleeping in the stable with the horse although, you're right, that might have saved you this time."

"Father, isn't there anything else we can do? Some added protection to provide for Gilly's safety?"

Gilly took her hands in a reassuring manner. "Desiree, I'll be fine. Besides, I leave soon to interview Commodore Barney, remember? In the meantime I'll keep a good lookout, I promise."

"We all have to keep our eyes wide open from now on, including you my dear," Pechin said to his daughter.

"Me? Why would I have to be careful?"

"If anyone wants to intimidate me they need only threaten you. They wouldn't try anything here at the office or at our home in Old Town. There'd be too many witnesses. But they might try something when you leave the house. Make sure your driver is with you at all times. I'm not trying to frighten you, Desiree, but you must promise me to use all caution. Why don't you go with the orphans to the summer estate?"

This time, Desiree gritted her teeth. "I'll not run away from bullies and ruffians. They have no idea who they're dealing with when they threaten a Pechin."

Her father exploded in laughter. "Ha! That makes two of us then, my dear."

"There's one thing that pains me, sir," Gilly interjected.

"Speak up, then."

"It's the Dooley home. All of the little treasures of Mrs. Dooley that mean so much to Michael and his father, I ... "

"Tut, tut, my boy, don't fret about any of that. Before you go south to see Barney, drop the house keys off at my office. I'll have someone assess the damage and make arrangements to clean, restore and replace everything. By the time you return all will be right again. Now, when are you meeting with Mr. Peabody?"

"We're to meet at the cooperage on Sunday at noon."

"Good, let me know what you find out. Peabody sounds like a thorough man. I want all the details, understood?"

*****

Gilly led Desiree out of the office. "Look, Dez," he said taking her tenderly by the elbows. The fact that he was touching her came so naturally to Gilly that he did so without it registering in his conscious mind. She didn't mind it a bit.

"Dez? Is that what you're going to call me, Dez?"

"Well, gee, I didn't really think about it. It just came out of my mouth. Is it okay by you if I call you that?"

"It's okay, darling. But no one else is going to call me Dez except you."

"Agreed. Listen, I don't much feel like going back to the Dooley place right now. What would you say to some spicy blue claws at Ole' Sally's on the wharf? We could wash it down with some cold ale."

Desiree looked down at her silk dress. "But, I'm not properly dressed for the wharf."

"Come on, *darling*. I'll make sure they give you a bib."

The restaurant was filled to capacity by soldiers and sailors. Somehow Sally found a table for them. She put down some newspaper on the table. There were no utensils, napkins, or tablecloths. Newspaper was used in place of all of these. Gilly asked Sally if she had a bib for Desiree. He pointed at Desiree's silk dress. Sally frowned. She took a sheet of newspaper and put it over Desiree's lap. She frowned again, then creased another and, before Desiree could object, stuffed it down the front of her dress between her breasts.

"There," Sally said emphatically. "That will hold you 'till you're stuffed with my crabs. This here place ain't the Baltimore Hotel, dearie. But, those stuffed shirts up in Old Town can't hold a candle to my blue claws neither."

Desiree and Gilly laughed at Sally's unceremonious etiquette. While they were giggling, a boy brought them two tankards of cold pale ale. They didn't order the ale. It's was just served automatically when blue claws were ordered.

"So, this is the wharf at dinner time," Desiree mused. "You should have told me to wear my buckskin shirt and trousers."

"You'll get used to places like this as you get used to me," Gilly said, sporting his winning smile.

"Mister, I think I'm going to like getting used to you." Desiree raised her tankard in a toast. Gilly lifted his in return. Deep inside each of them, invisible walls crashed down and left a pile of emotionally scarred rubble on the pine planking of Ole' Sally's. Desiree, who had hidden her heart behind silk and lace, and Gilly, who had dug defensive entrenchments around his own, welcomed an aura of mutual trust. They weren't afraid of being hurt anymore. They felt safe. They felt joy. The tavern may have been packed to the rafters, but they could neither see nor hear any of it.

Sally piled the spicy blue claws right on the newspapers covering the small table and laid down a knife and a mallet on top of the crabs.

Gilly saw the look of apprehension on Desiree face. "Have you ever eaten blue claws?"

"No, I – I haven't. They do smell delicious though don't they? Why do they call them blue claws when they are deep red?"

"They turn red when they're cooked. Now here's the important thing, you have to eat them fast or they'll get cold. I like them hot or cold, but some folks don't care for them if they're not warm. Are you ready to eat?" Desiree nodded her head, her chestnut eyes bulging in anticipation.

Gilly grabbed a crab and twisted off the legs and claws. He threw the legs over his shoulder careful not to hit the patrons at the table in back of him and put the claws to the side for later.

"What on earth are you doing?" Desiree was confused by his lack of table manners.

"This is how you eat blue claws. Now watch me and then you try."

He turned the crab over on its back and opened it with his fingernails. He tossed the top half over his shoulder and scooped out the gills from the bottom until he found the meat. This he promptly stuffed into his mouth. He used the mallet and cracked the claws, then deftly used the knife to separate the shell from the meat. Finally, he dipped the meat into a bowl full of melted butter and lemon. As he chewed the sweet crab, the juices and lemon butter ran from the sides of his mouth and dripped off his chin.

Desiree stared at him with raised eyebrows. "Oh, my, that's so disgusting it looks like fun!"

"Try it. Hurry up, they're getting cold."

251

Desiree followed his instructions to the letter. Soon, she was squirting crab juice and lemon butter all over the table, even onto Gilly. They laughed and ate and ate and laughed, washing it all down with cold pale ale. It was a feast as indelicate and messy as any she had ever enjoyed. She relished every moment of it.

After the newspapers were whisked away and the shells swept from the floor, Gilly shuffled his chair on Desiree's side of the table facing the bar. "Now the fun part starts," he exclaimed excitedly.

Desiree glanced around the crowed tavern. The sailors were dressed in their shore-leave finest: jaunty caps decorated with colorful ribbon, black-striped pullovers, white-duck trousers, and silver buckled shoes. The soldiers were also decked out: tall black shako hats with silver plates and leather straps underneath their chins, dress blue jackets with white facings, and gray pants with black bands on the sides.

As the customers consumed more and more ale, rum, and whiskey, Ole' Sally's could hardly contain the jubilant noise. Everyone was here to have a good time, away from marching orders, drills, laborious trench digging and, most of all, officers. This was their Friday night and nothing would prohibit them from enjoying it.

A group of soldiers in the corner of the bar started singing *Yankee Doodle Dandy*. Army musicians, dressed in red jackets and white pants, accompanied the singers playing fife and drum. Everybody joined in the chorus including Gilly and Desiree.

For the older patrons, the song brought back memories of the revolution. Old-timers told the younger ones stories of adventure and brave deeds. Some old fellows had served under Arnold and Montgomery at the siege of Quebec; some regaled tales of starvation at Valley Forge; some had marched with Nathanael Greene and Daniel Morgan in the great Southern Campaign; some had even sailed with the incomparable Joshua Barney.

This was what Gilly had been hoping for - to rekindle the latent fires of patriotic passion that can quickly be forgotten over the course of a generation. As the veterans remembered the pain and sacrifice that had won the nation's freedom a wizened gleam came into their baggy eyes.

They knew that their time and come and gone. Now America's fate rested on young, untested shoulders. The command officers for sure were no strangers to battle. Nearly all had fought against the British in the last war. Yet, it was these lads, some not old enough to shave, who would bear the cause of liberty against all odds. The old men also knew some of these boys would pay the ultimate sacrifice though they dared not mention it.

The army musicians struck up a rousing rendition of their favorite marching tune. All the boys in blue joined the familiar chords with lusty voices. They had trained with this song since they first enlisted. It was now as much a part of their military life as reveille in the morning. It was also their favorite song to sing after feasting on blue claws and ale. The proprietor could not refuse them a free round on the house since she thought the lyrics were meant to honor her.

> I'm lonesome since I crossed the hill,
>
> and o'er the moor and valley,
>
> such grievous thoughts my heart do fill,
>
> since parting with my Sally.
>
> I seek no more the fine or gay,
>
> for each does but remind me,
>
> how swift the hours did pass away,
>
> with the girl I left behind me.

The soldiers went on and on with chorus after chorus. Then they sang robust songs of war and melancholy songs of hearth and home. As the evening wore on they all knew they were approaching curfew. Just a few more minutes with comrades to hoist another tankard and share one last toast before they returned to camp.

Desiree was sleepy. She reached over and guided Gilly's arm over her shoulders and tucked her head beneath his arm and chest. Gilly's heart skipped a beat. He had dreamed of touching her light auburn hair. He longed for the feel of her soft curls in his hands. Despite the lingering smell of crabs that permeated Ole' Sally's, Gilly detected the alluring bouquet of lilac soap emanating from Desiree's face and neck. He gently placed his cheek on her head and sighed.

Desiree closed her eyes. The pale ale had taken its effect. But the sense of serenity warmly stirring in her heart was lit by more than a tankard or two. She felt contented. For the first time since she could remember, she felt happy.

The sailors refused to be outdone where vocal talent was concerned. After all, seamen were legendary for their sea songs and ditties. These tunes were their mainstay while working around the capstan weighing anchor. They hadn't any musicians with them but they were determined to trump the army.

The sailors coaxed a young lad to represent them and lifted him atop the bar. He had blond hair tied smartly in a well-greased tail that stretched to the small of his back. His merry green eyes sparkled, reflecting the light of the sooty whale oil lamps positioned around the tavern. Recognizing the acute responsibility in representing all of his shipmates, he doffed his cap and clutched it nervously. Then he gently closed his eyes and began his ballad.

'Tis the last rose of summer,

left blooming alone;

all her lovely companions

are faded and gone;

no flower of her kindred,

no rosebud is nigh,

to reflect back her blushes,

or give sigh for sigh.

I'll not leave thee, thou lone one!

to pine on the stem;

since the lovely are sleeping,

go, sleep thou with them.

thus kindly I scatter,

thy leaves o'er the bed,

where thy mates of the garden

lie scentless and dead.

So soon may I follow,

when friendships decay,

and from love's shining circle

the gems drop away.

When true hearts lie withered,

and fond ones are flown,

oh! who would inhabit

this bleak world alone?

There wasn't a whisper heard. Nothing had to be said. The song and its tenor said it all. The young lad climbed down from the bar and disappeared among the throng of drinkers. Slowly, every man placed their tankards on the bar and left the tavern in reverential silence.

Gilly pushed back Desiree's ringlets and with the palm of his hand tenderly raised her head underneath her chin. Her chestnut eyes were wide open. There were tears on her dimpled cheeks.

They said goodnight to Sally and followed everyone out the door. Desiree's carriage and driver waited in front. "Gilly, please be careful tonight when you go home."

"I will. I'll lock both doors and have Mr. Dooley's pistol beside my bed. If anyone comes to break in tonight they'll have a surprise waiting for them."

"Do you know how to handle a gun?"

"A rifle I do. A group of us from the orphanage used to go hunting on Saturdays in autumn thanks to some of the husbands of the ladies from the benevolent society. We'd leave on Friday afternoon and camp out overnight. The men taught us how to spot and stalk deer and shoot geese. I hope I won't have to use the pistol anyway. Will you be at the orphanage tomorrow seeing the little ones off?"

"Yes, I'll start early in the morning to make sure everything is in order. We're trying to make the children think that this is going to be a holiday. Are you at the cooperage tomorrow?"

Gilly grunted and sighed. "I haven't been paying enough attention to the business as I should have. I hope Richard is handling everything alright. Orders will be down to nothing soon because the military has all it needs right now. But, I'll go over the books anyway. Then maybe I could help you and the other women pack the kids up. Afterwards, I've got my own packing to do."

It was a soft night with a full moon. The sky was sprinkled with shimmering stars. They both looked up. "That was a sad song the sailor sang tonight," Desiree reflected. "It was sad and beautiful at the same time. I sensed the boys must have had mixed emotions as they listened. So hushed they all were you couldn't even hear them breathe." She turned to face Gilly and encircled her arms around his waist. "I wonder what it feels like to know that the battle is nigh? To know you might fall, or one of your comrades will, and leave you standing all alone, 'The Last Rose of Summer.'"

Gilly shook his head. He had felt the sadness and the beauty of the ballad, too. It did something to him. Yet, with Desiree here so near to his beating heart, he felt a sudden and magical compulsion. He placed his hands firmly on the small of her back. He lowered his face until their noses were touching. Then, he pressed his parted lips against hers. She did not refuse him. Instead, she returned his kisses with an ardent desire. A fire erupted in her bosom and the more fervently he kissed her the more eagerly she responded.

*****

Father John couldn't sleep. Even though the night air was warm, he wrapped a shawl around his shoulders and exited the rectory. As he aged in years, his body usually grew weary in the evening and, having a clean conscious, found no difficulty fading off in blissful slumber. Tonight, for an unknown reason, this was not the case. He walked down Market Street toward the wharf hoping to see moonbeams playing with the shimmering wavelets off the Patapsco.

As he made his way onto the wooden planks of the wharf he noticed something amiss. There was the faint light of a candle emanating from the window of the Dooley Cooperage. He glanced up at the night sky. The full moon was hanging lower in the heavens than it was when he left his door at the rectory. No one, he thought, would be working this late with only one small candle to see by. After what had happened at the Dooley home curiosity got the better of him. He neared the cooperage and saw that the front door was slightly ajar.

The door creaked on its rusted hinges. Even though his eyes were accustomed to the darkness he could see nothing save a shadow silhouetted on the planking of the floor from the soft glow of the candle. Suddenly, the flame was doused.

Father John did not remember the blow he took on his left temple. He was sent spinning around and around in an endless black vortex. The tunnel in which he spiraled started to become narrow and confining. There was no use in trying to fight the current that drew him through the abyss. It was all powerful. "Take me where you will, oh Lord," he said to the dark nothingness. "Be it done to me according to Thy word." He lifted his head and peered at the swirling cosmos ahead of him. Suddenly, he saw the pinhead of a white light.

Chapter 16: The Saint of Fells Point

As Gilly had told Desiree last night, he arose at daybreak, saddled Sarika, and proceeded to the cooperage to check on the books. He tethered Princess to the rail out front and fumbled in his pocket for the key. As he was about to insert it, the door opened on its own from the slight pressure of his left hand. The shutters were closed yet there was enough of the early sunlight seeping through the cracks to reveal the tragedy before him.

The entire front room was in shambles. The counter was knocked upside down, papers, ink wells and quill pens, and account books were strewn across the floor. It was if an earthquake had rumbled through the business, leaving nothing standing upright.

Gilly instinctively knew the cause of this mayhem. He felt the same way after he witnessed the destruction of the Dooley home. He put his hands to his face, rubbing his unbelieving eyes. "Not again," he muttered.

He bent over and placed his hands over his knees to quell the nausea that took hold of his stomach. A small rivulet of blood from underneath the counter made its way along the floor until it reached his shoes.

He sprang to the overturned oaken counter and seized it by the drawer sockets. It was heavy. He bent both knees and took a deep breath. He used every ounce of muscle, forcing it erect and tilting it towards the back wall. Finally, in desperation, Gilly heaved his body against it. The counter crashed against the wall showering him with splinters. Under his feet, Father John lay prostrate, bleeding from his head profusely.

A few yards from the cooperage there was a ship's bell on the quay used in case of fire. Gilly dashed out the door and yanked on the bell's rope. Its knell broke the silent, still sleepy wharf out of its summer, Saturday morning haze. It was a hefty, cast-iron bell and its peal could be heard all along the piers and deep into Fells Point. Gilly's heart was pounding so hard he could feel it through his chest, reverberating with each toll of the bell. Running back to the cooperage he knelt beside the priest's motionless body. He grabbed a towel from a hook under the counter and soaked it in a water cask. This he applied gently to the gash on Father John's head. He had seen a doctor take a pulse at the orphanage when some of the children were bedridden from different illnesses. He remembered what the doctor did and

261

placed his index and first two middle fingers against the priest's neck just below the jaw line. After agonizing seconds, he felt a slight beat and gasped in thanksgiving.

From all across the Point help came running. Shopkeepers, stevedores, saloon owners, mothers of the Point with children in tow descended upon the wharf. The Deptford Hundred, the Point's lone fire brigade, sent an engine pulled by a dozen men and boys. Seeing no smoke or flames, they stood beside the bell in confusion. Gilly ran out the door to see if any help had arrived.

"Here! Everybody! It's Father John! He's hurt real bad!"

The captain of the Deptford followed Gilly into the cooperage. Dozens more appeared in the doorway or peered through the now open windows. The captain shoved his way out the door and grabbed his lieutenant by the collar. "Murphy, take a horse from the station house and find Doc Williams. Tell him it's Father Moranvillè. Hurry it up. It don't look good."

"What's happened to him, cap?"

"Tell doc its life or death. Damn it Murph, hurry!"

Nobody dared move the body. Gilly, panicked, shouted at the crowd. "Any of you women know how to dress a wound? For God's sake he's bleeding to death!"

Mrs. Dougherty, the Irish midwife, squeezed her way through the doorway and knelt beside Gilly. "Holy Mother of God, Jaysus help him," she whispered.

When Doc Williams heard who was hurt, he didn't wait to have his horse saddled for him. He swung himself up on Murphy's mare in back of the lieutenant. "Move, Murph!" he ordered.

It didn't take long before all of the seafaring community of Fells Point had heard the news. Gabe, who was permitted to stay at the orphanage because of his responsibilities selling *The American*, ran to the church and rang the great bells that called the faithful for Sunday services.

Desiree, Mary Pickersgill, and the rest of the women from the benevolent society who did not accompany the children to the Pechin summer estate hurried to the rectory. News had it that Father John would be taken there.

Commodore Rodgers, who was dictating correspondence to Samuel at headquarters, heard the scuttlebutt from the sailors and marines under his command. Mr. Pechin, busy in his office as usual, was informed by his chief assistant, Bartlett, who didn't even bother to knock on the editor's door before entering. City officials, common laborers, fisherman, tradesman, servants and slaves, even the mayor received the news with, at first, a sense of shock and alarm, then anger.

Mr. Pechin's newspaper never published on weekends, but he decided this was a story too important to leave untold until next week. He barked for Bartlett to have the pressmen come to work and the delivery boys ready for a special Sunday edition. Then, Pechin rushed to his carriage and had the driver take him to the rectory. Gilly, he knew, would be there.

*****

It was almost midmorning when a train of people escorted Father John's stretcher to the rectory. The stretcher had been gingerly placed in back of the Deptford's new goose-neck fire engine. The engine had well-oiled springs on its axles. Doctor Williams thought this would be better than having the stretcher carried all the way down Market Street by hand. Williams directed that all the windows in the rectory be opened to keep the temperature as cool as possible in the blistering August heat.

The doctor complimented Mrs. Dougherty on her skills with the bandage she applied to Father John's head. Then, he ordered everyone out of the room to examine his patient more thoroughly. Everyone left to stand vigil outside the rectory – everyone except Gilly.

"Tell me, Doc. What happened to him? Is he going to make it?"

Doctor Williams ignored the question and continued on with his examination. Gilly sat down on Father John's leather chair and waited. A rosary was being recited outside and even though the faithful prayed quietly,

264

their whispers were still heard in the study. Williams frowned and glared out the window.

"If you want to be of any assistance whatsoever," he said to Gilly, "dismiss those people at once and fetch me a clean pot of boiling water."

"But they're praying for their pastor."

"Then tell them to go pray in the church. I want solitude and I want the boiling water and I want it now."

Gilly left the rectory. Upon seeing him, the crowd hushed in anticipation of news. He motioned for the rectory's cook, Mrs. Callahan, to come to him and asked her to boil some water. Then, he instructed the crowd as to the doctor's orders. In a moment they silently left the rectory grounds and filed into St. Patrick's Church.

When Gilly returned to the study the doctor had finished his assessment. A pot of steaming water lay atop Father John's desk resting on clean linen. Williams was busy suturing the wound with a needle and silk thread that he had immersed in the boiling water a moment ago. He gently applied a new bandage around the head and two others over the top of the skull and underneath the left and right sides of the jaw bone.

"The trauma was severe as any fool can see," Williams said, as he pushed his eye glasses up to the crown of his salt-and-pepper head. "He's in a coma, but breathing easily. How, I don't know. He should be dead. The blow was struck below the left temple adjacent to the ear lobe. His jaw is broken in several places. He has lost a great deal of blood. What has happened inside the cranium, which also sustained considerable trauma, is anyone's guess. I take it you didn't find him as I saw him when I came into the cooperage?"

Gilly shook his head. "No, he was pinned underneath the heavy oak counter. It must have weighed twenty stone."

"I trust the Deptford's men removed it carefully?"

"No, doc, I moved it myself."

The doctor gave Gilly's frame a quick size up. "Then have you added circus feats of incredible strength to your well-deserved reputation as a writer?"

"I don't know how I ... " Gilly broke off in mid-sentence. "Doc, what's to be done now? Should I send to the seminary for a priest?"

"If his Eminence, Archbishop Carroll hasn't been notified yet, and I can't for the life of me think why he hasn't since half of Fells Point is camped outside the front door or is inside the church, then inform the prelate at once. He'll decide whether or not to send a priest. The help Moranvillè needs now is outside of my purview. We can only see to it that the bandages are changed regularly.

"Watch out for any signs of infection and fever. Keep him as cool as possible. Wet his lips with water every fifteen minutes and sponge his body to keep his temperature down."

Williams reached into his bag and drew out a bottle of witch hazel. "Dab his face and neck with this every hour. It's an old Indian remedy. It might help with the swelling and help prevent infection if the Susquehannock Indian tribes know anything about medicine, which I think they do. If his pulse weakens or if you detect any other changes in his condition send for me immediately. I have to attend to a difficult pregnancy in Old Towne and will be some hours. My housemaid will know how to find me."

"Thanks, doc. I'll make sure everything will be taken care of just as you say." The doctor reached for his bag and proceeded to the door. He turned back with an inquisitive stare.

"Do have any idea who tried to murder him?"

Gilly's sullen face and angry, unflinching eyes stared back at Williams. "No, doc. But they must have thought it was me. Apparently, they don't like my well-deserved reputation as a writer." The doctor nodded and walked out.

*****

Mr. Pechin met Desiree, who was talking to Mary Pickersgill, outside the rectory. Gilly opened the door and raised his hands atop his brows to shield his eyes against the steady sun and survey another crowd who couldn't fit into the church and spilled out onto the rectory grounds. He spotted Desiree and her father and waved to them to come inside. He continued scanning the mass of people which grew ever thicker by the moment.

Gilly seemed frustrated. "Has anyone seen Mrs. Dougherty, the midwife?"

"She's gone off with Doc Williams," Mary Pickersgill said. "There's a lass in Old Town who has one that doesn't want to come out and join the rest of us."

"Mary, do you know anything about changing bandages and how to take care of sutures?" Gilly asked.

Mary nodded. "I've done my fair share doctoring if that's what you're after. As for sutures, I could sew up a man from the inside out if I had to."

Gilly ushered them in. Before closing the door he put his finger to his lips so the crowd could see he wanted them to be very quiet. Then he gave them a thumbs-up and pointed praying hands towards heaven. This gave the people a sense of hope and a command to continue on with their silent petitions.

Gilly went over the doctor's instructions with Mary and then joined Mr. Pechin and Desiree in the dining room opposite the study. Desiree jumped into his arms and kissed him on his cheek.

"Darling, I'm so sorry. My God, how could this have happened to the gentlest man on the face of the earth?"

Gilly was emotionally spent. He bowed his head atop Desiree's curls and let loose a few tears. Mr. Pechin waited a moment before speaking.

"Gilly, I know this is very difficult for you. To you, I suspect, Moranvillè is your father. The only one you've ever known. I, too, have come to regard him as the spiritual father of myself, my daughter, and this community. But, I must ask you … " Pechin couldn't put into words what he wanted to say.

"Mr. Pechin, I know what you mean. But, everything happened so quickly. I discovered his body just after sunup. The cooperage was destroyed. Whoever did this must be the same thugs who ransacked the Dooley home. They probably thought that Father John was me. Mrs. Callahan told me that Father John went out for a walk after midnight. She waited up for him but he never came back."

"Why didn't she alert someone?" Desiree asked.

"My dear," Pechin answered, "priests keep strange hours tending to their flock. It is not unusual for them to be called, like a doctor, at any hour whatsoever."

"That's what she told me," Gilly concurred. "He must have walked down to the docks and saw something or someone in the cooperage. Doc Williams said Father John should be dead. They hit him that hard. Then, they crushed his body with the big counter. They didn't mean to hurt him, or me, they meant to kill. They might yet succeed." Gilly cradled his head in his hands trying to think.

Mrs. Callahan swung open the door from the kitchen and poked her head into the dining room. "Would you care for a pot of tea to calm your nerves?"

"Please, dear woman," Mr. Pechin answered.

"Oh, and Master Gilly," the cook said between sobs, "with all the troubles I forgot to give you this. It was delivered early this morning." She handed him a letter. He slid it into his top pocket without questioning why a private letter to him would be delivered to the rectory.

Mr. Pechin approached him and put a sympathetic hand on his shoulder. "Son, I don't know if you can summon the courage to write about this, but, consider if you will, the immense implications of this tragedy. It affects not only yourself, but every Baltimorean soul who treasures freedom."

Gilly nodded his head in agreement. This would be the toughest writing assignment he had ever been given. "I'll write it right here on this table. I'm not leaving Father John alone. Not for one minute."

"Neither will I, father," Desiree said. "I'll stay here and help Mrs. Pickersgill."

"When you're finished, Gilly, send the copy with Desiree's driver to my office. We'll stay up all night until we can go to press. The story will be blanketed across the city tomorrow morning. The headline will be 'OUTRAGE!'"

Desiree went into the study and grabbed an ink stand, quill, and paper. While she passed the front door she detected a soft knock. She opened it and, after seeing who it was, curtsied. It was Archbishop Carroll.

"May I enter and see our servant John?"

"Please come in, your eminence," Desiree said. Gilly and Mr. Pechin saw the old prelate from the dining room and greeted him in the foyer. Mr. Pechin, who knew the archbishop well, heartily shook his hand. Gilly genuflected before him and kissed his episcopal ring. Desiree led the archbishop into the study. He knelt at Father John's bedside and prayed. Mary Pickersgill knelt with the archbishop by the bed while the others exited the study and quietly closed the door.

To their surprise, an odd looking man sat at the dining room table peering at them through thick eye glasses. "Mr. Peabody, what are you doing here," Gilly asked.

"The door was ajar so I took the liberty to enter. Please forgive my impudence. I am deeply sorry for the tragedy that befell you today. You have my utmost sympathy." They all joined Mr. Peabody and sat down at the table. Gilly pushed his writing implements aside.

"Do you have any light to shed on the situation, Mr. Peabody?"

"I do. But first please tell me how the good Moranvillè is faring. Is it as serious as I suspect?"

They all just nodded their heads. No words were required and the intelligence officer, sensing the somber atmosphere, added none.

"Mr. Peabody, my name is William Pechin," the editor said, extending his hand. "Allow me to introduce my daughter, Desiree."

Peabody rose and bowed, stiffly. "This is indeed an honor. I would not presume, however, to impose my person upon the sadness that prevails in this humble and holy abode were it not for the extraordinary circumstances which have brought me here."

"Proceed, Mr. Peabody," Gilly insisted. "Any information you can share on what's happened today will be appreciated. I am going to write about it for a special Sunday edition of *The American*. Mr. Pechin and I think what transpired today should be made known to all of Baltimore as soon as possible."

"What has occurred this morning is already known to all of

Baltimore and beyond for that matter. But, your story, Gilly, will help separate fact from fiction in case the enemy has plans to turn the tables on us and spread inaccuracies that will benefit them and cause damage to the defense of this city."

Peabody noted the perplexed facial expressions around the table and decided to answer their questions before they were asked. "Mr. Pechin, thank you, sir, for having the forethought to arrange for your special edition tomorrow. I believe this will, as I said, stave off any contingency the network of spies has in store for us.

"And now, if you allow me, let's get to the particulars. Where were you last night Gilly, and what time did you get home?"

"Desiree and I had dinner at Ole' Sally's. We left about ten o'clock."

"Did you have any plans on checking the cooperage last night after dinner?"

"No. I told Desiree I would go there first thing this morning, which I did."

"So, the intruders weren't expecting you. Still, who else would come into the cooperage at so late an hour but you?" Peabody seemed to ask this question of himself.

"Certainly not Father John," Desiree maintained.

"Certainly not the good priest, I agree with you Desiree. But not Gilly, either."

They all started to voice disagreement with Peabody's reasoning. "See here, Peabody," Mr. Pechin declared. "Of course they knew it was Gilly. Why, they threatened him on Friday night by destroying the Dooley home and leaving an ominous message."

"Yes, I heard about the incident. But they would have had Gilly followed last night. They knew he was on Thames Street. They also knew he would retire early, for such is his custom. In my business, one first learns to establish a pattern on persons of interest. Gilly has been watched for quite some time now. Not just by enemy agents but by me."

"You!" Gilly exclaimed. "Why would you watch me?"

"Not me, personally, Gilly. I had a few of my people follow you. Before you become too agitated, allow me to explain. I had you followed for one very good reason. I wanted to know who and how many of the enemy were *watching you*. Forgive me for my cloak of secrecy. It's become my second nature."

Mr. Pechin was becoming impatient. "Listen, Peabody, I'm a newspaperman. I deal in facts, not mere supposition. Why did enemy agents break into the cooperage last night or early this morning, and why did they viciously attack Father Moranvillè?"

274

"Had they known it was the pastor, they never would have laid a hand on him. If they were going to kill Gilly they could have gone back to the Dooley home and finished him off there, locked doors or not. They broke into the cooperage because they knew I was to meet Gilly there Sunday morning. They desperately needed to cause a ruse."

Desiree, who was silent and absorbing all this information, finally started to see Mr. Peabody's line of thought. "You mean they knew you would find something on Sunday at the cooperage. Something incriminating that would have identified them. So they ransacked the place to cause a diversion?"

"Very good, Desiree, that's it exactly. When an unexpected intruder entered while they were at their work, they assailed him without conscious. After all, the intruder could have been just a common thief. To add murder to their destruction of the premises could only further their intent to throw us into even more confusion, thus covering their tracks. These agents are, without question, thorough professionals.

"What they did not intend – in fact, what was the furthest thing from their mind– was to hurt Father John. This is where their luck has run out, completely. Your story tomorrow, Gilly, will reinforce in the minds of the people the scuttlebutt that has swamped the city today. It will confirm that an atrocious act has been committed against a cleric who is beloved by this city and across this state."

"So," Desiree surmised, "the tables have turned on *them*." She spun her head towards the study and sighed. "Even now, he serves his flock. Perhaps he really is what the people think he is: a saint in our very midst."

For a moment they said nothing. Then, Mr. Peabody rose to leave. "Are we still meeting at the cooperage tomorrow, Gilly? Or, perhaps, you would like to postpone."

"I'll be there if I can. If I'm not, here are keys. I managed to lock the door and close up the windows and shutters before we left this morning."

Mr. Peabody took his leave. The archbishop soon followed after delivering a blessing over the rectory and everyone there. Mary Pickersgill and Desiree decided to take turns at Father John's bedside. The cook brought another pot of tea to the dining room after Mr. Pechin left for his offices. Gilly finally took pen to paper and finished his story. It was delivered to *The American* sometime after midnight. The pressmen at the newspaper would be at into the wee hours.

Mary Pickersgill relieved Desiree at about three in the morning. She found Gilly awake sipping some tea.

"Any change?"

Desiree shook her head. "He's breathing, Gilly. At least he's breathing. My God in heaven, I've never seen anyone so badly hurt before. To think this could happen to Father John after everything he's meant to Fells

276

Point and to all of the people here is … "

"There's a blanket and pillow on the chair, Dez. See if you can get some rest." He fingered in his front pocket, suddenly aware of the letter Mrs. Callahan had given to him earlier. "Funny, I didn't notice this before," he said.

"What?"

"This letter from Michael Dooley, it's addressed to me in care of the rectory. Why would Michael send it here instead of Thames Street or the cooperage?"

"I don't know. Perhaps he addressed it by mistake or he wanted Father John to give it to you."

Gilly opened the letter and rubbed his weary eyes. He read the first paragraph. "Oh, my God … "

"What is it, Gilly - sweetheart, why has your face suddenly turned white?"

Part III

"To know what you ought to do."

Chapter 17: Socrates and Plato

A spine-chilling peal of thunder cracked across Fells Point early Sunday morning sounding like the felling of a large tree as it slowly obeys gravity and crashes to the earth. Gilly had fallen asleep atop his arms on the dining room table. Mrs. Pickersgill sat next to him plying a needle and thread through a well-worn sock. Gilly awoke, as all Baltimore did, with the clamor of the storm.

The rain battered against the window panes of the rectory as Doctor Williams descended his carriage and struggled beneath an upturned umbrella toward the front door and let himself in.

He entered the dining room and hung his rain jacket on a hook. Mrs. Callahan brought him a towel to dry his hands and face. She was talking to no one in particular about how they didn't make umbrellas the way they used to.

"Well, since I've had no word from you I assume there's been no change," the doctor surmised.

"No, sir," Mrs. Pickersgill replied. "He's breathing like a baby, but he hasn't moved a muscle or blinked an eye since you left yesterday. By the by, doctor, how's the gal in Old Town, did she deliver the goods?"

"Two hours ago, Mrs. Pickersgill, the child finally decided to come out into the world. I'm sure it was a tough decision. What a time to take your first breath of Baltimore air with the British breathing down our own necks."

The doctor roused himself by vigorously shaking his head. "Mother and daughter are resting comfortably, which is a damn sight better than the likes of us. As soon as the mid-wife, Mrs. Dougherty, has had a chance to sleep, I'll send her to help with the dressings." Williams took his bag and entered the study. Desiree left Father John's bedside as he came in.

She glanced at the dining room window. "It's getting worse. I think the rain is blowing sideways. I'm wondering if my father still plans on getting out the special edition."

"Oh, I'm sure he'll wait on the weather and then put it on the street. No use in doing anything else now," Gilly mused.

Mrs. Callahan had been up all night with the rest of them. Nevertheless, she had been busy in the kitchen for hours. The fragrance of Brazilian coffee beans and the sweet aroma of fresh-baked pastry emanating from the kitchen filled their nostrils and moistened their mouths. The kitchen door swung on its hinges and out popped Mrs. Callahan muttering something about how chickens don't lay proper eggs these days. She put the coffee pot and a plate of fresh peach pastries on a side table and disappeared back to her domestic domain. It didn't take but a moment for the three tired souls to help themselves. As they ate and sipped, Gilly took the letter from Michael Dooley out of his top pocket and began to reread its contents.

"Would you read it out loud, Gilly?" Desiree asked. "I know I read it last night but I was half asleep. This coffee has given me something to go on this morning."

"It was like a dagger in the heart when I read it at three in the morning, Dez. Let me start from the beginning."

Vergennes, Vermont, Sunday, August 10, 1814

Dear Gilly,

I read with interest your last letter and had a long talk with Uncle Bob. It seemed strange to me that two men who had knowledge of the Dooley cooperage in the city of Cork, Ireland, decades ago, are now employed at our place on Fells Point. To Uncle Bob, it is more than strange, it is diabolical. I'm going to relate to you the story of how my father and Uncle Bob came to our shores as this will put the

282

pieces of the puzzle together for you nicely. In the meantime, it is urgent that you watch the new hires, <u>Sean O'Casey</u> and <u>Liam Dailey</u>. I repeat, watch them carefully. Do not trust them!

Uncle Bob and my father were just young boys at the time my grandfather was accused of secretly being in league with French spies. He ran the most successful cooperage in Cork City. Many tradesmen, coopers among them, were jealous of him. Uncle Bob tells me there were documents found in a Dooley barrel outlining a plan for a French invasion of Ireland, through or near Cork City, and enlisting the help of Irish revolutionaries.

At the trial, two young men who had found the barrel and reported the discovery to the police were the main witnesses. Their testimony, along with a host of trumped up, circumstantial evidence was enough to condemn my grandfather to the block. He was hanged for treason because of these two men. Their names were <u>Sean O'Casey</u> and <u>Liam Dailey</u>! This cannot be a coincidence!

After the trial, my grandmother, depressed and overwhelmed with despair, died of heart failure. My father and Uncle Bob decided to use whatever funds were left of my grandfather's savings and boarded a ship to America in the latter part of the War for Independence. They eventually settled in Baltimore after serving with Washington at the Battle of Yorktown.

Uncle Bob says these men are dangerous. They were paid to give damning testimony. What they're doing in Fells Point now during our Second War for American Independence is beyond our understanding. But, if they are the same people who were responsible for my grandfather's execution, then, Uncle Bob says, God help you, because you're going to need it. He wishes he could be in Baltimore to deal with these vermin himself.

Given this information, I know you will immediately recognize the true peril that surrounds you and our fair city.

Jessica and I, Uncle Bob and Captain Ken wish you all the best. Stay vigilant and pray for our combined victory on both Champlain and the Chesapeake. St. Thomas Aquinas, pray for us.

Your brother in the code,

Michael

Desiree propped her head up with her fists underneath her chin. "What are you going to do now?"

Gilly finished his pastry and helped himself to another cup of coffee. "I'm to meet Mr. Peabody this morning. He'll figure something out, Dez. If we had Michael's Uncle Bob here, I think the situation would take care of itself. At least now I know why the Bible was desecrated."

"What Bible?"

"The Dooley family Bible, Dez. It was kept in a cedar chest in the living room. I didn't mention this to you before because I figured it had nothing to do with me or my stories. It was personal. It was directed against the Dooley's. The Bible had been – um, it was – someone had peed on it, you see."

"You're right, darling. That was personal. It's certain, then. O'Casey and Dailey did it. The Bible was a message for the Dooley's, not you."

Mrs. Pickersgill, who seemed to be paying attention only to her basket of socks, could hold her tongue no longer. "I've known Bob Dooley these past twenty years. They'll be no safe place on earth for those new hires of yours. When he gets home he'll track them down, mark my words. In the meantime, you two had better watch your step. These low-down skunks have the blood of a priest, if not a saint, on their hands. If they can do what they did to poor Father John, they'll not think twice about cutting the veins of your lovely throats, and that's the truth of it."

Doctor Williams joined them in the dining room. He immediately went to the side table and poured a cup of coffee. "The good news is there's no change in our patient. The bad news is we need to start thinking about getting something into him. Without water, he cannot be with us long. His jaw, gums, and facial tissue are all swollen. This will continue to get worse. Forcing liquids down his throat while his mind is comatose would only trigger a spasmodic reaction. We'd only succeed in drowning him."

"Are there any options at all?" Desiree asked, pleadingly.

"Are those people still praying in the church?"

"You bet, doc. There was a candlelight vigil all night. Now they're setting up shifts. They'll be at for as long as it takes," Mrs. Pickersgill said.

"Good. Have them keep it up - because that's our option."

Gilly left them and entered the study. Father John's face had turned deep purple and was twice the normal size. Gilly removed Istvan's locket from around his neck. He kissed it and gingerly slipped it around Father John's neck.

He knelt down beside the bed and folded his hands. "May the Irish Madonna shed her tears on you, *mon ami*."

The storm which struck so suddenly at dawn quickly abated. Gilly walked down Market Street following the footsteps Father John took just two nights ago. He kept his head down while he trod over the slippery cobblestones. As he passed Market and Bank Streets he heard the familiar cry of "EXTRA! EXTRA!" The cry came from Gabe who was standing on top of his wagon. "EXTRA! OUTRAGE COMMITED! FATHER JOHN NEAR DEATH!"

It wasn't too long ago that Gilly was in Gabe's shoes. Gilly wondered if Gabe recognized the full importance of this day's headlines, excited as the boy must be to hawk an extra, let alone a special Sunday edition. Gilly continued his trek down Market Street. There was too much going through his mind to consider and analyze any one thing in particular. His success as a writer for the newspaper, his newfound love for Desiree, the rampage of the Dooley home, the wicked assault on Father John, Michael's letter, all of these things flitted through his consciousness like noisy seagulls competing for scraps of leftover bait tossed from a fisherman's dory.

Underneath the surface of his mind's eye was the war and the ever looming threat to his beloved city. And now the threat was all too apparent. He had been a facilitator for that threat, he thought. If it were not for his ambition to write for the newspaper much of this would never have happened. He had left his responsibility to take over the Dooley Cooperage to follow his own self-interest. Why couldn't he have paid more attention to the obligations he had sworn to uphold? Would Michael see his actions as a noble pursuit of a dream or simply a dereliction of duty? Were his hands also stained with the blood of a saint - of a kind, pious soul – of his lifelong mentor?

Mr. Peabody saw Gilly's hunched frame slowly making its way towards the quay. For the first time in weeks, Gilly was walking with a noticeable limp. Peabody waited for him under a creaking sign that read: Dooley – Cooper. The intelligence officer sensed the burden weighing upon the young man's shoulders. He feared that this morning, he would only add to it.

"Good morning, Gilly. Is there improvement at all in the good Moranvillè's condition?"

Gilly took the keys to the cooperage Mr. Peabody offered him. "No, sir. No change I'm afraid. Father John is still critical." He slid the key into the lock and opened the door. Peabody noticed something but kept it to himself.

The carnage appearing before them was unchanged from yesterday morning. The priest's blood had puddled and thickened on the hickory wood flooring. Mr. Peabody produced a large magnifying glass from his valise and went right to work. Gilly sighed and shook his head. How would he ever explain this to Michael?

He let open the shutters and jimmied up the window sashes caked as they were from years of soot and sawdust. They'll be no more orders filled by this business for quite some time, he thought.

"It's just as I expected," Mr. Peabody said, wiping his eye glasses with a handkerchief. "The work room is in shambles. I'll find no thumbprints in there to help us."

"I don't think you're going to need thumbprints." Gilly said, handing him Michael Dooley's letter. Peabody wrapped the wire frame of his glasses around his ears and read.

"A most interesting letter, Gilly. It's a pity it hadn't arrived sooner. Much damage could have been avoided."

"You mean Father John?"

"Yes, I do. But that's behind us now. Let's keep our eyes on what we can gain from this inglorious mess, not on what has eluded our grasp." Peabody stepped toward the shattered oaken counter and withdrew its main drawer. He pulled out a ledger and delicately fingered through its pages.

"That's a record our clerk keeps of the hours worked by the Smith brothers, and, God help us, O'Casey and Dailey."

"Where is your clerk?"

"It's Sunday."

"Where was he yesterday?"

"Richard wasn't here when I found Father John. But he wouldn't have been anyway. It was too early."

"Has he made any attempt to contact you since then?"

Gilly knitted his brows. "No, he hasn't. I haven't heard from him at all."

Peabody went to the front door and examined the lock. "Richard has a key to the cooperage doesn't he?"

"Of course he does. He opens and closes shop all the time. I'm too busy to be here ... "

"Yes, don't fret about it, Gilly. Richard depended on the fact that you were busy working and writing for the newspaper. This gave him a free hand, you see."

"A free hand to do what? You're not insinuating ... "

"No, Gilly, I'm not insinuating anything. You see the lock here? The bolt is completely intact. There are scratches around the metal facing and the wood is chipped on both sides but that was for show. This lock was opened by its key, not forced with some kind of lever."

"It was O'Casey and Dailey. They must have stolen the key from

Richard!"

"No, they didn't have to do that. They…" Mr. Peabody stopped in mid-sentence. He stared over Gilly's shoulder. "They received the key from Richard Snipes or he was here with them. Isn't that right, Samuel?"

The commodore's personal secretary was standing on the wharf a few feet in front of them. He had circles underneath his reddened eyes. His mouth was agape, but he could not speak. In his hands he held a writing tablet.

*****

Mr. Peabody's carriage took them to Hampstead Hill to see Commodore Rodgers. During the drive, Samuel had opened up and told them everything he knew. Richard had disappeared. All of his things at the boarding house were gone. Sean O'Casey and Liam Dailey weren't anywhere to be found. Peabody hadn't asked any questions. He simply listened with his eyes closed, clutching the notebook.

"It's all my fault," Samuel lamented. "I was the one responsible for hiring O'Casey and Dailey. I had recommended Richard to you, Gilly. As God is my judge, I never thought he would be in league with the British."

Samuel gazed out the window of the carriage as they rode through Old Town. "I knew Richard well when we were boys. We went to school and grew up together. He was more of a pacifist than I was. He was deeply committed to his faith. I never knew anyone who possessed such a deep understanding of language. Richard was a true scholar.

"When we were boys, he used to quote Cicero and Cato. He could read *The Republic* in the original Greek. For fun, he pretended to be Socrates to my Plato. He would drill me with questions in search of the truth. He was the teacher. I was his student."

Gilly listened to Samuel's recollections with intense interest. He knew Samuel was in shock, or close to it. He could see the pain in Samuel's eyes. It was the worst kind of pain, Gilly thought - it was the pain of betrayal.

Mr. Peabody opened his eyes. "Did you ever suspect your cousin?"

"I don't really know that I suspected him of anything at all. I was happy to see him after all these years. We were so much alike. I missed his companionship. There were things I could tell Richard that I would never dream of telling anyone else.

"When he came to Baltimore after leaving Elizabethtown, I was elated. He said he wanted to leave teaching for a while. His plans were to find a job and support himself, even though he had inherited a great deal of land and livestock from his parents. But, that was Richard. He had to make his own way, you see. When he first arrived we would spend hours at night sipping tea and discussing the classics: Homer's *Iliad* and the *Odyssey*, anything written by Ovid or Virgil. Richard's favorite quote is, I think, what defined his mind:

"All literature, all philosophical treatises, all the voices of antiquity are full of examples for imitation, which would all lie unseen in darkness without the light of literature."

"Cicero," Mr. Peabody said.

"Yes, sir, Cicero again. The classics were to Richard a beacon to guide the inquisitive mind. He said all of the questions, or at least most of them, had already been asked and discussed by the ancient minds. When I heard Michael Dooley and Gilly talking about the Code of Aquinas at the cooperage it filled me with the same kind of passion for truth which filled Richard's every waking moment. But, Aquinas was something new to me.

"We discussed the code a great deal. He thought it was an excellent model for self-enlightenment and encouraged me to delve into its mystery and pursue its meaning in my own life.

"What he could not understand was my decision to join the navy and act as Commodore Rodgers' personal secretary. He did not see how it was possible to justify this with the meaning of the code. Of course, I felt just the opposite. My meditations on the code led me in my decision to leave the cooperage and join the armed forces. I recognized that this is what I ought to do. That this was divine intervention in my life. What Aquinas was talking about, what the code meant, truly entered into my heart and soul. To me, this was my purpose and I felt it within every sinew of my body.

"Richard, as I said, didn't see it that way. He was against the war. Not just our Second War of Independence, but any war whatsoever. It's not that he didn't believe in fighting for what's right. He did, but not physically. He said a true general was one who fought without fists. He was determined in his mind that freedom should be won by other means. In principle, I concur - which is why Commodore Rodgers promised me I would never have to point a gun at my fellow man. But, while this may be a practical approach for an individual, I confess its application for a nation is purely hypothetical. As I said, I never consciously suspected Richard. But, since you have asked me, I must admit feeling uncomfortable in Richard's strong opinions and vehement opposition to slavery. I myself, and most Quakers I know, are against slavery. Richard, however, was obsessed with its abolition. There was nothing he wouldn't do, no act so atrocious, no deed so abhorrent, outside of murder of course, to end the blight of slavery in America. Yet, murder may have been the result of his efforts. And the murder of a sainted man who cared more for mankind than any I've ever known."

Samuel had spilled every conscious thought about his cousin he could muster. He sat back in his seat and stared at Gilly and Mr. Peabody, looking for answers he did not possess. The driver opened the hatch on the carriage's box and bellowed "Rodger's Bastion coming up, sir."

"Thank you, Carl," Mr. Peabody said. "And now, Samuel, let's examine your cousin's parting lines to you written on one of pages of his notebook which he left conspicuously for you to find before vacating his lodgings. Peabody positioned his eye glasses on the tip of his nose.

My dear Samuel, thank you for everything you have done for me. You're heart and your mind will forever abide in my bosom as an anchor of pure grace in this corrupt world. By the time you read these words, you will know of my treachery. I didn't mean for it to end this way after all the kindness and generosity you have bestowed upon me. For this, my dear cousin, I am most exceedingly sorry. If you can reach into the tender recesses of your large heart and find a refuge of forgiveness for me there, then I will be content even to my last breath. I can travel with you only so far, Samuel. Remember, *Amicus Plato, sed magis amica veritas* (Plato is my friend, but truth is a better friend).

"Indeed," Samuel said. "Richard thought he found his truth. He had heard, as everyone did, about the British raising and training a brigade of black soldiers, all former slaves. Richard couldn't contain his enthusiasm. I suppose he thought, if the British won the war, they would free even more American slaves."

Mr. Peabody shook his head in frustration. "Your cousin is a very naïve man. The British are hardly liberators of anyone. Just ask the Irish or the

Asian Indian. Ask the millions addicted to the seed of the poppy in China.

From the tone of this letter, Samuel, Richard sounds as if he's a clueless

schoolboy, not a serious scholar. Did he actually believe the British wouldn't

use every device in their power to bring as much violence to this country as

possible? I wonder if he even knows of the outcome of the rampage of the

cooperage. He sold his soul to a devil who promised him the world. His

decision was outlandish and immature. God help him when he comes to the

realization, which he certainly must someday, that he contributed to nothing

but heartache and misery. I'm sorry for you Samuel. But, I cannot hide my

contempt for the actions of your cousin."

Samuel said nothing. He put his head between his knees trying not to
vomit.

Chapter 18: The Cipher

The midwife, Mrs. Dougherty, arrived at the rectory just in time for tea. While she filled her cup she also filled Mrs. Pickersgill in on all the details of the difficult delivery in Old Town. Desiree, half asleep, stood her watch in the study. She had hoped by now there would be some sign that Father John was improving. But his condition hadn't changed. As Doctor Williams had predicted, the swelling had increased. Yet not as much as it could, had Williams not ordered the application of the witch hazel. Moreover, there was no sign of infection. Perhaps the Susquehannock Indians knew something about medicine after all. The doctor had also assured them that the priest was feeling no pain while in a coma. This, at least, was a blessing, Desiree thought.

The afternoon sun poked in and out of the remaining cloud cover from the morning storm. It shone, piecemeal, through the western window of the study. By chance, one of its rays rested on the locket Gilly had slipped around the neck of Father John.

Desiree wondered about the locket. It didn't appear to be a religious object. It was just a small, round, glass encased, pewter trinket, about the size of a silver dollar. There appeared to be some sort of cloth on the inside, a browned fragment of a woolen garment perhaps. Maybe it belonged to his mother. Usually a locket contained a snippet of hair from a loved one. But this was definitely a homespun fabric.

It was getting hotter in the room. The storm had brought only a morning respite from the scorching Maryland sun. She opened the windows and unlatched the shutters. There was singing coming from the church. The hymn sounded familiar. Now, she remembered. It was the tune Father John had been singing and humming to himself when he was pruning his roses. That was the day Desiree's life had changed. It was the day Father John had told her about the Code of Aquinas. After that everything happened so quickly.

Had she really been the self-serving, manipulative, spoiled young brat who thought boys were her personal play things? Yes, she answered herself. She was certainly that and much more. And then she talked to Father John. Somehow, he found a way to penetrate the inflexible walls of selfish

298

obstinacy that surrounded her head and heart. For years, her father had tried and failed. In the end, he simply gave up trying and gave into Desiree's every demand.

Father John, on the other hand, didn't really try at all. How did he do it? She recalled his story about the roses, about them blooming according to the dictates of nature and not at the whim of men. He chastised her with his narrative on Michael Dooley and Jessica Farmer; about the love that blossomed between them because of the prayers of Mrs. Dooley, and the promise she exacted from Father John on her deathbed. After Father John laid his hands on her head and blessed her, the roses in Desiree's own life began to bud and flourish beyond anything she had ever dreamt before.

And, it all started with a song. The psalm she first heard from the lips of this blessed priest and that now wafted on a warm breeze into the study. Look up at the night sky, he advised her, and see the stars and the planets moving with a purpose because they were under authority. Then, he asked her if she was also under authority. For most of her life, Desiree actually believed she was the authority. Things were different now.

She glanced back at the locket resting on the priest's chest, moving ever so slightly up and down with the cadence of each silent breath. It was his mother's locket, Desiree decided – a mother who watched over every beat of her son's heart. She smiled and raised her head. Behind the bed there were roses in full bloom in a pretty vase that were placed in front of a small altar to the Holy Virgin. She looked down at the locket and then up to the statue on the altar again. She suddenly had a strong feeling that the locket was more than just a keepsake.

*****

Samuel had managed to collect himself when they entered headquarters. He took his seat behind his desk and busied himself with some paperwork. Commodore Rodgers was in his office with Generals Smith and Stricker. Mr. Peabody made his report.

"Is there anything damaging the spies could have obtained before they crawled their way back to their British masters?" Stricker asked.

Mr. Peabody was studying Richard's notebook. Gilly, looking over Peabody's shoulder, found this interesting because all the pages of the notebook were blank except for Richard's farewell missive to his cousin. The intelligence officer removed his magnifying glass from his valise and inspected the blank pages. He brought his nose closer to one of the pages and sniffed.

"Well, I'll be ... "

"What is it, sir," General Smith demanded. "What do you see in those pages?"

Mr. Peabody readjusted his wire rim glasses and glanced up at the officers before him. "Nothing, gentlemen. And that's the holy truth. This methodology is so antiquated I would never have looked for it unless there was nothing else to look for. Why, it's positively brilliant."

General Smith became agitated. "Stop speaking in riddles, Peabody. What do you mean you don't see anything and that's the holy truth. What on earth is brilliant about nothing?"

"There are impressions on one of these pages." He lifted the page in question in front of them.

"I don't see anything at all," Commodore Rodgers said.

"Exactly. The preceding page has been torn out of the notebook. That was the page that contained the message."

General Smith started feeling foolish. "Very well, Peabody. I haven't the slightest idea what you're talking about, but, please proceed. We are all ears."

"Upon the torn page was written a message. It was written using a quill, but the pen was not dipped in ink. It was dipped in lemon juice. I can smell just a whiff of the lemon on the page with the slight impressions."

"Lemon juice?" Gilly asked, surprise in his voice.

"Yes, Gilly. It's a method as ancient as Caesar himself. No one has used this tactic for years. The lemon juice is, of course, invisible. But the quill has left a definite series of impressions on the next page."

Mr. Peabody spotted a candle on Commodore Rodger's desk. He took a match from his pocket and lit it. "Applying heat to the lemon juice that has seeped onto the subsequent page," he instructed, "may reveal parts of the message." Peabody carefully removed the page and held it a few inches above the flame. Within seconds, printed letters appeared on the page.

Gilly was amazed. "What does it say, Mr. Peabody?"

"That is still a mystery, I'm afraid. The author, who I assume to be Richard Snipes, wasn't as old-fashioned as I first thought. The lemon juice has only leached through part of the way to the next page. But, the impressions of the quill, when I have studied them through my microscope will fill in some of the blanks. At least I hope they will. Then, we will have our message or at least parts of it."

"You were right, Peabody," General Smith exclaimed. "This fellow is brilliant. Now go and get the rest of the message and return to us with the full text as soon as you have it."

Peabody shook his head. "I'm afraid it's not going to be that easy, general. The print revealed by the flame and some of the remaining impressions which will be discovered by my microscope can only yield a series of groupings. Subsets, if you will, of an enigma."

"You mean a coded message, Mr. Peabody," Stricker asserted.

302

"Well yes, in a way, general, it is a coded message. But, a mathematical one dealing with frequency of use based on the given language employed by the author."

"Gibberish, again," Smith cried. "For God's sake man, speak English."

"I will, General Smith, but the message, which is known as a cipher will not. The message is in a foreign tongue, one I am not at all familiar with."

Gilly suddenly remembered something Richard had said to him at the cooperage. It was something about Finno-Ugric languages.

"Mr. Peabody, could the cipher be written in Hungarian?"

*****

Richard had fled on horseback with Sean O'Casey and Liam Daily to a small farm on North Point, about twelve miles east of Baltimore. A ship's gig had been dispatched to retrieve the spies and bring them to the safety of a British sloop-of-war. They had finished their work in Baltimore, even though it had ended up badly due to the attack on Father John.

What the Chief of British Intelligence had hoped for was an erosion of confidence by the American fighting men in their commanders. Generals Smith and Stricker, Commodore Rodgers, and Major Armistead were all targeted for a campaign of rumor and innuendo questioning both their military competency and their personal character. Richard Snipes and the two Irishmen who worked at the Dooley cooperage had done an admirable job up until a few nights ago. They had even succeeded in obtaining some intelligence as to the fighting capabilities and defensive positions of the American forces.

One last piece of intelligence was sent just before the Irishmen had demolished the cooperage. Richard had written the message in his notebook using lemon juice. To further complicate detection, he used a cipher in a foreign language. A language the Chief of Intelligence, Henrik, would appreciate. Admiral Cockburn's intelligence staff had a key to the cipher and would be able to decode it easily. Richard had been very proud of this piece of intelligence.

His dream was to free the slaves. Ever since he was a boy, he felt total disdain for the plight of slaves he had seen working on the tobacco farms of Maryland. It wasn't just the dictates of his Quaker faith. It was something deep inside of him. It was a burning desire to dedicate his life in ending this brutal practice.

From his home in Elizabethtown, Richard established a network of correspondence among prominent anti-slavery advocates even before war was declared against Great Britain. His contacts included bankers, lawyers, businessmen, and a surprising number of public officials. Organization wasn't all that difficult. The Quaker communities in America, especially in Philadelphia, and fellow Quakers throughout Britain, banded together and

304

formed anti-slavery societies on both sides of the Atlantic.

But Richard was much too impulsive to wait for changes that would enable a political solution. He was totally opposed to sending blacks back to Africa as proposed by the American Colonization Society, regardless of the support they received from notables such as Thomas Jefferson, James Madison, and James Monroe. Richard knew many, if not most, of the free blacks in America were adamantly against this as well. Richard needed to be part of a direct offensive against slavery as an American institution.

When he had heard that the British were freeing and training former slaves to fight against their former masters, he knew he had to be a part of it. To his classical mind, it was a pure and noble pursuit of good versus evil.

The United States would drag its feet on the question of slavery for generations, Richard thought. It was an integral cog in the economic wheel of the southern states. Nothing, Richard believed, short of civil war would change the status quo. He did not desire civil war, yet he saw no other recourse.

There was already talk of secession in the northern states and cities. The war against Britain was thought of as unnecessary, even foolhardy. Plans were being laid by northern governors to negotiate a separate peace. The young Quaker construed this would inevitably lead to a war between the states. He concluded that, if there was going to be a civil war, he should take it upon himself to do everything he could to bring a division among the states as soon as possible. To Richard, that meant helping the British and helping them now.

He had voiced extreme anti-slavery sympathies to certain parties in Great Britain and Canada before war was declared. Over the past few years, he had invited a number of anti-slavery advocates to his farm in Maryland – some of them prominent British citizens. After Madison's declaration was narrowly approved by Congress, Richard received a visit from an artist who wished to paint slaves working the tobacco fields. The artist was also an intelligence agent.

From a window of the farmhouse on North Point, Richard saw a light flash on and off coming from just beyond the shore line. It was the signal from the boat that would take them to safety. He motioned for Sean O'Casey and Liam Dailey to go ahead without him. They waited a moment to see if he would change his mind and follow them out the door. He made no effort at an explanation and they didn't press him for one. They really never liked him anyway. They had been paid professional spies for thirty-five years. Richard was an idealist. The only ideal O'Casey and Dailey cared about was money. Richard nudged them out the door and quickly closed it behind them. He couldn't go – not after he had found out about the attack on Father John.

As soon as the two Irishmen had gone, Richard searched the farm house for something he needed. After finding it, he sat on a chair and reached into his jacket pocket. He pulled out a copy of Plato's *Dialogues*. Its subject was the trial and execution of Socrates. He used a pencil to underline some of the words on a particular page, then placed the book on the floor and stood on the chair. There being no hemlock, Richard used the rope he had found. His last thoughts were of the Code of Aquinas his cousin Samuel had endeared himself to. He asked for forgiveness.

*****

Sarika had worked up a good lather. Gilly had ridden his princess at almost a full gallop from Baltimore until he reached the stables where Mr. Pechin's prized horses had been transferred just west of the city. The horses were finished exercising for the day and were being led by the grooms to the temporary stables where they would be washed and fed. Gilly dismounted Sarika and waved to get the attention of a stable boy.

"Are these the Pechin horses?"

"They is, sir. Gettin' them ready for chow right now," the boy informed him.

"Is the Stable Master here?"

"He's in the shed right down this path. I can smell his cookin' from here."

Gilly thanked the boy and led Sarika down the dirt road to a dilapidated shed. There was smoke coming from the chimney. He knocked on the door while trying to catch his breath from his arduous ride. Istvan answered the knock.

"Te jó eg! Gilly Morrison!" Istvan wrapped his thick arms around his protégé. "You have come see me, igen!"

"Hello, Istvan. It's so good to see you again." Istvan saw that Gilly was as sweaty as his horse. "Come, Gilly Morrison. Sit and eat. I make favorite dish." The Hungarian called for the stable boy and told him to take care of Sarika.

Gilly took in the delicious aroma of goulash and helped himself to a seat at the small table. Istvan hurriedly placed bowls and spoons, milk, fresh bread and butter on the table. Gilly was about to explain the nature of his visit, but his stomach could not resist the simple feast before him. He ate and drank with relish.

"Ah, you no lose appetite. This is jó. I see you walk better, too. The Princess take care of you like child. I knew from beginning when you say she too feisty. Now, look at you and horse. Together, you make team."

"She's everything I've ever dreamed of, Istvan. You were right about her all along." Gilly wiped his mouth and smiled. "And you, Stable Master. You look well, too. Your horses are all safe here?"

"For time being, Gilly Morrison. We hear rumors. British everywhere, they say. So, if true, and enemy is everywhere, we stay here until we find where everywhere is."

They both laughed. Then Gilly's tone became serious. "I've come to fetch you and take you with me back to Baltimore, my friend. And we need to leave as soon as Sarika is rested."

Istvan saw that Gilly was not jesting. "Why, Gilly Morrison? Why you take me, old man, on road at night?"

Gilly reached across the table and grasped Istvan's iron-like hands in his. "Because, my friend, your new country needs you and she needs you right now."

Istvan had to think about this for a moment. It had been over a decade since an army had the need of his services. It was when Anton had first joined the Hungarian Hussars. Istvan was a different man then. He had a title and a great commission. Back then he still had hopes and dreams.

"Then, Gilly Morrison, while we travel I need tell you who I really am."

They rose just after midnight and saddled their horses for a long and difficult night ride back to Baltimore. Fortunately, there was a cloudless sky and a bright half-moon to help light the road. Along the way, Istvan told Gilly about his life in Hungary before he immigrated to America. Dawn was just breaking when they arrived at headquarters on Hampstead Hill.

Samuel was serving coffee to Generals Smith and Stricker, and Commodore Rodgers. The commanders were being briefed by their aids-de-camp. The small office was filled to capacity and, with the constant comings and goings of messengers and the din of independent discussions, seemed as busy as a marketplace. Mr. Peabody had been up for hours working with his microscope filling in some of the remaining letters of the cipher that the lemon juice had not exposed. He anxiously waited for Gilly's interpreter.

Rodgers was curious about something. He placed his cup of coffee on the desk and motioned with his head for Samuel to approach him. His secretary dutifully refilled the commodore's cup.

"Samuel," Rodgers whispered in his ear. "Yesterday, why did Gilly suggest that the code might be written in Hungarian?"

"Because, sir," Samuel whispered back, "my cousin was an accomplished linguist. Lately, he has been studying Finno-Ugric languages and dialects. Hungarian was of particular interest to him."

Rodgers nodded his head showing he had understood. The commodore knew his secretary had received a large blow when the news came to light that Richard was a traitor and a spy. Rodger's did not want to add to Samuel's discomfort after everything that had happened.

Gilly led Istvan into Rodger's office. Although the road's dirt and dust from their long ride showed on both of them, Istvan was a sight to

310

behold. All three commanders and their subalterns stopped their conversations and stared in amazement at the man who had just walked through the door.

Istvan was dressed in the uniform of a Hungarian cavalry colonel. The military men in the room recognized certain aspects of Istvan's dress. After all, the French, Germans and Hessians, Russians, Austrians, Poles, and even the British and American Armies had duplicated parts of the uniform because it was the personification of what all cavalry officers imagined themselves to be. It wasn't just colorful and well-tailored, it bespoke the swaggering, gallant, and audaciously handsome Hungarian Hussar: black-felt shako hat with diamond plate, leather visor and black cockade; a short-waisted green jacket with a high, scarlet red collar and cuffs; frilly, white linen shirt; creamy-white leather sheath housing a curved sabre with a brass hilt; skin-tight blue pants tucked into short, black-leather riding boots. This was pure military romance come to life, and Istvan's oiled, coal-gray handlebar mustache completed the costume and gave him the aura of a king.

He stepped, gracefully, into the office, removed his hat, smartly clicked his heels, and performed an elaborate bow. General Smith opened his mouth and was about to say something, but nothing came out. It didn't matter. Everyone in the room had their mouths agape as well.

"Gentlemen," Gilly said, proudly. "May I introduce Colonel Istvan Gèza, Master of the Horse to his majesty, Franz Joseph Karl, Holy Roman Emperor, Emperor of Germany and Austria, Apostolic King of Hungary and

Bohemia."

Istvan said nothing. He stood at attention like a statue. He would only speak to authority when directed to.

Rodgers rose from his chair and bowed. Unlike Generals Smith and Stricker, the commodore had traveled a good deal in his career and was familiar with the protocol and delicate temperament of European officers. "Colonel, you are most welcome here. If I can speak for the commanding officers … " Rodgers glanced at Smith and Stricker who nodded in agreement " … I want to extend our humble gratitude for offering your services to our armed forces. I am afraid we are in no position to offer you anything in the way of a commission. That would be up to our superiors in Washington. However, if you choose to volunteer your talents, we would consider ourselves more than fortunate that an officer of your status, with such impeccable credentials, would grace us with his august company."

Istvan was more than pleased. "I humbly place myself at service to your armed forces and to his excellency, President Madison. Please, convey to him my personal affection and esteem."

Rodgers civilly nodded his head trying not to smile. "When next I see the president, I will inform him of your sentiments. For now, colonel, if it is convenient, I believe our intelligence officer would like to have a word with you. Mr. Peabody, please take the floor." Peabody stood and waited for all of the messengers and aides-de-camp to leave the room before he approached Istvan.

"Colonel, I want to personally thank you for your assistance in this matter. Has Gilly filled you in on the details?"

"What you call details, I think I know. You have zeró?"

Mr. Peabody looked around the room, somewhat embarrassed. "I have a cipher, which I believe may be written in your language. Can you help us with this?" Peabody handed Istvan the page from Richard's notebook.

"Is zeró, igen? In my Hungarian, Mr. Peabody, cipher is zeró, is nulla. In English, mean nothing. You look at paper, you see nothing but letters. Letters make no words. They just letters."

Peabody smiled, "Yes, colonel, that's right. It means nothing unless you can decipher its meaning. May I ask, colonel, if you have any experience with deciphering coded messages?"

"Igen, Mr. Peabody. As Master of Horse for Emperor Franz Joseph, all couriers with dispatches come to stables for horses. Captured enemy messengers come with horses, too. We check horses for hidden dispatches – hidden in saddle, in reins, in stirrups, even in or under horse shoes. I see many secret messages. I know French, Prussian, Russian, all Croatian languages, so I try to decipher for army."

"Very good, colonel. Please try your luck with this message. Would you do this for us?"

"Igen. Istvan decipher for you. I need pencil and time."

Rodgers offered Istvan his desk. "Take all the time you need, colonel."

Gilly and the commanders left the room to Mr. Peabody and Istvan to crack the code. Samuel looked up from his desk. "Sir," he said to Rodgers, "do you think they will be able to make anything out of my cousin's notebook?" There was a trace of hope in Samuel's eyes as he asked this question. Perhaps, the cipher would help alleviate some of the damage Richard had done to the American cause and help restore a portion of his family's lost honor.

"I really don't know, I ... " Rodgers checked his opinion when he saw the expectation in his secretary's face. " ... Well, you can't win battles with doubts running through your mind. Let's just say that the well-groomed Hungarian colonel will bring us some well-deserved luck."

Chapter 19: Cups and Saucers

Father John winced when he opened his eyes. The pain just to move his eyelids was intense, and the sunlight in the room added to his misery. He saw Desiree sitting in his leather chair with her eyes closed and her hands folded between her breasts in silent prayer.

If Father John could smile he would have. Sure, the fervent look upon Desiree's face as she bowed her head in prayer made him feel like smiling but that wasn't all. He knew he had lost consciousness. For how long he didn't know. He knew he was lying in his own bed and that his bed was now located in his study. Somehow he felt good about these things. As if whatever happened to him was in some way a blessing. He remembered, vaguely, walking along the docks of Fells Point and looking at the stars. He recalled something about the Dooley Cooperage ...

315

Desiree opened her eyes, looked at the bed and could not breathe. She wanted to shout but nothing came out of her mouth. She dashed to the door, came back to the bed, kissed Father John's hand, ran to the door again, came back and kissed the locket, then scurried out of the room to tell Mrs. Pickersgill, Mrs. Dougherty, Mrs. Callahan, and anyone else within earshot "He's awake!"

*****

While Gilly waited for the cipher to be broken, he went in search of the Smith brothers. He found them under the lean-to having dinner.

"Master Morrison, come in out the sun," Elijah insisted. "Ethan and I were just sittin' here talkin' about what happened. We're awful sorry about Father John."

"The cooperage, too," Ethan added. "Any idea who did these terrible things?"

Gilly sat cross-legged down on the ground in front of them. He picked up a piece of straw and played with it in his mouth. "Boys, what if I told you that Sean O'Casey and Liam Dailey did it?"

The Smith brothers stared at each other in horror. Ethan began shaking his head. "It can't be true. Why, Elijah and I took to the two of them right off. They was regular fellas. We even tossed a few tankards back with them guys. I got Sean into the city brigade – that wasn't easy neither. They're

316

the best militia in the state. Elijah got Liam a place at the fort to take over for Samuel. We did everythin' we could to help Sean and Liam fit right in … "

Ethan's voice trailed off as the truth of the situation dawned on both of the Smith brothers, their culpability becoming apparent of their faces. Gilly continued gnawing on his piece of straw. "Don't fret boys. They made a fool of me, too. It wasn't just them either. Richard Snipes was the brains behind everything. He duped us and dragged his own cousin through the mud. Samuel took it pretty hard."

"Richard," Elijah whispered with disgust. "Richard, Sean, and Liam, they made us look like a horse's ass, didn't they? We just thought they wanted to pitch in and help like everybody else. Instead, they used us. We were blind men. We *let* them use us, and now Father John's payin' the price for us bein' so stupid."

Ethan tried to reason it all out. "Master Morrison, if they tricked Samuel, who's as smart as a book, no wonder they pulled the wool over our eyes. But, why did they hurt Father John? He never hurt nobody."

"They didn't know it was him, Ethan. They probably didn't know who it was. Father John was just in the wrong place. It could have been any one of us." Gilly grabbed a saddle bag sitting beside him and rested his head against it.

"How's the padre doin', Master Morrison, is he gonna make it?"

317

"Elijah, I just can't say either way. It's real bad. Doc Williams said he should be dead. They hit him that hard."

They were silent after that. Gilly's eyelids felt heavy in the afternoon heat. The long night ride with Istvan had caught up with him. He nodded off, the straw dangling from his teeth.

"Let him sleep, brother," Ethan said. "Looks like he needs it after everything he's been through. Let's go find Samuel and see if we can cheer him up."

In his dream, Gilly was standing beside a newly dug grave. It must have rained terribly the night before because the ground was thick with mud. There were many other graves, also fresh and just as muddy. No markings identified the dead.

The air was choked with smoke and gunpowder. Gilly could hear the haunting tattoo of military drummers far off in the distance. He saw the victory flag flying over Fort McHenry at half-mast.

Gilly had been crying, but there were no more tears to be shed. He felt guilty. "I should have warned you," he said to the grave. "I should have warned everybody. I wanted to. But no one was listening to me. Then they said it was all my fault. They said if I didn't write about it nothing bad would have happened. They said I riled up a hornet's nest."

Gilly collapsed on his knees, squirting mud up into his face and eyes.

318

"I didn't mean to do it. I didn't mean to let loose the hornets. I'm sorry. I'm so very sorry!" Something was kicking him in the leg. "That's great! Now their kicking me!"

"Sorry 'bout that, mister. I didn't mean to disturb your nap - you Morrison?" Gilly shaded his eyes with his hand and looked at the soldier grinning down on him.

"I'm Morrison."

"Brass says you better get your ass up to headquarters. If I was you, mister, I'd oblige 'em. They're pretty big brass!"

Istvan and Mr. Peabody had done it. The cipher was broken. Gilly ran past the sentry and slid on the sand sprinkled on the office floor to keep it dry. Everyone was there to hear the news.

"Gilly Morrison, that no way enter presence of superiors!" Istvan admonished him.

"Sorry, Istvan - err, colonel. I came as soon as I could. What does it say? Mr. Peabody, what's in the message?"

"We were about to find out when you barged your way in here." Rodgers said, smiling. "Go on, Mr. Peabody. Read it to us."

Mr. Peabody straightened his wire rim glasses around his ears and cleared his throat:

319

"American forces plan scuttling merchant vessels in harbor behind gun boats and barges mentioned in previous message. Vessels will be deliberately sunk after British bombardment begins on Fort McHenry and if said attack appears successful. This will prohibit British naval ships from entering main channel. Suggest sabotaging American merchant shipping at anchor before commencing attack on Baltimore."

"Then, they are going to attack us!" Gilly shouted. "This is definite proof, isn't it?"

Rodgers slammed his fist on the desk. "Damn it, Gilly! Keep your voice down. Richard and the Irishmen weren't the only spies among us."

"No they weren't, commodore," General Stricker agreed. "And this is not definitive proof of anything, Gilly. It merely shows the extent of their planning should they *decide* to attack. It also demonstrates the breadth of their espionage activities against this city. How else could Richard have gotten this information if he didn't have at least one more agent working in our very midst?"

"You're right, John," General Smith said. "The plan to scuttle our shipping was only known to the commanders, including Armistead. So the long arm of British intelligence has reached into this very room."

"There was someone else who knew of this plan besides us," Rodgers said, as he rested his long legs up atop his desk and stared directly at Gilly.

"I knew of this plan, gentlemen," Gilly confessed, "only because it was my idea."

"What?" General Smith exclaimed. "What do you mean your idea, Gilly?"

"I mentioned it to Major Armistead when I visited the fort for an interview some weeks back. The major told me not to tell anyone else about it and that he would suggest it to the commanders. Upon my word of honor, gentlemen, I swear to you I have never told one soul about this idea since that day."

Mr. Peabody coughed, conspicuously. "May I, gentlemen?" General Smith nodded.

"Gilly, did you ever suggest this to anyone else before your interview with Major Armistead? Perhaps to Mr. Pechin?"

"No. The idea never really occurred to me until after I got to the fort and was looking at the channel. After I proposed it to Major Armistead I promised him that everything we talked about in the manner of military preparedness would be kept in the strictest confidence. I knew this is what I ought to do."

"Then, you never brought this up afterwards, maybe in a casual way or, since it was such an insightful suggestion, as an innocent boast to Desiree Pechin?"

Gilly had enough. He stepped in Peabody's direction with clenched fists.

"Ha! Ho! Ho!" Istvan laughed. Everyone in the room, including Gilly and Peabody turned their faces to the elegantly dressed Hungarian. "So, Gilly Morrison, you have new princess, eh? Ha! Sarika must be very jealous," he said musically wagging a finger in Gilly's direction.

The colonel marched to the center of the room and faced the commanders. "I know boy, Gilly Morrison, like I know horse. I break cipher for you, for my new country, and for President Madison. But, I break neck of any man who not trust boy's word. End of discussion, igen?"

Mr. Peabody faced Gilly and extended his hand. "As I choose not to have my neck broken, please take my hand and forgive me for any aspersion I may have cast upon you, sir. You have been more than helpful to me throughout my investigation since the very beginning. We'll find this other spy in due time, Gilly."

Gilly beamed a winning smile and whistled through his teeth. "I'm sorry, too, Mr. Peabody. I know you're only doing your job."

"This is jó," Istvan said. "Now, gentlemen, since Hungarian cipher

322

broken, I wish inspect American cavalry and offer humble assistance. I wish to talk to horse and men."

"By all means, colonel," General Smith said with relief. "Talk to as many horses … " the general paused for just a moment, somewhat confused, " … and men as you like. Now, gentlemen, let's discuss what we can do to make sure our merchant fleet stays afloat, where it belongs for the present, in Baltimore harbor."

*****

Thomas Swann awoke with the sea gulls minutes before daybreak. He was a paid military observer serving at Point Lookout, on the very southern tip of St. Mary's County, in Maryland. It was a good place to observe any shipping sailing up and down the Chesapeake. From his post, Swann could see the eastern shore of the bay quite clearly. Since Point Lookout lies at the confluence of the bay and the Potomac River, an observer could effectively monitor enemy movements threatening Washington, Annapolis, and Baltimore.

Swann lit a fire and put a kettle on the grating to brew some tea. Then he gently kicked his cat. "Get up, Missy. If I got to go to work then you do, too." He bent down and petted her sleepy face. "You're a lazy hussy … yeah … that's my good girl." The cat purred in appreciation.

Missy was his sole companion. If he wasn't talking to her, he would have been talking to himself. Talking to the cat was at least more sociable. Swann hadn't seen much action lately. Last year, a British force of two to three thousand infantry landed on Point Lookout to raid American coastal villages and free the slaves. Swann had to move inland until the British foraging parties departed. Since then, Swann had little, if anything, to report to his superior, Secretary of War John Armstrong, in Washington.

He yawned and stretched out his arms. The eastern sky was a bit brighter now. He could see the outline of land that was the far shore across the Chesapeake. The dawn was slowly making its debut for the day, arrayed in a golden haze. Last night, the sunset turned the sky into a fiery-red furnace. Swann giggled to himself remembering the old saw: "red sky at morning, sailors take warning; red sky at night, sailors' delight."

"Ha!" Swann laughed. "They don't know anything, them sailor boys, do they Missy? Smells like rain to me."

The kettle started to hiss. He poured the boiling water into his tea pot and added a couple of scoops of leaves. While it steeped, Swann took his spyglass and swept it over the bay from north to south. There was enough daylight now to inspect the water.

Swann gulped. "Missy, you ain't never gonna believe this."

*****

Desiree ran outside the rectory door as Gilly dismounted Sarika.

"Darling, oh my darling, he's conscious! Father John's eyes are opened!"

"What!" Gilly exclaimed. "Dez, is he all right, I mean in his head, is he all there?"

"I hope so. Doc Williams is with him now. Come on, darling, let's see."

Desiree took no notice of the bags under Gilly's eyes and the caked-on road dust that soiled his trousers and turned Sarika's mane and tail from white to leather-brown. In turn, he didn't notice her disheveled hair and red-rimmed eyes. They ran into the rectory and entered the study hand-in-hand, happy at the news.

Doctor Williams was carefully administering laudanum mixed with brandy and water to Father John. He glanced at Gilly and Desiree as they came into the study.

"You two need a bath, a change of clothes, and some sleep. See that you get it, starting with the bath." The couple, unaware of their physical appearance, looked at each other and shrugged.

"How's he doing, Doc?" Gilly asked.

"He's in immense pain. I've given him some of the strongest opiates I have in my possession after filling his gullet with as much water as possible. The opiate will allow him to rest. He's quite alert, or will be for a few minutes until the laudanum takes effect. If you have anything of import to tell him, do so now." Williams looked at them sternly. "That means it has to be of the utmost importance or don't bother to talk to him at all, understood?"

They shook their heads in unison. Father John also understood. He stared at Gilly severely. He desperately wanted to communicate something. His eyes were pleading for recognition. Desiree noticed immediately.

"Darling, he's trying to tell you something. Look at his eyes. They're begging you to do something."

Gilly approached the bed and laid his hand upon Father John's chest. Inadvertently, he touched the locket. He lifted it in front of Father John's eyes. The priest blinked.

"Father, do you want me to take away this locket?" Father John blinked again. Doctor Williams backed away as Gilly undid the clasp. A look of contentment appeared on Father John's face. His eyes took on a glassy, dreamlike quality. He closed his eyes and breathed deeply before falling asleep.

"It must have been the locket," Desiree offered. "Did you see the change in his expression the moment you removed it?"

"Yeah, Dez, he became calm the second it was lifted off his chest."

"He did nothing of the kind," the doctor stated flatly. "The opium just now filled his brain and induced him back to a comatose state."

"Oh, my Lord, doctor," Desiree protested.

"Not to worry, young lady. This time the coma is controlled by the chemical from the poppy seed. He'll rest until some strength comes back to him, unless other complications develop. But, nothing medicine has done, either from the Susquehannock or from my little bag of tricks, has brought him back to us. In my professional medical opinion, it was the prayers I heard coming from the church today that brought him back to us. I said last night that was our only option. I stand by that diagnosis."

Williams walked to the door. "Do as I advised," he ordered Desiree. "Go home and sleep. Then come back to the rectory to relieve Mrs. Dougherty and then Mrs. Pickersgill in turn."

Gilly and Desiree walked outside together. Gilly held the locket in his hand. He stopped, put it around his head, and tucked in into his blouse.

"The locket is yours, then Gilly?"

"No. It's on loan. It belongs to Istvan, you know, the Hungarian who's in charge of your father's stables? It was a present to him from his mother." Gilly explained the history of the locket and how it ended up around the priest's neck. He also told her about Richard and the cipher, his long ride to bring Istvan back to Baltimore, and how Istvan had come to his defense earlier today at headquarters.

"I knew it had to do with someone's mother. I had no idea it represented so much to so many people. I'm glad Father John wanted you to have it back." She turned and looked at the rectory. "It seems the locket has done its job in there."

"Yeah, Dez, it sure did. I think Istvan's mother would be proud of what it did for Father John."

"Now, about Mr. Peabody," Desiree said, her temper riled. "You can tell him from me that, even if I knew about the plan to scuttle ships or some such nonsense, I would never betray a confidence. We Pechins are good at keeping secrets."

Gilly took her into his arms. "There's one secret this particular Pechin is going to have a hard time keeping to herself." He kissed her with a passion not usually seen on Market Street.

Desiree was going to scold him for making such a scene in public, but she was having a difficult time catching her breath.

"Now, go right home Mistress Pechin and lay those pretty curls down on a nice, soft pillow. I'll picture you doing just that when I finally close my eyes tonight." He kissed her again. This time she forgot she was even on Market Street.

*****

When Gilly opened the door to the little house of Thames Street he smelled goulash. Before leaving headquarters, he asked Samuel to escort Istvan back to the Dooley home where he was invited to stay for as long as he wished while he was in the city. Istvan wasted no time preparing the evening meal.

William Pechin was better than his word. Gilly had not even begun his journey to see Commodore Barney yet the house was already neatly cleaned and nearly repaired. Pechin even had some of Mrs. Dooley's furnishings replaced - including the cherished Pillar and Scroll shelf clock, from Plymouth Connecticut. How Pechin managed to find one in Baltimore was beyond Gilly's imagination.

Gilly smiled at his Hungarian friend as he opened the kitchen door. The savory aroma of veal and paprika filled his nose and moistened his mouth.

"How is horse, Princess?" Istvan asked.

"She's fed and snug for the night out back," Gilly said.

"How is girl, princess?"

"She's ... " Gilly found it difficult to find the right words to express his love.

"She's still in here?" Istvan said, finishing Gilly's sentence as he pointed to the center of his chest. Gilly just smiled. In fact throughout the whole meal he found it hard to do anything else.

After dinner, Gilly and Istvan shared their views, alternately, on horses and girls. Eventually, their thoughts turned to the war.

"Entrenchments on hill not good enough," Istvan maintained. "Need more men, better trained; need more cannon, better men to sight targets; need sabre for cavalry, horsemen no have sabre. British like to flank weak points in line. Scare militia with bayonet charge."

"I know, Istvan. The commanders have tried but they don't have much to work with. It's a good defensive position though, don't you think?"

Istvan frowned. "Americans must watch English tricks. British have navy. With navy they move army. If wind good, they move army quickly anywhere they want. Istvan show you." He got up from the table and went to the cupboard. He came back with some wooden spoons and forks, also some porcelain cups and saucers.

"Saucers like cities." He placed the saucers lengthwise along the table one at a time. "Here, Baltimore saucer." He moved down the table pretending it to be farther south and a little east. "Here, Annapolis saucer." Down at the end of the table and more toward the center was the final saucer. "Here, Washington saucer." Then he held up the spoons and forks in his hands. "Spoons like artillery - these all your cannon, not much cannon. Forks

330

like infantry – each fork a brigade." He spread the spoons and forks around the saucers.

Istvan held up the cups. "Cups like English ships. They carry English army." He moved the cups up and down the length of the table as if they were sailing the Chesapeake, then raised his bushy eyebrows. "No jó, Gilly Morrison. Cups move up, cups move down. Saucers no move. Spoon and forks move slow."

"What about our cavalry? They, at least, can move faster than infantry on foot."

Istvan threw up his hands in frustration. "Cavalry no have sabre." He looked down at the table and shook his head. "No jó. American army spread all over table. Cups can float and move, Gilly Morrison, saucers cannot."

*****

Thomas Swann cursed Missy because she insisted on playing with the leather strap of his spyglass as he was attempting to number and identify the massive enemy fleet. He saw ships-of-the-line, transports, bomb ships, frigates, schooners, sloops-of-war, and others. Finally, he stopped counting. He fired off a note saying there were at least forty-six ships and gave it to a dispatch rider. Point Lookout was seventy miles away from the nation's capital.

Chapter 20: Bladensburg

Mixed reports were coming in at a rapid pace from Washington. William Pechin, sitting at his desk and Gilly, hovering over his shoulder, were studying a map of the western shore of the bay.

"The couriers must be digging a trench from here to the Potomac and back again. They ride up and down the turnpike as if they were on a string like a yo-yo," Pechin said. "And every report contradicts the one before. If there's one thing I've learned being a newspaperman all these years is not to trust a damn thing. Not even if it's been collaborated by two different sources."

He stretched his neck and double chin to glare behind him at Gilly. "Son, if you hear something a dozen times I swear you'll hear it a dozen different ways. The trick is to hear it from the horse's mouth. To hear the news direct from *the authority* responsible – not an underling or a friend of a friend who happens to know a distant cousin. Get what I mean?"

"Yes, sir. You mean never report a rumor."

"Arrg! That's not the half of it. I mean never go to print even if your source is the president himself."

Gilly was confused. "If you can't believe the president, who can you believe?"

"No one! Remember, the president is primarily a politician. Office holders, and seekers of the same, lie as a matter of course. They have to or they'd never get elected. People expect them to. Besides, the president's information is only as good as the people who report to him. Most of them are politicians, too. So don't trust anybody who feeds off of the public trough for a living."

"Then, Mr. Pechin, what is it you want me to do?"

Pechin pointed his finger on the map, down the Baltimore-Washington Turnpike. "You see here, Gilly? I want you to go to Bladensburg, just north of the capital. From there you can get news going to and from the string on the yo-yo. You can also find out where Commodore Barney is and then go and talk to him."

Gilly had planned on going further east, meeting up with Barney's

Flotilla closer to the bay before the incident at the cooperage delayed his departure. But, now things had changed.

Pechin traced his finger on the map. "Word is the British fleet is sailing into both the Potomac and Patuxent Rivers – at least part of the fleet. No one knows for sure. Point Lookout reported as many as fifty ships congregated at the mouth of the Potomac of few days ago. Since then they've dispersed. Sending ships this way and that could all be part of a plan to stretch out our defenses. They could hit Washington, Annapolis, or even, God forbid, Baltimore."

"Like cups and saucers," Gill thought aloud.

"Like what?"

"Nothing, sir."

"Well, then talk sense. I want you on the road to Bladensburg by tomorrow. You'll be near enough to us to come back if you have to. You'll be close to the capital if you have to go there. Plus, from Bladensburg, you can make inquiries and try to find Barney and get a story. That's the horse's mouth I talked about.

"Keep abreast of the dispatch riders – where they're coming from and what their destinations are. Talk to the soldiers. Not the ones going into battle, because soldiers aren't told anything reliable when they might come face to face with the enemy. Talk to the ones coming *from* an engagement.

Now that's news and it's real.

"Send reports back to me with the couriers. I'll pay top dollar for good information – make sure the riders know this. Stay at Bladensburg for as long as you deem necessary. You'll be the eyes and ears of *The American*. Take the coach so you don't kill your horse – your ... "

"My Princess."

"Your Princess - have her tied onto the rear of the coach without a saddle. She's comes from good stock and will serve you well when you need her. And, you're going to need her to get back to me when things get hot."

Pechin looked down again at the map. He let his temper get the best of him and slammed his fist down on the desk in complete frustration. "If only we had more time," he whispered. He stood up and put his hand on Gilly's shoulder. "Son, is there any service I can do for you while you're away?"

Gilly didn't have to think on the question. "About Father John, Mr. Pechin, would you ...

"He'll have everything he needs. You have my word."

"Desiree ... "

"I now have a daughter a father can be well proud of thanks to you and Moranvillè. Still, you know how stubborn she is. It'll take an army just to keep her in the city and not follow you down the turnpike. But, she'll be busy

335

nursing Father John and," Pechin raised his eyebrows, "this morning she mentioned something about a hospital."

The next morning, Gilly sat down at the bar at Ole' Sally's and ordered breakfast. Sarika had already been fed her favorite Timothy hay at the Dooley house and was now tethered outside to a hitching post. The palomino sensed an urgency in her prince. She also saw the traffic clogging the streets from Fells Point to Old Town. A rifle battalion, five hundred strong, and two artillery companies towing four and six pound cannons rolled down Market Street. The militiamen were part of the 5th Maryland, known to folks in the city as "the dandy regiment" because they were comprised of affluent young men. They were marching to fife and drum, dressed in blue jackets with cotton-white cross-belts, and singing merrily about "the girl I left behind me."

Gilly heard the familiar tune while enjoying a fried ham steak, crispy potatoes, and dipping his bread into two large egg yolks. Sally poured him another cup of coffee. "I hope they'll be singin' like that when they come marchin' back." She glanced out the window and laughed. "Just look at the crowds of people cheerin' them on. If I didn't know better, I'd a thought it was the Fourth-of-July."

Sally was old enough to remember the last war. She folded her heavy forearms across the bar. "Why do the young ones fall for it, do you suppose?"

Gilly wiped his mouth with a napkin and slurped from his mug. "You mean the soldiers?"

"I never see the old ones singin' and that's a fact, Gilly. I suppose it's always been that way. Why, it wasn't too many years ago my Jerry marched down Market Street singin' like that. It was Bob Dooley, the connivin' scum of a man who talked my Jerry into joinin' up in the fight against Cornwallis. Told him he'd make a fortune bein' a scout for General Washington."

Sally wiped a tear from her eye with a swollen, arthritic hand. "He never made a fortune, poor Jerry. He died of the dysentery they said. He's buried somewhere near Cowpens. But, he was as proud as any of the boys marchin' down the street this mornin' on their way to God knows where. Saints preserve 'em."

Gilly paid for his breakfast and gave Sally a big kiss on the cheek. Outside, he patted Sarika on her nose before walking down to the rectory at St. Patrick's. He had hoped to see Desiree there but she had not yet arrived. Mrs. Pickersgill was attending to Father John when he knocked gently on the door of the study.

"Well if it isn't the famous writer himself who's come to see us," Mary joked. "If you've come to have your confession heard, you're late. We've just had a breakfast fit for King George – chicken broth and rum – spoon fed and swallowed courtesy of myself and Mrs. Callahan's kitchen."

Gilly grinned, showing almost all of his white teeth. Mrs. Pickersgill smiled as she took her tray and rose to leave the room. "You two boys have a nice chat. Mind you, Father John, don't let the conversation be too one sided. This young buck has the gift of the Irish if the sky-blue eyes and the curly red locks are any indication."

Mrs. Pickersgill left the room but quickly ducked her head back in with a warning. "Himself is a bit uncomfortable at the moment. Doc Williams will be here shortly to dose the poppy seed. Don't be long, Gilly. He's a might sore from swallowing the broth and needs to shut his eyes."

Underneath his bandages, Father John managed something of a smile. His face and neck were still painfully swollen. Gilly took a seat in the leather chair.

"It's started." Gilly didn't need to explain. "I'm being sent to Bladensburg to cover the story. Before I leave, I wanted to talk to you about what happened that night at the cooperage. Are you up to it, Father? Or should I wait until I return and you're better."

The good priest blinked his eyes once, his signal for "yes," then held a steady gaze. Gilly took a deep breath. "It was the new hires, Sean O'Casey and Liam Dailey. On the day they attacked you, I received a letter from Michael Dooley telling me that these same men, who were originally from Cork City, in Ireland, had given false testimony against Michael's grandfather. Bob Dooley said these men were paid British informants. Their sworn statements led to the execution of the grandfather and, untimely, the death of his wife from a broken heart. For some reason, I don't know why after all these years, they desecrated the Dooley family Bible when they tore apart the house on Thames Street. That's a story only the Dooley's will be able to explain to us.

"Bob Dooley and Michael's father left Ireland and finally settled here, in Fells Point, as you well know. Michael told me his Uncle Bob was a drunkard and a brawler. This information might help to shed some light on why he became that way.

"Two brothers, Father - one who lives by the code and one who has refused its precepts – this tells me just how much someone has to willingly apply the code in order for it to work. In his letter, Michael told me that his uncle has started talking about it and wishes he could finally adopt it into his life. That, in and of itself, may be a miracle.

"Anyway, O'Casey and Dailey tried to kill you. The civilian in charge of military intelligence here in Baltimore told me they probably didn't know it was you who came into the cooperage that night. He said that you were simply a means to an end, which was to cover up their tracks leaking vital information to the British and spreading horrific rumors about the officers in charge of our city's defenses.

"For all we know, they've gone back to the British. But, there's one thing more you need to know. The Irish coopers weren't acting alone. There were at least two other persons who were involved in the treachery. One, we now know, was Richard Snipes, Samuel's cousin." Father John closed his eyes; a different sort of pain swept across his complexion.

"Richard used me, the Smith brothers, and Samuel to do his dirty work. We were all so involved in what we wished to do that we never noticed. His reasoning was that if he helped the British, somehow he would help end slavery in America. Samuel said Richard was adamant in his opposition to slavery and would do anything to effect abolition. I'm quite certain that had Richard known it would hurt you, he would never have provided the keys to the cooperage to the thugs who did this to you."

Father John opened his eyes and blinked again. Whether it was in agreement with Gilly's sentiments was impossible to tell. Perhaps, Gilly thought, it was a general absolution for all parties involved.

"Before I go Father, would you please give me your blessing?" Extending his index finger, the priest made the sign of the cross. Gilly blessed himself. He withdrew Istvan's locket from under his shirt and kissed it. Father John blessed this also.

*****

The coachman secured Sarika to the rear of the carriage and Gilly climbed aboard and took his seat. To his chagrin, he was the lone passenger. "Everybody's going in the opposite direction," the driver yelled to him through the hatch below the box seat after they had gotten underway. "You and the militia are the only fools heading south!"

340

"How long until we reach Bladensburg?"

"Who knows? The turnpike is full of soldiers and provision wagons going south and anybody with a brain in their head moving north."

"What's your name?"

"Name's Eustace ... you Morrison?"

"Yea. Call me Gilly."

"Wasn't going to make this trip, Gilly. I kind of figured on staying away from John Bull, if you know what I mean. But the boss tells me you're a *special fare*. He says William Pechin was going to buy this rig outright if I didn't drive this team today."

Gilly laughed. The way Eustace called him a "special fare" was almost comical. He felt like saying he was just an orphan on a picnic ride, but held his tongue. "I'll tell you what, Eustace. You get me and my horse to Bladensburg as fast as possible, and I'll see to it Mr. Pechin makes it worth your while."

"Say no more, Gilly. But I've got to keep in back of the militia until they make camp for the night. It's no use trying to get around them. Tomorrow morning we can go on ahead to Mike's Tavern. That's about twenty-five miles. Mike cooks up a mean Irish stew and he has the best cider anywhere. We'll spend the night there and be well in front of the militia all

341

the way to Bladensburg. Does that suit you, Gilly?"

"Okay by me, Eustace. I'm getting hungry already."

About five miles outside the city, the militia came to a halt and made camp. Eustace pulled over to the side of the road while Gilly went to see what was wrong. He found the commanding officer bawling out orders on how the encampment was to be set up.

"Colonel!" Gilly shouted. "Why have you stopped?"

"Orders! Damn them!" the colonel complained.

"But you're supposed to be on the way to Bladensburg in case the British attack Washington."

Lieutenant Colonel Joseph Sterett, a middle-aged farmer, who Gilly had seen coming to and from headquarters looked at Gilly with skepticism. "Who are you?"

"Gilly Morrison. I'm with *The American*."

"Morrison...yea, I've read your stuff. Pretty good stuff, too. You going to report on the invasion for the newspaper?"

"Yes, colonel, anything of interest you can tell me will be helpful. If you want, I'll keep your name out of it."

The colonel looked around him to make sure none of his

subordinates were within hearing distance. "It's this damned Winder ... you know ... the guy Madison made a Brigadier General?"

"Sure. He's was put in charge of the defenses of Washington and Baltimore. The commanders in Baltimore, as you know, don't think much of him."

"That's the one. This morning, he sends us orders, hot from Washington, you know what I mean?" Gilly nodded his head. "We're to form the regiment and get down the turnpike to Bladensburg like our life depended on it. We're supposed to join up with General Stansbury's brigade who left before we did. A few minutes ago, a dispatch rider hands me a marked satchel – an official bag. I open it and I'll be damned. Now, Winder tells me we're to slow down. To take our good old time getting to Bladensburg. This morning it was get down here quick; now it's the opposite. The only thing I can think of is that maybe Washington isn't really the target. Maybe it's Baltimore or Annapolis. Who the hell knows?"

"Cups and saucers," Gilly said underneath his breath. "Thanks colonel, I'll see you in Bladensburg." Before Eustace got underway, Gilly flagged down a courier riding to Baltimore. He gave him a note to be delivered to the editor of *The American*. The courier would be well paid for his trouble.

Even though they didn't arrive at Mike's tavern until after midnight, Gilly had Eustace harness the team well before dawn. After a hard ride they

343

finally reached the picturesque village of Bladensburg nestled on the eastern side of the farthest reaches of the Potomac. But, nobody was there.

Eustace drove his coach up to Main Street. The neat brick houses and the few shops in town were empty. Gilly got out and looked around. "There's plenty of tracks that lead over here." He pointed to the river where a wooden bridge crossed the shallow waters of the Potomac. "That must have been the Maryland Brigade under General Stansbury we heard was well ahead of the boys from Baltimore we left with on Sunday. Looks like most of the townsfolk high tailed it out of here when they heard the news the British might be on the way. After what the redcoats did to the other towns up and down the bay, I can't blame them for leaving."

"Hey, Gilly," Eustace said. "There's a livery stable up the road apiece. My company uses them to get fresh mounts. I'm taking my team up there to get them something to eat. I'm sure your palomino is hungry, too. You want to jump inside? Maybe we can find something to eat ourselves."

"Yeah, Eustace, no point in standing around here."

The livery was abandoned, but there was some fresh hay for the horses. Eustace saw to the grooming and feeding while Gilly took a look around. There was a farmhouse a hundred yards away with smoke coming from the chimney. Gilly walked up and banged on the door. When it opened, he was met with a blunderbuss staring him right in the face.

344

"I told you soldier boys I ain't going nowhere! Now you skedaddle off my property or I'll blow that pretty face of yours back to last Sunday!"

Gilly whistled and held up his arms. "We're not with the army, lady! We just came down from Baltimore. My friend's over at the livery, feeding the team. I was looking for something to eat – honest I was."

Behind the blunderbuss was the kindest, sweetest old lady Gilly had ever seen. "There's biscuits and gravy on the stove. Take what you want. Any sign of them army boys?"

"No, ma'am, not a lick; looks like General Stansbury's brigade has come and gone. There's a regiment of militia, the 5th Maryland, which should be here shortly, though. They were behind us on the turnpike."

"So, what are you doing in Bladensburg? Everybody else has turned yellow and left town. Everyone except for me, that is. I ain't going nowhere and you can't make me either."

"Don't want to make you do anything you don't want to do, ma'am. I'm here for *The American* - it's a Baltimore newspaper. I'm looking for Commodore Barney. I need to talk to him for the paper."

"Are you looking for Joshua? He's busy making a nice welcome for the redcoats. Last time he sat at my table he was going to fight a duel out back in my woods. The sheriff chased them off before Joshua could kill the man. Last I heard Joshua was down at Pig Point with his gun boats. That's as far as

345

they can go by water. My guess is he's planning on giving the British a little surprise."

"Yes, ma'am, I'll take the biscuits and gravy. I'll say hello to the Commodore for you, ma'am, whenever I see him. Oh, I'm sorry, what's your name?"

"Name's Henrietta - you just tell Josh that 'Old Lady' Henry says he's welcome anytime. That may not be long, either. I say he's on his way here now."

"Why would he come here?"

"For the biscuits and gravy, you dang fool!"

"Yes, ma'am, but won't he be busy guarding the capital?"

"Josh and I talked about that already, right before his duel. Josh says the British will have to march right up Main Street here in Bladensburg. He says there's no other logical way to cross the river. Why, I could cross it myself with a bucket of water on my head and wouldn't spill a drop, bridge or no bridge. The river runs too deep anywhere else. 'Sides, Winder's not as stupid as he looks. He'll have the other bridges blown before the redcoats get to the river. Joshua says the British know that already, too. Nope, if the redcoats want Washington bad enough, they've got to come right through here."

As Gilly and Eustace enjoyed their meal, Stansbury's brigade came back over the bridge into Bladensburg, all fifteen hundred of them. They filled the town and then headed for high ground just to the east. At the same time the 5th Maryland stumbled down the turnpike onto Main Street. They had been marching all day in suffocating heat and were sweaty, dirty, and exhausted. In just a few hours, the tiny village had become a hub of military activity. What's more it would soon become the focal point of the war.

Gilly and Eustace bunked that night in the carriage at the livery. In the morning, Eustace was anxious to get back to Baltimore. He said his goodbyes and drove his team north towards the turnpike. As the coach rambled away, Gilly became aware that the village was deserted again. The Maryland Militia wasn't to be seen anywhere in town or towards the east. They must have moved out during the night, Gilly thought.

Gilly took Sarika by the reins and walked her back to town. He was thinking on what "Old Lady" Henry had said about the British coming through Bladensburg when he spotted a cloud of dust. He mounted his Princess and galloped down Main Street stopping at the foot of the bridge that crossed the Eastern Branch of the Potomac. Looking over his shoulder he thought he saw the glint of bayonets. "It's them," Gilly said.

As Gilly crossed the bridge, an army scout quickly came up behind him. Both horse and rider were drenched in sweat. "Redcoats is right on our tail!" he shouted.

"Let's go, Princess!

Gilly galloped to the other side, riding abreast of the scout. After they nearly crossed, the scout put up his right arm and reigned in his horse. Gilly pulled Sarika to an abrupt halt. Just ahead of them were three riders.

"My God!" the scout whispered, "it couldn't be." He waved his riding glove trying to get their attention. The gentlemen turned their horses and approached the scout. "Sir, the British have taken Bladensburg! They're right behind us!"

"Where's Winder?" the smallest of them demanded.

"Up on the hill I guess, sir." The three riders put their horses to flight over the grassy knoll in front of them.

"Who was that?" Gilly asked the scout.

"Madison."

"Madison? Madison who?"

"President James Madison! And if you don't want to get shot, you'd better get off this bridge!"

Sarika struggled to get up the slope. There, Gilly saw the American lines, nearly all of them Maryland militia, including Colonel Sterett and "The Dandy Regiment" that marched out of Baltimore three days ago. The

Americans were still trying to assemble on the field when they heard the British drums and bugle calls down in the village. Gilly rode passed General Stansbury. The general was standing on his stirrups, yelling at his officers. "Why is the bridge still standing! Why hasn't it been destroyed?"

From the crest of the hill, Gilly could see more American militia coming up the road from Washington. There were marines placing heavy artillery along the road, seemingly as a last line of defense. He saw a naval officer directing the positioning of the cannon wearing a blue jacket with gold epaulettes. "Barney," Gilly thought aloud.

He could have tried to ask President Madison or General Winder or General Stansbury a question, sought some kind of comment, or begged for any of sort remark from them and sent the answer by courier to Mr. Pechin. But, he needed to speak to the "horse's mouth," and that was Commodore Barney.

Below his position, Gilly saw the American artillery open fire with six-pound shot directed at the British infantry charging the bridge. The British faltered and then charged again. Gilly could see the Marylanders pouring musket fire into the enemy lines. The British Light Brigade stormed the bridge once more. Their men jumped into the shallow water on both sides of the bridge. Each minute - every second - saw more red and white uniforms streaming onto the American side of the Potomac. The first American line fell and ran. Their officers pleaded with them to make a stand. Still more enemy infantry crossed the river, forming lines, advancing, and flanking American positions.

Gilly saw Colonel Sterett on his horse, and the Maryland 5th Regiment gallantly holding their ground. Gilly watched in horror as the young Baltimoreans were being flanked on both left and right. He remembered them singing, dressed in their finely tailored uniforms marching proudly down Market Street only a few days ago. Now he saw them being cut to pieces. His first reaction was nausea. His second was anger.

Finally, it was hand-to-hand combat, bayonet-on-bayonet as the British regulars rushed up the slope. An order to withdraw pulled the "dandies" off the field else they all would have been slaughtered or captured. This meant the inevitable collapse of the American second line of defense. Gilly couldn't wait any longer. He slapped his heels at Sarika's belly and practically flew down the Washington Road straight for Barney's position.

General Winder watched his army disappear before his very eyes. The militia from the first two lines retreated down the Georgetown Road and in a half-dozen different directions after that. From a now safe position behind the fighting, President Madison sent a message to his wife, Dolly, back in Washington. He told her to leave the city.

When Gilly reached the sailors and marines, he found Barney leaning against one of his eighteen-pound guns. Gilly dismounted. "Commodore, my name is Gilly Morrison, I'm with *The American*."

Barney smirked. "Welcome to our little war, Mr. Morrison. You must be a tough one to be traipsing around a battlefield on a pretty palomino looking for a story. Are you tough, Mr. Morrison? And how is that stick-in-the-mud editor of yours, Bill Pechin? Still at it day and night flying the Republican colors?"

Gilly looked with panic back at the road behind him. He saw a massive line of redcoats marching behind a Union Jack fluttering in the breeze. "Sir, I just witnessed the collapse of the first two American lines. You're the last hope for the defense of the capital."

"Yes, Morrison, so what's your point? Do come to it quickly, I fear our interview will be a short one. Did you come through Bladensburg then?"

"We arrived yesterday."

"Did you happen to see an old woman who owns a farm just outside of town?"

Gilly was dumbfounded. "If you mean 'Old Lady' Henry, then yes, I did. She gave us some biscuits and gravy. She says to tell you you're welcome anytime. But, commodore, the redcoats are … "

Joshua Barney laughed. He pointed his spyglass across the field. "Well, Mr. Morrison, now that you've tasted the best biscuit and gravy on this side of the Mason-Dixon and you've seen the total incompetence of the American War Department, I'd say you have a story to send back to Bill

Pechin. Now, if you'll excuse me."

Barney barked at his marines as they sighted the eighteen-pounder exactly where he wanted. Then he had a few words with his marine commander, Captain Miller. The commodore strode to the rear of the gun and pulled the lanyard sending grapeshot directly down the middle of the road. When the smoke cleared the road was empty. There wasn't a redcoat left standing in front of them. The British attempted two more frontal assaults with the same results. "Now, they'll try to flank our right," Barney said. "Are you ready, Captain Miller?"

"Sir, how can you hold them?" Gilly asked incredulously. I saw them coming by the thousands through Bladensburg. The front lines have disintegrated, there's no one behind us."

"Again, Morrison, I ask you – what's your point?" Barney could see that Gilly was shaking. "Is this the first time you've seen men go down in battle?"

"Yes, sir. I – I don't see how they can do it. I don't know how you can be so calm when all around us are men screaming and dying, and right now I don't feel tough. In fact, I'm so scared I can't feel anything."

"I'm not calm at all … " Barney peered into his spyglass. "No, Morrison, inside I'm a ball of nerves like you are. But a captain has to stand firm on his quarterdeck or his men will never fight for him. He pointed his glass at the British lines coming over a ravine. "There he is, sir. By God, it's him."

"Who?"

"That rascal, Cockburn." He gave Gilly his glass. "See, the naval officer behind their lines? He's the one who forced me to blow up my little fleet of gunboats the other day. I guess he's sore that I had my men do his work for him. I rather think he wanted to destroy my boats all by himself. Now, he's come to see me again."

Gilly saw the British admiral through the glass. "It's 'The Great Bandit!'"

Barney grabbed the glass back. "The Great Bastard, I call him. If he wants a naval war I'll show him how." With a wide sweep of his arm, Barney waved his flotillamen and Captain Miller's marines forward. They counterattacked in mass as if they were boarding a ship, pistols at the ready, cutlasses dancing in the air gleaming in the sunlight, sailors screaming like bloodthirsty savages. The British line staggered back to the ravine in confusion. The overall British commander, General Robert Ross took the field and ordered reinforcements. He also ordered a charge on the American left defended by stalwart Marylanders.

For a moment everything hung in the balance. The Americans had the initiative. Gilly thought they just might be able to hold after all. But, it was only for the briefest of moments. For some inexplicable reason, General Winder ordered a retreat back to Washington.

Some of the American officers were in shock upon receiving the order. Some refused to leave the field. Barney and his men, who weren't informed of Winder's retreat order, kept up the fight. Suddenly, Gilly saw the commodore seize his leg and stagger forward. Barney quickly turned his head on all sides to see if anyone had noticed he had been shot and then he stared hard at Gilly.

"Morrison, don't you say a damned thing. Remember, you're on the quarterdeck now." Gilly nodded his head.

"Sir," Captain Miller said, completely out of breath. "They've withdrawn the wagons! Winder's ordered a retreat. They took everything with them. There's no more ammunition to fight with!"

Barney was furious. He was also losing a lot of blood. He wiped the sweat off his brow and fell near his cannon. "Get out!" he ordered. "All of you get out!" He looked at Gilly and smiled.

"Did it ever occur to you, young Mr. Morrison, that there would be a time in your life when you instinctively knew what you ought to do?"

Gilly stared at Barney incredulously. How could he have known the words of the code at such a dire moment? For a split second Gilly froze.

"Miller - get the men out of here and take this tough young man with the palomino with you," Barney barked. "Get him a gun if he wants one. We could use a few more men like him."

The men tried in vain to move their commodore back, but Barney waved them off with his sword. "Damn you Miller, I gave an order."

Captain Miller lifted Gilly onto Sarika's saddle and took the reins. The last Gilly saw of Commodore Barney, he was sitting next to his precious eighteen-pounder. His leg was spurting blood. With his sword in his hand, he waited for Cockburn. He was still smiling.

Chapter 21: The Storm

Gilly was tired, hungry, and still dazed by the day's events when Sarika trotted up to Mike's Tavern. He loosened the stirrups from his feet and slid down the saddle. He was happy to be on the ground after the hard ride from the outskirts of Bladensburg. He massaged the small of his back and his bottom with his hands. His body was so sore it hurt just to touch it. Even though it was past midnight, the tavern door was opened. He could hear loud voices inside. Gilly removed the bit from Sarika's mouth and stroked her mane.

"You did really well today, Princess. Mr. Pechin was right. I needed your strength. Thank God you gave it to me or we would never have been able to get around the redcoats and back on the turnpike. I'm sorry you had to see what we saw today. You're amazing, girl. You never failed me. Not even during the worst of it when other horses were sacrificed. I knew you heard their cries of pain just as I heard the screams of the wounded soldiers. The commodore said I was tough, but you're the one with all the guts, my Princess. Now, we're both exhausted. Let's get something to eat and get some rest, okay? We've got an early day tomorrow."

Gilly kissed Sarika's nose. He tried not to remember the fighting, but the sights, sounds, and smells of the battlefield whisked into and out of his mind by their own volition. He tried putting it out of his mind as he rode north, passing carts and carriages, women and children, cows and goats, but to no avail. He knew these things would be with him for the rest of his life. Sarika seemed to know it, too. She gently licked the tears streaming down his face.

As soon as Gilly entered the tavern, everyone stopped talking. No one needed to ask him where he had come from. They could tell by looking at him. Mike drew him a tall tankard of cider. "Do you feel like talking about it, son?"

"I will for a bit. Just send someone to tend to my palomino. Give her a good rubdown and the finest Timothy hay and apples you got. I'll settle up with you in the morning." Gilly could feel the anxious stares all around him. "How much do you know, Mike? I'm too tired to be going over everything. God, I never felt this way before. I'm just dog-tired, Mike."

"We heard our boys ran like rats on a sinking ship. And that … "

"Stop it!" Gilly shouted, pounding his fist on the bar. He took a long draw of the cold cider and wiped his mouth with the back of his hand. This calmed him down. "Not everybody ran, Mike," he said with conviction. "Our boys fought with bayonets against the regulars. I know because I was there. Most of the running was done by that damned Winder. He ordered the retreat. Right when Commodore Barney had the British bottled up in the ravine by the Washington Road. Oh, the redcoats out soldiered us all right. Those were the same infantry that beat Napoleon. They were battle-tested on the fields of Europe. But if Winder had only rallied the militia to take a stand behind Barney's guns, and then threw them back into the fight, we could have held. Winder orders a retreat, just happens to forget to tell Barney and his men, and then also forgets to tell the men where to retreat to. There was no rallying point for the men to get back into the fight.

"We had the high ground. Those British infantry had been marching all day long. They were worn out. Our boys were still coming in from the countryside. We could have drew the redcoats farther in and then cut their supply lines. But, that damned Winder orders a retreat to nowhere. He leaves the field with our boys still out there fighting with nothing left to fight with. Don't talk about our boys like that, Mike. You've got no right to talk about them like that."

Mike refilled Gilly's tankard. No one in the tavern said a word. Gilly rubbed his eyes and brushed his red, curly hair back over his head. "After that,

358

there wasn't anything left to stop the redcoats. When I was up the turnpike a piece, I saw the fires being lit. I guess they burned Washington like they burned Havre de Grace and all the other towns on the Chesapeake going on over a year now. When are we finally going to stand up like Barney did, and the boys from the 5th, and stop the bastards, Mike?"

The cider took effect immediately. Before Gilly's head slipped down onto his chest he had already passed out. Mike and some of the men carried him to a cot and gently put a pillow beneath his head.

Despite his words to Sarika, Gilly didn't wake until late morning. Mike's tavern was full up. The straggling militia who had fought at Bladensburg made their way slowly up to Baltimore. Some of them stopped for a cold cider and a plate of Mike's famous Irish stew. Gilly listened to them at the bar, cursing Winder, cursing Madison, and cursing just about anything they had a mind to. They were also frightened. As more and more of them passed or piled into Mike's, all the talk was of British retribution. Word was the redcoats were still burning down the capital. The fearful question was what city was next? The answer, of course, was Baltimore.

Gilly mounted Sarika and got on the road at noon. The sky was overcast and grey which matched the mood of everyone travelling north. Gilly didn't stop and talk to the soldiers as he normally would. He didn't want to hear about the battle over and over again. He was there and saw with his own eyes what had happened. More importantly, in his young mind, he saw what

359

could have happened.

Behind him the clouds darkened and the wind picked up a bit. Growing up in Baltimore he was used to fast changing weather. In fact, anyone from Washington or anywhere in the bay area could spot a nasty summer storm in the making. Along the turnpike, men looked up at the sky to make their own assessment. They could have gone off to the side of the road and try to find a farmhouse to take cover or pitch a tent or fashion a lean-to. But all the soldiers and Gilly, too, wanted to get back home. Besides, it was so intolerably hot that some wind and cool rain would ease their way.

Sarika, who had been amicably trotting along, stretched her neck to turn to the southwest. She snorted and picked up her gait. Gilly was writing his story for *The American* in his head and took no notice.

Quite suddenly, the leaves on the trees rustled with a freshening breeze. This brought Gilly out of his reverie. He glanced back at the sky. There was a mass of black clouds streaked with an eerie shade of green coming down the roadway. He could feel the wind whipping around his back, taking his shirt tails with it. Then, a lightning bolt was followed by a loud clap of thunder. There was no rain as yet, so the wind propelled the road dust airborne. As the wind increased it took with it sticks and small branches.

Gilly saw a group of soldiers taking cover in a ditch on the side of the road. He dismounted Sarika and grabbed her by the reins. "Come on, Princess. That's a good girl. Follow me down here." She shuffled her hoofs sideways to get down into the ditch.

He removed a blanket from his saddle bag and tucked it underneath his arm. All the while, Gilly stroked her mane and gently talked in her ear. "Sleep, my Princess. Let's sleep now." Sarika first sat down, then, as Gilly continued to pet her and talk in her ear, she placed her head on his lap. Gilly placed the blanket, flapping in the wind, over Sarika's head and put his own head on top.

The storm turned into a tempest. Gilly had closed his eyes. He didn't see that the day had turned into night. The wind no longer howled, it screamed. Yet, Gilly remained calm. If it was a twister, and he thought it probably was, there was no use in doing anything but staying exactly where he was, shielding his Princess. He had heard the roar of the cannon and the cries of dying men and horses. This, he supposed, was nature's response to hell on earth instigated by human hands.

Then the rains came. Torrents of water fell from the sky pelting the road and quickly filling up the ditch. After a few minutes the wind abated, but the water kept rising. Sarika twitched. She innately sensed the danger. Gilly removed the wet blanket and she sat up, but Gilly struggled. His boots were stuck in the mire. He reached for a root to pull himself up, but it gave way. For the first time since the storm began, he felt panicked. The rain poured down so hard it was impossible to see. What was once a safe haven from the wind a few minutes before had become a fast moving stream. Its current was so powerful it moved Sarika's body dangerously close to Gilly. He couldn't move his legs and it was useless to try and remove his boots.

"Help us!" Gilly cried from the bottom of the ditch. This time, it was Sarika's turn to act calmly. She rose on all four hooves while at the same time putting her head underneath his waist. Using her strong neck muscles she picked him clean out of the mud. A group of soldiers, who had already extricated themselves, had heard Gilly's plea for help. They quickly formed a perpendicular line from the road to the ditch. The last man grabbed Gilly's hand and Sarika's reins. They heaved in unison and, in a horrifying moment that seemed a lifetime, brought boy and horse over the berm.

Without a word, the soldiers patted Gilly on the back in a reassuring gesture, then resumed their trek back to Baltimore. Mike and everyone else can say all they want to about those men running away from battle, Gilly thought, as he watched their backs through the falling rain. They'll always be the bravest of men to me. Gilly, Sarika, and the long line of soldiers, many with their heads bowed low in despair, slogged their way home. Home - despite the mud, somehow that felt good.

Late the next night at the Dooley house on Thames Street, Gilly took care to tend to Sarika, even to pick her shoes. She had been through just as much as I have, Gilly thought. With weak legs he stumbled up the stairs and fell into his bed. "No dreams Lord. Please no dreams."

*****

Desiree had everything organized. At least she thought she did until Gabe told her about the blood. She had been busy the whole time Gilly was away reconstructing the orphanage at St. Patrick's into a makeshift hospital. She had purchased new cots and bedding, bandages and linen, drapes and bed curtains, needles and surgical thread, sharp knives and saws (dreadful things) and every medication and drug known to Baltimore's apothecaries.

"Blood? What about blood?" she asked Gabe.

"The blood that gets on a nurse's uniform."

"What about the blood that gets on a nurse's uniform?"

Gabe breathed out a theatrical sigh. He had been Desiree's assistant for the past week and she had been a hard taskmaster. She was a perfectionist and wanted everything done right the first time, but only after tedious and time consuming analysis. So, when just this once she missed something, Gabe was more than pleased to let her know.

"When soldiers are wounded they get bloody," Gabe explained. "When they get bloody, the nurses get bloody."

Desiree cocked an arched brow and stared at the orphan with derision. "Well?"

Gabe tried not to smile. "Look at how you're dressed, Mistress Pechin."

Desiree wore a light-blue, cotton dress with a low-cut square bodice and short sleeves, the waist tied right below the breasts. She had her hair pinned up in a bun, like many women when the weather was hot. On her feet she wore a pair of dainty, pink slippers. It finally dawned on her what was wrong. "Oh my goodness, I forgot all about the aprons. How could I, really. What on earth was I thinking?"

Gabe grimaced. "You bought the aprons yesterday, ma'am, they're in the closet. I was thinking a uniform would be more practical."

Desiree clapped her hands. "Brilliant, Gabriel! Uniforms are just the thing. You are a dear. Now, run down to the dry goods store and purchase three dozen uniforms, the kind nurses wear, and, oh, kerchiefs to be worn on the head and pinned in back. Charge it to my account. Off you go, now. Scoot, and be back directly."

Gabe shook his head as he left the orphanage. Next time, he thought, I'll keep my mouth shut.

*****

"There's talk of capitulation, then?" Gilly asked Mr. Pechin.

"More than that, son. The whole city was on fire with the rumor that the British were already on the march, up the turnpike, to take the city from the southwest. I don't mind telling you I was apprehensive myself. It's the only spot the city is completely vulnerable. Thank God that didn't happen.

364

Maybe it was the storm that saved us after all. Point in fact, I know it was. No army could possibly have marched through it. We've been given a providential reprieve. And, I'm not a man who often credits the divine for earthly favors. You came through it, I take it, despite the difficulties?"

Gilly whistled. "It was the worst I ever saw, sir. No wonder the British left Washington after such a short occupation. If they felt anything like we did coming back from Bladensburg, I'd say they just wanted a warm bath and dry place to sleep. By the way, sir, did you like the story I sent you?"

Pechin looked at this morning's edition of *The American*. On the front page was Gilly's story about the battle next to the lead article on Commodore Rodgers' return to the city. The three commodores: Rodgers, Perry, and Porter, had gone down to Washington to fight the British during the naval withdraw from the attack on the capital. They had fought with distinction. Now, Rodgers was back in Baltimore to help in her defense.

"Your story on what really happened at Bladensburg and Rodgers' return will quell the tide of any talk of capitulation, Gilly. But believe me when I tell you it was touch and go. Even members of the town council were crying for terms of surrender to be drawn up. The destruction of the capital scared the hell out of a lot of people in this town."

"What do you want me to do now, sir?"

"Nothing. Word is the British Navy is moving out of the Chesapeake.

They could be going to Bermuda to regroup and then hit us again at their leisure. My gut still tells me they're going to come here. They hate Baltimore and everything she stands for. Have you had any more news from Michael Dooley in New York?"

"No, sir."

"The British didn't send all those troops down the St. Lawrence for nothing. The attack on Washington, as you know, was only a piece of their overall strategy. I venture they try and take Lake Champlain and then threaten all of New York. American representatives, notably Henry Clay and John Quincy Adams, are in the Netherlands, at Ghent I believe, negotiating a peace treaty. Another British victory will spell the end of this country as we know it. So, whether it's New York or Baltimore or, God forbid, both, we would have no cards whatsoever to play with at Ghent. If I were the British I'd take the Ohio Valley and shipping rights on the Mississippi. That would leave them with all the riches on this continent and make us poor country cousins for the next hundred years. Let me know if you hear anything from Dooley. In the meantime, I want you to take some time off. You look horrible."

*****

For the first time in his memory, Gilly tried to do something he had never done before: relax. In the mornings, he took his bait box to the Patapsco and bagged rockfish by the score. Afternoons were the perfect time to go riding with Sarika out on Patapsco Neck, the peninsula that stretched from the

366

city all the way to the bay with plenty of woodlands to keep horse and rider cool in the summer's waning days. Evenings were spent with a book, reading by lamplight under the stars in back of the Dooley home.

It worked for three days. Although there was no sign of the enemy, Gilly was still on edge. His newly found leisure time turned to helping Desiree at the orphanage, cleaning and repairing the cooperage, visiting the rectory, and spending time with Father John who was mending quickly. It was at the rectory that Gilly received a note from Mr. Peabody asking to pay him an immediate visit to his home in Old Town.

"Hello, Gilly. It's good to see you again. I understand you've been given some time to compose yourself after the fiasco at Bladensburg."

"I haven't composed anything in over a week, Mr. Peabody, and it's killing me. What's going on?"

Peabody drew his chair up to his desk and gave Gilly a serious look behind his thick glasses. "I just received word the British fleet has been spotted in full strength passing Annapolis and moving up the bay."

Gilly squirmed in his seat. "I knew this lull couldn't last long. But I've heard nothing about it."

"No, you wouldn't. The alarm has not yet been sounded. My boss, Major William Barney, has a system of lookouts posted at points along the coastline with a relay of riders every ten miles. The news comes first to intelligence and then to the commanders. I suspect things will get pretty hectic around here whenever General Smith alerts the city. But, there is something else I needed to talk to you about before all the hubbub begins."

"Make it quick, Mr. Peabody. I've got to get to the newspaper and report this to my editor."

"I understand. Listen Gilly, Richard Snipes' body was found at an abandoned farmhouse on North Point. Apparently, he committed suicide by hanging himself."

Gilly pressed his lips together. "Does Samuel know?"

"No. I thought it best if you would inform him."

"Thank you, Mr. Peabody. I will do so directly after I see my editor. Did he have any personal effects that I may give to Samuel?"

Mr. Peabody handed Gilly a burlap bag. "These are his clothes, a timepiece, some currency, and a book on the death of Socrates, written by Plato in the original Greek. The book was found on the floor directly beneath the chair on which he was standing before he kicked it aside and suffered the consequences. In the book there are words and phrases, ostensibly from Socrates, that are underlined. They are incongruously but not haphazardly strung together. This caught my eye since I have a mind trained to reveal patterns and, hopefully, make some sense out of them. However, my Greek is not what it should be. I took the liberty to have the words translated. I've

368

made a copy of the words for you." He handed Gilly a piece of paper.

"You know, don't you Gilly, there is another spy out there. This individual is close to the commanders or at least one of them or the information revealed in the cipher your Istvan solved would never have been obtained by Richard Snipes. These underlined words may be a clue to help us."

"Why would Richard construct another puzzle? Why wouldn't he just write down who the spy is?"

"I don't know the answer to that. Perhaps it was because Richard promised the spy total anonymity. Perhaps the British do not know the identity of the spy any more than we do. And, perhaps this new puzzle was Richard's only way to help us after he found out about Father John, not knowing which side would find his body hanging from the rafters first. What better way to redeem himself than to choose, from antiquity, an amalgamation of seemingly obscure passages from the greatest philosopher in human history. Socrates was his hero. Yours is Aquinas. May I venture to say he designed this stratagem, in a moment's notice, so that you, and only you could break the enigma? Richard, I think, finally understood the Code of Aquinas. His very last thought may just have been "to know what you ought to do."

Gilly stuffed the paper inside his shirt and rose to leave. Mr. Peabody walked him to the door. "Show this to Samuel. He will be more apt to talk to you after hearing of his cousin's fate than he would to me. Now, go and do your job. If anything comes from this please contact me immediately. The fate of this city and this nation may be crammed inside your blouse."

"C'mon girl," Gilly said to Princess, "let's move!" Gilly galloped all the way to *The American*. He banged on the editor's door and walked in. Pechin was with his assistant, Bartlett.

"Look who's here, Bartlett. Our prized story teller who, I think it safe to say, has had his full of taking orders from my daughter on how to run a hospital."

"Mr. Pechin, I've just come from Peabody. The enemy fleet has been sighted moving north from Annapolis."

Pechin jumped to his feet. "Bartlett, get the pressmen back. It looks like another special Sunday edition. Gilly, hop back on your damned Princess and get me a story. I want something … " Pechin paused, searching for the right word. "Fresh! Something – anything, I can publish by midnight!"

As ordered, Gilly hopped on Princess and raced up to Hampstead Hill. With the respite from a British attack in recent days and the fact it was a weekend, many of the militia had gone home to their families. Still, the commanding officers and their staffs were busy, too busy to see Gilly. He couldn't even get in to see Samuel. Gilly left the burlap bag with the sentry. He spent the next couple of hours interviewing newly arriving volunteers from Pennsylvania and getting their reaction to the news. It wasn't the story Mr.

Pechin expected, Gilly thought, but it was different and the headline about the enemy ships moving north on the bay was the real story anyway.

On the way home it began to pour. Lightning split the night sky and the heavens opened up to soak Gilly and Sarika all the way down Market Street. Gilly patted Princess on the head. "Don't worry, girl. There won't be any ditches for us tonight." When he saw a light on at the rectory, he pulled up on the reins and dismounted.

Desiree was in the study talking to Father John. She was modeling a new nurse's uniform in front of the mirror when Gilly knocked and walked in.

"Dez, the battle hasn't started yet. You can save that uniform for when it's really needed – and that might be in a couple of days if the news holds true." Gilly took a towel and wiped the rain from his face and his matted red hair. He looked again at Desiree and squinted his eyes. "Hey, you didn't by any chance have that uniform altered did you? It looks like it was made for you."

Desiree blushed. "Well I did ask my seamstress to…" The two of them went on like that for a few minutes while Father John sat upright in his bed trying to read his breviary. He laid his book on his lap and smiled. He was wondering when the ceremony would be. Then he resumed his prayers.

Gilly sat on the leather chair and sighed.

"What's wrong, darling? You look bored," Desiree asked.

"Of course I'm bored. And I guess you've heard the news about the British fleet? You know, the one that's probably headed for the Patapsco?"

"Well of course. Everyone in the city knows by now. Don't be silly. But General Smith has not sounded the general alarm. So, he must not be certain yet. Now tell us what's wrong."

Gilly lifted his head and gave a sidelong glance in the pastor's direction. "Evening, Father," he said with a forced smile. "What's wrong? I'll tell you what's wrong. The entire British fleet is headed straight for us and I'm about to go home and go to sleep. That's what's wrong. Why, at Bladensburg I was in the middle of everything. Here, I'm of no use to anyone. Even my story for the paper tomorrow wasn't very interesting. About the only thing I did today that was remotely … " He reached into his blouse and pulled out a piece of paper.

"What's that, dear?"

"Something Mr. Peabody gave me today. Dez, I'm sorry. I should have told you straight off. Richard Snipes' body was found on North Point. He – he hung himself, Dez." Father John put his breviary down again.

"What?" Desiree covered her mouth with her hands.

"He left this book about Socrates lying on the floor near where he … Anyway, the book was written by Plato. It's about the death of Socrates. Richard underlined some words on a page of the book. Mr. Peabody says they might be a clue as to who the spy is that was working with Richard. I tried to give Samuel some of Richard's effects and talk to him about the underlined words but I wasn't able to see him. Peabody wrote down a copy of the words for me."

"You mean it's a mystery?"

"Yeah, I guess so. The book was written in the original Greek. Richard underlined certain words and phrases before he died. Peabody thinks that only I, or those who accept the Code of Aquinas, can discern its true meaning. Here are the underlined words:

the last and worst evil

but the oracle made no sign of opposition

I have drunk the poison

a chamber

the hour of sunset was near

soon the jailor

you know my errand

have patience

the debt shall be paid

is there anything else?

"What on earth? Gilly, how is anyone to make sense of such nonsense?"

"I don't know, Dez. I don't think Mr. Peabody does either. That's why he wanted me to talk to Samuel about it. He seems to think that Richard did this to somehow vindicate himself. That this is what he "ought to do." But, if you ask me, it sounds kind of eerie. You know, Richard left this underneath his body. Peabody says Richard did this to help us after realizing the consequences of his treason. That he deliberately made it a puzzle because he didn't know if the British would find his body first, or us."

Desiree raised a finger as if to make a point. "So, Richard thought that the British wouldn't be able to solve this puzzle and that we could." Gilly and Desiree stared at each other hoping one of them could provide an answer. The answer was provided by a strained voice.

"'The last and worst evil' refers to Timothy."

Slowly, Gilly and Desiree turned their heads to the bed. Desiree, somewhat confused, asked the priest a simple question she never expected to be answered. "I'm sorry, Father. But did you just say something? Because you haven't made a sound since … "

"Second Timothy," Father John said, weakly. "Chapter three, verse thirteen."

Gilly went to the bookcase and removed a Bible. He paged through the New Testament. "But evil men and imposters shall wax worse and worse, deceiving and being deceived," he quoted.

"And the oracle that made no sign of opposition," Desiree said, although almost in a state of shock at hearing the priest speak. "Is an oracle like a seer?"

"No, *mon ami*, a seer reads – interprets – signs. An oracle receives them. An oracle is a portal. Now, children, Moranvillè is tired. Go to Monsieur Peabody, whoever he may be, and talk to him about this tomorrow. Now, turn off the lamp and go home. I am tired and must sleep."

Chapter 22: The Battle of Baltimore

Sunday, September 11

Desiree had her driver stop at the Dooley home to pick up Gilly.
They were going into Old Town to try and find Mr. Peabody. It was a quiet
Sunday morning. The houses of worship were full of soldiers and their
families. The militiamen were still on leave and had plans to spend the day
visiting with friends and sitting down to home cooked meals.

The headline in *The American* about the British fleet being cited
moving up the coast had everyone staying as close to home as possible just in
case. Gilly's story about the Pennsylvanians had elicited some good humored
jokes about strangers racing into Baltimore to save the city only to find its
inhabitants peacefully going about their business.

376

One Pennsylvania private serving in the 111th Infantry, Anthony Keefer, was so proud of his regiment he bent Gilly's ear talking about its rich history. "We was started by old Benjamin Franklin," Gilly quoted the private in his story. "Our motto is 'No Step Backward' and we aim not to until this here battle is done, and then we can go and step backward toward Philadelphia the way we come down."

Private Keefer's profession was a ship's caulker, but he also worked in a family smokehouse business along the Delaware River. Gilly reported that he brought a basket of smoked herring with him "so the good people of Baltimore could taste what real fish is like." Gilly took a liking to Private Keefer and introduced him to the Smith brothers. A strange twist of fate would later bring the three privates together into the maelstrom of war.

Desiree's buggy pulled up to Mr. Peabody's small brownstone in Old Town. He had heard the clip-clop of the horse's hooves on the cobblestones and was at the door to greet them.

"You've come just in time," he said. "I was just brewing some tea and waiting for the general alarm."

"It's official, then?" Gilly asked.

"Yes. General Smith has just now made a determination that the city is in jeopardy. Please do sit down Mistress Pechin; it is my honor and privilege to welcome you to my humble abode." They sat in a little parlor opposite his office. Peabody poured some black Irish tea into dainty china cups and offered Desiree a chocolate torte.

"I am an avid bachelor," he said to Desiree. "My needs are few and my wants go unfulfilled as it should be. But, I have a weakness for sweets. I am the confectionaries best customer."

Gilly grew a bit impatient. "Mr. Peabody, how close is the British Fleet?"

"They are gathering now at the confluence of the river and the bay. They will disembark, I should think, early tomorrow morning in the fog of darkness and land as predicted on the shores of North Point before sunrise. So, there is no need to rush about looking for a story for your newspaper, Gilly. The British will present themselves when time and tide allow. That leaves us with a civilized cup of tea and a delicious mystery to unravel."

"Oh, I agree," Desiree said taking a bite of the chocolate torte.

"Well I – I don't," Gilly stammered.

Desiree frowned. "Perhaps he's right, Mr. Peabody."

"Look," Gilly insisted, pulling the piece of paper from his pocket, "we were with Father John last night going over the words from Socrates, when, all of a sudden, Father John says something!"

"It was a miracle," Desiree said.

"It was heaven sent, anyway. He said that the 'last and worst evil' referred to Timothy, uh – 2 Timothy, 3:13."

Mr. Peabody grabbed his bible and looked it up. "Interesting, 'evil men and imposters … deceiving and being deceived.'"

"Couldn't that be the spies?" Desiree thought aloud. "Richard would have included himself after what happened to Father John. Richard, O'Casey and Dailey were all imposters, and Richard was certainly deceitful."

"And deceived by his own plans," Mr. Peabody said.

"But the oracle that makes no opposition," Gilly pressed. "Father John said that the oracle is a portal."

Peabody grinned. "A portal is an opening, of course. An opening without any opposition is exactly what I thought the unnamed spy would be. This spy acts with impunity because of his rank or access to something important, or both."

"And 'I have drunk the poison.' Richard is telling himself he knows what he did was wrong," Gilly said. "Richard admits his guilt before he kills himself. Now, what about the next one? - 'A chamber.'"

"A chamber could be a room, couldn't it?" Desiree offered.

"Or a place where ammunition is found," Peabody surmised with certainty. "The chamber of a weapon holds the cartridge in place before firing."

"'The hour of sunset was near,' is the next part," Gilly said. "So, we have a time frame to work with. What's going to happen after the attack begins, and maybe the treachery we're expecting, will be before the sun goes down. Makes sense to me, Mr. Peabody. If the invasion force lands, as you say, at dawn, then they will be in position to assail us by nightfall.

"'Soon the jailer,' whoever that person is," Gilly went on, "will do something."

"The jailer," Peabody guessed, "will act soon upon or near sundown."

Desiree finished explaining the next three lines. "'You know my errand ... have patience ... the debt shall be paid.' That's all about Richard. His errand is to hang himself, which we now know. We must have patience with him while we try and solve this mystery. And, he pays his debt to us and to the country and his cause with his own life."

Mr. Peabody concurred, nodding his head. "The last line answers itself: 'is there anything else?' The answer is no. Everything we need lies here before us. We must only identify who the 'jailer' is and by this identification we will know where the treachery will take place. Do we all agree with this summation?"

"Yes," Gilly and Desiree said in harmony.

"Then, Gilly, get to Samuel to see if he has any idea who the 'jailer' is. Don't wait for me if you don't have to. Tell Samuel that I'm sorry I judged his cousin a little too harshly. No, never mind, I'll tell him myself when time permits. But the time for tea, cakes, and civilized conversation has ended. Mistress Pechin, I'm afraid your hospital may be needed by this time tomorrow, certainly within the next forty-eight hours."

When Gilly and Desiree got into the buggy they could hear the church bells ringing throughout the city. The general alarm had finally been sounded.

****

Desiree had Gilly dropped off at the Dooley home on Thames Street and then went directly to the hospital. When the general alarm was given, thousands of Baltimoreans went to predesignated positions. Whether it was straight home to tend to the children or to military defensive positions in and around the city for the militia, everyone seemed to know where to go without any questions. Unlike Washington, Baltimore's Committee of Vigilance and Safety had seen to every last detail. The city's citizens didn't wait for the federal government to help them.

The orphanage-hospital at St. Patrick's was no different. The women from the St. Patrick's Benevolent Society who were not with the orphans at "Tranquility," the Pechin summer home, reported for duty. Doctor Williams would take charge upon his arrival. Mrs. Dougherty and Mrs. Pickersgill were to be the head nurses. Mrs. Callahan had volunteered to serve meals to the patients. Gabe would supervise the orderlies.

Gilly was right when he said his contribution to the war effort would be with his pen long before any attack on Baltimore took place. Now, he would be tasked with a different contribution. With the help of the Code of Aquinas, Gilly and Desiree were ready.

Hundreds of miles to the north, on that very same day, sailing on the small bay outside Plattsburgh, New York, on the shores of Lake Champlain, Michael Dooley was, too. The Battles of Baltimore and Plattsburg had begun. The fate of the young United States of America would be decided decisively, almost at the same hour, and world history hung in the balance.

****

Monday, September 12

Thousands of militia marched into Baltimore. They came from all over Maryland, Virginia and Pennsylvania. General Smith had congregated a force of ten thousand men at the defenses on Hampstead Hill even before Bladensburg. Now, their numbers swelled beyond imagining. The overwhelming majority of these, part-time soldiers, were young and green, and as such, untested. Major Armistead had Fort McHenry manned and ready before the general alarm was given. Soon, merchant ships from Baltimore would be sunk in the middle of the channel barring the Royal Navy from entering the harbor.

Gilly arose early on Monday morning and rode Sarika through Old Town. He was on his way to Rodgers' Bastion at the heart of the American line. After what Mr. Peabody had said, Gilly was itching to ask Samuel about "the jailer." He also wanted to see what the commanders' next step would be. Mr. Pechin would want to know.

Samuel could only spare a minute to talk to him. Headquarters was buzzing with messages and Samuel needed to approve all official dispatches. They walked outside away from prying ears.

"I'm sorry about your cousin," Gilly said with compassion. "I would have told you in person but they wouldn't let me see you."

"Thank you, Gilly."

"I know you're incredibly busy, but have you had a chance to look at the book Richard left behind. Did you notice he underlined certain words?"

"I noticed. I could see he was trying to tell us something. He must have found out, of course, about Father John. Richard probably thought the priest was killed. He would have become overwhelmed with grief and self-loathing. He believed in his cause until his cause betrayed him. Unlike Socrates, he no longer believed in the truth of his own convictions.

"I know, my friend."

"Most of the words are self-evident, as you probably already know. The one that perplexes me is 'jailer.' I have no idea what he meant by that. In the book, of course, Plato's dialogue concerns the last speech by Socrates. The jailer brings the hemlock that Socrates must drink. Socrates had been convicted and condemned for corrupting the youth of Athens by introducing strange ideas. But, we know now these ideas weren't strange at all. They were rooted in timeless truth. A truth Aquinas certainly understood. That is why I was intrigued by your discussions with Michael Dooley concerning the code. The code is also a timeless truth. There is more, much more, to learn from both Socrates and Aquinas. Truths that my dear cousin didn't comprehend."

Samuel shrugged his shoulders and shook his head. "There is something I know with certainty, that Socrates believed his duty was to question false wisdom and false authority. That he sacrificed his life. He did this for the truth. He did it as a lesson, a final one, for his students and all of us who regard him with such esteem as Richard did. And Richard followed his example. Instead of fleeing for the safety of the British fleet, Richard, like Socrates, chose to accept the consequences of his actions. Socrates, although innocent, drank the poison forced on him by an imperfect authority. Richard, in self-condemnation and under his own imperfect and warped authority, used the rope because, unlike Socrates, Richard was guilty of corruption.

"Why Richard underlined the words, 'the jailer,' is as much a puzzle to me as it is to you. Clearly, he is warning us about something that is going to

384

occur soon, within the next few days anyway. It is Richard's way of atonement, I think. I pray you can see clear to solve this mystery before it is too late."

"Thanks, Samuel. I know this has been very difficult for you. If you should think of anything let me know. In the meantime, I'd like to find General Stricker."

"He left yesterday afternoon. He's gone up the Philadelphia Road with the City Brigade and then down Old Log Road or North Point Road as some people call it. The Smith brothers are in one of his companies. Lately, they have taken on the role of scouts."

"They've gone out to meet the British?"

"In a way, yes. General Smith wants some intelligence as to the enemy's strength. He also wants to check the British on their way down the peninsula, to keep them somewhat off balance and perhaps inflict preliminary damage. In any event, if the main body of the British Army is delayed that will give General Smith precious time to reinforce Hampstead Hill. Volunteer militia are still pouring into the city.

"General Stricker's headquarters is only about seven miles away at the Methodist Meeting House. Reports are that the British Army under Major General Robert Ross and Colonel Arthur Brooke, and augmented by sailors and marines under Vice Admiral George Cockburn, landed at North Point before dawn today. I'd say we should be receiving reports about an encounter by midday."

Gilly whistled. "Cockburn! So the old bandit's at it again - or the 'Great Bastard' as Commodore Barney called him. Thank you, Samuel. I'm sorry to have disturbed you. I'm going to ride out to the meeting house and see for myself how things are going. You wouldn't happen to have an extra spyglass around here would you?" Samuel walked back to his office and grabbed one from his desk. "Thanks, Samuel. Listen, if ever you should need me in the next few days, leave a message with Desiree at St. Patrick's. She'll be at the hospital."

"I will. As for me, I've already received permission to return to Fort McHenry when the shooting starts. Commodore Rodgers will have no need for a secretary in the field of battle who cannot shoulder a weapon. But, I have helped build most of the defenses at McHenry and know its strengths and weaknesses. I'll go to the fort and help them there." Gilly nodded and turned to leave.

"Gilly, wait." Samuel put his arm on top of Gilly's shoulder. "Everyone knows you were in the middle of the fighting at Bladensburg. Some of the officers here thought you were crazy to place yourself in such a dire situation in quest of a newspaper story. It didn't surprise me at all. I knew at the time that's where you would be and, more importantly, what you ought to do. But please, for the sake of those who love you - try to stay behind the

386

lines this time."

It took Gilly several hours to reach the meeting house. General Stricker had already formed his line of battle awaiting the enemy. Gilly found out that a cavalry unit and a rifle company were sent ahead as an advance party to observe the British and harass their progress. Despite Samuel's plea to remain behind the American lines, Gilly spurred Sarika farther down the road. Fearing he was getting to close, Gilly dismounted and tied Princess to an oak tree. He cautiously crept through a wooded area to the right and spied the men of the rifle company. He knew the Smith Brothers were with the advance party.

"You, mister. What are you doin' walkin' in back of us like that?" The whispered voice came from a tree branch above Gilly's head. He looked up to see the green uniform of an American rifleman.

"I'm looking for Ethan and Elijah Smith," Gilly whispered back.

"Did their mama send you or was you just out for a walk?"

"My name's Morrison. I'm with *The American*."

"Which one? We're all Americans here except those fellers in front of us. Elijah and Ethan are to the right, 'bout twenty yards. Don't spook 'em or you're liable to git kilt."

On the right were three figures with their backs to Gilly. They each had their rifles balanced on tree stumps aimed at a small clearing ahead. As he inched closer, Gilly recognized them as the Smith brothers and Anthony Keefer. Gilly cracked a dry branch crawling to their position.

Ethan, the nearest one to him, swung his rifle around and pointed it in his face. "Master Gilly, what on earth … " Ethan picked up a twig and threw it at his brother. Elijah came crawling over.

"I'm just here to see what you boys have been up to," Gilly whispered.

"Then, you've come at a good time," Elijah said. "You see that little hill dead ahead about a hundred yards? There's been redcoat officers and some guy in a blue jacket millin' around up there for the past two minutes. I had a bead on one when you cracked that stick. I think Anthony's been eyin' them up, too."

"What's a Pennsylvania private doing with you so far up this road?"

"He got permission. They say he's the best duck shooter in Phillydelphia, so the captain said he could come with us. This here's the fella you introduced us to the other day, remember?"

Gilly reached into his jacket and pulled out the spyglass Samuel lent him. He trained it on the hill. He would have whistled if he could. "That's a general up there, boys." Just then, several shots rang out from the woods to their left. The general's horse raised its hooves in the air and arched its back.

The officer fell of his mount and slipped to the ground. In seconds, gunfire erupted from both directions. The British Light Brigade advanced by twos on the American skirmish lines driving them out of the trees and into a panicked flight.

"C'mon Ethan. You too Anthony!" Elijah shouted. They stood and ran for cover towards the thicket behind them. Gilly scrambled to his feet. He saw Ethan and Elijah fall at the same instant directly in front of him. They were both shot in the back. Gilly rushed to them checking for a pulse on the neck; first Ethan and then Elijah. There was none.

Gilly knew he had to leave them. It sapped all of his strength to lift himself off the ground beside their bodies. He took one step before a musket ball ripped through his left thigh and sent him to his knees. Anthony Keefer, hiding behind an oak, slung his rifle over his shoulder and dashed into the open. He grabbed Gilly by the waist and made for the roadway. After a few steps, Gilly began hopping on his right leg. "The horse, Anthony! Get us to the horse!"

Anthony shoved Gilly onto the saddle and then mounted behind him. The British Light Brigade burst from the trees, knelt, and took aim. Sarika didn't wait for a command. She galloped down the road just as a volley of musketry hurled their leaden balls through the air.

The first volley missed them. But the second line of light infantry now stepped in front of their comrades and raised their weapons. There was a picket fence about fifty yards in front of Sarika. Behind the fence was Baltimore's finest militia, the City Brigade, in full strength. The militia stood and aimed their fire around Sarika just as the second line of British infantry squeezed their triggers. Anthony Keefer was knocked off the saddle. A musket ball had shattered the butt of his rifle and had enough velocity to carry him off of Sarika's back. He rolled on the ground, quickly got up and ran to the safety of the fence.

Sarika was undaunted. The fence, about five feet high, loomed ever nearer. Gilly was lying across the saddle trying desperately to hold on to the stirrup leather. Sarika was no jumper, but she gauged the height of the fence and the length of her stride perfectly. When she leapt over, a hearty cheer from the City Brigade rang across the field. But, Sarika didn't stop running.

There were at least a-half-dozen attempts to stop the palomino by soldiers and civilians alike during her long gallop back to Fells Point. But Sarika was determined. She knew her prince was hurt and she was taking him where he needed to be. Gilly somehow managed to stay on the saddle despite losing consciousness twice.

The hospital at St. Patrick's was receiving more of the wounded as the army field hospitals started filling to capacity. Before the attack on Father John, Desiree had never seen suffering. Her whole life had been cushioned against anything uncomfortable. Pain was not reality – death was for other people. Dressed in her fitted uniform she was a godsend to young men who yearned to see something beautiful and angelic after living hell. She played the part well, as any accomplished actress would. In her heart, however, she was stabbed by each new wound she saw.

Sarika wasted no time getting the attention of the orderlies who were busy unloading stretchers from the line of ambulances parked on Apple Alley. She simply bypassed them and trotted through the front door. Sarika balked every time a nurse tried to take Gilly down from the saddle; obstinately pawing her hooves, snorting with displeasure, whinnying in frustration - until Sarika saw *her*.

Desiree had run to the foyer to see what the ruckus was. She held her hand to her lips, quelling an urge to scream. In a moment, she had Gabe carefully removed Gilly's motionless body from his saddle and put him on a stretcher to be taken to one of the few empty beds. As an orderly grabbed Sarika's reins and started to back her out the door, Desiree whispered in the horse's ear "thank you, Princess."

*****

Tuesday, September 13

Gilly thought he was dreaming. He had just opened his eyes and Desiree was smiling at him with a cold compress in her hands. "How did I ...
"

"Shhh, darling. Doctor Williams will be here in a moment.

391

"But what about ... "

"Shhh."

Since he couldn't have his questions answered, Gilly tried to remember what he was doing at the hospital. There was something about Princess and how he couldn't make her stop. That was a silly dream, Gilly thought. Why would he be riding Sarika lying on a saddle like a sack of cornmeal?

"That was quite a ride you had last night." Doctor Williams said, while checking Gilly's leg underneath the bed sheet. How bad does it hurt?"

"Not bad, doc. It stings like hell though. But that leg has always hurt since I was a baby. Can anyone tell me what happened?"

"The ball went clean through your thigh. You were fortunate. It missed the femur and any major blood vessel. Still, you could have bled to death if you didn't have your leg pinned under the flap of the saddle. The orderly tells me they had to pry your fingers from the stirrup strap. So, you must have been pulling on that the whole time. This drew the flap tight around your thigh and provided enough compression to stop the bleeding. I'll write about this to the medical journal after this is all over. For the time being you need rest and a few weeks for the wound to heal."

"Thanks, doc. But what happened? Did the British break through?"

"Not yet. Stricker fought them to a standstill. He retreated last night to Hampstead Hill."

Williams continued on his rounds. Desiree came back to replace the compress and found Gilly's eyes shut. There was a trickle of tears running down his cheeks.

"Darling, are you all right. Is the pain too much? I'll fetch Doctor Williams back. He can give you something."

"No, Dez. No laudanum for me." Gilly wiped his face with the bed sheet. "I just remembered. The Smith brothers were killed yesterday. I need a clear head if I'm going to be of any help."

Desiree was pouring a cup of water when an explosion rattled the building. Most of the water splashed onto Gilly's cot. Everyone in the hospital, including Doctor Williams, stopped what they were doing. Desiree's nerves, already taxed by the screams of wounded soldiers, overwhelmed her. She quickly put her hands in her apron so no one would see them shaking.

Gilly sat up and put his right hand into her apron, squeezing her cold fingers. "It's just a ranging shot, Dez. The British are establishing their distance to the fort. Don't be scared, as long as the fort holds we are in no danger here. It might be a good idea to batten down the hatches though. Secure anything that moves. There's going to be a lot more of that kind of thing today."

393

"Thank God we moved the children."

The blast came from the bomb ship *Volcano* about two miles away from Fort McHenry. It was a 200-pound shell that exploded short of the fort. *Volcano* and her sister bomb ships *Destruction*, *Aetna*, *Meteor*, and *Terror* sailed closer. A dozen other ships including small frigates and rocket ships joined them. The combination of their fire-power would shake the very foundation of the city's infrastructure.

"Dez, when's the last time you slept?"

"I – I can't remember. A while, I guess."

"Find yourself a cot and go to sleep. Once the British find their range they won't stop until we surrender or they run out of shells. Go on, Dez. You've had a rough time of it."

"I think you're right. My shift is over now anyway unless the ambulances come back with more wounded." Desiree leaned over and kissed him.

"Save that for the honeymoon." William Pechin, dressed as impeccably as ever, stood in front of them with a scowl on his distinguished face. "Gilly's right, dear. The worst is yet to come." Desiree tried to smile and left with her hands still in her apron.

"Tell me, Mr. Pechin, in all honesty, do we stand a chance?"

Pechin shrugged his square shoulders. "You should know better than anyone. You saw how our boys fought at Bladensburg."

"They fought scared," Gilly said. "There were so many orders and counter-orders it's amazing that they could fight at all. There's one thing that I was more than encouraged by, though."

"What's that, son?"

"Despite the chaos, they never questioned authority. Not during the battle. The mischief Richard and the Irishmen instigated in our ranks bore no fruit whatsoever."

"Thanks to you I think, Gilly."

"No, Mr. Pechin. Thanks really go to the British. The attack on our nation's capital made the boys angry. Besides, the boys now know what to expect if they should fail. That'll make them stubborn. They'll do anything to prevent that from happening to their homes and they'll stand tall to defend their families. Right now, Mr. Pechin, I'd say they're like a pack of army mules."

"Can you write about that, son?"

"Yes sir. About that and what happened yesterday. The Smith brothers, the ones that worked at the Dooley Cooperage, were killed. I saw them go down. But not before one our sharpshooters took out their general."

"What general?"

"General Ross, I suppose. It happened so quickly. I saw him get knocked off his horse. I don't know if he's dead, but he was definitely shot."

"I can't report that if it's not confirmed. Too bad, that would give us an edge. Do your best Gilly. Not that you haven't always done that. Now I know why your nickname is 'tough.'"

Gilly blushed. "You're really going to print tonight?"

"Without question, I'm going to put a newspaper on the street or I'll be damned. After all, if we lose this battle, it'll be the last edition I'll ever publish."

*****

Tuesday Afternoon, September 13

The bombardment of Fort McHenry began in earnest. Shells, rockets, cannon fire, even incendiary devices known as "carcasses" filled with gunpowder pitch, and sulfur, rained down on the fort's garrison of about a thousand men without obstruction. Major Armistead tried to return fire, but the fort's cannons could not reach the ships of the Royal Navy, now anchored two miles away.

General Smith's defensive force had grown to almost 20,000 men and 100 pieces of artillery. Their line stretched out for over a mile and they were well dug in. Commodore Rodgers held command of the center with his marines, seamen, and Baltimore privateers. The British Army, now under command of Colonel Brooke and accompanied by Vice Admiral Cockburn and his marines, played a chess game with the Americans. They first threatened a flanking maneuver northwest of the American line. Then they formed in force at the center. Each move was parried with another.

Admiral Cockburn fumed that he had not convinced his superior to attack Baltimore sooner, before the fortifications on Hampstead Hill had been completed and well before those stupid, little forts Babcock and Covington were in place. Still, the Admiral thought, the navy should be able to take Fort McHenry. And on the outside chance that didn't occur in the next few hours, Cockburn had one more agent in position to finish the job.

Colonel Brooke decided on a night attack. This would blind the American artillery and allow the British to attack with the bayonet at close quarters wielded by seasoned veterans against unproven militia. But the attack could never be successful if Fort McHenry held. Now, everything depended on Armistead.

Lying awake in his cot, Gilly felt a familiar ache in his left leg, which had nothing to do with the musket shot he took yesterday. This was a pain he had felt since childhood and a precursor to severe weather. Both the American seamen at Rodgers Bastion and the topmen on the British ships-of-war who had served long enough sensed it, too. It would soon become a classic nor'easter, a large storm and the bane of coastal seafaring towns from Virginia to Canada.

Despite the rain that drenched the city, the attack on Fort McHenry was intensified. Bombs burst in mid-air above the fort while rockets zigzagged in every direction leaving a trail of smoke and sounding like an eerie whistle before exploding.

The constant barrage woke Desiree. She went to Gilly's cot and put her head down on his chest. He gently stroked her chestnut hair as he did that night at Ole' Sally's. Desiree, safe in his arms, nodded off. But Gilly couldn't quell the sounds of battle in his head, let alone those leveled at McHenry. The bombs came in increasing frequency now. Sometimes two or three were over the fort at the same time and exploded simultaneously. The noise was deafening.

Through it all, Gilly had written his story and sent it by courier to Mr. Pechin. He thought about what his editor had said and wondered if this was going to be his last story. If the British entered Baltimore, *The American* would be the first building to burn.

Samuel poked his head behind the bed curtain and saw Desiree asleep in Gilly's arms. "Is it all right to speak to you?" Gilly motioned with his head for Samuel to come closer. "I'm going to report to the fort, Gilly. I heard about Ethan and Elijah. I'm sorry for your loss. They died as heroes." Samuel bowed his head for a moment.

Mrs. Callahan brought in some soup on a tray and kicked Desiree in the leg for her to move. "Get up Dearie. I've brought our young man something hot and it won't do for you to be gettin' in the way with those brown locks." Desire lifted her head and brushed back her hair. "Now mind me, Master Gilly, this isn't my soup," Mrs. Callahan warned. "If it were there'd be a might more chicken in it. Honestly, I don't know if they make chickens as they used to or cooks for that matter. But eat it anyway lad, it'll help get your strength back."

Gilly nodded in appreciation. He took a sip of the broth and winced. "Mrs. Callahan, who made this, it's horrible." Suddenly, Gilly dropped the spoon into the bowl. "My God, I think I know where 'the chamber' is! And the 'jailer,' I know who he is, too! We've gotta get out of here! Samuel, I'm going with you. Have you got a horse?"

Samuel's mouth was agape. "I – I have a wagon. You know who the 'jailer' is?"

"Yes! I do!" Gilly frantically threw off his bed sheets.

"Mrs. Callahan, take this tray back, but thank you dear, dear sweet lady. Desiree, help me get dressed! Samuel, you'll have to carry me to the wagon!"

Despite Desiree's protests, Gilly got out of his cot and managed to slip on a pair of trousers. She was still protesting when Samuel lifted Gilly in his arms and headed to the wagon on Apple Alley. Desiree followed them voicing every possible objection. Samuel whipped the horses as the wagon lurched sideways and disappeared out onto Market Street. Desiree watched them go as she stood on the front steps of the hospital. She was completely drenched by the torrential nor'easter, but didn't seem to notice the rain at all.

"It's what 'you ought to do,' darling. Isn't it?" she stated proudly.

*****

Samuel drove the team of horses at breakneck speed. It was getting late. It was difficult to gauge when sundown would occur. It was already dark because of the storm. As they neared the fort the sky lit up from the incessant flare of rockets pummeling Whetstone Point. Samuel screamed the question "Who's the jailer!" But Gilly could not hear him.

They galloped into the fort ignoring orders to halt from the sentries. They would have been fired upon except for the fact that this was an army buckboard driven by a uniformed warrant officer. Gilly pointed to the powder magazine next to the officers' quarters. Samuel reigned in the horses and stopped the wagon in front of the magazine's fortified door. Gilly propelled himself off the wagon, landing in the thick mud of the compound. Samuel grabbed him by the waist and together they used the weight of their bodies to ram the door.

McGuiness, Armistead's cook, was crouching inside the room with a round, black object in his right hand and a closed copper lantern in his left. He turned toward the entrance when Gilly and Samuel stumbled through. His face was contorted with both astonishment and fear. McGuiness opened the small door to the lantern and lit a fuse stemming from the black object. It was a grenade. They rushed him. Using his tall frame and athletic legs, Samuel shortened the distance between him and the cook. Samuel hit him in squarely in the chest with his head, jarring loose the lamp from the cook's hand. It bounced off the brick floor and landed near a keg of gunpowder. Gilly saw that the candle inside the lamp was still burning. He pounced on it and scrambled to his knees. Using his right arm and leg, Gilly crawled out into the compound and threw the lamp into the rain and mud.

Inside, Samuel was struggling with McGuiness for possession of the grenade. The timed fuse was growing shorter. The cook used the grenade as a blunt weapon. He struck Samuel with it repeatedly, blooding his face and breaking his teeth and nose. Samuel was close to losing consciousness. McGuiness saw his opponent wobble and took advantage. Using all his strength he swung the grenade at Samuel's head. The Quaker clerk, who had forsworn violence all his life, dodged the blow and grabbed his assailant's arm. Using the cook's own momentum, Samuel threw him over his shoulder and onto the brick floor. Then he wrapped his strong fingers around his throat and crushed the cook's windpipe. Samuel staggered outside with the grenade. The fuse was still lit, it could not be extinguished. Samuel hurled the grenade in a high arch above their heads. It exploded harmlessly in the air.

Gilly had fallen into the mud. It was raining so hard he could barely make anything out. He cupped his hand over his eyes to see his friend. What he saw was the face of a ghost. "I killed him," Samuel gasped. Gilly desperately wanted to say something to him. To somehow relieve the utter horror and shock visibly expressed on Samuel's countenance. But there were no words. Suddenly, a shell screamed down onto the fort and crashed through the roof of the magazine. For some reason, known only to a higher authority, the bomb failed to explode.

Major Armistead was informed immediately. The contents of the magazine, over three hundred barrels of powder, were removed by a line of men acting like a bucket brigade. Still dazed, Samuel found the power to do what 'he ought to do.' He took the point position in the line and helped move the powder.

One of the officers asked Armistead if it was wise to subject the barrels to the driving downpour thereby making them useless should the British try and storm the fort by land. Armistead looked at Gilly, lying in the mud - shirtless, shoeless, clutching Istvan's locket. "Those are Dooley barrels, lieutenant," the major said, matter-of-factly. "We can depend on them."

Epilogue

"How did you know it was the cook?" Mr. Peabody asked. He was seated next to Gilly at the long, polished mahogany table. The intelligence officer and Gilly had joined the Pechins for a formal dinner at the editor's house in Olde Town. It had been almost a week since the Battle of Baltimore.

On the morning of September 14, 1814, the British abandoned all hope of punishing the city as an example to the world. It was also the morning where a Victory Flag was flown over Fort McHenry demonstrating what a free people could accomplish when they are filled with a noble resolve. All eyes and ears were fixed on Gilly as he tried to answer Mr. Peabody's question.

Gilly whistled through his teeth. "Mrs. Callahan tipped me off. She served me some awful chicken soup that she said was not her cooking. For some reason, don't ask me why, that made me think of Major Armistead's cook and his disagreeable nature. I remembered McGuiness telling me he was the cook for the county sheriff before he was fired. Samuel's presence at the hospital must have triggered two and two together in my mind because he was headed to the fort to help in her defense. Later, Samuel told me that some of the men at the fort actually nicknamed McGuiness 'the jailer' because he slept in the guardhouse. Mr. Peabody guessed that 'the chamber' was a place where they stored ammunition. At the fort, the guardhouse is right next door to the powder magazine."

"Amazing," Mr. Peabody said before taking a sip of expensive, Portuguese wine. "And I was sure it was someone in authority. Especially, since this man knew about the plan to scuttle the merchant ships in the harbor."

"He had guided me down to the shore line outside the fort when I went to interview Major Armistead," Gilly recalled. "As I was talking to the major, McGuiness took a nap on a flat rock using his apron as a pillow. I suppose he didn't really nap at all."

"The information McGuiness heard that day was like a gold mine to him," Peabody said. "He was probably in league with Liam Dailey, who had taken Samuel's place volunteering at the fort. In any event, the information was passed on to Richard.

"I made some inquiries afterwards and found out McGuiness had vowed revenge against the city for his dismissal. He was also in dire need of funds. Payment was to be made after he ignited the powder magazine and made his escape. That was the reason behind the long fuse on the grenade. Had it exploded in the magazine, the whole fort would have gone up and the British would have then sailed nearer to the harbor. Gilly's idea to scuttle the merchant ships would have prevented the Royal Navy from getting any closer, but they were close enough to concentrate their guns on Hampstead Hill. Our surrender or our annihilation would have quickly followed."

"And if the shell which penetrated the roof of the magazine had exploded," Mr. Pechin added, "the British would be enjoying this fine meal instead of us."

"This is true," Peabody concurred. "Admiral Cockburn had his agents draw up a sketch of the fort well over a year ago. They knew where the powder magazine was and they also knew it was not bomb proof. McGuiness was simply a backup because they were convinced at least one of the hundreds of shells fired on McHenry would do the job. One did, of course, but by God's grace is was a dud."

"How is Samuel holding up, Gilly?" Mr. Pechin asked.

"Okay, I think." Gilly stretched his leg out on the Ottoman the butler had carried in from the parlor to ease the pain from the musket wound. "He's been spending a lot of time talking to Father John. The two of them have

405

become very close. I have a hunch he's going to be fine in the long run. He's left the navy, although Commodore Rodgers pleaded with him to stay on and serve with him in Philadelphia. Every day, he comes to the cooperage and helps me out with fixing the place up. He's already planning a new workroom. He thinks business will be picking up soon."

"Father John is recovering as well," Desiree said, cheerfully. "His speech is improving every day. The swelling has almost all disappeared. He said this whole thing has made him a better preacher because he must speak slowly and use less vocabulary." They all laughed at this. "Father John said it will make him more like his favorite saint, Francis of Assisi, who said something like 'preach the gospel at all times and when necessary use words.'"

Mr. Pechin laughed the loudest. "If I followed that advice, I'd be out of a job."

Desiree cleared her throat and flashed her eyes at Gilly.

"Mr. Pechin, speaking of jobs, I must tell you I'll – I'll be leaving mine," Gilly said, slowly.

Pechin was dumbfounded. Desiree quickly filled the void. "Father, I've never known you to be at a loss for words before. Gilly, darling, tell them about your lunch today."

Gilly blushed and quickly glanced at Mr. Pechin. "I had the honor of

406

meeting Mr. Key this morning. We decided to have a bite to eat and we went to Ole' Sally's."

"You know Frank Key?" Mr. Peabody asked.

"I just met him today. I read his 'Defense of Fort McHenry' in the *Patriot* this morning. *The American* is going to print it when we can get enough of our pressmen back."

"We would have printed it first," Mr. Pechin huffed. "But some of our employees are still in the hospital. It's not fair that we didn't have a go at Key's poem."

"Mr. Peabody, how do you know Mr. Key?" Gilly asked.

"I went to school with him at St. John's, in Annapolis, for law of all things. That's when I discovered I wanted to catch people who broke the law, not defend them. Frank was born to defend. Maybe that's why the poem he wrote about the defense of this city rings of such truth. What, may I ask, did you and Frank talk about?"

"Law school. He thinks I would be an ideal candidate. He's read my stories in *The American*. He said that the power of words can also be used in defending our constitutional liberties and that there are few higher callings. St. John's isn't very far away," Gilly said, glancing at Desiree.

"And what about your dream, Gilly," Mr. Pechin asked with more than curiosity. "You were born to put pen to paper. You proved that with your stories for *The American*. You can't let talent like that rot on the vine."

"He's never going to do such a thing if I have anything to do with it," Desiree said. "Gilly's a writer and he will continue writing or he won't have me."

Gilly blushed a second time. "Then, I will keep writing, Dez."

Mr. Peabody, leaned over and whispered in Gilly's ear. "Before you leave, you and I must have a discussion about that code you referred to. Perhaps Samuel would like to join us."

"Desiree, too," Gilly whispered back.

After dinner, the butler handed Gilly a letter. "A special military courier delivered it to the rectory at St. Patrick's. Father John though it best to have it sent here," the butler said.

"Who is it from, darling?" Desiree asked with anticipation.

"It's from Michael Dooley, dated September 11th, on board the flagship *Saratoga*, outside Plattsburgh, New York. This may be news of the British invasion from Canada we've been waiting for Mr. Pechin. May I read it aloud?"

"By all means, son."

408

Dear Gilly,

I trust everything is well with you and that you're
business with O'Casey and Dailey hasn't caused you or our
fair city any pain. I haven't much time to put on paper all
the details that have transpired of late here in New York.
Commodore Macdonough has allowed me to include this
letter to you in the marked case that is being sent to Navy
Secretary Jones. Since the official dispatch service will pass
through Baltimore on the way to Washington, you will be
the first to know of the events that have transpired here.

We have won! Our little fleet has beaten the British
in Plattsburgh Bay! Lake Champlain is ours! Since the
British cannot control the lake, their army of 14,000
regulars must turn back to Canada. There will be no
invasion of our country from the north.

This is a blessed victory, Gilly. But it came at great
cost. Captain Ken was killed in the battle. He fought with
bravery and distinction. His loss is sorely felt here as it will
be in Fells Point.

Jessica and I, and Uncle Bob are fine. We are more
than fine since I have my father back! Yes, Gilly, it's true.
He was forced to serve in the British fleet as a carpenter.

We found him aboard the British flagship *Confiance*. He was wounded in the battle but not severely. He sends you his love as do we all.

Our plans are to come home as fast as we can. Please give our love also to Desiree, Father John, Samuel, and the Smith boys.

Gilly paused for a moment and held back a tear. Desiree came over to him and put her arms around his shoulders.

I know you, too, are facing the enemy. We heard about Bladensburg and Washington. Perhaps you are being tested now or have already been thrown like kindling into the black furnace of war. If so, Gilly, stand fast by the code Aquinas is teaching us now. Know that, although our part in the great drama may be little, it is our duty to know what we ought to believe; to know what we ought to desire; to know what we ought to do."

Your brother in the code and by our mixed blood,

Michael

*****

Ghent, Kingdom of the Netherlands

December 24, 1814

One of the American Commissioners, John Quincy Adams, son of a president, strolled down the cobblestoned Graslei along the Leie River pondering the day's events. It was almost midnight. Colorful candle Christmas lights from inside the grand merchant buildings adjacent to the river reflected off the serene water. The still air was laden with moisture. As a Massachusetts man, Adams knew it would soon snow. From a distance, he could hear the bells of St. Nicholas' Cathedral usher in the blessings of peace.

He was apprehensive, but not altogether displeased about the treaty he had just finished negotiating. People back in America, he thought, probably wouldn't like it. The terms of the treaty ending the war between the United States and Great Britain granted *status quo ante bellum* (the state existing before the war). It meant no winner, no loser. Everything would be as if the war never even took place.

Adams smiled. On paper, he thought, it will look like nothing has changed. In reality, he knew things had changed a great deal and would continue to do so. Before the battles of Champlain and Baltimore, the British negotiators had legitimate aspirations of substantial territorial gains. Now, they simply wanted the war to end. If Americans had not stopped the enemy in New York and Maryland what would have happened at the negotiating table? Would the union of the states have survived? By virtue of the status quo the American Republican experiment had been allowed to continue.

411

On his way back to his rooms it started to snow. Maybe, Adams thought as he walked and wondered, the treaty wasn't such a bad thing after all. Perhaps it was a gift - a Christmas present for the future.

HISTORICAL NOTE

During the pivotal year of 1814, Commodore John Rodgers spent most of his service in Philadelphia, not Baltimore, although his service south of the Mason-Dixon Line was paramount. The construction of Rodgers Bastion on Hampstead Hill began with his arrival in Baltimore on August 25th. By the 28th, he was officially put in command of all naval forces in the city. His presence in Baltimore was a godsend after the humiliating American defeat at Bladensburg and the burning of Washington.

Major Armistead ordered the huge flag that was to fly over Fort McHenry after the battle a full year before the attack. For the purpose of creating an even greater sense of urgency in this novel, Mrs. Pickersgill is taxed with getting the job accomplished in much less time.

As in any war, there is the crucial element of military espionage. Mr. Peabody, of course, is a fabrication, but not his methods. Unlike the War for

Independence, where British intrigue played a major role in defaming competent American officers, there is little evidence of this stratagem in the War of 1812. Character assassination was chiefly the bailiwick of opposing political operatives and their sympathizers in the American press. Intelligence, however, did play a key role in the battles fought in the War of 1812, including Admiral Cockburn's assessment of the vulnerabilities of American forts, specifically of Fort McHenry. The chief of intelligence for General Samuel Smith was Major William Barney, son of hero Joshua Barney. His professionalism was a great asset to American defenses.

Finally, the meaning of the words of St. Thomas Aquinas, taken from his *Two Precepts of Charity* and used as a family and individual code by the novel's characters is not only the moral backbone of this story, but a guidepost for human endeavor in this or any age.

415

www.ingramcontent.com/pod-product-compliance
Lightning Source LLC
Chambersburg PA
CBHW060138260626
47160CB00001B/22